ALSO BY LINDA HOWE STEIGER

FOG

TERROIR

A Morgan Kendall Wine Country Mystery

LINDA HOWE STEIGER

"It's still magic, even if you know how it's done."

—TERRY PRATCHETT, *A Hatful of Sky*

CONTENTS

1 AN INVITATION

"**B**ut this is Uncle Jules I'm talking about, Morgan." Kit's eyes pleaded as he leaned towards her. They were sitting over the dregs of an early dinner in Formerly's Bar and Grill looking out across the little downtown plaza and into the redwoods of Creekside Park. It was midsummer. The day had been long and unusually hot for Quarry Canyon. Now, however, a cooling fog was beginning to drift over the coastal mountains and roll into town as Kit and Morgan waited for Morgan's son, Talies. A breeze blew through the open bay window and ruffled the dark curls at the back of Morgan's neck. She shivered, reached up, and smoothed away the tickle.

"Uncle Jules?" Morgan asked, noting the lovely blue of her companion's eyes and the little moue of distress under his grand and drooping moustache. Such a handsome fellow this 'Kit' Carson Jalesco. Fiddling with a curl, she recalled the story of how he'd received that name from his father. Meanwhile Kit was pleading on and on. Finally, when he paused, she asked absently. "And am I supposed to know this uncle of yours?"

"He's not my uncle. Indie's. Have you not been listening?"

"There's Russian dressing on your upper left." She waggled a finger towards the imminent drip hanging from the end of his graying moustache.

Kit frowned and sent his tongue out to explore. Mopping his whiskers with a napkin, he went on, "She's afraid for the old man, see? Strange things have been happening at the winery. She sounds scared."

"Your ex-wife possesses a fertile imagination, does she not? Didn't you tell me that her paranoid fantasies were what triggered your divorce?"

"I did say that. But there were other reasons as well."

Morgan bit into her buffalo burger and chewed thoughtfully, watching the emotions wash across her friend's face as he explained how this time Indie's story might well be true. She finished her burger and leaned across the table. "What I don't understand is why she calls you. If she seriously believes her uncle's life is in danger, she should talk to the police."

Kit responded as if he'd been slapped. His mouth flattened to a line. His shoulders collapsed. Morgan could almost hear the hiss of air escaping his ego. She was well aware that Kit himself had once qualified as "the police." But he was retired now, thanks to a gimpy knee. She sighed, pushing aside a twinge of guilt. The man needed more objectivity when it came to his ex-family—emphasis on the "ex."

She pulled out her smart phone and checked the time. "You know, if Tally doesn't turn up pretty soon, we'll miss that show he wants us to see in San Francisco. I'm texting him again." Then she laid her phone face-up beside her wine glass and glowered down at it, as if expecting something to explode. The phone remained still.

Kit observed this operation but made no comment; instead he picked up where he'd left off. "Because she doesn't think they'd pay attention to her, that's why. And because Jules himself blows everything off. I think we should drive up next weekend. Look around. Talk with folks. It's Jules' eightieth. A perfect excuse. Nobody would be surprised that we turn up for the party. I'll fix it with Jules, or Indie. We can bunk in one of the guest cottages for a few days. It'll be fine."

He paused, expecting Morgan to say something, but she remained as silent as her smart phone, so he continued. "You're right. I am no longer officially 'police'—just a lowly part-time gumshoe. I can't sprint after crooks anymore, but I'm still a pretty good detective. It's not all that outrageous that Indie ask me for help—I mean, ask us. I did tell her I'd try to bring you along." Kit's voice trailed off. Morgan's eyes remained glued to her phone. He took a sip of wine and waited for her attention to shift back to him.

Finally Morgan lifted her eyes. She grimaced, chin out. "What did you just say, Kit? We? Us? You cannot mean this coming weekend . . ."

"I do wish you'd try to focus a little on what I'm telling you."

"But I do—most of the time I do!" She smiled weakly, but said nothing more about Talies being late or how his delayed appearance produced visions of cars spinning out of control on the freeway. Bleeding bodies. Crunched up metal littering the pavement. His ancient Honda flying off the upper deck of the Richmond bridge. Splashing into the Bay. Gurgling to the bottom. She knew hers was an excessive response. And she knew that Kit knew that it was really more about Artie than Talies. Artie, her beloved husband, Talies's father. Artie had been killed in a fiery car crash during a rain storm in the Santa Cruz Mountains. That had happened several years ago, but the pain remained as fresh as if it had been yesterday. And the memory always arose when Talies was late, which fortunately didn't happen all that often. But when it did, Morgan had to fight to control still raw feelings of loss, of hazard, of the general unpredictability of life. PTSD her therapist had said. Nearly unbearable at first, but she was getting better. Sort of. She smiled at Kit and drew a ragged breath.

"I'll be okay," she murmured, wrapping her arms around her shoulders and scolding herself, trying to stop staring at her phone as if it were some sort of life-line. She sent orders to her shoulders to relax. She drew another deep breath and forced the tension to leave her legs. Finally, she lowered her eyelids and took several long breaths of cool air, willing herself to step back from the precipice, tentatively, gently.

"Sorry about that," she said and changed the subject. "Did Talies say anything to you about tonight? I mean, it seems so strange to me—his taking us to some magic club. Feels out of character. He's usually Mr. Rational. Not that I mind, but it's at least an hour into the City, with all that highway construction. Of course, you know that. I wonder if he thought about it." Her eyes crept stealthily to her phone. Her thumbs twitched as if poising to make another text.

"No. But I'm sure he'll brief us when he arrives." Kit watched her side step her demons and pitched his voice to exude calmness. "He will be here soon. No worries. Probably a little more traffic than he expected. Or maybe he stopped for something to eat. That young man does have an enormous appetite." Kit's eyes drifted across the room, which was rapidly filling with diners and drinkers. Three sweaty hikers were settling themselves, and their gear, at a neighboring table.

Morgan picked up the wine bottle and refilled her wine glass. Then she offered to refresh Kit's. "More?"

"Sure. But could we please try to get our plans settled before Talies shows up? Do you need for me to repeat anything?"

"No. I got the gist. Your ex-wife feels scared. There's to be a birthday celebration up in wine country this weekend at her uncle's place. You want me to go with you . . ." Morgan reached across the table and touched his hand. Kit enfolded her fingers in his, and rubbed them fondly.

"So?" he asked. "Will you?"

Morgan felt loath to commit. She drew back her hand. She didn't like Indie. She didn't like this gig. She had other matters on her mind.

Kit sipped his wine and tried to look wise, tried to signal he was immune to her negativity. "Indie said everybody's coming, even her brothers from LA. We'll be able to talk with the whole family about what's been going on up there. It'll be fun too! I'm sure you'll enjoy yourself, Morgan."

"Fun? I thought this was about work."

"It is. But can't we have fun too? I haven't seen Indie's brothers in years. I like them—they're amusing. You'll like them. And, I know there'll be a behind the scenes tour of the winery. Jules loves to walk guests through his vineyards. Half the town will show up for his party. It'll be a great show!" Kit chuckled about something and grinned to himself. "Those Romanos! They're hilarious! They talk all the time! And joke around a lot. I wondered if that's not what this thing with Jules is really all about—some sort of joke, you know?" He snorted, and grinned again. He reached across the table and began fiddling with her fingers, again. "Oh, lighten up, Morgan, please. Come with me. We'll have a great time!

And even if we are working, working together will be fun. And maybe you'll even pick up a little about my former life. Meet some of the people I used to know. . . ."

But Morgan wasn't buying Kit's spiel. Not just yet anyway. In fact his approach was making her uncomfortable—this invitation seemed neither fish nor fowl. She didn't like how he braided together the personal and the professional, although she couldn't find the words to articulate exactly what was wrong with it. Was she being a bit simple? She murmured, "I'm not sure I understand what my role would be up at your uncle's—"

"Indie's uncle."

"Oh. Right. Indie's uncle. But, look, Kit—you make these people sound like they're your family. They aren't. It makes me feel awkward. They're your ex-wife's family. And I have zero desire to make friends with *them*. Anyway, it's unethical, isn't it?"

Kit sighed and pulled back his hand. He cleared his throat, stroked the end of his drooping moustache. "Maybe. I see what you are saying, but it's complicated. I am aware, as you have so accurately observed, that I might be having some trouble separating personal feelings from professional business. . . ."

"Precisely! That's what makes me uncomfortable."

"To be honest, it makes me a little uncomfortable too. But that's my point."

"What?"

"I know what I'm proposing to do may look unethical. I mean, me taking on an investigation of my ex-wife's family. But I have no choice." His picked his words carefully. "See . . . it makes me furious to think someone—anyone—would want to harm Jules. I can't believe anyone in the family would do that. And I don't want to ignore something that might be a danger for Jules. Protecting Jules, not soothing Indie's anxieties, is what I'm about. And by the way, it's not just Indie saying these things. It's Tinker too."

"Tinker?"

"Right. See how I keep forgetting you don't know these people? But that's a *good* thing I think. Your being there will keep me honest, keep me from giving in to my feelings, my preconceptions."

"And who's Tinker?"

"Ah. Tinker is Indie's cousin. She's Jules' youngest. She and her family live at the winery too. Actually, Jules has two daughters, and they both live on the estate. And his son, and all their children—at least the younger kids do—and his sister-in-law, and her family too. There's a lot of family." Kit paused as if remembering something about this family, then went on. "Anyway, point is—Indie says Tinker is worried about Jules too." He paused again. "Indie's a little vague on details. It always makes me crazy, but I can't believe, she'd make the whole story up. Not when it's Jules. Did I tell you Jules practically raised her after her mother died?"

"No, my friend, you did not. How about—you run up to Buckthorn by yourself and sort the problem out? You don't really need to involve me!"

"But I do! I thought you understood: if I go alone, I have no integrity. You just said so yourself."

"But . . . "

"Oh, come on, Morgan. I'm trapped! Damned if I do, damned if I don't. Don't you see? Whether I like it or not, this is my family. I can't just ignore them. I don't think I ever told you, but my mother was some distant cousin of Rickie's. They found each other again when I was about six or seven. I used to visit Buckthorn as a kid."

"Wait a minute. Rickie?" Morgan had no idea who Kit was talking about.

Kit however pushed right on through. His mind became mired in the past. "Yeah, I remember playing with Eddie when we were boys. We chased some goats through the vineyards. . . ." He grinned at the memory. "Then my dad changed jobs, and we had to move away. It was years before I saw Jules again. For crying out loud, Morgan, Buckthorn is where I met Indie! Certainly I told you that!"

Morgan shook her head—no, he had not.

Kit went on. "Right, but that's a whole 'nother story. Although maybe it would help explain why I'm so stuck on doing this. I can't not, see? But I know I have some pretty strong opinions about this crowd too. I think I know what's going on, and who's doing it. But I am also aware we'll need some sort of evidence, if we're going to do anything about it. And evidence is what I mean to get. Oh, come on Morgan. Dammit I need your help!"

Morgan's jaw had literally dropped as he had been speaking. It was the first time Kit admitted he was related to one of California's oldest and best known vintners, the Romano clan. Why hadn't he said anything before? Or maybe he hd. Was that why he was at the Art and Wine Fair, where they'd first met one another. Now she felt like a fool.

Meanwhile Kit dug himself deeper into his own personal hole. "I need you so much on this, Morgan! I need your eyes, your ears, your brains. You're not all twisted up with memories like me. You've got the right sort of intelligence, and that dogged curiosity of yours . . ? You're so good at sussing out people's secrets. You can be objective. I'm not so sure about myself. You read people. This is not flattery. It's true! Frankly, I thought about asking you for help almost the moment Indie called me about Jules, and that was . . . six months ago?"

"Six *months* ago? You never said anything. . . ."

Kit nodded sheepishly. "I know. I know! I guess I hoped it would go away. I was so busy. Those two big cases. You remember. I'll never get this agency of mine off the ground if I go dropping cases. But now I'm free. Like a bird. And Indie's so damned insistent."

Morgan frowned. She did not like the sound of what Kit was telling her. It had the tell-tale sound of sucking mud. And he was being inconsistent—sinking deeper and deeper into his ethical hole. And she? She felt as if she were stepping off a cliff, only to fall into a swamp filled with alligators, or worse.

"I know, I know," Kit went on, misreading the sour expression on her face. "I *am* sorry to intrude on your time. You are busy. But I don't have anyone else to turn to, and I *do* really need to do this. Look—Jules and Rickie are *great*—I love them. I *admire* and I trust them, both. With my life! But I worry about what I'm getting myself into. I mean, what if one of them tells lies? Not that I believe either one would ever lie to me, but if they did, would I catch the lies? When I interview strangers, for work, now or back when I was a cop, it wasn't difficult to suss out the liars. But with these two? It feels like how you and Talies are—I'll bet you don't recognize half the lies Talies tells you."

"What?! Talies never lies to me!" Morgan felt deeply insulted, for both herself and for her son. Then, in half a moment, she realized Kit was probably right. But she let it go, asking instead, "So who is this Rickie person?"

"See, like I said—you don't know these people!"

Morgan scowled.

"Well, that's the point, isn't it? You can't pre-judge them. Although you could miss some of the subtleties." He frowned and pulled absently on the drooping end of his moustache. "Maybe you'd be more comfortable if you knew a little more about this group—a little introductory info—names, relationships, a *little* of their histories—before we go in. It can be confusing: they are a big family." He was gazing into her eyes, pleading. He reminded Morgan—suddenly—of her friend Izzy's lovely Black Labrador when he wanted to be taken for a walk. Oh please, please, please, please! those eyes seemed to say. Morgan had to admit, she found both that dog and this man difficult to resist.

"Let me try this again," Kit went on. "Indie's got these brothers, see. I always liked her brothers. They're crazy, funny guys. A little unpredictable maybe. Actually, to be honest, I never seriously trusted any of them. In fact, I doubt I'll get anything useful from them about what's been going on up at Buckthorn, or who might be responsible. They're not what I'd call 'observant people'. Not like Jules or Rickie, who are both solid as rocks. They always know what's going on, whether it's right in front of your face or behind the scenes. They're amazing! Their words are gold. You can bank on what they say being true. Unlike Jack, of course. Well, can't say I ever liked Jack. Or trusted him. Although some folks do." Kit seemed to shake off some shadow from the past.

"Slow down, Kit. You're confusing me. You still haven't told me who this Rickie is . . . and now there's this Jack fellow? Are these guys Indie's brothers?"

"See what I mean?" Kit grinned, laughing at himself. "I know them all so well. But no. *Rickie* is Jules' wife! *She* is definitely *not* one of Indie's brothers. Like I said before—a distant relation of my mother. 'Rickie' is short for *Ricarda*. '*Mia cara Ricarda*' Jules calls her, when he's feeling affectionate, or when he's seriously irritated with her." Kit stifled a private chuckle at another long past incident. "Simply put, Rickie is Indie's aunt, her great aunt—and she is one fine lady! Jack is Rickie's nephew, Jules' too, of course. Not Indie's brother—her father! Jack is Eddie's son, see? His only son I might add. His only kid in fact! Not that he's a kid any more. Eddie of course is long dead. Indie does have a bunch of brothers though—or at least they always felt to me like a 'bunch'. We used to call them 'the sons of Jack'." Kit rolled his eyes. "Now where was I?"

"Eddie? Sons of Jack? Should I be taking notes? Dear, I'm not sure I'm following you."

"Oh, don't worry. You'll catch on. Let's see—maybe I should start again, at the beginning—and maybe that should be with Irene."

Morgan frowned. Maybe they'd had too much wine with their dinners.

Kit pursued his train of thought. "Irene was married to Jules' older brother Eddie, see. But like I said, Eddie died, a long time ago. Irene however is alive and well. She lives up at the vineyard too. Actually there are two dead Eddies in this family—that is to say, two Eduardo's. But I'll get to that in a minute. I'll stick with Irene for now. Irene is mostly known as '*Nonna*'. That means 'grandmother' in Italian. But maybe you already know that. She's Indie's grandmother—and her brothers' grandmother too, of course. Which is why they all call her '*Nonna*'. Actually a lot of people call Irene '*Nonna*', as you will discover. I generally don't, however. I certainly would *not* want Irene for *my* grandmother. She's a *real* piece of work, that old lady is. She must be pushing ninety by now. Very Old World sort. Like I said, Jack's her son. Her only son. Jack's a piece of work too, but in a different way. Smarmy, you might say. I always thought Jack was a real . . . mmm." Kit laughed uncomfortably and glanced over his shoulder at three rather scruffy hikers, who, having caught his eye, hoisted their beer steins in greeting. Morgan realized they had been openly eavesdropping on their conversation, which is why Kit now touched his moustache in a way that shielded his entire mouth as he whispered a long, rather unkind, descriptor of Jack.

Morgan found herself stifling the giggles at all this. She stole a peek at her still silent phone. Ten whole minutes since she'd texted Talies.

"Oh come on, Morgan. Tal's fine! Trust me. He's just a little late. Oh, please say you'll help me. You can see how much I need your help! I feel obligated to these folks, to Jules especially. He's been very good to me over the years. I've simply gotta go up there."

"So you said."

"And there's something else." He paused as if struggling for words. "It's Bailey, see. My kid. Indie's got him up there. Right in the middle of whatever's going on. It makes me jumpy. He's so young! So innocent! He's just the kind of kid to be in the wrong place at the wrong time. I need to make sure he's safe, if nothing else. Surely you can understand that."

"Oh, I do. But from one helicopter parent to another, why don't you drive up tomorrow and extract your son? Take him back to your place. Take him camping. Take him wherever. And tell Indie to have the cops look into whatever is going on."

Kit looked pained. "Easier said than done."

Morgan grunted, but said no more, as Kit continued to talk round and round his subject, laying out every card in his hand as he tried to gain her sympathy and her compliance. Meanwhile Morgan sat scowling and trying to identify the source for her ambivalence. She wanted to help Kit, she truly did, but she felt so wary.

When at last Kit seemed to have talked himself out, Morgan leaned forward, rested her elbows on the table, tented her fingers under her chin, and asked carefully, "Have you considered that this could all be a ploy of Indie?"

"A what?"

"Well, it strikes me that your ex-wife might have concocted this whole Jules-is-in-danger scenario as a way to get you back into the family fold, so to speak. You are a very attractive man, and this sounds like a perfect set up to draw your attention. If you go, you'd be on her turf again, feeling all protective about her uncle Jules, and all worried about your Bailey, not to mention being slightly off the mark with too much birthday wine and birthday cake. Seems to me you'd be a sitting duck for one of her machinations."

"Wait a minute! Are you jealous?" He sounded surprised.

Morgan frowned; she'd surprised herself too, with her own boldness. She temporized. "You know, I do have work obligations myself. I was honored by an invitation to join an American Library Association panel on internet security for public libraries. I was planning to use the weekend to prepare my presentation."

Kit's face fell about a mile. "Look, I don't think Indie's making a play for me. And even if she were, I wouldn't be interested. No—I truly believe she thinks these threats to her uncle's life are real. Or are you getting even here, for that time I bailed on you, pleading my work obligations. I said at the time I was sorry about that, Morgan, and I truly am. But yours was a cold case, and this is, potentially, quite a hot one. I'm convinced it needs looking into. Maybe I've given you the wrong impression about Indie—she doesn't always make things up. Her intuitions can be surprisingly accurate. Oh come on, Morgan. Say 'yes'. Please."

Morgan sighed. Despite her words, she could not seriously believe that Kit would let himself be taken in by his former wife— at least not for long. Still, her gut churned at the prospect of becoming involved with Indie's extended family. In fact, it felt like sheer madness.

"How about I sleep on it?" she said finally, reaching across the table to take Kit's hand in hers.

"Of course!" His voice cracked with relief. "How about we talk again day after tomorrow. Brunch? I need to take care of some things in the office anyway, before we can head up to Wine Country." He rubbed her fingers gently and wrapped his gaze around hers. The little breeze kicked up again, freshening the evening air and drawing Morgan's eyes towards the dancing redwoods outside the window. Suddenly, she drew her hand away from Kit's and pointed across the plaza towards a familiar, long-legged figure striding rapidly in their direction.

"Talies!"

Talies raised his arm saluting her. Morgan waved back. Kit signaled to Mike the barman for their bill. A moment later she was jumping up and down, throwing her arms over her head and shouting, "TAAHL-yes! TAAHL-yes! We're over here!"

But the man who pushed through the door of Formerly's and

hurried towards their table was not Talies. Nothing like Talies. He was blond, not dark haired. Short and stocky, not lank and towering. Fortyish, in dusty hiking boots. Not a twenty-something in cross-trainers. A wide-brimmed Australian hat. Morgan blinked as if several frames of a film had been awkwardly skipped over. She turned and stared across the now empty plaza. No sign of Talies. Had she been hallucinating?

The stranger bumped her elbow as he shoved his way towards the bar. Morgan scanned the room, eyes wide open, mouth agape. Where was her son?

2 SHOW TIME

Mike, his bald head glowing in the hot pink light of the bar's neon sign, was talking animatedly to the stranger in the Australian hat. He motioned broadly with one arm, stabbed the air with his hand. Morgan figured he was describing the route back to the main highway. She felt like an idiot staring at them, so she picked up her cell phone and rapidly texted her son.

"Mom!" came a voice behind her.

She whirled around.

There, laughing at her discombobulation, stood Talies, grinning. "Did you see that guy jump in front of me as I opened the door?! What a rude son-of-a-bitch." Talies dropped his backpack on the floor and pulled up a chair and nodded to Kit. "Traffic sucked on both sides of bridge!" He plucked a slice of pickle from his mother's plate and dropped it into his up-turned mouth. He shivered with pleasure. "I love these home-made ones!"

"You're late," said Morgan as he crunched down another pickle. "Did you not eat?"

"I'm fine. Stopped off for a burrito." Suddenly he looked over his mother's shoulder and stared at the back of her head. Leaning towards her, he fingered her hair. "What have you been up to, Mom? How'd this get here?" He held out the brilliant yellow quail's egg. It looked plastic.

"Wha . . ?"

"Baulk, baulk, baulk." Talies cackled, mimicking the cluck of a cartoon hen on her nest. He grinned again.

"Talies . . ." said Kit suspiciously.

"What are you up to now? Some sort of magic trick? What is going on with you?" asked Morgan.

"No worries, folks. Just putting you in the mood for tonight's show. Did I tell you I got an A in methods, Mom? Truly a difficult course! I'm kinda glad I didn't do criminal justice after all, that I got stuck into psych. Good old Bezerkley. Guess they did the right thing by me."

"That's nice, dear. But what does your choice of major have to do with tonight's event? Speaking of which—shouldn't we get moving?"

"Plenty o' time, Mom. Watch this. I'm going to make this little guy disappear now." He closed his fingers slowly around the yellow plastic egg. Morgan watched, her lips pursed, as Talies passed one hand back and forth over the hand closed over the little egg and mumbled something unintelligible. Then he cried, "Voila!" and opened his hand. The little yellow egg still lay on his palm. Talies' face fell. "Shit," he muttered. "Must have gotten the spell wrong. Not so easy this magic business." Grinning, 'though not at all sheepishly, he tossed the little egg lightly back and forth between his two hands, arcing it higher, and higher with each toss. "Okay, watch this one. I'm pretty sure this will work."

As the egg-shaped object came closer and closer to the ceiling, the heads of Kit, Morgan, and the hikers at the next table, bobbed up and down watching it, their mouths open. They became half-mesmerized following the bouncing egg. "There. Did ya see that!?" said Talies.

All eyes remained glued up on the ceiling. No egg anywhere in sight. "Where'd it go, Tal?" asked Kit, looking around.

Talies held his empty hands out. "Pretty good, huh? I disappeared it into the thin air!" Talies grinned a victory grin. The hikers applauded. Morgan and Kit frowned.

"So where'd you hide it?" asked Morgan, her eyes darting across the nearby tables and over the floor. No sign of that infuriating yellow egg.

"Not telling. You figure it out."

Morgan's forehead became deeply furrowed; her eyebrows formed into a V. Talies was being annoying. She did not like this kind of mystery. She made movements as if preparing to leave. Talies ignored her and hitched his chair towards Kit. "Actually, I've been thinking about magic a lot recently—sleight-of-hand, you know. I think it's a useful skill for detectives. Here, I'll show you another interesting one." Talies extracted a shiny silver quarter from his jeans.

Morgan groaned and puffed out her cheeks, but Kit leaned back into his chair and folded his arms across his chest. He was prepared to play along.

"I think you'll like this. Give me one of your hands, please," said Talies.

Kit stretched an arm out. Talies placed the coin on Kit's open palm.

"Now, close your fingers over it. Make a fist. Good. But really clamp down on it, because I'm going to use magical powers to remove that coin." As Talies spoke, he helped Kit fold his fingers over the quarter, then stroked them gently. "That's right. Squeeze down. Don't make it easy for me!"

Kit squeezed till his knuckles paled.

"That's pretty well clenched," remarked Talies. "You might want to loosen up just a little, so you don't get a cramp. Ah. Perfect." His manner resembled that of a physician preparing a patient for some delicate piece of possibly painful surgery. Satisfied with how Kit was holding the coin, Tal rose from his seat, gave his arms a little shake, as if to get the kinks out, and flexed his fingers—first on one hand, then on the other. He gave Kit's shoulder an encouraging little squeeze and added a few more tender strokes to Kit's clenched fist, saying "All secure in there?"

Kit nodded, his eyes intently on his own closed hand.

"Excellent! Okay! Let's do it! Keep your eyes on that there fist. Don't blink. I'm now going to extract my coin. I promise, this won't hurt a bit. Well, at least not that much." Talies cackled slightly as he raised both of his arms over Kit's head and began oscillating them in a snake-like pattern as he lowered them slowly down towards Kit's out-stretched arm. He hovered them over Kit's fist while making a series of curious, rhythmic movements and mumbling what sounded to Morgan like lines from Edward Lear's Book of Nonsense. Finally, with a thoughtful expression, Talies began massaging the air over the fist, as if feeling around for a lump. Suddenly, he jerked and grabbed into the air above Kit's right ear, as if to catch a fly moving at warp speed away from their table. With a sigh of satisfaction, Talies stepped back and folded his arms across his chest, carefully keeping both hands hidden in his armpits. Then, grinning like the Cheshire Cat, Talies resumed his seat and proclaimed, "Did it!" One of the hikers started to applaud.

"No you did not!" said Kit, who was still tightly squeezing his fist around the magical coin. "I've got the coin. Your hocus-pocus failed again."

Morgan's eyes darted back and forth between them. The three beer-drinking hikers leaned closer.

"Well, I disagree," responded Talies calmly. "Although. . . . Well, I did catch it on the fly. I suppose it's a tiny bit possible the darned coin took a weird bounce. Let's have a look." Slowly Talies unfolded his own arms and opened first one fist, then the other. In neither one was the coin. Talies blinked ingenuously. "Shoot! I thought I had it. Like I said, it was moving pretty fast. Might not have reckoned the arc properly. Let's look in your hand, Kit, just to be sure."

Kit shook his head, continuing to clench his fist tightly closed. "I don't need to look, my young friend. I can feel it in there!"

"Indulge me, sir. I don't want to lose my quarter. Might need it for . . . well . . . for a parking meter somewhere."

One by one Kit lifted his fingers. His eyes grew wide. He stared at his palm.

No quarter!

Morgan blinked. "Okay, Tally. So where is it?" The three hikers stared too. One of them nearly toppled off his chair. By this time Mike had stepped over to watch, an amused smile on his face.

"Gee whiz! I wonder where the darned quarter got to," said Talies goofily lifting the wine bottle to see if the coin might be lurking beneath it. He checked under his chair too, and under the table, under a napkin, behind both his own ears. "Wait! I see it!"

Morgan's eyes followed Talies' pointing finger.

"That's our quarter, isn't it?" Talies said. "On your left shoulder."

Kit's head swung around as he slapped his hand on his own shoulder and grabbed the elusive piece of silver. He did not look amused. Indeed he looked seriously annoyed. "You did some sort of quick change thing again, didn't you?"

The hikers had collectively dropped their jaws. If there had been a fly buzzing around, it might have sailed right into one of those gaping mouths just to have a look around. Mike stepped back behind the bar.

"Nope. My coin!" crowed Talies. "I had only the one. A 2010. See?"

"You got me good, my man. What's the trick?"

"No trick. Just science really. I'll do it again. See if you or Mom can use your detective skills to figure out what happened."

"Okay. Do it again," said Kit extending his arm impatiently. "But this time I'm going to put some sort of mark on the darned thing, so you can't do a quick change on me."

"No prob." Talies dug into his backpack. "Voila!" He held up a paper of little sticky red dots. Kit removed one and stuck it in the middle of the quarter. Then they ran through the trick again. Morgan watched Talies's hands carefully, certain she'd see how the "magic" worked this time around.

But she didn't. Nor did Kit. Nor did anyone else.

"Very clever, Tal. But why did I feel it so clearly on my palm?" said Kit, removing the quarter from his shoulder and verifying the dot.

"Okay. But maybe Mom would like me to do it on her first?"

"No. Just tell us," said Morgan tartly, checking the time on her cell phone.

"If you insist," Talies responded sweetly. "We learned this trick in cognitive science class last fall. My professor is actually the amazing magician we're going to see tonight! Wait till you see him. His tricks are based on brain science." Then Talies told them, in gory detail, about something called a sensory after-effect known as 'shadow perception'. Talies admitted he had only pretended to put the quarter in Kit's hand. In reality he had palmed it while simultaneously pressing his thumb into Kit's palm in such a way

17

that it would feel to Kit like a coin. He told them it had taken him weeks of practice to get this part of the trick right. "It's like what happens when you blink after someone takes a flash photo of you," he explained. "The neurons don't work at the speed of light, so the brain continues to see the image of the flash for a several seconds after the flash of light stops hitting your retina. Some people think the flash gets burned onto your retinas, but that's not correct. It just takes a few seconds for your brain to receive the message that there is no more flash going on. Same thing with this coin trick—assuming I get my thumb pressure correct. But what I think is really cool is that even after you know all about the science, the trick still works! You can't help not being fooled! Crazy, huh?! Some tricks are built into the structure of the brain!"

Kit stretched his hand out again, ready to test the validity of Talies' hard to believe assertion. Meanwhile Morgan signaled to Mike for the bill, which he handed to them as Talies went through the trick again.

Kit shook his head in disbelief as he picked the quarter off his shoulder and checked for the red dot. He kept his other hand closed as his looked thoughtfully first at the coin, then at his fist. Finally he threw the dotted coin onto the table. "Damn! You're right! It does feel like that coin's still in there, even though I know the feeling is only an illusion!" He chuckled at the weirdness of science, and opened his fist. "What?!"

There, in the middle of Kit's palm, lay the quarter with the red dot.

Talies began to laugh, crazily.

"Tal . . ." Morgan sounded a warning note.

"Must have done something wrong, again," whined Talies, assuming a sad face.

"Twit!" said his mother, handing Mike her credit card.

"Sorry, sir," Tal said, although clearly he was not the least sorry. "But seriously, guys, magic's only partly about taking advantage of loopholes in human perception; it's also about surprising you by managing your expectations. My professor, who also teaches a graduate course in criminal justice, says some crimes can be like that too. So that made me think—magic would be a good skill for a detective. And I am determined to be a detective, a good detective. It's already been pretty helpful on my summer job."

"In my experience, most crooks aren't that clever," Kit responded. "Most leave a fairly obvious trails of clues—if you know where to look."

"But that's what I said, isn't it? Knowing where to look. Knowing not to be fooled by what one only seems to perceive."

Morgan slipped her credit card back into her wallet and gathered up her belongings. "Come on, Talies. I don't know what you two are talking about now. What does magic have to do with your summer job in a coffee shop on Telegraph Avenue, just tell me that! Unless maybe you are using it to induce those wonderful caffeinated aromas."

Talies tossed her an impish grin and winked at Kit as he hoisted on his backpack.

"Boys? What you are not telling me?"

"It's a long story, Mom. Like you said, we need to get going. Wouldn't want to miss Jorge."

"Jorge?" Morgan asked, as they hurried across the downtown plaza. "Do we need to pick up someone on the way into the City?"

"No, no. Jorge's my professor. The awesome magician. His performance starts at 9:30, so I hope it won't be too wicked hard finding a parking spot near Union Square."

"No worries," offered Kit. "I know a place."

"Cool!" said Talies.

"If not magical!" Morgan added under her breath.

"Look, guys! Olympia's doing Trojan Women next month," said Morgan, gawping at a poster outside one of the theaters near Union Square. "The box office is open and there's no line; let's get tickets." She reached towards the handle of the lobby door.

"Please. Not now, Mom!" said Talies, taking her by the elbow and propelling her rapidly through the gaggle of play-goers, tourists, smokers, and buskers crowding the sidewalks along Geary Street.

"How much further is it?" asked Morgan, panting slightly as she freed herself from her son's grip to leap across Jones Street, narrowly avoiding a dented delivery van as it careened around the corner.

"Sheesh, Mom! You're gonna get yourself killed. The place is up there. Other side of the street. Next block. The Somerset Hotel. There's a small performance space in the basement." Talies nodded towards a faded purple awning flapping over the entrance to one of the Tenderloin's less inspiring residency hotels.

As Morgan's eyes sought their destination, Kit gently drew her arm through his own and guided her around a trio of the great unwashed preparing to shoot up in full view of the theater-going public.

"We cross here," instructed Talies when the traffic light changed. They moved as a phalanx past some selfie-taking Millennials outside a thumping dance club.

"Magic Show Tonight" read the banner hanging from the fire escape. A blue arrow chalked below it pointed down the alley. Talies hurried ahead to wrestle open the heavy steel door; then with a nod to the scrawny security guy fooling with his phone, he led them towards a murmur of voices. They filed through a second heavy door, propped open with a paint can, and descended a narrow stairway into a small, dimly lit basement room, furnished with motley second-hand couches and odd chairs. A low platform jutted from the back wall—the stage. About a hundred people filled the room, standing or sitting around, chatting among themselves, ordering drinks from a make-shift bar, waiting for some signal to take their seats. The low stage was hung on three sides with black curtains. In fact, the whole room had been done up in black—black painted walls, black ceiling, even the cement floor was black. If there had been a twirling disco light and some giant speakers, the room could have been taken for a night club. But instead, there were high-end theater spots on tracks spidering across the ceiling. As Kit and Morgan got their bearings, a disembodied voice boomed—"Please take your seats. Our show is about to begin."

Waving off a young woman with a drinks tray, Talies maneuvered them towards a cushioned loveseat of uncertain color—more dark grey than blue, or perhaps green, or dirty teal. The loveseat was angled awkwardly close to center stage. "My favorite seat," Talies told them, patting its lumpy cushions. "Not too uncomfortable. You get a really good view of his hands. Be sure to keep your legs back though, or you might trip the performers. They use the door over there, and the step here, to get on and off stage." Morgan and Kit settled down and carefully tucked in their legs. Talies folded his long body into the corner of a nearby, somewhat longer, sofa on which perched a pair of pencil thin, dark-eyed Asian girls, whom he seemed to know.

Almost immediately the house lights dimmed, and conversation ceased. The room grew as black as the back of a cave on a cloudy night. A minute passed. Then another minute. Nothing happened. The audience grew restless—shifted in their seats, rustled, coughed, whispered to one another. Then, just as Morgan was wondering whether a fuse somewhere had blown, three beams of bright white light shot from the ceiling spots to illuminate a small circle near the front of the black stage. Morgan's leg jerked against Kit's. "Whoa! That surprised me," she whispered. The audience became deeply silent.

As her eyes adjusted to the light, Morgan became aware of a tall, dark-skinned man standing at the front edge of the stage. He was so close to them, she could have reached out and stroked the velvet hem of the dark cloak that wrapped his body like a chrysalis. He felt a little too close. Instinctively, Morgan leaned back, disconcerted by the realization that to get to where he stood now, this man would have had to pass within inches of her own toes and she had completely missed that. She drew back her feet, wondering whether in fact this magician had simply materialized out of thin air. It was weird. She licked her dry lips and swallowed as she stared fixedly at the man on stage.

He stood quietly, giving Morgan, and everyone else in the room as well, a few moments to absorb his fascinating aspect. He seemed to float half an inch above the stage floor. He was all in black—his chrysalis-like cloak, his high topped boots, even his hair—a long tangle of dark Medusa-like dreads. African American, of course, although his clean-shaven skin seemed unusually dark, enhanced perhaps by cosmetics. Morgan noticed the kohl that encircled his eyes. His brows were dark too, and thick—also enhanced? At any rate, his brows crossed his forehead in a ruler-straight line, rather in the manner of a Frida Kahlo portrait. The only relief from all this black were the small, green lensed spectacles perched at the end of his nose. Dark eyes peered benignly over them at the hushed audience. Morgan noticed a flash of bright blood red—the silky lining of the cloak's stiff collar. Its color perfectly matched the magician's red painted lips. She found it difficult to take her eyes off this figure, although, to be frank, there was nowhere else to look in that palpably dark room. Morgan watched the rise and fall of the magician's chest as he breathed in and out, thus confirming for herself that this was a living man, not an effigy. She observed tiny drops of sweat glistening on his grease paint. The effect was mesmerizing, slightly off-putting, like some cross between Wizard of Oz and Count Dracula. She twisted around, her eyes seeking the whites of Talies' eyes. She mouthed— "Jorge?" Talies nodded. Morgan laid a hand on Kit's reassuring knee.

Slowly, after what seemed to be an eternity, but which was in fact only a minute or two later, Jorge began to move. He unwrapped his great cloak. He bowed to the audience, very slowly and with great dignity, deeply from the waist. Four times he bowed—first to the center, then to the left, then to the right, and then to the center again. Slowly he spread his arms wide as if drawing down a blessing from above. For a moment he lowered his head as if in prayer.

When he looked up, he intoned, "Good evening, my friends." His voice was deep, and kind. There followed a burst of generous applause. "Welcome to my Magic Show! Prepare yourself to be amazed!"

With great solemnity the magician raised one arm over his head and pulled a glass of red wine out of thin air. He toasted the audience, but did not drink from it. Then he raised his other arm and pulled a second glass of wine out of the air—white wine this time—and toasted the audience again. From the edge of the stage, he presented the glasses with great courtesy, to the two girls sitting beside Talies. Talies grinned and nodded to his professor. Morgan whispered in Kit's ear, "Wish I could do that!"

And so began the magic show. Morgan's eyes followed the magician's every move, as she tried hard to see through his many illusions. But, alas, not even once during the next ninety minutes did she witness anything other than a series of perplexing impossibilities. Several times Jorge stepped out of character to explain (without the corny accent) how a particular trick was done, revealing its basis in some aspect of neural physiology or human psychology. "People will always miss the difference between the Eight of Spades and the Eight of Clubs, if I do this," he said at one point in a card trick. "They can't help themselves. It's how human vision works!" Or, "This trick always makes me feel like Obi-Wan Kenobi making use of the Force to get you guys to do my will. Remember that scene when he speaks to the storm troopers? Even though the troopers are on a mission to find Luke and the droids, Obi-Wan convinced them not to notice what's right in front of their eyes." Jorge went into some detail about this, as if he were teaching a class back at Berkeley, and then repeated the trick. Even after learning all about the mental quirk that made the trick work, Morgan still couldn't prevent her being "forced" to do the magician's will, nor could anyone else in the audience for that matter. It felt strange. Were all humans really as weak-minded as those ridiculous Star Wars storm troopers? Morgan decided she was not fond of magic.

When the show let out, Morgan, Kit, and Talies linked arms again as they dodged through the crowds spilling from the Geary Street theaters and bunching in the doorways of clubs, bars, and restaurants as people jockeyed for post-performance tables. At the corner of Mason and Geary, a barbershop quartet of homeless men balanced on the curb, crooning "I Left My Heart in San Francisco." Pedestrians paused to listen or to toss quarters and dollar bills into their plastic bucket. Somewhere, over the rumble of traffic, a saxophone whined the blues.

Morgan hunched into her parka against the chilly summer wind that blew in through the Golden Gate and across the City. She felt tired and still half-wrapped in the after-effects of that strange magic show, with its ever-shifting light and dark and its flashes of color and noise. That basement room had been claustrophobic, and its soft couches uncomfortable. And that whole cascade of tricks had left her feeling more than a little annoyed, if not edgy, for she had fathomed none of what she had watched. She yearned for time to think quietly about what she'd witnessed, and to digest its meaning before she could begin to respond to Talies's expressions of excitement and delight.

Finally Talies did stop emoting about his professor's amazing feats. "So how about we get something to eat? There's some good pub grub only a block from here." Her son was hungry, as usual.

"Not for me," said Morgan. "That show left me feeling weird. It was as if the ordinary rules no longer applied, though I suppose we could do some bacon and eggs at home. How do you feel, Kit?"

"Either way's fine—home or here," Kit replied peaceably.

Talies easily yielded to the suggestion of home cooking. "Anyway," he said, "I need to get an early start in the morning. Work's been pretty busy." He peered over his mother's head to catch Kit's eye. "See what I mean about tricks and crimes, Kit? Magic is great training for a detective. Helps sort illusion from reality. Don't you think?"

"Let's talk the philosophy later," said Kit evenly. "Right now magic seems to me more about doing things too fast to be seen— or maybe it's simply our old friend misdirection. You know—the old 'Hey, look up there!' while I pull the ace out of my sock."

"Okay. We'll talk later. But don't you agree magic is a lot more scientific than most people think?"

"Whoa, watch out there, friends," said Kit dodging to avoid the cluster of tourists stopped to make phone videos of the quartet. Then he responded, "I'm not sure, Talies. The linkage between magic and crime seems tenuous to me."

"Isn't it yet another example of people seeing what they want to see, or what they expect to see?" put in Morgan. "Nothing new about that. Hate to say it, but I wasn't exactly enamored with Jorge's show. For one thing, my eyes didn't appreciate the speed of those flashing lights. And all the staring I did, trying to see into, or under, or through the multiplicity of trick upon trick. What a stream of surprises! I still feel twitchy."

"But Mom. . . ." Talies, however, never finished his sentence, for there was a sudden squeal of brakes, an ominous thump, then the gentle tinkle of glass spilling on pavement. Someone screamed! Someone else screamed—louder. A profane curse rang out. And,

24

all too soon, there was a general eruption of sound and motion, worse than any magic show, as people tried to see and sort out what had happened, where, and to whom. The quartet of singers stopped mid-phrase. People shoved people, with some folks pushed into the street, others, in the opposite direction. Voices shouted contradictory instructions. Horns blasted. Traffic came to a dead halt. Someone screamed again.

Kit, Morgan, and Talies dropped arms and stepped up into the doorway of a small art gallery as they tried to locate the nexus of action. Kit rose onto his toes, like a meerkat on lookout. "What the . . ." he muttered and disappeared into the crowd. Talies followed in his wake. People lifted cell phones over their heads, made videos of what had happened, then bent over their devices and busied themselves posting their videos to social media.

Morgan watched Kit's head bob slowly towards where the front end of a white van had come to rest halfway up on the curb, one headlight smashed against the lamp post. A voice of authority commanded, "Everyone, please, step back." One of the singers shouted, "Man down! Man down!" The crowd swelled. It spilled onto the pavement, forming a wall around an open space beside the van.

Morgan heard someone shout, "Over here, girl! Help me get him up." A few moments later, she watched a sort of wave pass through the crowd as three people—two women and an elderly gentleman—left the scene of the accident. "Excuse us. Excuse us," said one of the women, as they crossed diagonally through the now grid-locked intersection and disappeared behind a line of stopped buses.

"Man down! Man down!" one of the singers was still shouting, although by this time he was standing in the middle of the street, waving his arms importantly, diverting, or perhaps confusing, the traffic. A couple of cop cars pulled up in a cacophony of sirens, horns, and flashing lights. The professionals took over. An ambulance screamed to a halt. Two more cop cars arrived.

"Come on," Kit said, reappearing at Morgan's side. "There are sufficient Samaritans here. Let's get ourselves out of this place. Where's Talies?"

They stepped back up into the doorway to look for him.

"What happened?" asked Morgan, scanning the crowd. "Could you see anything? Anyone?"

"Some poor guy was lying in the street. Looked like one of the singers. But I'm not sure. I saw something strange though—I thought . . ."

He was interrupted by Talies, bursting from the mass of onlookers. "I couldn't see a friggin' thing," he said. "Anybody hurt? Anybody dead?"

Kit shrugged. "Unclear. A man seems to have been hit by that van. People were trying to help him. But did you happen to get a look at an old guy sitting on the curb?"

"Nope. Sorry. I didn't. But I did see someone I . . ." Then he shook his head and swallowed his words. He looked confused.

"Kit? Talies? What's going on? What did you two see?" asked Morgan.

"We should get on the road," Kit said.

3 INTO WINE COUNTRY

It was nearly eleven and almost a week later when Kit picked her up in his big SUV. The morning fog had nearly dissipated and the temperature was rapidly rising towards bone melting sauna. Morgan tossed her overnight bag onto the backseat and climbed into shotgun position. She leaned forward and cranked up the air.

"Thanks for fetching me," she said, stifling a yawn as Kit backed down her driveway and maneuvered out onto the narrow mountain road. She held her breath as he executed a tight three-point turn, barely missing the redwood that had lifted up the pavement. She crossed her mental fingers that no biker would come speeding down the mountain at just the wrong moment.

"Remind me to stop at Izzy's shop when we get back," she said. "I think the book I ordered must be in by now. It's for my dad's birthday."

"Would you like to stop now?" Kit replied as they circled the downtown plaza.

"Not really. A few days won't matter."

Traffic was its usual stop-and-go on the main route out of town. By the time Kit merged onto northbound Highway 101, Morgan was fussing with her phone.

She looked up and cast a smile in his direction. "I realize I must have sounded reluctant about making this trip when we talked about it the other night. But I want you to know that now I am looking forward to our adventure together—very much. It's been a long time since I was up in wine country. I'm very much flattered you want my help looking into Indie's uncle's problems." She touched his forearm lightly to underscore her goodwill.

Kit mumbled something about "not flattery," looked quickly back over his shoulder, and changed lanes. Morgan said nothing more, although she still wished they were heading towards a nice simple murder investigation involving total strangers. She sighed. Wine country would be lovely, of course, and the food and drink undoubtedly delightful, the mid-summer weather seductive. If only Indie and her family weren't part of it.

"By the way, I like your new road beast," she said, patting the leather-wrapped dashboard.

"Actually this belonged to my old aunt. I borrowed it from my cousin. Her son bought it for her last year, then this year had to take away her license. Said she was a danger to herself and others on the road."

"Is this what they call a 'suburban'?"

"Dunno. Just a big SUV to me. I didn't pay that much attention. Supposed to be safe."

"Well, it makes me feel like a queen anyway, perched up here. I might become a danger to myself and others too, if I had the chance to drive a thing like this. Do something crazy off-road, you know. Anyway, I texted Talies that he could use my boring old car while we're away. The weather person said it will be even hotter this weekend and Tally's old clunker has no AC. I told him he could come home to sleep too, if he wants. It's usually a little cooler in Quarry Canyon than in Berkeley. I cannot imagine working an espresso machine all day in this heat. Makes me sweat just thinking about it. No doubt the grapes where we are going will be enjoying themselves though—basking in the sunshine, ripening, making sugar." She twisted her body so the dashboard fan blew directly on her neck.

"Global warming I suppose," she went on, kicking off her sandals. She leaned back in her seat, and closed her eyes. "They say the heat won't break until next week. Reminds me of summers on Lake Michigan when I was a kid. Ugh, I hated that weather! So muggy. Like a steam bath. Dad always claimed it made people go a little crazy. I wonder if heat has anything to do with what's been happening up at Buckthorn. A kind of summer madness? Max will probably spend the entire weekend under the front porch, poor yellow kitty! I hope my neighbor remembers to fill his water bowl." Morgan yawned once more as she stared at the traffic ahead. "Maybe I should text Tally to check on Max. He could drive over even if he doesn't sleep at the house. Or I could ask Izzy. . . ."

Kit grunted, but his attention was more focused on navigating traffic than on making conversation.

Morgan's mind turned to her friend, Izzy Folger, who owned a bookshop on the downtown plaza. It was Izzy who had finally convinced Morgan to accept Kit's invitation for this winery gig. With a little help from Naeve Casey, that is. Izzy and Naeve were Morgan's two dearest friends. Ever since Artie's death, their primary goal seemed to be steering her towards another committed relationship. But Morgan wasn't interested in finding a replacement for Artie. And she wasn't very interested in getting more involved with Kit, certainly not when he was still at the beck and call of an ex-wife who was very much among the living. Naeve and Izzy had refused to buy her excuses. And so, for three long nights over the past week, they had talked and talked and talked, crumbling her excuses to dust. Finally, she had caved. Cried "Uncle." The trip to wine country with Kit would at least be better than their endless nagging. Then Izzy had gone on about the Northern California spas, how relaxing they were, how restorative they could be, how Morgan should spend more time that way. "I hate soaking in hot springs," Morgan murmured out loud as she thought about those long conversations.

"What?"

"Oops. Sorry. Just thinking about something."

"No prob," Kit said placidly, his eyes intent on the road. "Matter of fact, I don't like soaking either. I worry I'll fall asleep and drown. You know—we could go over to one of the Mendocino beaches if you feel the need to cool off—after the party I mean, after we figure out what's going on, after we save everybody who wants saving." He grinned as he glanced at her. "There's usually a breeze at the coast. Although that part of the ocean isn't so great for swimming—rip tides—sharks—you know the drill."

Suddenly his head snapped back over his shoulder. He jerked the wheel, first one way, then the other. Then he stomped on the gas and changed lanes as a silver Beamer roared around on their right, going about a hundred miles an hour.

Morgan gasped and braced herself on the dash.

Kit swore. "That guy's got a bug up his behind!" It took almost five minutes for his driving to return to normal, although his eyes kept darting to his mirrors. Suddenly, he mumbled something crude and jerked the wheel once more. He hit the brakes—hard. A long black Mercedes with darkened windows shot by on their left.

"Sheesh!!" Morgan grabbed at the dashboard again.

"Maybe you were right about heat and craziness!" Kit growled, rubbing his chin. He forced a smile. Then he rolled his eyes and chuckled happily about something. "Of course there's always the caves."

Caves? Morgan had no idea what he what he was talking about now, but she did feel a change in his emotional weather.

"By the way, you should prepare yourself for a few inconveniences," Kit continued. "In the accommodations, I mean. Last time I was up at Buckthorn . . ."

Last time? Morgan wondered when might that have been.

" . . . the cottages didn't have air conditioners. Just a couple of noisy fans that did nothing much. Jack tried to get Jules to put in a pool once. Not a terrible idea, but it didn't happen. Water is too precious in the valley to waste on luxuries like swimming pools; I remember Rickie telling him that in no uncertain terms. Tinker didn't want a pool either. She hoards water for her veggies. I admit—it does get hot up there at Buckthorn. Most of the family seem fairly immune, however, even into triple digits. Except for Indie. Indie hates the heat. She wilts. She's like Jules—he spends much of the summertime in the wine caves."

Kit's good nature had returned. Morgan observed his shoulders relax, his driving become less tense, as he chatted on about their destination. She didn't like interrupting the flow of his words, but she did feel a somewhat urgent need to sort out the various members of Indie's family. "I know I should remember what you told me before about these Romanos," she said at one point. "But I'm still a bit fuzzy. I recall something about 'Tinker', and 'Jack', but I've completely blanked on 'Rickie'. Would you remind me who he is?"

"She. Don't worry. It's my fault. I can be clearer."

"Good. Anyway, didn't you say my not knowing was part of why you wanted me to come along?"

"Yes, I did say that." Kit lifted an eyebrow thoughtfully. "But I also agree it could be helpful if you had at least a passing acquaintance with the main characters before we arrive. Just the basics though. It would give you a running start."

Morgan agreed, expecting him to start immediately, but Kit needed to make a few more highway moves. He slowed to dodge the remains of an exploded truck tire in their lane. Then there were the dozen or more black plastic garbage bags spilling bath towels and baby clothes across three lanes of pavement. Bits of fabric flew across the windshield, like oversized milk weed seeds escaping their ripened pods. Kit growled as he jerked the SUV from side to side. Then he hit a major pothole only to encounter a fender bender in the middle lane. Grimly he remarked, "This is not going to get any better. Let's skip over to the back roads. What do you say? We have plenty of time."

"Fine with me."

"Great! This part of the North Bay used to be my stomping grounds, during my cop years. I've driven every inch of blacktop up here, and half the dirt roads too. Indie and I had a little place outside Guerneville for a while. We explored a lot of wine country, found some places tourists rarely visit."

"So where is Buckthorn? Are we close?"

"Not really. Buckthorn's maybe forty or fifty miles northeast of here, as the crow flies. It could take us several more hours if we go the back way, which is what I've suggested. It's fairly remote, near the intersection of Napa, Lake, and Yolo counties. In the shadows of Mount Saint Helena, you might say. Nearest civilization is a crossroads tasting room, and a mom and pop shop. Nearest real town is probably Calistoga, although some folks trek all the way down to Napa City or over to Santa Rosa. Buckthorn backs up under one of the eastern palisades of the Mayacamas." He pointed with one hand. "Or maybe those are the Vacas. I get them mixed up. Jules can tell you though. He's quite a geology buff. Good! This is our turn."

Kit exited the highway, went right, then left, then slowed down to search for an un-marked road. Soon they were driving through vineyards, not another car in sight.

"Makes a fair amount of wine at Buckthorn, Jules does," said Kit at last. His voice had softened as their road trip calmed down. "Good, drinkable stuff. You won't find Buckthorn wines in chain stores of course. They don't have that kind of volume, though I gather Eddie . . ." Kit stopped abruptly and smiled in her direction. "Sorry. I meant to say, 'Indie's cousin Eddie'. He would like to—umm—increase Buckthorn's wine production, or so I gathered. Eddie oversees the wine-making operation." Kit paused again, as if considering an additional remark about Eddie, then he continued. "It might be useful for you to know that the Eddie you will be meeting this afternoon is named for his grandfather, Eduardo Giuliani Romano. He's the guy who started Buckthorn, back in the Thirties, after the repeal of Prohibition." Kit sent another grin towards Morgan as he went on. "The family sometimes refers to him as 'Big Eddie.' Dead now, of course. Big Eddie's parents came over from Tuscany, back when he was a little tyke, about Bailey's age I think. It was right after the First World War. They spent a year or so in Chicago where Big Eddie's dad worked for the railroads. Then they came out to California—to the Central Valley first, then, later, to the Buckthorn Valley."

Kit stopped at a Y-intersection and looked around, as if searching the fields for some hidden landmark. It all looked the same to Morgan—miles and miles of vineyards in all directions. Kit finally opted to go left. He drove half a mile, then changed his mind. The road was narrow, so he drove in reverse all the way back to the Y. There he turned around and took the right-hand option. "Gets a little confusing back in here," he explained. "Doesn't help when people take the road signs down. They think it keeps the tourists out." He snorted a half laugh and rolled his eyes. "Now, where was I?"

"Jules' son Eddie . . . and Big Eddie, his father?"

"Yes. So Indie's cousin Eddie is Jules' second born. He's named for his grandfather, Big Eddie. No. That's not quite right. I forgot someone. There's another Eddie in this mix. Jules' older brother is—was—an Eddie too. He would be our current Eddie's Uncle Eddie. I suppose you might call him Eddie Junior, but nobody ever did, to my knowledge. I cannot not mention him. He's dead too however. Killed at the end of the Korean War—Pork Chop Hill." Kit launched a sort of half grin in Morgan's direction. "Confused yet?"

"Only a little. Let me see, there are—or were—three Eddies in this family. Two of them are dead—that would be Jules' father and Jules' brother. The Eddie I will be meeting is Jules' son. He's alive and kicking."

"Very good. You get an 'A'! Those dead Eddies still haunt the vineyards. Anyway, you might like to know that when Big Eddie bought property in Buckthorn Valley, it was all planted in prunes and walnuts. He pulled out most of those trees and put in vines. Some of the original rootstock is still around—they call it the 'mother clone'. By the way, there's a year-round creek under the palisades, spring-fed according to Jules. Icy cold too! A couple of waterfalls, if it rains sufficiently in the winter." His eyes twinkled. "We could go paddling in the creek if you like—quite different from soaking in a hot spring."

Morgan flipped him the bird.

Kit grinned and continued in his teasing tone. "Bailey likes a good water fight. A little rock hopping. Frog catching. Quite the thing on a hot day. Hope you packed a suit, or maybe we can find one for you to borrow."

Kit soon became caught up in his reminisces of past visits to Buckthorn. Morgan's eyelids drooped; she fought the urge to sleep. What he was saying included little that would be useful for the job at hand. She yawned loudly. Too many late nights with Izzy and Naeve. She dozed, then finally her head sank awkwardly against the shoulder strap of her seat belt and she fell fast asleep.

Twenty minutes later she woke with a start—she'd left her wedding ring at home on the bathroom sink! She'd never done that before! She closed her eyes again, mimicked sleep as her mind searched for why or how she could have done such a thing. Perhaps the heat had made her a little crazy—or forgetful. At any rate, there was little she could do now. But without her ring, that finger felt exposed, alone, naked even. She tucked her hand under her thigh and decided it was time to see where they were.

"Gugh . . . umm," Morgan's tongue lapped away a bead of drool at the corner of her mouth. She slit open her eyes and kneaded out a crimp in her neck. Then she straightened her shoulder belt, and slowly sat up.

"It's about time you woke up, sleepyhead. There's stuff to see."

They were moving now at low speed along a different narrow road. On either side vines hung heavy with fruit. To the west were rows of trellises as far as the eye could see. To the east, more trellises, all the way to the foothills of the Mayacamas. Ahead of them was the hazy shimmer of Mount Saint Helena, that ancient volcano marking the upper end of Napa Valley. And north of that, Morgan knew, several more ridges of the Mayacamas joined together, then opened out, embracing the smooth waters of Clear Lake, a nineteen mile long, half a million years old, geologic fluke. They rode in silence for a while, admiring the panorama. Morgan thought about the varied landscapes of northern California—the folded ridges of the coastal mountains, the valleys of the Napa and the Russian rivers, differences in micro-climate and terrain and geology and soils making so many different terroirs, as the French would say. Little wonder California wine growers produced so many different and excellent wines.

"Why are the vines on the right neatly pruned and tied onto their wires," she asked, "while those on the left snake out in all directions. Do they need to be pruned? Or are they a different type of grape?"

"I don't know. Different varieties of grape makes sense to me. Or maybe it's different vineyard practices. Hard to say. How do the berries look?"

"Berries? You mean 'grapes'? There are loads of them. But what I don't see are people. Does nobody work the vineyards in summer?"

"Oh, they work them. Just not out in the baking heat of a hot summer afternoon. Sometimes they work at night. It's cooler. I know pickers frequently do nights. It's better for the berries, and the people."

"Well, there's a great deal I don't know about viticulture. Maybe I'll pick up some information at Buckthorn. At the moment all I know is that these vineyards are very beautiful. Hard to believe anything even mildly threatening could happen in such peaceful-looking countryside." Suddenly a wave of happiness washed across her consciousness. She nearly laughed out loud.

"Not much traffic out here, that's for sure—except a bicyclist or two," said Kit, giving a wide berth to a grey haired spandex-clad gentleman who was pedaling casually down the middle of the road. The man waved as they went by.

"Friend of yours?" asked Morgan.

Kit shook his head. Next, they passed a cluster of ranch houses, a few long barns, and then more fields, indeed field after field, of grapevines, their branches spread along the shoulder-high trellises like the legs of dancers stretching at the barre, as the berries soaked up the sun's energy and quietly made sugar.

"What's that?" asked Morgan, pointing towards a four-sided wooden tower that rose on the margin of a vineyard. "Looks like the base of a Dutch windmill, but it has no sails. Some sort of silo?"

"Nope. It's a tank house."

"A tank house? Look! There's another one! Why's it so fat on top?"

"The tank house is a type of water tower, sits over a wellhead. The base protects the pumping system and that fat part, as you call it, houses a redwood holding tank, at least they used to. It's enclosed to minimize evaporation. Anyway, that's why the top story has that overhang. The tank house was part of an irrigation system, back in the nineteenth and early twentieth centuries. Also provided the family's drinking water. It's all different now. Systems are electrified, wells are deeper, and holding tanks are no longer needed. But there are still lots of tank houses around. People like them. Part of the regional heritage, you might say."

"There's another one! It looks brand new!"

"Yup. I didn't say people didn't still build tank houses, or rehab them. There's one at Buckthorn. Jules took out the holding tank years ago and turned the fat part into his office. Julie took it over after she and Dennis got married; they remodeled it—put in a bathroom and a small kitchen."

"Julie? Dennis? I don't recall your mentioning those names."

"Oh, I probably didn't. Julie is Jules' oldest—Eddie's big sister. She and Dennis lived in the tank house while they built themselves a real house, down the road from Jules and Rickie's place. I think the tank house is used for guests now. It's very quaint."

"Look! Another one. Next to that barn. I never noticed tank houses before. They're everywhere, aren't they? Hey! That's an eagle! Two eagles! I mean, three!"

"Big enough wing spread certainly."

"There's an eagle's nest in that tree!"

By now, the road had turned eastward, and they began to climb the ridge, following a winding, well shaded, nearly dry canyon. Vineyards gave way to pastures, for cattle, and goats. They saw a horse corral, and a flock of sheep. As the road became steeper, the landscape became increasingly forested, with madrone, native oak, pine, even a few redwoods.

"Ever been to the Petrified Forest?" asked Morgan as they passed a small sign.

"Once. When I was a kid. I liked the geysers better though. Petrified trees are disappointing, if you ask me—they don't move much."

"What happened anyway? Saint Helena erupt umpteen million years ago? Knocked everything flat then buried a forest in volcanic ash?"

"Sounds right. But I'm vague on such matters. Jules is the expert. Would you like to stop somewhere for a drink? We have time. How about an ice-cream? And we could finish our chat about the Romanos without distraction."

"Sure. I mean, that would be very nice, thank you. I confess, I do want to know what I'm getting myself into. By the way, when do we get to the real Napa Valley?"

"Pretty soon. It's on the other side of this ridge." Kit slowed down, turned, and they bounced a hundred yards up a dirt lane. He drew to a stop in front of a rather rough looking roadhouse perched on a sort of shelf above the creek canyon.

"I used to think this was a stop on the pony express, when I

36

was a kid. I s'pose it's possible, but I likely made it up. Come on."

Heat smacked Morgan in the face when she opened her door and climbed out. "Holy cow, it's hot out here!" Laughing, she stood for a moment and simply looked around. Kit headed off immediately towards the dilapidated roadhouse. Morgan decided to see what lay below in the canyon. She crossed the road and slid down the embankment, landing on a ledge, from which she could see into the nearly dry stream bed. She gazed for a moment at half a dozen turtles dozing on a log that dammed the trickle of water to form a shallow pool. A seventh turtle tried to clamber onto the log, but his efforts only spun the log and all the turtles splashed into the water.

By the time Kit reappeared, Morgan was sitting at a picnic table under a massive live oak tree, frowning at her cell phone. "No signal," she announced.

"No ice-cream either," he said, putting on the table two huge iced teas, a hunk of delightfully moldy local cheese, and a package of crackers. He sawed energetically at the cheese with his pocket knife as Morgan chugged half her tea in a single gulp.

Ten minutes later, their thirst and hunger assuaged, Kit took up the Romano story again. He seemed a bit more organized, carefully ticking through the major players as if they were characters in a play.

"Stop me if I repeat myself," he said. "I'm not great with kids' names—and some folks' partners may have changed since I was last at Buckthorn. Indie and I used to get up fairly often—for family gatherings, or to help with crush or bottling. Indie always seemed a bit annoyed by my friendship with some of her family, but I'll enjoy getting to know Jules and Rickie again." He winked as if annoying Indie was a game he rather liked to play.

"At any rate," he went on cheerfully. "The Romanos! They've been at Buckthorn since the early Thirties—I think I told you that. Big Eddie, who established Buckthorn, had two sons. The older son was called Eddie—I told you that too—and then Jules came along six or seven years later. Eddie fought in the Korean war. He died on Porkchop Hill in '53, leaving behind a young wife—Irene—aka *Nonna*. Their son Jack was born a few months after his father was killed, so father and son never actually met one another. All very sad, but not all that unusual. Irene must be pushing ninety by now. She's a bit deaf I hear (ha-ha)—has some health issues, but as feisty as ever. To tell the truth, I can't imagine Irene dying—she's way too stubborn, and too mean! She never remarried, or took a lover, as far as I know. Although I could be wrong. But for public consumption she lived only for Jack, and later, for Jack's kids."

"Doesn't sound like the happiest of lives," remarked Morgan. "A war widow, raising a kid by herself. I'd bet she was lonely. I'd also bet there was some man, or men, somewhere, in the background. Did she work? I mean professionally?"

"Not outside Buckthorn. And as far as I know she still lives in the little house that Jules built for her after he took over Buckthorn in the Sixties. We pass her place as we drive in. It's in the middle of a vineyard. Maybe you're right about her being lonely, I really couldn't say. I'm not sure where Jack hangs out these days. His first wife died, as I may have said. The flu. Indie told me that Irene nursed her through to the end. That wife's name was Carolyn. She and Jack had four kids, in rapid succession, including, of course, Indie. The kids were all young when Carolyn passed. Jack remarried quickly—Gail, her name was—something of an odd duck. She was Carolyn's physician, believe it or not. She didn't like kids much, according to Indie. And she didn't drink wine. I have no idea why Jack married her. Gratitude maybe. Anyway, she landed a big research position in San Francisco at some point, and simply moved out. Irene took over Jack's boys after Gail left, and Indie, who was maybe seven or eight, went to live with Jules and Rickie. Jack camped out by himself in one of the guest cabins down by the creek for a while. Licking his wounds, one presumes. Did I ever tell you about Indie's brothers?"

Morgan shook her head. "Not really."

"Well, she has three of them. The oldest is Aaron—he's a screenwriter down in LA, or at least last I heard; he's married and has a bunch of kids. Then there's Bowie—something of a ladies' man. Always had a string of girls following him around, even in second grade! Bowie's been married two or three times, as far as I know. He's a pilot—small planes mostly, for corporations. He's lives down in the San Fernando Valley. And then there's River—

he's my favorite among Indie's brothers. He used to have a partner, name of Paul. They were a great pair. I hope they're still together. Nice fellows."

Kit paused, reflecting briefly; then he went on. "I never got to know Gail really—she came to our wedding though. I don't know if she and Jack ever got divorced, legally. She always seemed just sort of 'out there'—in the background somewhere. You know what I mean? Indie didn't like her one bit. She and her father used to fight about her, like cats and dogs. The fights settled down when Gail moved out. Now Indie's one of Jack's greatest advocates. I always found that a little surprising. Jack is an arrogant bastard, if you ask me! But I don't want to prejudice you."

Morgan nodded sagely. "Losing one's mother when young can be pretty hard. I wonder if Indie and Irene ever figured out how much they had in common—both being single moms—you know?"

Kit shrugged. "No idea. Indie didn't like her, that's all I know. I did think it was remarkable that Irene has stayed on at Buckthorn. She could have gone anywhere! Done anything she wanted. But she didn't." Kit shrugged again. "But nobody ever talked to me about this kind of stuff. Let sleeping dogs lie, I always say."

"So, how did Gail get on with Rickie?"

"They seemed to tolerate one another, although it always seemed to me there was something not quite right between them." He frowned, as if trying to dislodge a long buried idea. "It could be that Rickie just never got over Carolyn's dying like that. Or maybe she didn't like how Gail moved out. I don't really know. It's all speculation on my part. And like I said, nobody talked to me about this kind of stuff. Indie, however, is singularly devoted to her uncle."

"So you said."

"She'd have a break-down if anything happened to him."

Morgan nodded, sensing an increase of discomfort in Kit.

They sat in silence for a few minutes. Finally Kit stood up and put his hand around his empty glass. "Would you like some more tea? I would."

"Yes, please."

"Are you okay with all this? This stuff I'm telling you?" he asked upon his return.

"I'm okay with it. I was just thinking about the two families though—Jules' side and Indie's side. You mentioned about Indie's brothers, how they're not that involved in winemaking. What about the rest of Indie's family? Her father Jack, for instance. And what about Jules' kids, and their families."

"Well, Jack is very involved in the wine business. Always has been. Fancies himself Jules' equal. Of course he's not! Indie told me Jack has his own brand these days, but he travels for Buckthorn wines too—restaurant sales and advertising placements, that sort of thing. River used to manage Buckthorn's tasting room in San Francisco; he still does as far as I know. Hope so anyway. He's a competent guy. So was Paul for that matter. Julie, Jules' oldest—remember?—and her husband Dennis handle the finances for Buckthorn and oversee the marketing strategy. Julie and Tinker are in charge of the estate's tasting room and the tourist stuff. Tinker used to help her sister some, with the books. I'm not sure she still does. Eddie handles that part of the wine-making operations that Jules' doesn't. Buckthorn also has a professional winemaker; she probably still reports mostly to Jules. Something of an uncomfortable situation, I suspect. Anyway, we'll see. There are various nieces, nephews, and many grandchildren—most of them work in the cellars when they're old enough, and are not in school. Indie's brothers live and work in Southern California, like I said. They don't play a big role at Buckthorn, but everybody turns up for crush. Even old Gail helped out a couple of times, early on, or so I have been told—and Tinker's husband comes most of the time. They live on the estate too. He's an architect though, designs wineries among other things—Phil Sasaki."

"Phil Sasaki!" gasped Morgan. "The guy who won the Pritzker Prize a few years ago? Who did that big mixed-use development near Larkspur Ferry? That Phil Sasaki?"

"Yeah. I always forget Phil's got kind of a Reputation."

"Wow! I'm impressed. I love Sasaki's work! We tried to get him to do our library renovation, but we couldn't raise enough money to cover his fee. He's very pricey. I remember how he handled that big dispute over wetlands in Florida, lots of big shots got involved. Made national news. He's pretty creative. I always think of Phil Sasaki as one of the good guys. You know? So he's part of this family. Interesting."

"Can't say I know him very well. He wasn't around much when I was—always flying off somewhere. I heard he did some nice winery stuff in France. And he did oversee Buckthorn's big expansion a decade ago. By the way, Julie's husband is another name you might recognize—Dennis Giardini. His family is based out in the Central Valley; their wines are everywhere, as far as I can tell. I always wondered whether the Giardini's might try to swallow up Buckthorn one day."

"Hmm . . ."

Kit went on. "Julie was right out of high school when she and Dennis got married." Then he stopped and did a kind of eye-roll thing before continuing. "And their kids are—see if I can get this right—Yoko, Adena, and Mork! So Santa Cruz! Their kids must be in their twenties by now. Julie used to have her eye on becoming general manager of Buckthorn one day, even though it was Dennis who got the business degree down at UC Santa Cruz. Eddie went to Davis of course. He got the degree in enology—that's 'winemaking' to me and you. A sociable type is Eddie—friends with all the up and coming youngsters in the Valley. Very good friends with that guy who got famous selling really cheap wine—the Giardini's big rival—can't think of what he called his brand at the moment. You know who I mean though . . ."

"You mean Old Cole Cab? That's Mike's house wine!" Morgan laughed.

"Yeah. That guy. Ben Coleman. Eddie's best friend—or used to be. Wine Country is a small place—'incestuous', some say. Everybody knows everybody else's business, that's for sure. I suppose we should keep an eye out for business rivalry as the source of Jules' troubles. Did I tell you that Eddie lost his wife, Nicole, a couple of years ago? Some sort of flying accident. I never understood quite what happened. Nicole was an ace pilot. She took me up a couple of times in her Cessna. I even thought about getting my own pilot's license." He paused again, shook off something else he thought about saying, and grinned sheepishly across the table at Morgan. "Sorry, I seem to be digressing. You probably don't need to know all the gossip. And probably I need to find the restroom. Excuse me a minute. Tea runs right on through me."

Morgan watched him trot towards a shed-like structure behind the roadhouse. Perhaps from the physical discomfort, or perhaps from something else. At any rate, he was smoothing his moustache and smiling upon his return.

"This is taking longer than I expected," he said. "We really should be going."

"I'm ready whenever you are."

"Just a couple more things. I'll make it fast. One is that Eddie is a pleaser—that is, he doesn't like upsetting people, even when it's necessary. And he tends to be secretive." Kit tugged briefly at his moustache again, as if considering, then rejecting, another comment on Eddie before continuing.

"I had a hunch once that Jules wanted to pass leadership of Buckthorn to Eddie when he retired, rather than to Julie, or to Dennis, who are first in line so to speak. Jules is old school: he may well believe that the wand should go to a son, not to a daughter. I doubt Julie agrees. Anyway, last I heard, Jules was still solidly in control at Buckthorn—he still makes all the big decisions, and many of the small ones. His primary advisor is Roberto Padilla, his long-time vineyard manager. I think we should try to get a line on what Jules is thinking about succession at Buckthorn."

Kit stared absently into space for a moment. "I could go on and on," he said finally. "Endlessly, I suppose. I haven't covered half what I'd like to, but it's probably enough, for now. We will need to keep our eyes and ears open. And, I should add. There's a lot more than just family to watch out for."

Morgan nodded. "Lots of money in wine these days. Lots of connections."

Kit snorted. "Speaking of money. For what it's worth, here's one more name you might recognize—Rachel Suttermann. Her family goes way back—way, way back—remember Sutter's Mill?"

"I certainly do."

"They're all about gold, as well as the wine. Can't be a better pairing than that. Rachel is Buckthorn's winemaker. She's also Ev Wolfe's granddaughter. Evelyn Wolfe is Jules' long time best friend.

He's a very good winemaker too. Owner of Bob Biker Wines. Bet you've drunk your share of those."

Morgan nodded. "Yup. Small world, isn't it."

"Oh my yes. And one big happy family."

"Well then, maybe it's time to go meet them."

Kit frowned, his eyes resting on his empty tea glass. He leaned down to rub his leg as if bothered by a sudden stiffness in the knee. Then he said slowly: "One last thing."

"Mmm?"

"I don't want to overwhelm you, or prejudice you."

Morgan nodded, encouragingly. Kit drew his mouth into a thoughtful pout and stroked an end of his drooping moustache.

"Kit, what is it?"

Kit grunted something as he played with his facial hair. Morgan waited patiently. "Look," he said after a moment or two. "Indie called me the other night."

Morgan braced herself—Now it comes, she thought to herself.

"I was surprised. I mean I'd already told her I was coming up, with you or without you." He rested his eyes in Morgan's. "I'm not quite sure . . . well, it's more than just a few strange, potentially dangerous accidents happening on the estate that have her concerned. Tinker actually saw someone attack Jules. He was nearly killed."

"Then she really should call the police."

"No wait, I'm not done. Remember in San Francisco? Last weekend? That van that jumped the curb? The man lying in the street?"

"Are you saying that man was Jules? But . . ."

"No. Not him. But almost. Do you remember my saying there was an elderly gentleman sitting on the curb? And that two women pulled him up and hustled him off?"

"I couldn't see over the crowd. And no, I don't remember."

"Well, I only got a glance, but that old man looked familiar. I thought it was a freak resemblance, at first." Kit paused, then spit out the rest. "Truth is, Indie phoned me in the middle of that night. I'd just gotten home and into bed. She was hysterical. She said Jules had been attacked in Geary Street—by a van. Tinker and Tinker's daughter Samantha were there too. The three of them had gone into the City to see The Lion King and were walking back to the car when it happened. A van came speeding right at them, out of nowhere. Jules won't admit he was hit, she said, but Tinker thinks he was. They got him away pretty fast, but Sam swears the van was aiming for her grandfather. Sam's only sixteen, but she's no fool. Indie, of course, wanted me to drop everything, and come up instantly. But, well . . . I wanted to wait to see if you would come with me."

"Oh my God."

"I didn't tell you before because I didn't want to put pressure on you. I couldn't get back to sleep. In fact, I haven't slept well all week. And Indie—well, you know what she's like."

Morgan sat very still. Her heart was pounding. Her hands were trembling. "Oh my God," she whispered again as an icy chill prickled up the back of her leg.

4 BUCKTHORN

A glory of red roses wrapped the stone pillars marking the road in. Morgan read the sign as Kit sailed on by—

BUCKTHORN ESTATE WINES
TASTING ROOM
SATURDAY AND SUNDAY 12-5 PM
WEEKDAYS BY APPOINTMENT

"Isn't that . . . ?"

It was several miles before they could swing around.

"Well, it looks different than it used to," Kit growled, slowing as he approached Buckthorn Road for a second shot, from the opposite direction. "Those pillars are new. I was watching for an old barn, with a collapsed roof. It seems to be gone."

Buckthorn Road was only one lane wide, but it was freshly paved. Kit drove slowly up and over a small rise, then down through a canyon, then back up into a forest of evergreens and native oak, as they climbed towards the top of a ridge. Poison oak grew rampantly along the roadside, its leaves already turning purple. Morgan opened her window and breathed in the fragrance of hot rock, pine needles, acorns, dry creek bed— chaparral, with notes of lavender, rosemary, and thyme. The symphony of smells evoked memories of happy summer drives with Artie so many years ago. Just before the road began its final descent into Buckthorn Valley, Kit pulled into a turn-out and came to a stop. They stepped out and pushed their way through some shrubs to look at the view.

"Beautiful isn't it?" Kit laid his arm around Morgan's shoulders and pulled her closer. Then with his other arm outstretched, he began to point out highlights. "That's where we are going. Buckthorn. Where Indie grew up. . . . Look at the shape of this valley, and those rocky cliffs. There are only a couple of ways in and out. Trucks use the easier road, down there at the southern end. And, do you see that dirt track across from us? Zig-zagging up the palisade? That's one for the hearty, winding its way through that scrubby stuff towards Tinker's place . . . up there on the ridge line. Very contemporary. I like it. All the glass! Phil's doing, of course. There's a good paved road down from their place into the next valley."

And, indeed, the valley below them did have a comfortable basin-like shape, rimmed around by rocky palisade and arched over by the vast blue Western sky. The valley floor, somewhat rolling, was mostly a carpet of emerald corduroy—vineyards.

"Loverly," murmured Morgan, her eyes playing across the scene. "Reminds me for some reason of an old, hammered tin washbasin of my grandmother's. Its bottom was lumpy like that, but from use. Grandma bathed me in it when I was little. I recall sitting there in my bathwater, Grandma frowning down at me, and me crowing with delight as I wiggled and splashed my bathwater onto the floor—little earthquake maker she called me! I expect this valley suffers regular earthquakes too." She smiled to herself, imagining the vines dancing in California's regular rattle and roll. She wondered, did the wine bottles dance too? Did barrels crash and roll across the winery's floor when the earth moved?

"What's that down there?" she asked Kit, pointing towards a large stone building of two or three stories, nestled back against the palisade on the other side of the valley.

"That's the old winery. Built in the mid-1880s, I believe."

"Are those olive trees?" She pointed towards two rows of gray green trees following a long access road that ran from

Buckthorn Road over to the stone winery.

"Um-hum."

"What's with the scaffolding?"

"Probably the new tasting room Jules told me about. Or maybe they're just repointing the stone. Looks like they're getting ready for crush anyway. See? They've put up the canvas roof." He directed her eyes towards an arrangement of large white canvas sails shading a concrete platform abutting one end of the winery.

Morgan grinned. "Looks like a party tent."

"Not really. The canvas protects operations on the crush pad. Keeps things a bit cleaner and the staff a lot cooler. See the load of new barrels back in there? And what a collection of lugs! I wonder where they'll park the bottling truck this year."

"Lugs? Bottling truck?"

" 'Lugs' are what we call the plastic boxes that pickers use, to lug their berries in. The bottling truck is nothing more than mobile bottling line. It's pretty slick. The whole family turns up to help. Buckthorn doesn't produce enough wine to have a permanent bottling set-up."

"I see," said Morgan as she studied the outline of the stone building. "Looks like there are three stories. What happens upstairs? Do they store wine up there? Or are there just offices?"

"Too hot up there to store wine. Heat rises, you know." Kit suddenly stepped away from her and squinted out across the valley. "You can't see it very well from here, but behind the winery is a loading dock and beyond that there's a big old door into the mountain. That's where they age the wine. Buckthorn's wine caves. Perfect temperature and humidity. Jules had the whole winemaking operation re-imagined some years ago. Phil did the design, of course. They enlarged the old mining tunnels significantly, made a series of rooms to be filled with barrels. They also removed the flooring of the upper levels of the winery at that time and installed some very modern, stainless steel fermentation tanks. In the old days, they'd do crush on the top floor of the winery, believe it or not. There was a ramp where the loading dock is now, so the horses could drag up the wagonloads of berries. After crush, they relied on gravity to move the juice into the maceration vats below then into redwood fermentation tanks on the ground floor. Today, of course, it's all electric pumps. Hoses everywhere. And crush is done outside. You'll see. Jules hung onto his old redwood fermentation tanks though. Says he likes the flavor they give reds."

"You said mining tunnels? What were they mining?"

"Probably looking for gold at first, like the Forty-Niners. Chinese workers dug out the tunnels. By hand, if you can believe! The same guys who laid track for the transcontinental railroad. Jules' put his wine barrels in those tunnels in the Thirties and Forties, and later had them dug out even more. You'll see. Saves on air conditioning."

They stood for a few more minutes studying the layout of Buckthorn, then Kit directed Morgan's eyes towards the other end the valley, past some vineyards and an apple orchard, towards the cluster of other homes and farm buildings.

"The old Victorian down there is Irene's place. And across that road is Julie and Dennis's place. Something of a McMansion, I think. And up there, at the end of the pavement, is Jules' place, the old homestead. I love the wrap-around verandas. We call it the Big House. There's an arbor out back. See? Along the far sides of the flagstone piazza? That's where the birthday party will be." Morgan's eyes followed his finger point.

"I'm not sure how old the Big House is. Do you see that adobe front bit? And the barn out there beyond the garden? Jules told me they were built for General Vallejo."

"Really? I thought General Vallejo lived in Sonoma."

Kit shrugged. "He did. But he owned thousands of acres all over this part of Northern California. Probably had several houses, back when we were still part of Mexico. Anyway, the longer leg of the Big House was built well after General Vallejo's time. It's mostly a long string of bedrooms. Jules and Rickie added a few more, and a couple of bathrooms. Indie and I used to stay in a suite out at the end. I don't know who uses all those rooms now. Rickie wanted the verandas. Said she needed a veranda on both sides of her house so she could sit in the shade and watch the sun rise as well as set on the vineyards."

"Oh, look, Kit! There's the tank house!"

"Yup. And straight across from us, out beyond those apple trees, you can almost see the little stream I told you about. Behind the guest cottages. I expect we'll be staying in one of them. And, hey, look! It's still there! See? On the other side of the arbor, just behind the garden, that little cottage that's sort of set off from the others? Tinker lived there for a while, until she married Phil and they built that glassy place on the ridge. When she moved out, Indie and I moved in. It's where Bailey was a baby. But just look at Tinker's place. Interesting, don't you think? The views must be outstanding!" He pointed towards the top of the ridge and a strange, oddly shaped, mostly glass construction from which one could surely see not only down into Buckthorn valley but also out, in all directions, probably as far as the Sierras.

Morgan nodded. "So where do the vineyard staff live?"

"Oh. Well, some of them live in town, but Roberto and many of the others stay down at the southern end of the valley. There's a small village of manufactured homes, and some RVs, down there. It's easier to get into town from that end of the valley." Kit looked up at the sun. "It's getting on. We should be going. They'll be expecting us."

"Look," said Morgan. "It's another golden eagle. I wonder if she's one of the ones we saw before." They watched as the great bird circled high over the valley. "And that up there must be Mount Saint Helena," said Morgan finally.

Kit nodded in affirmation.

Suddenly two ravens began to caw. Their cries echoed off the walls of the valley. Then the eagle dropped down, like a rock, grabbed a critter off the valley floor, and flapped off with its talons full of fur.

"Wow! Did you see that?" said Morgan, instinctively stepping back into the shadows. A few minutes later, with a final look over her shoulder, she followed Kit back to their borrowed SUV.

As they drove slowly off the ridge and out into Buckthorn Valley, Morgan asked, "So, did they ever find gold in these mountains?"

"Not that I know of. Only quicksilver. But that's really a question for Jules."

"Quicksilver is the same as mercury, isn't it?"

"Yes."

"So why not call it that?"

"I don't know. Quicksilver's a liquid . . . could be the only metal that is. It moves, looks alive, I guess. Sort of. 'Quick' is just an old word for 'alive'. It's very silvery too. Why do you ask?"

"Just curious. You mentioned the Gold Rush and that got me to thinking about how valuable wine has become—more valuable than gold, it sometimes seems! I was playing around on the internet in the library last week, and—can you believe it?—somebody shelled out more than a quarter of a million bucks for a single bottle of hundred year old champagne. And old pessimistic me thought—what if when you popped that cork, and the champagne had gone to vinegar. What a downer that would be! Made me laugh. People do crazy things, don't they?"

As Kit drove out onto the valley floor, Morgan stared down row upon row of vines, all heavy with ripening berries. She wondered—mildly—how do winemakers make white wine from such dark grapes? Or did they? Perhaps white wine was made only from green grapes. She opened her window to smell the sweet fragrance of ripening fruit and realized the huge gaps in her wine knowledge. She promised herself to ask someone that question about white wine.

Mid-valley, Buckthorn Road came to a Y intersection. To the right, through an allée of gray-green olive trees, lay the old stone winery. In the other direction was their destination, the Big House. Kit turned left.

He slowed to a crawl as they passed Irene's, so they could both ogle it. At first glance, the house seemed deserted. The blue paint was peeling and the gingerbread trim, worn and crumbling. The small fenced-in front lawn was filled with faded plastic lawn chairs, children's toys, and rusting tools. A gnarled, half-dead apple tree leaned over the roof of the front porch. A long black hose stretched from a spigot near the front steps towards a healthy patch of pole beans, tomatoes, and a short row of leafy greens. Purple hollyhocks bloomed luxuriously.

"The so-called Little House," said Kit as their vehicle crept past. "Jack used to live out back—in the carriage house. He may still."

"Does this whole valley belong to Jules?"

"Most of it, as far as I know. Up to the top of the palisade anyway, where Tinker's house is."

Diagonally across the road sat another house, set well back into a neat, very green, front lawn surrounded on three sides by vineyards. The house was very large and of an unremarkable design. "Julie and Dennis's place," said Kit as they drove by.

"Pretentious" was the word that came to mind as Morgan stared at the glassed-in swimming pool.

"Umm," was Kit's comment.

The pavement ended in a graveled area at the front of the Big House. Kit pulled up on the grassy verge. He had barely opened his door, when a wiry gray and white terrier charged out from under the veranda, barking furiously. "Shut up, Whiskey," said Kit evenly. "We're just family. Hush. Good dog. Nothing to bark about now." Whiskey quieted mid-bark and began to sniff Kit's extended hand. A moment later the little dog was wagging his stumpy tail so rapidly his whole body swung back and forth, as if to say "Oh! Right! Right! Now I recognize you—Hello! Hello! Hello! So glad to see you! So glad to see you!"

"Good boy. It's only me. No worries—I'm not a ghost." Kit squatted down and began to fondle the dog's ears. "Now sit, Whiskey. Be still." Whiskey plumped down on his haunches, although his tail kept thumping away on the ground, and his eyes held firm on Kit's face as if to ensure this man was who he said he was and wouldn't disappear in a puff of smoke.

Meanwhile, a silent phalanx was forming behind Whiskey, consisting of a yellow lab, two shepherds—one of them pure white—and a stocky brindled mutt with a distinctly large black nose.

"Hello, boys and girls," said Kit conversationally to the dogs. "So, who's your new friend with the big nose? And where are your people at?"

Kit opened the back of the vehicle and began unloading their luggage. Morgan climbed down from her seat. A moment later they were engulfed by people of all sizes. Everyone began talking, or yipping, at once.

A barefoot woman in hot pink shorts came out of the house and stood quietly above them on the veranda. Her golden hair hung in a single thick plait down her back. Indie. The only person at

Buckthorn Morgan recognized. Morgan waved briefly. Indie ignored her, saying instead, "Late again, Carson." She sounded annoyed.

Suddenly, around the corner of the house, came Bailey, flying at top speed, arms spread wide. He crashed up against his dad. Kit dropped the luggage and swept his son into his powerful arms. "Hey, old man. Glad to see you too!"

Bailey grinned like a hyena as he patted his father's cheeks and pulled on the ends of his moustache.

"Ow!"

"Bailey! Stop molesting your father. Get over here. Now!" commanded Indie. "Let them get their stuff up onto the veranda at least."

Kit set his son on his feet and started once more to gather up the luggage. Bailey, however, ignoring his mother's command, grabbed at his father's hands and started dragging him away. "Come on, Dad. Come on! You gotta see the baby goats."

"Inna minute. Inna minute."

Morgan stood to one side and watched as a swirl of people began to appear. They came from all directions, all of them talking at once. Who were all these people?

"Hey, Kit. It's been a while, bro!"

"Thought you'd never get here, old friend. We opened a good red for ya."

"That your new gal?"

"Kit, we need to talk."

"How are you, Cuz? How's the old knee treating you?"

"Glad you could make it, Kit-o! Dad's half soused already but he's looking forward to seeing you."

"Leave him alone, people," commanded an old lady stomping out of the house, assisted by a three-footed medical cane. Her wrinkled face beamed a welcome. "Let the man get his stuff together before you attack."

"Hey, Rickie," said Kit, as he came up onto the veranda and threw his arms around the old lady. He kissed her solidly on both cheeks. "It's been a long time. Thanks for inviting me—for inviting us—to Jules' party."

Rickie's look said she knew quite well why Kit was here, but

52

she wasn't going to mention that. "And this must be Morgan," she said hospitably. "I'm Rickie Romano. And this," she said, waving to the crowd below them on the gravel, "is our family." The crowd became quiet as Rickie pointed at each person with her cane, introducing them to Morgan and Kit.

"Over there, that's Julie, my oldest. I think that pie must be ready by now. Would you go see to it, dear?"

"Sure, Mom. See ya later, Kit."

"That's Dennis, her husband. I don't see Eddie around. He must be down at the winery. Anyway, over there's Phil, my son-in-law. That tiny woman with the big baby on her hip is my younger daughter, our little Tinker. And that little thing peeking through Tinker's legs, is Desidera, my great grandchild. Hard to believe, isn't it? But I don't see Jessica . . . where's that daughter of yours, Tink?" Rickie shook her head as she scanned the crowd. "Oh well. This family's hard to keep track of." She went back to her introductions. "Ah, over there, with the frilly apron over her jeans, that is Emma, my granddaughter-in-law I suppose you'd call her. And there's Eddie's Lucy, another of my grandchildren." She looked down and added, "And these two tykes sitting here at my feet . . . They are Josh and Ellie. Twins. Eddie's youngest." She ruffled the hair of each one as she said each name. "Where's your daddy gotten to, urchins? I thought he'd be here to greet his old friend."

The twins shrugged in unison.

Rickie glanced over her shoulder. "I expect I don't need to introduce Indie. Jules is still out back, under the arbor, getting drunk. You're so late, Kit dear. Was the traffic bad? We thought you might not make it before moonrise."

At this point Whiskey let out a sorrowful yelp, as if to remind his mistress of his own presence. "Oh yes, I nearly forgot the four-legged beasts. Let's see now—this one is Whiskey, of course, my alpha male despite his being so small." She said "Whiskey" in the Italian way—Whee-skee. "And Fred—he's the yellow lab. Getting a bit old, poor thing, and slow, half deaf too. That one's Dewey. Dewey, what are you doing?" Dewey was trying to get his nose into Morgan's duffle bag. "For heaven's sake! Get over here, you big lunk." She slapped her thigh a couple of times and the dog trotted meekly to her side. Then nuzzling his head into her hand, he succeeded in making Rickie lose her balance.

Kit grabbed Rickie's elbow and steadied her. "Hey, take it easy, dog," he said.

"Tinker, would you do something with this critter, please? Take him back to the barn where he belongs," said Rickie reestablishing herself. She gave Dewey an affectionate pat on the head as he was led away; then she smoothly continued her introductions. "And that mutt's Little Lupo. He'll put that big nose of his into everything too—some of it's pretty unsavory. Fred's his best pal. Mutt and Fred, we call them. I suppose we should have called Fred, 'Jeff'—except we found out that he's really a she. Her puppies came as quite a surprise! I can't get used to that sex change." Rickie sighed at the idea of a transgender dog. "And this big clumsy thing is my sweet Aida, happy Aida." She put her hand on the head of the white shepherd. "Too many dogs I suppose." She tsked softly with her tongue, then turned her eyes back to the human group before her as if taking roll. "Now where's Zoe? I don't see Zoe. Anybody seen Zoe? Lucy, dear, do you know where Zoe is?"

Lucy was nearly three. She removed her thumb from her mouth and used it to gesture vaguely in the direction of the barn.

"I see. Thank you, dear," murmured Rickie as she turned again to Morgan. "And that one, back there behind everyone, skulking around, all in black, with the nose ring and the kohl-lined eyes—that's Angel, my grandson Ben's Gothic girlfriend."

"'Goth, Gram—not 'Gothic'," muttered Ben, as though he had already corrected this error a dozen times that day.

"And finally—" said Rickie, unfazed by her grandson's correction, she used her cane to point over everyone's head towards a thin, somewhat wild-looking girl, lurking at the edge of the vineyard. "That's my granddaughter Samantha—Sam we call her. Tinker's youngest. She turns sixteen this fall. Not as old as she thinks however." Samantha was studiously not looking at her grandmother. "The rest of 'em are—oh—scattered around the place somewhere, hiding out, pretending to work. Up to no damn good. But that's enough for now, I think."

"Well, thank you, Mrs. Romano," smiled Morgan. "You have a wonderfully big family—"

"Rickie, please."

"Yes. Thanks, Rickie." Morgan corrected herself. She turned towards the loosening crowd of family and said, "Hullo everybody. Thanks for inviting me—us, I mean—me and Kit—to Buckthorn, to the party. Forgive me if I don't remember all your names right away."

"She'll get to know you all soon enough," added Rickie as the family began to drift away. Rickie put a hand on Morgan's elbow and steered her towards the front door, murmuring, "I can't remember their names myself sometimes, and I was present at all their births!" Then she looked around over her shoulder and called, "Bailey, help your dad gather up that stuff. Indie, tell them where they sleep. Come along Morgan, we need to go meet Jules."

Rickie led Morgan down a wide hall, through a restaurant style kitchen, and out the back door, across another veranda onto the sunny flagstone piazza. At the far end of this piazza, under a vine-covered arbor filled with bees and butterflies, at a plank table littered with remnants from lunch, lounged an old man with a bottle, like some reprobate king out of an old play.

By the time Kit finished taking their luggage out of the car, he was alone. He looked down at the pile of their stuff, wondering why they'd brought so much. Even a bag of fresh fruit, which Morgan insisted would go bad if she left it behind. He sighed. Had his instinct been right? Was this Romano business going to take more than a few days?

"You might as well put it all back in. You'll want to drive down to the tank house," called Indie coming through the front door, adding quickly. "But come up here first. We need to talk."

Kit followed her towards the shady corner of the Big House. "You look well," he said, leaning back against the stucco wall and folding his arms across his chest. He gazed at his former wife, checking her from head to toe. It had been a long time since he'd studied her at this range. She'd grown thinner, but was still beautiful—good bones, good body. She looked strong as a young ox, anything but fragile. He caught himself staring at the bulge of her small breasts under the loose tee shirt and dragged his eyes to her face. Her skin had an attractive rosy blush. Sunshine always suited her, he thought. He watched a bead of sweat roll down her cheek. She flicked it away, then nervously undid her braid and rearranged her golden hair into an imperfect knot at the back of her neck. She moved closer. He felt the heat of her now, smelled the faint fragrance of her shampoo.

"I thought she wasn't coming."

"I told you I asked her."

"You're late. Rickie expected you for lunch." Indie vibrated with irritation. Her body was so close, Kit could easily have taken her into his arms. He resisted, wondered at the strength of this urge. He offered no excuse for his—for their—tardiness.

"So, what are you going to do?" Indie asked.

"Do? What do you mean?"

"I mean—while you're here. What are you going to do about it. She'll be in the way. She doesn't know us. They'll suck her in. She'll confuse everything."

"She'll be fine."

"More trouble than she's worth. I feel it. You know I feel things."

Kit ignored her provocations. "Where's Jack?" he asked. "You said your father would be here. And your brothers? Aren't they coming? Has anything else happened since we talked? Anything I should know about?"

"Dad's around somewhere. You just missed him. He's been in New York. He's exhausted. Probably gone for a nap. Or down at the caves. It's cooler there, you know. Uncle Jules hasn't been treating him nice. And my brothers will get here when they get here. You know how they are. Why do you care about them? They have nothing to do with Uncle Jules' problems."

"What are you going on about? My being here was your idea, remember? And why are you so hostile? You know I know what to do."

Indie scowled. Suddenly she reached out and ran a long finger lightly up his arm and looked into his eyes. "Oh, what do you know about anything, Carson? About my ideas? About what I feel? What I know?"

Kit blinked. He paused for a heartbeat, then said quietly,

"Well, do you have something to tell me? Has something happened since we talked? Another . . ?"

Indie shook her head. Her eyes filled with tears. "Oh, go join your new lady friend. Get Uncle Jules to tell you whatever."

For a moment Kit thought she was going to burst into sobs, but instead, abruptly, she pulled herself together, turned away from him, and called out in an entirely different voice, "Bailey! Bailey! Bring those baskets of tomatoes into the kitchen. Now! You've got more than enough. And don't let the goats out again, please." She disappeared into the house.

Nothing changes thought Kit, sighing as he walked onto the sun-bright piazza. Under the arbor Morgan was engaged in appreciating Zoe's kitten, while Zoe's grandparents—Jules and Rickie—were engaged in appreciating Zoe. He wondered whether Morgan had noticed his encounter with Indie.

Jules lifted an arm in welcome. "Hey there, stranger! Glad you made it!" Kit leaned down and bussed his cheeks. Jules neither looked nor sounded like a man in serious danger, but then Jules was not one to scare easily, nor was he one to wear his feelings or his thoughts on his sleeve. Kit studied the old man. He had certainly aged. Although still thick, his hair had turned snowy white since they'd last seen one another. His shoulders were unbowed; he still held them straight, although they seemed somewhat shrunken in both breadth and girth. His face seemed drawn, more wizen than Kit remembered. His eyes were bright still, but somewhat sunken into their sockets. No wonder he hadn't quite recognized Jules on the street in San Francisco. Nevertheless Jules seemed a man in control rather than a man over whom a dark shadow lurked. Or at least so Kit hoped.

Or was he being overly optimistic?

Eight years ago Jules had seemed young—eager, full of energy and enthusiasm about his projects. Surely, back then he would have run out front to meet them. Perhaps Jules had been ill. Or perhaps Kit was simply surprised by the inevitable signs of eight decades of hard living, and hard working. Or, perhaps, that series of mysterious accidents had taken a toll. Indie said Jules brushed off these events as if they were insignificant. Kit promised himself to make no snap judgments.

Kit also wondered, as he watched Jules fussing over his granddaughter and her kitty, how much his old friend knew. Probably knew more than he let on. Perhaps the whole family knew more than they said—Rickie in particular. He'd need to be crafty to get much out of them, circumspect. Neither he nor Morgan wanted to tip off a perpetrator until it was time to do so. And of course there remained the possibility that there was, in fact, nothing to investigate. Indie was worried about her uncle—that much was clear—but Indie was always worried about something. Kit remembered her telling him that Tinker was also concerned, although she'd also said, oddly, that Rickie was not—that Rickie was too deaf, maybe too dotty, to be worried. That did not seem right. Clearly, Rickie too had aged; however from what he'd seen so far, she was neither deaf nor dotty. Could he, should he, trust his ex-wife's view of things? Trust what she said about what had happened in San Francisco? Was there something sinister at Buckthorn? Or was Indie's imagination still not in good working order? Could Morgan be correct about Indie's being up to no good? Kit sighed, poured himself a glass of wine, and sat down next to Morgan.

When he looked up, he caught Rickie's eye. She had been studying him, but he couldn't read her expression. He turned away. Zoe too was studying him. She was still holding her kitten but standing now beside her grandfather. He made a note to himself that Morgan seemed already at work, worming her way into the family's affections.

"Hi," said Morgan softly. Her face told Kit she had observed the scene with Indie. "Tinker said we sleep in the tank house," she said.

He nodded.

Morgan looked at Zoe, who was leaning against her grandfather's arm and snuggling her face in the kitten's fur. "Zoe," she said gently. "This is your Uncle Kit." Zoe looked up and eyed him "Zoe says she doesn't remember you at all, Kit, but she would like to be your friend. Zoe recently celebrated her eighth birthday. And her kitten is named Fluff. Fluff is almost eight weeks old. Isn't that right, Zoe?"

"Hello, Uncle Kit," Zoe murmured gravely.

"Hello, Zoe. You were very, very little when I last saw you. You must have been no more than eight weeks old yourself."

Zoe gave Fluff an affectionate squeeze and then extended the little cat towards Kit. Kit rubbed its ears. Fluff mewed.

"Zoe is Eddie's daughter," continued Morgan. "She's the twins' big sister."

At this point Fluff began mewing insistently, struggling to free itself from the child's grip.

"Maybe you should give Fluff back to its mama now, Zoe," offered Jules. "She's probably hungry."

"OK. You gotta go home now, Fluff. Say good-bye." Zoe waved the kitten's front paw towards each adult in turn. Then, she gathered up the twins, Josh and Ellie, who had been hiding under the long table, and instructed them to bring along their kittens too.

As Kit and Morgan watched the children amble through the garden towards the barn, a young woman hurried across the piazza towards them. She was about thirty years old, and dressed in skin-tight jeans and a checked shirt with rolled-up sleeves. In her outstretched hands she bore before her two small glasses of red wine. These she placed in front of Jules and then stood back, expectantly.

"What do you think?" she said as if picking up a conversation they'd been having only moments before.

Jules picked up one glass and swirled it gently, breathing in the wine's aroma. He swirled and smelled a second time, and held the glass to the light and inspected its contents. Nodding, he swirled and sniffed yet again. Finally, he took a slow sip, held the wine in his mouth, sloshed it around a bit, then quickly spat in a long arc towards the base of the old vine behind him. He smiled, grunted mildly, but uttered no words. Then, as everyone watched, he performed the same ritual with the second glass of wine.

"I prefer the first," he said. "Lingers a bit lighter. Less jammy. Better balance. Not too, too much oak. And I like the fragrance. The old barrels, I presume?"

"Umm," the young woman nodded. "Agreed. But they're both all right, I think. Should I schedule the bottling truck?"

"First, do your chemistries. Let me know the results. But good work, Rachel." He paused to taste one of the glasses a second time. "Don't filter either one of these, or add any more fines, please. I want a natural wine." Then, with a glance towards Kit, he said, "Rachel . . . this here's Bailey's father—Indie's former husband—Carson Jalesco. Generally goes by the name of Kit. Don't ask why. Kit, this is Rachel Suttermann, my winemaker."

Rachel and Kit shook hands.

"And this Morgan," Jules continued. "They're here for my shindig."

"Hello," said Rachel, reaching out to shake Morgan's hand. "Sorry, I can't sit. We're pretty busy right now." She turned back to Jules. "Andrew Frye could turn up this weekend. I tried to put him off, since you're going to be busy with family and all. But he's was being difficult. He's full of himself, that man. Thinks he's a prince, like Parker. Nosy too. Keeps asking questions about how I do stuff. Oh, that reminds me—that new cellar rat you hired—I don't understand why you took him on. He's bright enough, but he asks too many questions, doesn't pay attention to what he should be doing. You might want to reconsider before we get to crush."

Morgan thought Rachel's tone self-important, if not rude. For one thing, she had utterly failed to acknowledge Rickie's presence, although Rickie, like Jules, had also tasted the wines, and nodded, nodding her agreement with his assessment. Rachel acted as if Rickie didn't exist. Morgan studied the young woman's face, wondering what Rachel knew about the events they'd come to investigate.

Meanwhile Jules was attempting to soothe his winemaker's ruffled feathers with regard to Andrew Frye. He harrumphed a good bit, and told her, "You worry too much, my dear. Whatever you work out with Frye is fine. He knows his stuff. Don't let him stress you out. You'll spook the ferment. Your grandfather told me he often works in the vineyards around Bordeaux. I know he'll like our wines. You'll see. And this blend of yours," he said, pointing at one of the glasses she had brought to him, "is very nice."

Rachel preened under his compliment.

"What's a cellar rat?" whispered Morgan to Kit.

"Tell you later."

"Oh, Jules, I forgot," Rachel said, picking up the two glasses as she prepared to leave. "Grandfather called as I was heading over here. He needs to talk to you. Said it was urgent."

Jules nodded, commenting to Rickie as Rachel disappeared around the side of the house. "She a little too serious I think. Gets so anxious. It is just wine after all." He turned to Kit and Morgan explaining, "Rachel's my friend Ev's granddaughter. You remember Ev, don't you Kit? She's very talented. Got a Davis degree last year, but . . ." Rickie tapped him on the arm, stopping whatever it was he might be going to say. Jules seamlessly shifted gears. Years of practice, thought Morgan, watching their silent conjugal communication. Jules went on, "Her grandfather and I trained that palate—before she went off to school. Her mouth's as sensitive as a good hunting dog's nose. She could go far, if only . . ."

His words were cut off by the sound of angry voices inside the house. The shouting pounded higher and higher until it sounded slightly mad. A look passed between Rickie and Jules. Rickie pushed herself up with her cane and stomped slowly towards the kitchen door. Jules' eyes followed her.

"It's getting to be too much for her," he remarked after Rickie disappeared. "That's our first daughter in there—Julie—giving what-for to the caterers." There was a crash, a tinkle of glass, more shouting, then a boom and more angry voices. Jules sighed. "Poor dear. She needs to retire from all of this, but she claims the continued drama keeps her young. I do not believe her." Gradually the shouting quieted. Jules sighed and emptied the rest of a bottle of wine into his tumbler. "Tinker thinks we should go on a long cruise," he scoffed. "That'll be the day."

Whiskey, at his master's feet, snorted in his sleep.

A breeze ruffled through the flowery arbor. Insects hummed. Kit swatted away a pair of bees. For a few long minutes no one said anything, content simply to listen to the summer music of chirruping children, twittering birds, the distant grind of a motor, an occasional yelp, a slamming door, the fall of petals.

"Jules," said Kit finally. "Indie told me about what happened to you and Tinker and Sam last week in the City. I'd like to hear your side of the story."

Jules took his time replying. In the end he said only, "I saw that man go down, poor fellow. Was he hurt?"

Their conversation was interrupted by car doors at the front of the house. Whiskey lifted his head, listened, then ran off, barking his ferocious territorial bark. The rest of the dogs materialized following in their leader's wake.

"Hard for anyone to sneak up on us with that crew on duty," chuckled Jules. "Might be my nephews. I do hope it's not another carload of lost tourists." He leaned forward in his chair, as if meaning to rise. Then instead he sat back, saying to Kit, "Let's talk later about these matters, okay? How about a walk in the vineyards when the sun drops and the air cools a little. Before supper?" He turned to Morgan. "Have you ever walked a vineyard, my dear? In summer? I'd love to show you mine. I walk it every morning, and sometimes in the evenings as well. Keeps me youthful, and alive."

"Once," said Morgan, "when I was young. Friends of my parents had a vineyard on the north shore of Lake Michigan." She glanced at Kit. "I think Kit and I would relish a walk with you, and a talk. Do we have time to put our stuff in our rooms first?"

"Certainly. No rush from me." Then he began to muse. "Papà came to Chicago with his parents. From Italy. Tuscany. He must have been about Zoe's age. Granddad worked on the railroad. It was a long time ago. Never been to Chicago myself, or seen any of the Great Lakes. Didn't realize they made wine that far north—ice wine perhaps?" He grinned, and looked at the sky. "Well, my boy," he turned once more to Kit. "Tinker told me she was putting you two in the tank house. I'll meet you in an hour or so out at the barn. Take yourself a bottle of white from the ice chest over there. It's a nice, not too alcoholic, thirst quencher."

And so, with a mild groan, Jules finally rose off his chair. Halfway across the piazza, he turned. A curious expression flitted across his face. Then he winked at them. Morgan glanced at Kit, hoping for an explanation. Kit's mind was elsewhere.

5 LESSONS IN WINEMAKING

Jules was talking quietly with a greying man in overalls and wide brimmed hat when Kit and Morgan rounded the corner of the barn. Then Jules turned and stared at a terraced vineyard on the slope above them.

"*Eh, bueno, Patrón.* I won't tell young Eduardo right away. Go see it yourself. My boys will have it all fixed by tomorrow though."

Jules frowned.

"Ah, there you are," he said as Kit and Morgan drew closer. "Kit, you remember Buckthorn's vineyard manager . . ."

"Of course I do." Kit extended his hand. "Carson Jalesco. Hello, Roberto."

"And this is his lovely lady," added Jules. "Miz Morgan Kendall. Morgan, meet *mi mano derecho, Señor Padilla.*"

Roberto's forehead furrowed.

Morgan too extended her hand.

"Roberto and I have worked together for nearly forty years. He is the soul of these vineyards—a true master. Without him, and his team, Buckthorn's vines would be in serious trouble. He understands their personalities, their magic. He is without equal."

"*Todos somos iguales a los ojos de Dios,*" murmured Roberto under his breath—We are all equal in the eyes of God. Then, with a slight nod, he began to make polite but ordinary conversation in impeccable English. A few minutes later he hurried off.

Jules chuckled. "I confess, I wouldn't want to live any longer if Roberto were to leave Buckthorn. He receives constant offers from other growers—some of them very generous! But so far—thank the good Lord—he continues to oblige me with his presence. In my opinion he is the best vineyard manager in the county, or for that matter, anywhere in California. He always knows exactly what's going on with the vines. No fooling him. Now, what were we three going to do? A walk in the vineyards, then, I believe, you have some questions for me. This way please. Let's see how the berries are ripening."

He set off at a surprisingly sprightly pace for a man about to celebrate his eightieth birthday. The years seemed to drop from his shoulders as he moved through his vines, tenderly inspecting a leaf here, a leaf there, sometimes adjusting a stem or carefully picking off a few leaves to ensure that each cluster of grapes was bathed in maximum sunshine. Morgan and Kit stayed close as he described what he was doing, and why. Soon their three heads were bending as one, in consultation.

"These are some of our oldest vines," explained Jules. "They go back almost as far as I do. My parents planted their first vineyard before the war, in the spring after the repeal of Prohibition. Just look at these stems! They are as twisted and gnarled as I am."

"What variety of grapes do you grow?" asked Morgan.

"Well, these here are Sangiovese. They came from my grandfather's vineyard in Italia. My father grafted them onto our native pest-resistant rootstock, *vitis rupestris*. Being Californians, you are probably well aware that has been standard practice since the phylloxera epidemic. Sangiovese may not be as popular as Cabernet, but my father claimed that for him Sangiovese was the taste of home." Jules chuckled. "He liked his Brunello. 'Twas magic in the bottle, he always said."

"Brunello? I've never heard of it," said Morgan.

"Ah. You've not been to Tuscany then," said Jules.

"No, but I would like to go, one day," she replied.

"Me too, if I live so long. I've never been, although I still have family there." Jules went on, "Brunello. *Brunello di Montalcino*. My father was born in Val d'Orchia, south of Siena. Tuscany is beautiful countryside! *Papà* said you could see Montalcino up on the hilltop from where he grew up. It's a hill town, built by Etruscans, he told me, hundreds of years before the birth of our Lord. In other words, they've been making wine there since the beginning! It humbles me. Brunello is very famous in Montalcino. Here in California? Not so much. It's . . . well, it's very expensive. If, that is, you can even find a true, natural Brunello any more; even in Tuscany I've heard that's getting difficult. A lot of fakes out there unfortunately. A lot of scandal."

With a wry smile, Jules glanced up at a passing wisp of cloud in the blue, blue sky overhead. "One of my cousins emailed me recently. He still lives near my parents' old place. Such goings on in Tuscany! Apparently the wine police caught a well-regarded vintner blending his Sangiovese with Merlot! Hard to believe, but, money conquers all, I suppose." Jules produced a look of mock horror. "My son Eddie wants Buckthorn to make Brunello again. He planted a great deal of Sangiovese down at the other end of the valley a few years ago. Brunello ages well, you know. Eddie claims it will bring a high price at auction. I wouldn't know about that, but it excites the boy." Jules shook his head slowly. Morgan wondered why Jules didn't seem to believe in this dream of Eddie. "Which reminds me—I do believe there's still a couple of bottles of my father's '52 in the library. It had a very good nose. I'll see if I can find one for you."

At this point Bailey came charging up the road. He grabbed Kit's hand as he slid to a halt. "Can I come to the library with you, Uncle Jules? I finished all my books!"

"I'm not talking about that library, young man. It's only my collection of dusty old bottles of wine." He winked at Kit and Morgan. "And I mean to taste every one of them before I go home again."

"But you are home, Uncle Jules, aren't you?"

"Uncle Jules is referring to his family's home, back in Italy," suggested Kit.

"No. I am referring to my final home. Up there." Jules' eyes moved again towards the wide blue sky. "Our Home in Heaven is what I'm talking about. Perhaps that's where I'll be going when this life is over." He smiled strangely.

"Oh, I get it," said Bailey, with a questioning glance towards his father. "But you're not going to die yet, are you Uncle Jules? I don't want you to die. I'll miss you."

Jules ruffled the boy's hair, but said nothing more about dying.

Suddenly an impish grin spread across Bailey's face. "Momma says I'm a bookworm. So can I come and taste what's in your library?"

"You are a scallywag," said Jules, taking Bailey's hand in his. "Come, walk with your old uncle. I'll tell you a few secrets about the grape."

Kit looked at Morgan, raising his eyebrows as if to say, So much for our having a long private talk with Jules. Morgan shrugged and nodded back over her shoulder. "Looks like more company coming."

Sam stood at the edge of the track, some thirty or forty feet behind them, monitoring the progress of her cousin Ben, whose red head bobbed towards them through the vineyards a dozen rows away.

"Hey, Grampy," Ben called as he drew nearer. "The berries in this patch seem almost ripe! Rachel's going to let me to do the brix."

"That's nice," said Jules, motioning for both Ben and Sam to join him. Then as they walked along together, Jules demonstrated how to adjust the vine leaves to maximize the amount of sunshine hitting the grape clusters. He halted at the base of a well-worn track up the palisade "Come along," called Jules to his little ducklings as he took Bailey's hand and turned up the first switchback. "Let's see what the critters did up here last night."

Jules paused mid-way up the palisade. He looked out across Buckthorn Valley as he caught his breath. The scene was magical, bathed in the glow of the westering sun. Ben and Sam immediately pulled out their cell phones to check the quality of the reception.

"Put those things away, you two. Look around yourselves." Jules extended his arm towards the tapestry of vineyards in the valley. Kit winked at Morgan, as Jules began explaining to the next generation of Romanos how to recognize, from a distance, which variety of grape was which by noting subtle differences in leaf color and foliage texture—the Chardonnays in the vineyard over there, the Cabernets there, the Zinfandels, the Merlots, the Pinots there, there, and there. "And down beyond the mobile homes, if you squint, Bailey, you can see your Grandpa Jack's Mustard Seed vineyard. See how the color tells us immediately that he's planted Cabernet?"

"Why plant so many different varieties?" asked Morgan, who was standing next to Jules. "Or is that a silly question?"

"Not silly," replied Jules, glancing at Ben and Sam who were now busy posting photos of the valley to social media. "You might say it's so we can make all the different wines we like."

"Well, I was thinking about the Brunello business we were talking about before," said Morgan. "I guess I'm still confused."

"What confuses you, my dear?"

"Well, for one thing, what does 'Brunello' actually mean? It's not a variety of grape, is it? You said Brunello wine is made from one hundred percent Sangiovese grapes. So why not call the wine Sangiovese? Like a Cabernet, or Chardonnay? Those wines are named after their grapes, aren't they? Or is Brunello simply another name for Sangiovese?"

"Yes and no," Jules chuckled. "'Brunello' in fact means 'little brown grape' in the Tuscan dialect. I suppose it could be applied to other clonal varieties of grape too, except that it's not, at least not in Tuscany. 'Brunello' is what locals call their own clonal variety of Sangiovese; it's grown only around Montalcino. There are other varieties of Sangiovese besides the Brunello."

"Umm. And why would someone want to add Merlot to it? Wouldn't that ruin the wine?"

"In my opinion it does," said Jules. "And many Italians agree. They're very careful about their naming conventions over there. Blending in a measure of Merlot wine mellows the density of flavors in your typical Brunello. It homogenizes the wine, so to speak; some think it makes the wine more palatable and thus more popular. Brunello can be a bit persnickety about where they will grow well. Merlots are more easy-going. Another idea is that by blending in some Merlot, one can stretch out the Brunello, as well as increase the overall predictability of the taste and behavior of your wine, if you can get away with it."

"Like adding water to stretch out a thick bean soup when

more guests than you expected turn up?"

Jules shrugged. "Maybe. Blending is a great art. It's complicated."

"Well, how about 'clonal variety'? What does that mean? I have so many questions! I'm even a bit embarrassed to ask some of them."

"Don't be embarrassed, dear."

"Okay, I'll try. So, I was thinking about what Ben said a few minutes ago. Why on earth would one make bricks in a vineyard? I don't get it."

Jules laughed out loud. "That's an easy one! Ben was talking B-R-I-X, not B-R-I-C-K-S. They do sound the same. And you're not the first one to be confused by winemakers jargon. However, 'brix' is what we call the lab test for sugar content in the grape. It's named for some German guy—Herr Brix I suppose it was—the guy who developed the test. Scientific types use it to determine whether or not the grapes are ready to pick, that is, whether the berry has made enough sugar to start the process of fermentation. Rachel and Eddie rely on brix tests. Me? I'm old fashioned. I put a few berries into my mouth. Here." He handed Morgan and Kit a few berries he had picked as they were out walking.

Morgan made a face and spat her two berries on the ground. Kit swallowed his quickly.

Jules laughed out loud. "They don't quite pass the readiness test, do they? Should be sweeter?"

"I want to taste too," said Bailey. Jules handed him a berry.

"Ugh!"

Jules nodded, and continued his lesson. "So, let's talk about 'clonal variety.' That somewhat oxymoronic phrase refers to the fact that wine growers use cuttings rather than seeds to produce more vines. Cuttings can be either planted directly into the soil, or grafted onto what we call rootstock. Why do we clone? The motive is to achieve predictability in fruit production, and thus in the wines. You do know what a 'clone' is, don't you?"

Morgan nodded. "An exact DNA replica of the parent."

"Cor-rect! Now, grapevines are very adaptable. And natural mutations occur from time to time, even with clones, thanks to differences in environment, or disease, and even between parent stock and the cutting. That means even among clones there may be variations. And that's what makes wine growing so interesting. Indeed, there is sometimes enough variation between the parent stock and clonal stock that you get an entirely new variety! There's more diversity within the different grape varieties than most people realize. Rachel told me that the horticulturalists down at her university have identified something like thirty-four or thirty-five distinctly different varieties of Chardonnay grapes growing here in Northern California alone. Alert! All Chardonnay wine is not the same! That number of varieties of Chardonnay may seem like a lot to you, but back in the old days, I'm told, they had as many as a hundred, or a hundred and fifty, different clonal varieties from the same rootstock! Hence growers like me tend to be hawk-eyed in the vineyards these days. We are very careful with our varieties. I can tell you that at Buckthorn today we are growing six different Chardonnays, and that for our estate Reserve Chardonnay we actually blend several of these together. You do know what *terroir* means, don't you?"

Morgan, who was trying to take in what Jules had just said, nodded uncertainly.

"In my opinion," Jules went on, "that word is over-used by certain wine snobs, even as the concept behind it remains valid!"

"*Terroir* refers to the micro-climate and local geology of the vineyard, doesn't it?" Morgan asked. "It's the idea that small local differences affect the flavor of the grapes grown there. I mean differences like whether the soil is clay or sandy or has a lot iron in it, or —as some say—even the type of manure that's spread, as well as differences like elevation and slope which then affect temperature or rainfall or the amount of sunshine on a particular vineyard. Right? Doesn't knowing about *terroir* help explain why two wines made from the same variety of grape but grown in two different vineyards will produce wines that taste differently? Am I close?"

"It's a bit more complicated than that, but not too bad," said Jules. "If you grow the same clonal variety of grape on two different terroirs, you should expect some modest difference in the wines produced. But grapevines are amazingly adaptable, and clonal varieties can mutate quickly in response to terroir differences. And then of course it's not all about the terroir either. Differences also occur because of how the wine was made, including variables like when the grapes are picked—how ripe or unripe the berries were—to how long the winemaker chooses to ferment and in what sort of tank or barrel and what chemicals are added or not added. And there's that whole business of blending. Winemakers are always trying to achieve their own idea of the perfect balance among flavor, acidity, and intensity. So they may sweeten a Cabernet with a little Merlot, for example, or add handfuls of oak chips to a ferment. The possibilities are really endless. In some cases, the winemaker will even obliterate the qualities of terroir in order to produce something that tastes like someone else's award winner!"

"Wow," said Morgan. "I didn't realize."

Kit was grinning. He'd heard this lecture several times before.

Jules went on. "Yes, winemaking has always been more of an art than a science. Science just enlarged the winemaker's toolbox, so to speak. And to my mind more is not always better. And there's always trade-offs, and even among clones, there can be a lack of predictability. Like I said before, mutations can happen quickly, at least with some varieties. Take those Pinots down there." He pointed across the valley. "They do it almost before one's eyes. Really! Some years they drive poor Roberto crazy. It's what keeps this business interesting, and makes it fun too!"

Morgan looked at Kit, whose grin had now spread from ear to ear.

"Don't get the idea that wine growers sit around waiting for their grapes to develop some quality they really like." Jules was on a roll now. "No, we growers are control freaks. I certainly am! So is Roberto. So is Rachel, for that matter. If we doesn't produce berries we like, we'll tear the vines out! Or we'll dig them up and replant in another location—a slightly drier field, for example, or a sandier one, where the roots have to scrounge deeper for water. Roberto and I do think that scrounging makes berries more intense. Tinker does the same thing with her tomatoes—she calls it dry-farming. Anyway, she minimizes the amount of water she lets them have. It makes for smaller tomatoes but also a more intensely tomato flavor, she thinks. And, of course, now we have global warming to contend with, which will make environments we thought were settled, change in many ways—hotter, wetter, drier. We wine growers will need to adapt along with the vines."

"I have another question," said Morgan. "You talk about rootstock. Why don't you grow grapevines from seeds, like pole beans, for example? Are grape seeds infertile?"

"I've been asked this question many times. The answer has to do with control. Grape seeds are not infertile, but they are unpredictable. Think about how variable human reproduction is. And I read recently that scientists are now saying that even identical twins have lots of genetic differences. The thing is, seeds offer far too many possibilities. If Mama Nature were to take over the vineyards, there'd be no way to predict the quality of wine production from year to year, and you can't run a winery business that way! I mean, just look at those three back there—all of them from the same family." He nodded over his shoulder at Ben, Sam, and Bailey, as if the differences among these cousins clinched his argument.

None of these cousins was paying any attention to Jules' discussion of viticulture. Each was absorbed in his or her smart phone. Bailey was playing a video game, grunting as he exploded alien spaceships. Ben was bouncing to a beat coming through his earphones, while practicing some complicated dance steps among the rocks on the hillside. And Sam was scrolling at warp speed through her social media pages, pausing only to post a quick comment or a photo she'd just taken.

Jules looked up at the sun and calculated the time. "Clones are more predictable, although even clones can vary. But I've said more than enough! Just remember this: Roberto and I must watch our vines carefully. If one of our fields starts producing berries we don't like—we rip out the vines—and burn them—or plant them somewhere else."

Morgan was stunned by this sudden display of ferocity.

"On the other hand, if we like the berries we're getting, we may choose to clone that stock and try it elsewhere. But don't get me wrong. We aren't constantly moving our vines around from year to year. Some vines are very reliable. I could show you a couple of fields where the vines still produce the way they did when my father planted them seventy years ago. You do realize I hope that a newly planted vineyard can take up to twenty years to reach mature production? That's a long time. Winemaking is all about time, you see. Time and patience. Watchfulness. Care. Both in the ground and in the bottle—which is perhaps a story for another time. Now, I can see by the sun that our time is getting on. Dinner is still a few hours off, but we'd better move along. These old legs won't carry me forever. I am well past my prime. Or maybe it's only this birthday party business that's getting to me."

Indeed, as Morgan studied his face, Jules did seem to have grown a bit paler than when they had started out. Was this only his age showing? Or was he not feeling well? Or simply had they been standing too long in the sun? She passed him the bottle of water she carried in her pocket.

"Uncle Jules, you're gonna like your birthday party!" broke in Bailey. "I know you will. Mama says so."

"Yes, I probably will, my boy." And, with these words, Jules turned and took Kit's offered arm, and the six of them climbed the rest of the way to the upper vineyard, where Jules lowered himself with a great sigh onto a long bench that had been ever so strategically placed in the shade of a live oak.

"Put that game away, Bailey," he called out. "Come over here. Let's see if you learned anything this afternoon. Can you identify the type of grapevine planted in this vineyard here?"

"It's Cabernet, isn't it?"

"Right you are! And we do grow lots of Cab here at Buckthorn. Samantha, Ben, stop skulking around and put away those phones. I want the three of you to do a little brix test for me on my berries."

"How do we do that, Grandpa?" asked Ben.

"The old fashioned way. Go pick a few berries and we'll taste them. But watch out for the poison oak. And be gentle, my children. Don't bruise the clusters. Get me a few as well. We need to consider picking this patch too."

The youngsters trotted off on their errand, returning in a few minutes.

"All right. Now, taste your berries. Don't say anything, but take your time and consider quietly what's in your mouth. Then, come over here, and whisper to me what you think. I want each of you to form your own opinion."

Morgan and Kit smiled as they watched Jules give a last lesson of the afternoon. Sam's response seemed to please him most.

"Now scat!" Jules said suddenly, clapping his hands. "School's over. Ben, I know you've got chores in the barrel room. And you two, run down and tell Grammy we'll be back in time for our suppers."

"So," he said, when they were alone at last. "That's enough of my hobby horses. It's your turn. You have questions."

Kit got straight to the point. "Tell us, please, what happened to you in San Francisco?"

"What do you mean?" asked Jules ingenuously.

"I believe you know what I mean, sir."

"Yes. All right," he said. He and Sam and Tinker had stopped to listen to the quartet of singers on the way back to the car after seeing "The Lion King." He had stooped down to put a bill into the tip bucket when a van lost control and swerved onto the sidewalk. He'd jumped to one side, lost his balance, and sat down, rather hard, on the curb. Jules thought one of the quartet had been hit. It amounted to nothing they didn't already know, or guess.

"Next thing I knew," Jules went on, speaking quickly and discounting any sense of danger. "People were crowding around, shouting. Very chaotic. Very dramatic. Tinker and Sam hoisted me up and hustled me off before the police came looking for witnesses. I wasn't hurt. And I certainly didn't take what happened personally. I did ask Tinker, however, not to say anything about it to the family, as they've been upset by some incidents already at the winery. Not that I saw any connection between those accidents and this van thing. Of course Tinker immediately told Indie, and her mother, all about it. And the story was out. Tinker spun what happened out of proportion, as usual. My family wanted to call the police. I forbade them to do so. It was ridiculous. I was tired. I went to bed." He looked up at the sky again, smiling the kind of strange smile that made Morgan wonder whether or not he was being entirely truthful with them. She watched Jules watching Kit's response to his statements, but Kit's face remained unreadable.

Morgan tried a different tack. "What about those other

incidents? Several struck us as being fairly unusual, and dangerous. And it seems like there have been a lot of that sort of thing recently, with you as target. I'd worry, if I were your family."

Jules rubbed his chin, and glanced at Kit. "I know. Yes, there have been a few accidents around the winery lately. But please understand, both my dear daughter and her cousin are pessimists by nature. By which I mean they can be trusted to make the worst of things. Tinker reads too many thrillers. She sees bad guys in the bushes. I'm not a fool. I take good care of myself. And I do realize that you two are here to check certain things out. Which to my mind is far preferable to calling the local cops. So, I appreciate your coming up—your presence will get the ladies off my case for a few days at least. Kit, I don't know if you know that I suggested Indie give you that call, after she got all over me. My dear boy, I haven't seen you in years. I certainly wish your visit to Buckthorn were for different reasons. But try not to take Indie too seriously. And now that you are here, I hope you'll try to relax and have a good time. I am relying on you to do what you can to settle my family down, of course, but please keep it in the family if you can. Trust me—I know there is nothing going on at Buckthorn that you need to worry about."

"So how do you explain the rags stuffed into the cave's ventilation system? Or who locked you in? I was told you could have asphyxiated," said Morgan.

Jules groaned. "That was a big non-event. I was only half an hour late for supper. I misplaced my key. Rachel came by; she let me out. The cellar rats had been cleaning the air ducts. I put them up to that—I thought a baby bat might have fallen down into one of them. I guess that idea upset the lads. Anyway, I was personally never in any danger."

Kit didn't buy it. The bat suggestion was preposterous, and Jules well knew why there were the air ducts—to vent the carbon dioxide and ethanols produced by the slow ferment of wines stored in the cave. And Kit was also aware that Jules liked to experiment back in his workroom with open-vats for the primary ferment. Toxic emissions were inevitable. Locked in with the air ducts blocked, Jules could have gotten into trouble. Indeed, for an old man with asthma and a possible heart condition, it might have been big trouble. Why was Jules shrugging this off?

Morgan, too, felt skeptical. She wondered whether Jules protecting someone. But who? Why? Clearly, Jules wasn't going to say. Nor could she trust Kit, given his obvious partiality to his ex-wife. Morgan decided she'd need to sniff around on her own. Perhaps get Sam's view about that van accident. Sam seemed an observant girl, and like her grandfather, nobody's fool.

"Your family seem very concerned about you, sir," said Kit gently. "Is Buckthorn in some sort of financial trouble? Are you? Is there something about the business you don't want your family to know? You could tell us. It would help our investigation. We can help, if you let us."

Jules frowned. He looked back and forth between Kit and Morgan, then laid down the law. "Let me tell you something, my young friends. And I want you to really hear me. The only thing that's going on at Buckthorn is a loss of the old work ethic. There's too much carelessness." He spoke slowly, as if he were speaking to his grandchildren. "Buckthorn is a family-run operation. That means I must hire my children, my relatives. They all care deeply about the winery, but there is a danger of complacency in this practice. They don't always maintain a professional attitude in their work. They know that Buckthorn has always been profitable. They know there's no threat of bankruptcy, or a takeover. They have nothing to worry about financially. So they grow lax. They get caught up in their own concerns. They know I will always be here to catch their mistakes. But I won't always be here. That's the rub. They need to learn to be responsible. It's important to seal the bung holes on the barrels properly after drawing out a little wine. Otherwise air gets in; the wine is oxidized and must be thrown away. It's important to check constantly on fermentation. If it goes on too long, the batch gets ruined and must be thrown out. It's important to scrub the vats completely clean. If they're not clean, the wine will take on a bad taste. It's important to always check the hoses for breaks. If no one pays attention, gallons of good wine can run down the drain. Air ducts must be kept clean too, and open—no rags left behind. Someone might die! It happens. Of course there have been conflicts among us about how to operate this winery. That's normal in a family like mine. I do realize values are changing. Traditions are changing. But I don't have to like it, or to tolerate it. Yes, these accidents do concern me. But that's all they are! Accidents. Accidents that shouldn't have happened. But you waste your time, my dear, dear boy, looking for evil in this garden. It's not here. Trust me. You and this fine lady would do much better to use this opportunity to enjoy yourselves. It's been a long time since you visited us, Kit. Isn't it time you became reacquainted with your family? So much has changed since you last visited us."

Kit knew he was being put off, and he very much disliked being put off. Like Morgan, however, he was forced to conclude there was little to learn from this old man, at least now. He knew Jules could be very stubborn. He knew he was on his own.

Jules, looking suddenly grim, swatted away a bee that had landed on his sleeve. "Bees! Even they have become a source conflict in this family."

"How so?" asked Kit.

"We need them in the vineyard, of course, and in the vegetable garden, and in the orchards—to ensure that a good quantities of fruit will be set. But Tinker keeps moving her damned hives around. I never know where I'm going to run into bees. Trouble is I've become very allergic to their stings." He fished through the pockets of his barn coat and began displaying various items. "But I'm not dotty. I always carry an epi-pen . . . and an inhaler . . . and my anti-venom kit. That's for the rattlesnakes. I've never been bitten, but Roberto has. So watch out when you climb around in these hills." Jules began to heave himself to his feet, his face precluding any further questions. "I need to check something in my vineyard before I head down. Want to come along?"

"But of course," said Kit offering his arm again. Jules took it and began chatting again about wine as they made their way slowly towards a far corner of the terraced vineyard. "The ancients were right, you know. Wine is a gift from the gods—whichever god or gods you happen to believe in. And winemaking is a sort of divine magic comprised of time, weather, and human genius. Man has been making wine since Neolithic times, or perhaps even the Paleolithic. It's hard for me to understand all the current whoop-de-do, as if wine had been suddenly discovered. And the snobbery that's involved. Is one truly a more important person for owning a bottle of 1973 Chateau Montelena Chardonnay? That was pretty good Chardonnay. It certainly deserved to win. I might even have a bottle of it somewhere in my library. We should open it, see if it's still drinkable. It might well have turned to vinegar by now."

The man's scallywag's grin reminded Morgan suddenly of Bailey's.

"You do know the story of that tasting?" Jules continued.

"We rented the movie," said Morgan. "A blind tasting. The Napa winemaker beats out the French ones, much to the consternation of the French. That was the first time, wasn't it."

"Not really," said Kit. "That film exaggerated a bit. The French knew all about California wines long before the Seventies."

"You are correct about that," added Jules. "California has been trading vines back and forth with the French for at least a century. But that damned tasting event represents the beginning of the end for old-timers like me. Others think of it as the beginning of The Best Years. They say it put California wines on a par with the Big Boys from France." He scoffed. "But for people like me it marks the beginning of over pricing, over development, and far too many movie celebrities building fancy wineries."

They paused as they stepped up into the terraced vineyard. "Welcome to Domain Poison Oak," said Jules. "I was feeling pretty cranky the day I chose that name, but there was a reason." He picked up a long stick and used it to lift a looping branch of poison oak out of the way. "The soils are thinner up here. The vines produce an intense Cab that I really like. However, over the years, I have become very allergic to the poison oak. I do my best to let it alone, however it does function as a sort of child deterrent." He laughed. "Julie installed those cute red roses down there at the ends of the vineyard rows. She claims they impress tourists, because of tour guides like to say they provide an early warning system for aphids and fungal infection. But there are much better ways. . . ." He let out a yelp, teetered, and nearly fell as his knee started to collapse. Kit leapt forward, and then nearly fell himself due to his own game knee. But he did manage to grab Jules' elbow in time, and to help him extract his foot from a deep hole he had stepped into.

"These damned holes!" Jules growled. "They'll be the death

of me."

He tested his foot and ankle tentatively; Kit did the same for his sore knee. Luckily neither one had sustained much damage. Jules, however, reached down and tucked his pant legs into his boots, before pacing rapidly down a row of vines, his strength having miraculously returned upon entry into this favorite vineyard. "Watch your step, my children. And follow me." He shouted over his receding shoulders. "Let's see what Roberto was telling me about."

"What's going on?" whispered Morgan to Kit. "Do you think he's slightly mad?"

Kit rolled his eyes and kicked some loose soil into the hole, and then stepped quickly but carefully down the row in Jules' wake. "He's certainly has become more eccentric," he murmured.

"Well, I like the roses at Buckthorn," Morgan called out to the receding Jules. "I think they make a beautiful contrast with the vines."

Meanwhile, Jules seemed to be looking for something. Suddenly he found it. He stopped and began to inspect the stems of several vines, which were waving around in the breeze like sailors drunk on a Saturday night. His mouth flattened. His expression grew hard. Carefully he extracted a long trellis wire from the tangle of vines and held it up for Kit and Morgan to see.

"What happened?" asked Morgan drawing to his side.

"Roberto told me some of these wires had been busted off. He blamed our local critters—a large buck, or possibly the wild boar, on a rampage. But he couldn't find any scat."

By this time, Kit too had caught up and was also inspecting the broken trellis wire. He inspected a second row of vines. "These cuts over here look too clean to have been torn by an animal. Could it be vandalism? Looks like a sharp cut, made by shears, or a wire cutter."

"Who the hell would climb all the way up here to deliberately cut down my trellises?" asked Jules, annoyed. "Roberto thought it was probably critters, and so do I. He thought it was wild boar." Jules gently re-twisted a broken trellis wire and lay a vine back into place. Sucking on his bloodied finger, he surveyed row upon row of damaged trellis wires. Ten minutes later he finally admitted, "Does seem a bit thorough for boars."

Meanwhile Morgan and Kit began scouring the soil for signs of culprits, buck or boar— prints, scat, hair, fabric caught in a wire. But they found nothing other than a few human footprints that were probably Jules' own boots, their shoes, or Roberto's. Near the entrance to the vineyard they did find some other prints—perhaps a grandchild's. But no large critters.

When Morgan raised her eyes. Jules was watching them, intently.

6 DOWN THE HOBBIT HOLE

Fifteen minutes later they were heading back down the slope, this time on a path that seemed to lead towards the old stone winery. They had failed to discover anything conclusive about the source of the vandalism at Poison Oak, and Jules had pronounced his vines not much damaged. Roberto would finish trellis repairs in the morning. He flat out rejected Kit's offer to install motion sensing cameras. Morgan stayed out of it. Instead, she simply pulled Jules' arm through her own and helped him navigate down the stony track, keeping her eyes out for fallen rocks and unexpected holes. Kit walked protectively next to the old man's other shoulder, ready to lend a hand should he start to tumble.

Conversation turned to the Romano family's early years in California. Morgan asked Jules about the death of his brother Eddie.

"It was very sad," he replied. "New wife. New baby. *Papà* was beside himself. You know the story, don't you, Kit?"

"Pork Chop Hill, wasn't it?"

Jules nodded, then retold the whole thing for Morgan's benefit. "My parents came into Buckthorn Valley from the Central Valley—Lodi—they grew grapes out there right through Prohibition. They produced a great deal of plain grape juice, and a fair amount of holy wine—for the Church, you know. They shipped the concentrated juice back East . . . for home winemakers. Home winemaking was legal, and quite popular, for a while. My parents crushed whatever they could get hold of for that wine base, let it macerate briefly in the skins for color, then sent it off by the boxcar-load. I suspect that base made terrible wine. At any rate, it was *Papà* who discovered this remote valley. He hunted boar around here, with some cousins."

"I gather Buckthorn wasn't the first winery in this valley, though," commented Morgan.

"That's correct; however, by the time my parents got here, the old winery had fallen into disrepair, and the vineyards had been planted with fruit trees. And the buckthorn was rampant. It was major work to clean it out. Then we brought planted vines from Italy. He said he intended it all for my older brother and me. He dreamed we'd run the estate together. That didn't happen, of course. America went to war in Korea, and my brother was killed near the end of it. I was about eight when he died—younger than Bailey is now. It was very sad. I still think about Eddie every day of my life. A part of me wishes my father's dream had come true." Jules patted Morgan's hand fondly. "I idolized my brother. I was so proud of his being a soldier. I always felt guilty about what he had to give up." A tear glistened as Jules looked across the green valley below them towards something no one else could see.

"Anyway . . . ." He sniffed. "Eddie's wife never remarried. Irene. You'll meet her tomorrow, if not before. Poor woman. She can be a terrible nag sometimes, but she has every right to be bitter. She never got over Eddie's death. So pointless it was. She quit high school to marry him. Then along came the baby. Jack. My nephew. He's much more like her side of the family than ours. Eddie never knew his son. Nor did Jack, of course, ever know his father."

They stood still for a moment, staring across the valley below. It was late afternoon; the sun was low in the sky. A full moon hung large over Mount Saint Helena. Birds called back and forth. Swallows swooped up and down the face of the palisades, chasing bugs, twittering. A peaceful scene thought Morgan to herself. Too peaceful for long-held grudges . . . or vindictive acts. But appearances can be deceiving.

Jules brought their steep descent to a halt in front of a small door, nestled into the hillside, half hidden by the low branches of a spreading live oak.

"A hobbit hole!" exclaimed Morgan. But it was a hobbit hole with a steel-barred security door of the type more frequently found protecting doors in rough urban neighborhoods.

"Bats," said Jules, pointing to the smear of guano that decorated this entrance. Absently, he plucked some dead blossoms from a pot of geraniums hanging in the oak and flicked them into the weeds. "I rather like bats. I put three bat houses in this tree once, but the ornery critters never deigned to move in. They prefer the crevices in that little overhang up there—not to mention the vent covers of my air ducts."

"Where does this door lead?" asked Morgan, noticing that it had also been fitted up with a shiny new brass locking device.

"The mine," replied Jules. "Actually these hills are riddled with mines. It was all about the cinnabar, you know."

"Cinnabar?" said Morgan, glancing towards Kit as she recalled their earlier conversation.

"That's right. Cinnabar ore is found throughout these hills. It's what makes those ledges up there so reddish. Not to mention this dirt here. Cook up the cinnabar ore and it yields quicksilver. Some say where there's cinnabar, there's also gold. I don't know if that's true. I do know, however, that cinnabar is toxic, and if there is gold in it, it's both expensive and dangerous to refine. Placer mining is a better bet. Easier. Safer too. The streams do most of the work of washing gold out of the mountain. All you needed was a pan. That's how the 49ers went after it anyway. I don't know what they pulled out of this here mine. Maybe it was cinnabar, maybe it was quicksilver, maybe it was gold, maybe it was nothing at all." Jules shook his head and grinned, as if he knew some secret. "Something magical about dreams of gold, don't you think?"

"So why the big lock?"

"Oh, that," he chuckled. "Rickie found out that Zoe and the twins were up here exploring the tunnels a couple of months ago. She threw a fit. Had Roberto install the security door, and the lock. I suppose it was a good idea. Keeps the critters out. If you know the trick, however, it's easy enough to open. I doubt Zoe is quite up to it yet." He reached above the door, fiddled some sort of latch, and the security door popped open. "There's a whole maze of tunnels down through this mountain. The framing is rotting away.

No wonder Rickie wanted to keep the little ones out. Some of the supports have collapsed, and there are some darned steep shafts to fall into. My brother and I used to knock around these tunnels a good bit when we were kids. We had a few scary moments. Would you like to have a look?"

"You bet," said Kit, following him into the tunnel's entry area. Morgan was right behind, declaring she too was up for a bit of adventure underground.

"Hey, it's really cool in here—temperature-wise I mean," called out Kit. "Oh, Susanna," he sang enjoying the echo. "Are you sure there isn't any gold left in these rocks? On a day like today, I could get into becoming a miner."

Outside was bright with sunshine, but inside, the tunnel was dark, pitch black even. Jules pulled out a small LED light and clipped it to his hat. "I always carry one of these. Follow me," Jules said, squeaking open a second rusty metal gate and turning down a side tunnel. "I'll show you a secret."

The tunnel grew narrower, and steeper, as they went back into the mountain. They stepped carefully down several rickety wooden stairways. Morgan lost track of the turns as they followed Jules' dancing light. The air was thick with spider webs, dust, and mold, but the floor of the tunnel was surprisingly hard-packed and clear of both loose rock and rotting timber. There were no signs of bats. "Watch on your left," Jules called back over his shoulder, pausing with one hand poised against the tunnel's wall. "There's a year-round spring behind these rocks. It gets a little slick underfoot."

They descended steadily, down through tunnels that seemed to cross and re-cross themselves. Occasionally, they had to duck very low or squeeze sideways to get through a tight place. Morgan hoped Jules knew his way out as well as he seemed to know his way in. To her, it all looked the same. A maze. She shivered at the thought of an earthquake. Another reason to want that security gate installed.

After what seemed like several hours, but was probably no more than ten or fifteen minutes, Jules made a sharp turn to the left and squeezed through a set of fat wooden posts propping up the tunnel's roof. The posts looked new, Morgan thought as she

83

followed him. They came out in a small sort of room with some shiny steel jacks holding up a real ceiling. The space was filled with an array of buckets, concrete sacks, metal bars, broken hoses, tools, and other industrial detritus.

Morgan glanced around.

"End of the line," muttered Kit to himself, wondering if this pile of trash was the 'secret' Jules wanted to show them.

Jules, however, seemed to be in perfect control. He reached around the mess and pulled a small lever that opened a low metal door. "Mind your heads," he warned, ducking his own head slightly as he stepped through.

Morgan went next.

Then Kit. "Ouch!" Kit cried, smashing his elbow on the door frame and stumbling over a pile of white plastic buckets. Jules flicked a switch outside the little door and light displayed a long underground barrel storage room. Along the neatly cemented walls ranged tiers of oak wine-barrels, on their sides, in sets of interlocking wooden frames. Both ceiling and floor had been cemented too, and everything had been white washed. "*Hoc est corpus meum*. That's 'hocus-pocus' to you." Jules chuckled, clicking shut a numeric lock outside the low door they had just come through. He re-piled the plastic buckets Kit had kicked over and placed them in front of the door, more or less obscuring it. "Welcome to the wine caves of Buckthorn," he announced. "Here rest the juices of the grape in quiet and temperate comfort as they metamorphose into a gift from the gods."

"Well, I'll be," said Morgan.

"Neat trick," chorused Kit. "Who else knows about your little backdoor?"

Jules winked. "Our secret. Staff believe it leads nowhere more interesting than a storage closet." And sure enough, posted on the outside of the low door was a faded tin sign that read, "No entry without permit. Hazardous Materials."

So that's why getting locked in the cave didn't concern you, thought Morgan to herself, wondering at the same time how many other such secret doors there might be in these caves.

The barrel room where they had found themselves gave onto a second barrel room, and that onto another, and another. In fact,

Buckthorn's extensive wine caves consisted of a veritable labyrinth of barrel-lined rooms, dug back under the rocky palisade.

As they passed along, Morgan and Kit read off the wine notes chalked on the barrel ends. Soon Jules was again extolling the skills of his young winemaker Rachel Suttermann. "Despite my recent remarks about wine blends, you should realize that Rachel's blends are for the most part quite magical. That's because of her exceptional winemaker genes. My friend Ev Wolfe is her grandfather. He's an excellent winemaker, nearly as good as I am. Her mother was no slouch either, rest her soul. And luckily Rachel inherited the family palate, and the family sniffer. She's a marvel at creating exquisite blends. Almost as good as me. I taught her much of what she knows. She's been . . . like a daughter to me." Then he added dryly "I'd let her take charge of my own reserve, if only she'd . . ."

But he got no further, for the lights in the wine cave sudden began to flicker, then went out. There was a terrible crash. Then a long, low, rumbling sort of clatter, as if a freight train were rolling through the wine caves. Morgan wondered whether a ceiling in one of the mine tunnels somewhere behind the barrel rooms had fallen in.

Someone shouted, "Watch out!!"

Curses reverberated. There was a second crash and more low clattering.

"GODDAMMIT!"

"I told you those barrels weren't stacked right!!"

"You friggin' idiot!! There's wine everywhere! It's the good stuff too . . . thousands of dollars . . . "

"SHEE-IT!! I didn't . . ."

"You didn't what?! You are an asshole!"

Jules quickly switched on his headlight and remarked in a bemused tone of voice, "Just some wine barrels falling down. I hope no one got hurt." A moment later, they heard the whine of a generator, and the lights fluttered back on. Morgan cocked her head. Who else was in the cave? Where had the crashing occurred? There was something about one of the voices . . . but the echoes had disoriented her. Kit seemed to be paying little attention to the noises. Did stacks of barrels often fall in a wine cave?

"If only she would what?" Kit asked Jules.

Jules did not respond immediately. He was fiddling with his LED. He took it off his hat and clipped it onto a tether inside his coat pocket. Then he asked. "What do you know about biodynamics?" he asked.

"Biodynamics? Isn't that a New Age version of organic gardening? Sustainable farming?" responded Kit.

"No," said Jules firmly. "But let's sit here on this bench for a moment. My old body is hurting after all that climbing around." He sat down and began massaging his calves. Kit sat down too. After his interaction with the pile of buckets, both his knee and his elbow were hurting.

"First off," began Jules after a few moments. "Not to be crude, biodynamics is more about bullshit than cow manure, if you ask me. A publicity stunt, not a science, although there are those who'd disagree with me. Biodynamics is designed, I believe, to open a new market for wine among the more gullible, half-cracked consumers. My young winemaker Rachel, despite her talent in the tasting department, bought into this cock-a-mammy nonsense a few years ago."

"Not complete nonsense, I heard," said Morgan, noticing that the noises in the cave seemed to have ceased. "And I heard it was based on science."

"You're not from the Republic of Berkeley are you?" asked Jules narrowing his eyes.

"Not me, but my son's a student there."

"Too bad," said Jules. "Let's hope he doesn't succumb to all the hocus-pocus in that air."

Kit raised an eyebrow. "Can you explain?"

"Sure. Biodynamics is one of your more recent fads among wine growers, but it actually began back in the twenties, invented by a German, or maybe it was a Polish, spiritualist who called himself a scientist. There are all sorts of aspects to this business, but for wine growers, it comes down to cow manure and moonlight. Perform the proper rituals in the vineyard, plant bull horns filled with cow manure in holes when the aspect of the moon is right, and vines will be more disease resistant, more productive. Or so they say." He laughed humorlessly.

Morgan gulped, recalling how Izzy swore up and down that wine made from biodynamically grown vines was far superior to any other wine one could purchase, even the gold medal winners that went for many bucks a bottle.

Jules went on. "Of course, you have to get the holes located properly according to the right astrological chart." He began to laugh again. "It's all bullshit and lunacy! It makes me so angry! Rachel bought into it all. Hence all the holes you'll find in the vineyards, including the one I stepped into up at Poison Oak. Claims she's a novice, can't get her astro-charts right. She keeps digging holes, and planting horns, then digging them up when the berries don't suit her and putting her manure-filled horn somewhere else. And sometimes she forgets to fill in the holes. I don't think biodynamics hurts the wine actually, but it is a hazard to those who work in the vineyard. We've had a couple of broken axles so far and some twisted ankles. Makes Roberto furious! I'm just a cynical old man, so all I see is a new way to con wine buyers into spending more money on a bottle of wine than it's worth. But Rachel was so insistent, and I got curious. So I even did some tastings. Trust me—there is no difference." He looked at Kit. "You doubt what I say, my friend?"

Kit remained silent.

Jules went on, harrumphing, "It's pure hokum! It is ruining a perfectly good winemaker. She should be focusing on real matters. Forget those planetary alignments and lunar schedules and bizarre rituals, I've told her. But she is one stubborn girl! She goes creeping around in the middle of the night. I caught her once using the GPS on her smart phone to locate a new hole. Pure lunacy and I don't seem to be able to stop it."

"Is that really what biodynamics is about?" said Morgan.

"That's pretty much it," Jules grunted irritably. "And I haven't said anything about Preparation 500 yet. That's the latest cock-a-mammy invention, by one of Wine Country's own! Just any old cow poop won't do now; you gotta buy their cow poop!" Jules grew quite red in the face.

"But what's the harm in it?" said Morgan. "I mean other than a twisted ankle or spending money you don't have to. Lots of people check their horoscopes. It's kind of fun."

"You're right, and it doesn't hurt the vines," responded Jules. "But I'm old. I don't have much patience for nonsense. I could ignore it, if it weren't so close to home. But it hurts my sense of living an ethical life producing honorable wines. That's what we Romanos are about. That's what I want to be the legacy of Buckthorn Estate. Biodynamics turns winemaking into a side-show, into a cult practice. A lucrative cult practice. Becomes like selling snake oil! I hate that! I'm not a wine evangelist, making a living off human gullibility. Look what they did to good old fashioned Christianity. Like the Taliban, or al-Qaeda did for Islam! Turning a beautiful idea into something evil. I'm not long for this world, my children, and biodynamics is not what I want to leave as the legacy of Buckthorn. I will make her stop!"

Jules so hummed with anger that he quite failed to notice the flood of wine running towards them from one of the side barrel rooms. As his tirade continued, he had stood up and begun pacing back and forth. Suddenly he skidded, awkwardly, and attempted to catch himself the wall. Only Kit's swift arm kept him from falling.

"Shee-it!" Jules growled under his breath. He looked down at the river of red wine. "What the hell is this?"

"You're hurt," announced Morgan, taking Jules' by his other elbow. "Your hand's bleeding."

"That's nothing," he responded. "Just age. Thin skin. I bleed easily."

Two young men skittered around the corner and came to a sudden halt. "Uncle Jules!" cried one of them. "Are you okay?"

Jules was sucking the blood off his bruised hand. Growling, he stuffed it into the pocket of his barn coat, then said, "And did you two cellar rats create this flood on the floor?"

Morgan stared at the young men. Her eyes locked onto one of them. She sucked in her breath. Her jaw literally dropped. "You!?"

"Mom! Uhh . . ." Talies eyes darted towards Kit as if to say 'Now what do I do?'

Kit muttered something on the order of 'Jig's up!'

"That's your mother?" gaped Cody. "What's she doing here?"

"Uhh. . . ."

Jules didn't bat an eye. "That's a long story, Cody my boy, and it does not concern you at the moment. Suffice it to say, mothers turn up, in the oddest of places sometimes. Often just when you think you're rid of them. It's a life lesson. You'd do well to learn it. By the way, your mother ought to be turning up shortly too. So, tell me, what happened? I assume the two of you will be clearing this up, immediately."

"Sorry, Uncle Jules. I was showing Talies here how to get to the top row of barrels so we could check the ferment, when the frame just broke!"

"Umm. We heard."

"But I never had that happen before. You know? We didn't do anything weird. Really! We were coming over here to see how far the flood spread."

"I see. And were either of you hurt when the cradles collapsed?"

Cody and Talies both said they were fine.

"And what's this?" Jules pointed towards pieces of a broken glass pipette in the puddle at his feet.

"Oh, crap!" said Cody, leaning down to pick them up. "That must be the wine thief. I wondered where it went. Must have bounced."

"Bounced? Goodness, how many barrels fell? And, which ones?"

"Only a couple. Well, maybe half a dozen? Ten barrels, tops. Twenty? Not that many, Uncle Jules. Honest." Cody looked like a dog waiting to be whipped. "They were your special reserve too. I am so sorry. Honestly, we didn't do anything I haven't done a hundred times before."

Jules' expression grew serious. "Well, you boys better get back to work. You've got some cleaning up to do. Cody, see me after supper, please. I'll talk you through fixing those broken barrel cradles."

Morgan glared after Talies as he and Cody hurried off in quest of buckets and mops. Then she shifted her glare onto Kit. "We need to talk," she said, reaching into her pocket for her smart phone. No signal.

Leaning on Kit, Jules rubbed at his leg and tentatively

stretched his hip. "Damn this old body." He was limping as they headed towards the main entrance of the caves, pausing briefly to point out the tunnel that led to his private workroom and Buckthorn's wine library.

The sun had dropped behind the ridge of the western palisade by the time they left the caves and stepped into warm evening air. "Another quote-unquote accident, sir?" asked Kit.

Jules said only, "Promise you won't say anything about this to the family. Let me handle it. I'll see you folks at supper. Eight-thirty. Under the arbor." He hobbled off to speak with Roberto, who had his head inside a large piece of machinery at the edge of the crush pad.

Meanwhile Morgan finally sent off her text to her son—"tank house tonight talk" followed by a scowling emoticon. Moments later her phone buzzed—"10 ok?" and a big red heart.

"All right, Mr. Jalesco," said Morgan, as they turned up the path to their quarters. "So why is Talies here?"

"Tell you later. . . but take a look at that," said Kit, directing her attention across the vineyard towards a stately old lady dressed all in black. She looked like something out of The Godfather. She was making her way very slowly along the side of the road towards the Big House. "Look who's coming to dinner."

7 TANK HOUSE CONFERENCE

Morgan left supper before the others and headed back to the tank house to await her son. It had been a long hot day. Leaning on the sill of the open window, she stretched out the kinks in her back and rested her eyes on the darkening vineyards, breathing in their fragrance. A critter rustled in the shrubbery below. At supper she'd drunk far too many glasses of red wine, eaten more than enough perfectly cooked pasta, and listened to more family gossip than she could readily absorb—so much bickering, so much noise, so much clatter from so many over-excited children needing sleep. Voices still jangled in her head—Eddie and Dennis and Jack and Julie, Tinker and Indie and Indie's brothers, and all those grandchildren and nieces and nephews whose names she could not keep straight. Everyone talked and talked, quarreled about everything, from why the San Francisco Giants had lost to the Los Angeles Dodgers to what would be a reasonable price for a good bottle of wine, and then about the very meaning of "good" itself when applied to wine. Her head spun.

And what had she learned from it all? Only that Romanos could disagree about anything. It took little to start them off. In fact, many of their so-called quarrels were so long-standing that even a casual squint of the eye, or a fractious tone of the voice, got someone going. This was a family of roiling and endless passions. And they seemed to enjoy their conflicts! Compared with the rest of the family, Jules and Rickie were calm, riding the waves of turmoil as if they were nothing more than ripples in a mountain stream.

Halfway through supper, Indie's brother Aaron had arrived in a cloud of noise and bustle, up from Los Angeles for the big birthday celebration. How could three people make such commotion, she wondered. Now she wracked her brain to recall the wife's name. Megan? or Jennifer? Or was Jennifer the daughter? They looked like sisters—both dark skinned and dark-eyed. African American maybe, or Mayan. She had no idea. Both were beautiful and youthful, in that costly Southern California way, the result of gym memberships, personal trainers, and every sort of spa and salon treatment. Some expensive cosmetic surgery too—at least on the mother's part—whichever one she was. And then there was that upright and silent old lady—the infamous Nonna. Morgan did notice that Rickie always called her 'Irene'. She herself hadn't yet had a chance to talk with Irene, but she would. Indeed she had a growing list of questions for Irene.

Abruptly Morgan's thoughts were cut off by the bang of the tank house door.

"Ma? You up there?" Talies took the steps two at a time, dropped his long body into the only over-stuffed chair, and heaved a groan. "Sheesh, I'm tired! Got anything to eat?"

Morgan pointed towards the bowl of fruit, then cut to the chase. "Why didn't you tell me you're working in the winery? How did this happen, Talies?"

Talies chomped into an apple, then with his mouth full of crunch said, "Kit said he would tell you . . . when the time was right."

"Well, he hasn't told me anything."

"So where is Kit anyways? He said to report to him when I got off. I figured he'd be here. Not sure how much he'd want me to say."

"Talies! I'm your mother! What does Kit have to do with the fact that you gave up a perfectly good summer job in Berkeley to come work in a winery? I thought you were all set."

"It's not like I've done something wrong, Mom. And I sure didn't expect to see you up here either. You never said anything to me about being here."

"Talies . . ." Her voice sounded a warning tone even as she realized what he said was perfectly true. But why should she tell him? This was different, wasn't it?

"Whatever," murmured Talies. "But please say it's not my fault if he gets mad, will you? I don't want to screw anything up. It's my first chance."

"What are you talking about? First chance?"

"Well, maybe three or four weeks ago? Seems longer ago than that. Kit said he had a job for me, at a winery. I thought 'Cool'. I didn't much like being a barista. Then he explained what he had in mind. And I thought, cooler and cooler! But then he said not to say anything to you about it, that he'd take care of that part. So I didn't. And here I am. A friggin' cellar rat in a winery, doing a different sort of grunt work under Rachel's eye while ferreting around, detecting things for Kit. Weird, but true. And I'm getting paid more than the barista thing." Talies grinned broadly. "It's awesome, Mom. I'm like undercover!"

"Has that man gone mad?" Morgan glared with annoyance at her son. She found the situation not awesome at all.

Poor Talies didn't know what to say next, so he stuttered something inane, ate his apple, and hated being at odds with his mother.

"Can I help?" said Kit from the doorway. He had been standing at the top of the stairs listening and trying to contain his amusement. Gently, he placed Morgan into a chair, then drew another chair next to her for himself. "Now . . ." he began quietly, "I tried to tell you the other night about my little deal here with Talies, but you were, shall I say, somewhat pre-occupied? Maybe I should have tried harder. But I got to thinking—maybe waiting is better. I didn't want you to go rushing off with me only because you were concerned about your son. Anyway, I didn't think there was much to worry about with regard to Talies. All he's doing is lots of washing of barrels and tanks, racking some wine, pushing stuff around—factotum in the wine cellars of Buckthorn. I don't believe . . ."

"What are you talking about?" spluttered Morgan. "I knew something was up! Talies wasn't acting like himself. And then he didn't want to stay over at the house while I was gone. And he wasn't answering his phone as quickly as usual either. He disappeared on me. I knew it wasn't traffic on the bridge that made him late the other night." She glared at her son. "You were driving down from Buckthorn, weren't you? Not just across the Bay from Berkeley."

"Busted!" responded Talies with a sheepish sort of grin. "But everything I said to you was true, Mom. And the reception is lousy up here. Maybe I need a different provider. And I do not text and drive!" His eyes sought out Kit's, hoping for support. "I don't think I've ever worked so hard as I have the last few weeks, Ma. This cellar rat stuff is totally exhausting! And on top of it, there's all the creeping I have to do at night—the spying! I love it, but it interferes with my sleep. . . ."

Morgan continued to scowl. Talies, still uncertain about what he should or could say, focused on his apple. Finally he pitched the core towards a bin, landing it with a noticeable clunk.

Kit's eyes found Morgan's. "Look, my dear, dear friend and partner in crime," he said, taking a long deep breath. "Don't blame Talies. It's my fault."

"I am well aware of that!"

"So perhaps you could forgive our little secret? At the moment, we three need to get on the same page. We need to work together for the benefit of all. I know, that sounds corny, but let me fill you in on some things. It's complicated. First off—Indie called me many times about Uncle Jules. I got so tired of her hassling me that I finally called Jules myself. I knew I couldn't come up here myself just then; and even if I could have, I was going to have difficulties. I knew it would be useful to have someone on the inside, so to speak. And Talies has been bothering me about his wanting to become a private detective . . . so I just thought. . . . I knew the weather has been unusually hot, and hence that crush was going be early. I suspected Buckthorn would be needing some extra hands to get everything done in time. That, at any rate, is the argument I spun to Jules at any rate. Jules figured out my real agenda as soon as I mentioned that Indie seemed worried about the spate of accidents and that I would like to come up. The man's no fool. It takes brains, as well as hard work, to make good wine."

"You can say that again!" put in Talies.

Kit silenced him with a look, then he continued. "Jules doesn't usually hire outsiders to help out in the winery. I was a little surprised how quickly he agreed with my idea. I could be wrong but I read that as a signal that Jules himself was worried about those accidents. Anyway, I told him Talies was your son, Morgan, and that you and I were friends, good friends. He already knew your name, probably thanks to Indie. I told him Talies was smart. He'd learn quick and provide an extra pair of hands as the winery got ready for crush. And he'd be an extra pair of eyes for me. Jules understood what I was saying. Talies started a few days later. Unfortunately, Tal still hasn't found out much. Don't get upset with me, Talies—I am well aware these matters can take time. Anyway . . . when I could see myself free to come up here, I wangled us both an invite to Jules' party. And here we all are!"

"But I don't see why you didn't clear it with me," growled Morgan, feeling both angry and betrayed.

"Come on, Mom, I'm old enough to run my own life. It's not as if anything is going to happen to me!"

Morgan glared at him.

Kit stepped in. "I just knew this might be a problem. I didn't say anything because . . . well, because I thought it would be best if you didn't know right away. Can we just leave it at that? Please?"

Morgan shifted her glare to Kit.

Kit sighed and added quickly, "I feel caught in the middle here. Talies and I both remember the first time he brought up his idea of becoming a private eye. You didn't seem comfortable with the idea."

"Because I wasn't. And because he told me he was going to go to law school."

At this Talies let out a kind of moan.

Kit battled on. "I'm not sure how to say this, but I think Talies is old enough to make up his own mind. He's very capable, this son of yours, and mature. Trust him. He was certainly being under-employed in that coffee shop. He worried about how you'd react to his accepting my offer. Which is why we both leaned towards trying out the winery business before we said anything. And I really did mean to tell you before . . . but obviously I . . . well . . . I didn't."

Talies was squirming in his chair by this time.

"So what am I supposed to do now?" said Morgan. "Ignore the situation? Or maybe, as you've got Talies snooping around the winery for you, I should just go back home?"

"Please, don't be like that. I meant it about needing your help. This case will need all three of us working together. We have different strengths. Frankly, after what I saw and heard today, I have realized already how right I was not to trust my own instincts, even with Talies in place. I'll get myself in big trouble, Morgan, without you."

Morgan felt somewhat mollified by this, but continued to frown as she eyed them both. And truth be told, she did feel like packing up and going back to Quarry Canyon, leaving these two to their own devices. On the other hand, she was finding she like Jules better than she thought she would, and several things about the situation had aroused her curiosity, including her sense that Jules wasn't being completely honest with them. Yes, there were some things she wanted to find out.

"All right," she said finally. "I will hold my peace . . . for now. And both of you . . . be careful! Let's just get on with it. I'm tired."

Kit and Talies both visibly relaxed.

"I don't know about you two," said Kit, his eyes darting back and forth, "but I didn't like either of today's so-called accidents. Did you hear about broken trellis wires up at Poison Oak, Talies?"

"Someone said a wild pig got in."

"Perhaps. A boar was Roberto's explanation. Or so said Jules. I thought the wires looked deliberately cut. And we saw no tracks, or scat. And about those barrels? Talies, did you have a chance to assess why the racks collapsed?"

"I did, actually. It looked to me like a couple of the uprights were nearly sawn through. The extra weight added by Cody and me, climbing up on top, was probably more than enough to break them. I'd guess whoever did the sawing intended the frame to break and wanted the barrels to come crashing down. I have no idea why. We both leapt out of the way pretty quick. It sure made a mess. We were lucky neither of us was hurt. All I could think was what if Jules had decided to check the ferment himself? He does that sometimes, Cody said."

"Mmm. Did you tell Cody about the sawn uprights?"

"No, sir! I did not. You were very clear that I should talk about that sort of thing only with you." He glanced quickly towards his mother. "Or now, with Mom too?" Morgan's grim expression lifted a millimeter.

Kit nodded. "Who has access to the caves to do that sort of damage?"

"Well, pretty much everybody goes in and out almost every day—Jules, all the rats, Rachel of course, Jack when he's around, Eddie, Dennis, Roberto, his staff occasionally, little kids, various people I don't know—friends of Jules maybe—any of the family really. You can probably rule out Nonna—I can't imagine her sawing anything—and maybe Mrs. Romano too. I've seen her down in the wine caves only a few times. Mostly when she is looking for Jules. I have seen a few tourists too, strangers, wandering around lost, if you can believe. . . . Doesn't happen often. I don't know how they get in. Anybody who sees stray people ejects them pretty quickly. Mostly they seem more panicked than devious. I also checked to see that the security still works back in the tunnels. The main door is usually locked at night. Maybe they should install some cameras."

"Cameras might not tell us much if the culprit's one of the regulars," said Kit. "Are you keeping an eye on Rachel like I asked?"

"Absolutely!"

"We heard today that she wanders around the vineyards at night, doing her biodynamic things. Have you noticed that?"

"A couple of times. She's fairly up front about it. I offered to help her a couple of times, to see what she actually does. But she says I'd probably be more of a hindrance. Can't say I understand this biodynamic thing. Looks like magician's gibberish to me, designed to impress and confuse. Jules sleeps in his workroom sometimes, when it get really hot."

Kit harrumphed. "We do need to get a handle on who or what is behind these so-called accidents that seem to target Jules. The list is getting too long to be simply a series of coincidences. It troubles me how little we actually know about what's happened.

Jules isn't telling us everything. I wonder who he's protecting. Indie, on the other hand, suspects Rachel, who is always in the vicinity. Any thoughts?"

Both Morgan and Talies shook their heads, so Kit began offering what he called "background."

"For one thing, I could never figure out why Indie and Rachel don't like one another, and Indie refused to explain. She said they played together as little girls. Rachel's mom went to school with Julie; and her dad was the son of Jules' best friend. Her parents have both passed away. Something happened because Indie was simply livid when Jules hired Rachel on as his winemaker. I couldn't figure it out. I thought at first Jules did it out of kindness. But I've heard she's a pretty good winemaker. . . . Oh, I would dearly love to know why Indie dislikes her so much. Or why she believes Rachel has it in for her benefactor."

Kit paused, snorting as if considering a puzzling scene from the past, then he went on, in rather the same vein. "It could be simple jealousy. Indie's prone that way. And she holds long grudges. Maybe they quarreled about a boy. But she still doesn't like it when Jules pays attention to Rachel. With this in mind, it does makes a sort of sense why Indie would blame Rachel for those accidents." He shook his head as if to loosen something hidden in a dark corner of his mind. "It seems to have gotten a little worse recently." He sighed. "Forgive me. I'm only thinking out loud."

Neither Morgan nor Talies said anything. Instead, they watched him pour a glass of wine, which he offered first to Morgan, then to Talies. Both refused. So Kit returned to his seat and drank the wine himself. "Anyway, Morgan, that's why I needed Talies to keep his eye on Rachel. She'll soon be made aware that he's your son, but family relationships are normal around here, and as far as she knows, he's no different from the other cellar rats. He works for her. He'll have an entirely different view from what you or I would have. And as a new employee, you know, he's supposed to ask a lot of questions. I have confidence that he'll suss a few things out. You know, she could have stuffed the vents, or caused those huge spills. But it's early days yet." Kit refilled his wine glass and smiled at Talies.

"But the van business? How could she have been behind

that?" put in Morgan quickly.

"Not easily."

Talies opened his mouth as if to say something, but changed his mind and snapped it shut.

"What?" asked Kit.

"That night," said Talies. "She said she had a meeting in town. That's why I didn't have to work."

"You should have checked if she actually showed up at that meeting before mentioning it," said Kit.

"I could try," said Talies. "But I'm not really sure which meeting it was. Sorry."

Kit grunted and let it go. He ploughed on. "Oh, and I ought to point out, for the record, that both Indie and her cousin Tinker have a long history of, shall I say, exaggeration. A flexible attitude towards the truth."

"You mean they lie," said Morgan.

He ignored her. "And I find it interesting that Jules won't admit to feeling even slightly threatened by what's been going on. Or maybe he's just a very good actor. I know if I was in his shoes, I'd be angry! Take those barrels this afternoon. Jules seemed almost serene watching two hundred cases of his personally crafted reserve wash down the drain. Those cases go for about three hundred bucks a pop! You do the math!"

"Holy crap!" gasped Talies. "Cody said that wine was worth real money."

"Right, so why didn't Jules seem to care?" Kit scratched his head, downed the rest of his wine, and answered his own question. "Because he's so focused on something else? That, anyway, is my guess."

"I wondered about that too. And you didn't flinch either. I certainly did!" said Morgan.

"Well, I've heard barrels fall before. Not often, but sometimes. Still, I did wonder. Jules seemed to be hiding something. Or protecting someone?"

"I had the same thought," said Morgan.

Kit studied her face, then went on. "Oh, that reminds me. When I pushed Jules into hiring Talies, I asked him to please be circumspect about Tal's connection with me, and you. I told him it was because I was worried about how certain members of this family would react, if they knew Tal was somehow related to me. Some family members may have taken sides in our divorce, and I didn't want any of that undermining of acceptance of Talies as an employee. I don't know whether Jules actually bought into that scenario it, but I do believe he has been fairly parsimonious with what he has said about Talies. I suppose he told Rickie of course. And Indie knows of course. Not that she would say anything. And after this afternoon's events, Cody's sure to tell everyone that Talies is your son and that you and I are an item, if for some reason they failed to figure that out." Kit sighed. "Anyway, we need to devise some consistent cover story for why Tal is here, and why he asks so many questions. It certainly won't help if it gets out that Talies is doing detective work for me. Any ideas?"

"How about staying fairly close to the truth?" suggested Morgan. "Maybe that you and I are friends, that when you learned my son was doing research on California's wine-making industry for one of his classes, you fixed up this summer job for him. That would at least keep Rachel from getting too annoyed about his questions."

"Good idea, Mom. And it's more or less what I already said. I'm the only one out in the winery who didn't grow up around here. They all know about winemaking. For them, working at Buckthorn is just one more bottom-of-the-food-chain summer job."

"So who else are you working with? Besides Rachel and Cody, I mean," asked Kit.

"There are a bunch of us. Mostly family—Mork and Ben and Tommy and Jorge and Adena. Jess puts in a few hours sometimes too." Then for the benefit of Morgan, he explained. "Jess's mom is Tinker. You know, Mom, being a cellar rat is not much different from being a barista. We wash everything! Everything has to be really clean, same as in the coffee shop. If it's not, the wine gets ruined. I mean, all the barrels and the tanks and the equipment, even the hoses, and the floors, and the walls! Yesterday Cody had me washing that huge canvas tent roof over the crush pad. Actually, that was a pretty sweet job, because the sun was so hot. We had a great water fight! And the other thing we do is racking."

"Racking?" asked Morgan.

"Yeah. Basically that means moving the wine from place to place. We syphon it off the lees and put it into fresh containers. The lees are gross, by the way, but they're good fertilizer. If you let the wine sit too long on that glop, the wine takes on terrible flavor, and the fermentation can gets out of control. Anyway, it means lots of hoses and syphons and pumps and stuff. And we wash all of it! And then there's the old barrels. Jules likes to reuse them, but Rachel and Eddie prefer new ones. So Cody and I sometimes have to break the old barrels down too. Did you know that wine gets into the barrel wood? Cleaning won't get it out. I also learned you can't put any old variety of wine into any old barrel. They're careful about that. Anyway, Mom, it takes me and Cody half a day to rack the wine out of one of those humungous casks. One of those transfers out into fifteen barrels! And I hate the syphoning business. I had a terrible time getting the hang of it. It's way easier with a pump, but for some reason Jules prefers syphoning. Oh, and sometimes Rachel lets us do some of the testing too, and the topping up. That's what we were doing this afternoon back in the barrel rooms. We were climbing the pile. Cody says climbing is easier than pushing the heavy ladders around. I guess I basically do what Cody does. I'm shadowing him, Mom. He's been a cellar rat for three years, and he's done it all! He even said he'd show me how to construct a barrel, if we have the time. Wouldn't that be cool?"

"Mmm," said Kit. "Last time I saw Cody, he was about ten." Then for Morgan's benefit he explained, "Cody is one of Indie's nephews. His parents are the ones who flew last night, from LA— Aaron and Jennifer, and their daughter Megan. Cody's been living with Nonna pretty much full time since he graduated from high school. I hear a lot about him from Bailey. He's a good kid, but I gather Cody's family is hoping our college student—Talies here— will be a good influence. That's why Rachel has us working together."

"Cody lives with Nonna only during winter," added Talies. "Summertime he bunks out in the mobile homes—we're roommates. We have talked a little about his doing UCLA undergraduate next year, then maybe transferring up to the enology program at Davis. He's a cool guy. Really loves the wine business."

Talies grinned as he reached for a banana. "Rachel says the bottling truck might come in next week, or the week after. We are getting ready for that now. I'm excited. Crush is early this year she said. What do you know about bottling trucks, Mom?"

"Not much, but I expect you're going to tell me."

Which is exactly what Talies did next, in great detail, while peeling then eating his banana. "I'm helping get the glass ready now," he bragged, "that's what we call the wine bottles here." Morgan was a little surprised by her son's enthusiasm about this winery job, although she was listening with only half an ear to much of what he said. When he mentioned Rachel, however, she tuned back in. "Rachel showed me some new labels she's had made," he said. "They're look sort of antique, you know? Anyway, everybody works on the bottling line—even the winemaker. Rachel's really cool, Mom. I like her. I know I'm supposed to be keeping an eye on what she does for Kit here, but I really can't believe she's responsible for the stuff that happened to Jules. And I don't know why Indie gets so on about her either. I think she's a good boss. And Jules always says nice things about her. She lets me do all kinds of stuff. She's nice. . . and . . . well . . ." He grinned. "She is seriously hot! She'll be bottling right beside me! She's really into wine, Mom. It's just about all she thinks about. And she works seriously long hours!"

"Which reminds me," said Kit. "Other than Rachel's temperature and her workaholic tendencies, have you found anything, even a small detail, that might put her into our picture? I am so hoping you've done a little more than check the security and admire your boss's attractions."

"Well, I am trying. But nothing definite yet," Talies replied. "Like I said, I ask her a lot of questions. I act like a dummy sometimes, interrupt her in the lab, follow her around, pretend I don't remember stuff. I want to see if she'll give me the same answer twice. My questions piss her off a little, so I'm glad we now have an official cover story." He grinned happily.

"What kind of questions piss her off," asked Morgan, recalling Rachel's comment about her 'stupid' new cellar rat. Something had certainly needled her. Perhaps something Talies asked about was a little too sensitive.

"Well, for example," said Talies. "I heard somebody say something about Buckthorn selling more wine than they produced. So I got curious. I started by wondering how much wine an acre of vineyard would produce. I asked Rachel. And she wouldn't answer me. She got all irritated. Said there are so many variables; there isn't an easy answer. I asked that question in different ways, but nothing worked. So then I asked how many cases Buckthorn produced last year, figuring I could do the math myself. I thought that would sound like an innocent enough question. But that turned out to be a sore subject for her. She hemmed and hawed. Gave me some bullshit about not having time to look it up. It should be right there in the database, shouldn't it? Another time, I crowded her about some computer software stuff, thinking it might be interesting to access Buckthorn's data files. I can make my way around most databases. I knew that wasn't so innocent. And she did get really huffy then. Told me to piss off!" He laughed at himself. "Later she came back and apologized, asked me why I wanted to know that kind of stuff. So I gave her the paper-writing line." He grinned. "Anyway, finally she said, when she has time, she'll teach me to input data for her. Then, she said I could look up what I wanted to know for myself. I thought that was cool!"

Kit seemed pleased with both Talies' initiative and his doggedness, as was Morgan, although Morgan was less certain where this information would take them.

Talies pitched his banana peel into the can, and yawned loudly. "So, folks. No obvious smoking guns so far. No terrorism, nothing like that. Only other possible line I found might be Rachel's environmental activism. She's pretty active with the watchdog types. You know—protecting the valley and the steep slopes and the rivers and streams, opposing development. Standard Bay Area NIMBY stuff, if you ask me. Cody told me though that the politics in Wine Country get pretty hardball at times. The Big Boys from the East Coast, and the Europeans, and even some Asians now, are buying up property around here. One of us should probably be keeping an eye on that stuff. Rachel seems to know a lot about it too. She goes to a lot of meetings and stuff. Knows people, Cody says. I'm not sure about all the politics stuff, but Cody thinks she's on the radical side. I don't know if that's true or not. And, she's into biodynamics. Whatever that's about."

Kit got up, pulled a pitcher of ice water from their little fridge, and poured himself a tall glassful. Then he went over to the window and stood looking out, pondering what Talies had said. "There's a lot of money in winemaking," Kit said thoughtfully. "It's big business, even for a small winery like Buckthorn, if you brand yourself right. But that's been true for some time now." He swirled the ice in his glass slowly and watched it melt. "Money," he said. "Follow the money. Always good advice. And, Talies, keep on Rachel. See if you can find out what's she's actually doing with those meetings she goes to. It could be there's a new development brewing that involves Buckthorn somehow. See if you can find what the local issues are. The problems. The threats. What does the Planning Board worry about. You might also ask her to explain biodynamics. I'd be interested to compare what she has to say with what Jules told us this afternoon. And I'd like to know who else in Wine Country is involved in this biodynamics movement. Get some details, some names, if you can. And I hope you took her up on the database offer."

"Oh, I did. I wouldn't miss that. But I don't get a lot of time to investigate. Rachel keeps us rats pretty busy. Of course she stays pretty busy herself." He made a point of yawning again. "We start at six in the morning! And, like I said, Rachel pulls all-nighters sometimes!" Then he yawned loudly again and began looking around as if he wanted to leave. "Boy! Am I tired!"

"Well, it is getting late—for all of us," said Kit. "Anything else you have to say? Anything useful?"

Talies stifled another yawn and stretched his long legs in front of the big chair and thought for a moment. "Just a couple of things. Maybe. I'm not sure what you're looking for. Anyway, I got to talking with Tinker a while ago. She told me about Nicole."

"Eddie's second wife," injected Kit quickly.

"That's a really sad story. Nicole was a pilot, Tinker said. Small plane. Lots of people have them up here. She was flying back from some wine thing in Fresno with Rachel's mom on board. They went down in a big fiery crash. It was just after the twins were born. Tinker thought Nicole had been drinking. I asked Tommy later what he knew about his step-mom's death. Tommy's a cellar rat too. He didn't say much except that the drinking part was mostly gossip. He told me his dad was still pretty broken up about what happened. The thing is, that doesn't feel quite right to me. I mean, Nicole died, like five years ago. Eddie's down at the winery all the time. He seems completely okay. He's always talking to Rachel about something or other. So a while back, I figured I'd ask Rachel about that little piece of gossip about Eddie's being still broken up. And wow! She nearly bit my head off! I suppose that was really too intrusive."

"Maybe she's still sensitive about her mother dying in that crash too," suggested Morgan.

"I don't think so, Mom. At least not from what I've seen," continued Talies. "Rachel's tough! A hard-hearted type. I think it was what I asked about Eddie. I mean I do have this sense that she and Eddie are a little more than friends. And if you asked me, he doesn't exactly act all broken up about Nicole. Get what I mean?"

"What do you mean?" asked Kit.

"I mean, when I see Rachel and Eddie together—they look like a couple, not like your regular old business colleagues. I didn't like to say anything to Tommy. I mean, if you asked me, Eddie seems pretty happy about not having Nicole around. You know?"

"Hmm . . . Rachel and Eddie, a couple? Interesting," murmured Kit. "We'll keep that in mind. Anything else? Anything more specific to the case?"

"Only that I'm teaching a little magic to some of the kids. I'm doing a show for them tomorrow night, right after the party. Come on by. I'm setting it up outside the entrance to the caves. Oh, and there was this other funny thing a while back—well maybe not so funny—but one of the pump hoses got cut my first week here. Out on the crush pad. Did you hear about that?"

Kit and Morgan shook their heads.

"Well, it looked cut to me, deliberately cut. So I went back later, after things had calmed down, to take another look. It seemed like a straight chop to the line rather than a tear in the hose sleeve. I took a picture with my phone." Talies fumbled with his phone and passed it over to his mom, who then passed it to Kit.

"I see what you mean," said Kit, handing the phone back to Talies.

"So at first, Cody thought the hose might have blown out, from wear and high pressure, you know? They do that sometimes, he said. But this one looked like a new hose. Later, Cody suggested maybe one of the forklifts ran over it. It didn't look like that to me either. Anyway, both forklifts were down for maintenance. We'd been racking off some wine barrels, and then all of a sudden—bam! Wine everywhere! I guess we screamed some pretty crude stuff. Rachel comes out of the winery at top speed. And she got really mad at me, as if it were all my fault! She said I should always check the lines before switching on the pump. But I don't see how that could help—I mean, if it was really a blow-out, right? On the other hand, if she was afraid someone might be messing around with the hoses . . . or she actually expected someone to be cutting hoses . . . well, then I could understand. But who sees a blow-out before the blow-out happens? Cody never told me to always check the lines. Anyway, we'd just washed that particular hose out, and it was fine. I dunno. Smelled a little fishy to me." Talies rolled his eyes, then squinted at his mother. "And, one other thing. Maybe you guys already know about this. But later, when we were cleaning up the mess from that hose, this huge swarm of bees got into a puddle of wine and started slurping away. I took a picture of that too." He handed his phone around again. "When Jules came out of the cave, this bunch of bees started stinging him. It was weird. Like he was wearing some sort of attractant. He really puffed up! All red. Started wheezing and gasping. It scared me. I've never seen anyone react to a bee sting like that. Anyway, Rachel comes dashing out of the winery and sticks this needle-thing into Jules, while the rest of us are standing around with our mouths open. Jules wouldn't let me call 911. She told me later he usually carries one of those needle things with him. She was surprised he didn't have one in his pocket. It's called an epi-pen. He has them stashed all over the winery—and even way back in the cave, although I've never seen bees in there. Now that I know what to look for, I see epi-pens everywhere! He's seriously allergic Rachel says. A couple of bee stings could kill him! Who knew?"

Morgan frowned.

"You've given us a lot to think about, Talies," said Kit. "Thanks. You had me worried there for a moment."

Finally Talies seemed to have run out of stories. He looked weary, and so a few minutes later his mother and his boss released him into the night.

After he left Morgan and Kit went outside and sat on some rocks at the foot of the palisade watching the moon progress across a star-filled sky. They were finishing off their bottle of wine, when Kit muttered, "I'd so much like to catch that woman in the act!"

"Which woman? Rachel?"

Kit shook his head, leaving Morgan to wonder just how much Kit had bought into Indie's perspective. She would need to keep an eye on him. Jules too had made her uncomfortable. He seemed open, but not completely candid about anything. Was he playing them for fools? Or was there another angle?

"I'm glad you installed Talies as a cellar rat," she said as they returned to the tank house. "That was a good idea. He gave us much to think about."

8 STAY CALM (AND CARRY ON)

Morgan and Kit woke to sunny skies and sounds of carpentry on the piazza, where Roberto and a crew of men were hammering together tables and benches for the afternoon's festivities. They went round to the front of the house, entering the kitchen down the long front hall. They stopped in the doorway. The kitchen seemed like chaos as more than a dozen people—both family members and hired caterers—unpacked and sorted through party equipment and prepared enough food for an army. All of the kitchen surfaces were loaded, in rather disorganized fashion, with party-related fare—the counters, tables, chairs, stools, even the tops of two restaurant-sized refrigerators. Orders barked back and forth.

"Get me the lid for that, will ya? No, the big one."

"Take that tray of glasses outside before they get broken."

"No! Stack the colored plates as if they were rainbows."

"We need at least a dozen pitchers for the wine."

"Did someone lock the dogs in the barn? That's all we need right now."

"Ask Mrs. Romano about that."

"Which Mrs. Romano?"

"Where is she anyway?"

"Hey, don't do that. The freezer's full up!"

"Oops. Sorry. Anybody know where I can find a mop?"

Meanwhile, children were zooming around getting underfoot, as they tasted whatever took their fancy and spat out the yucky stuff, giggling hilariously. The older ones were making sandwiches, snatching up slices of salami, getting peanut butter on whatever they touched, spilling milk, and generally functioning as tripping hazards. The adults seemed too busy to bother with them.

A huge pot of tomato sauce simmered on the massive cook stove. Whole loins of pork and beef and several legs of lamb marinated in plastic buckets on the floor as they waited for grill time. The largest salad Morgan had ever seen occupied a three foot long cutting board balanced between two stools. Underneath this board, a small child sat cross legged on the floor, munching an uncut cucumber and keeping her eyes on the swirl of legs going back and forth. The atmosphere of the kitchen made Morgan think of San Francisco's Ferry Building at rush hour, and the smells were outrageously wonderful.

Tinker crossed the kitchen towards them, holding in front of her two brimming mugs of coffee. "Here," she said thrusting both mugs at Kit. "It's all I can manage right now. Feel free to grab whatever you want from the trays." She noticed the little girl kneeling on a chair and dangling a string into the narrow space between the glasses cupboard and a sideboard covered with pitchers in various shapes and sizes. It was as if she were fishing for a reluctant trout. "Zoe! Take those kittens back to the barn!"

From the cellarway at the far end of the kitchen came a harried voice. "Does anybody know where Mom put the little Christmas lights?"

Nobody answered her because at that moment, Indie's older brother River and his partner Paul slammed into the kitchen through the door to the piazza. The hair of both men was standing on end and filled with bits of leaf and twig. They looked as if they'd only just survived a whirlwind. Their arms however brimmed with blooming branches of white oleander and their faces shone ruby red and gleeful. Indie cut them off as they headed for the sink. "Hey, Bro, you may not do that in here!" She pushed them back out onto the veranda. "And what are you trying to do anyway with those flowers? Murder us all? Oleanders are poisonous, you idiots."

"Heck, half the stuff in that garden is poisonous," growled River. "Like your deadly nightshade and the trumpet flower you love so much, not to mention the cycads and castor beans. My god,

Sister, even buckthorn is poisonous. Did you know that?"

"Juniper's poisonous too," added Paul with a huge grin, "And aren't those juniper berries I see floating in the marinade?"

"Poisonous only if you drink 'em with too much gin," countered River.

"Don't be ridiculous! Anyway, you can't go fixing your table garlands here in the kitchen. Throw those wretched flowers on the compost! And scrub your hands before you touch any of the food! Don't you boys know anything? Get roses, you big dummies!"

"Yoo-hoo . . . Rickie," called a woman poking her head through the front door. "Where do you want for me to put these oysters, dear? We have two coolers full up."

"On the back veranda, Cora. I'll be down in a minute."

Next, a bushy grey head appeared at the veranda door. "Mr. Romano around? These are for him."

"I'll take them," said Tinker, detaching a slightly damp toddler from her neck and handing her off to the nearest adult—Morgan.

"Well, hello," said Morgan to the child. "What is your name?"

"Lucy," said Lucy, removing her thumb from her mouth. "I want to get down."

"Certainly," said Morgan, standing the child on her feet. "Mama's over there. Why not ask if she'll let you help stir."

"No! Kitty!" Lucy pushed her way towards Zoe, who was now extracting a ball of wriggling fuzz from behind the sideboard. "I want kitty!" A howl ensued from kitty as Lucy got hold of its tail.

"No-no, Lucy," said Zoe. "Leave kitty be. Don't pull her tail. It hurts her. Come help me take the kitties up to the barn. You can carry Fluff, but don't squeeze her." Zoe pulled a docile yellow kitten out of the bib of her overalls and bundled it gently into Lucy's outstretched arms. Then she returned to the business of gathering up several more of her furry brood from various crannies. She tucked two more kittens into her overalls, and gave Lucy an encouraging push towards the back door. "Go. You go first. Wait for me outside. I'll be there in a sec. Don't let Fluff get away again."

Emma, Lucy's mother and hardly more than a child herself, watched this drama as she stirred the tomato sauce. "Don't let her get dirty, Zoe," she called after the older girl. "And keep her away from the goats. She's just had her bath. Lucy, you mind Zoe, okay? And be good." Emma placed a lid on the kettle and shoved it to a back burner; then, wiping her hands on her apron, she surveyed the kitchen as if it were a war zone. "Here, Mother. Let me take those." She dodged through the kitchen towards Julie, now panting at the top of the cellar steps, her arms overloaded with boxes. "Give me those. Mork and me will put the lights up. Jess'll do the other. By the way, where is Jess, Aunt Tinker?"

"Oh, I sent her and Desidera into town to pick up Phil. They should be back soon."

There was a heavy thump at the back door. A far from flat-chested young woman with green hair spikes, a nose ring, and a grape-vine tattoo snaking up her arm was backing herself and a loaded hand-truck into the kitchen. "Hey, Mom, where do you want the cases of wine?"

"I don't know, Adena. But not in here certainly," responded Julie. "Go ask Dad. He's out there somewhere. Or Uncle River. And remind Dad when you see him to remind Roberto to move Tinker's hives, like I asked him to."

Adena grunted and began struggling to maneuver the heavy hand-truck back outside and down off the veranda without toppling it over. Morgan gritted her teeth, envisioning tragedy. Fortunately, help arrived in the guise of a lovely, dark-haired Japanese woman, picking her way across the kitchen towards the back door, hands pressed to her swollen belly. Kiko was very pregnant. "Adena, wait!" she called. "Don't do that alone, honey. You'll hurt yourself. We'll help you . . . or Bowie will help you."

"No Bowie won't," declared Bowie, grabbing Kiko's arm to forestall her march across the kitchen. "That's a job for my lazy-ass brother. He and Paul are supposed to be doing the wine. Where the hell is River?"

"How should I know? He's not my brother."

"Hey, Kiko," called Tommy as he came into the kitchen from the front hall. "Looks like you're due any minute! Sorry I didn't get to see you last night." He glanced around the kitchen. "Wow! This place is a mad house!" Then he noticed his cousin who was getting herself into increasing trouble. "Hang on Deenie! Let

111

me do that. I'm a pro with these things."

"And as for you, Babe," Bowie said, literally turning Kiko on her heels and pushing her towards the front door. "You're going to Nonna's, where you'll stay out of trouble. I just dropped off Dylan and the twins, so you can help with their lunches and maybe snag a nap yourself. I gotta go find Dad. He's in some kind of urgent mode."

"Come on, let's go sit on the back veranda," said Kit, handing Morgan her mug of coffee and hooking a couple of the cinnamon muffins as Emma pulled them from the oven.

As Kit and Morgan stepped out through the kitchen door, a pair of middle-aged neighbor ladies in heavy dungarees pushed past them, juggling some very large plastic food containers, a jeroboam of Blanc de Blanc, a handful of birthday balloons, and an oddly shaped gift, roughly wrapped in silver paper and purple ribbons. "Rick-ee!" One of them shouted. "We're dropping off some goodies for your old man's party. Where do you want us to put them?"

Morgan and Kit settled themselves for breakfast at the far end of the veranda heaving a sigh of relief to be out of the center of activity but close enough to be able to observe all the comings and goings. Roberto's crew were finishing up even as the party set-up crew started to work.

"Kiko looks so young! And so pregnant," remarked Morgan.

"Yeah. Bowie's third wife, I think," replied Kit. "She doesn't just look young, she is young. This will be her second child, according to Aaron. We were chatting last night. She's some Japanese beer heiress, apparently. Rich as Croesus. He says the family doesn't quite approve of her, though she seems sweet enough to me."

"Do you think we should offer to help back in there?" asked Morgan, nodding towards the kitchen.

"We'd only get in the way."

Suddenly Indie slammed out of the kitchen and onto the veranda. She stood for a moment, hands on hips, looking around. Her body language read harried, exasperated, if not angry. "Where the fuck *is* Rachel? This is all her doing, again."

"Don't know. Winery?" replied Kit, calmly, even though it

was unlikely Indie intended anyone to answer.

Indie glared at him, as if she could easily have strangled him. Then she ran off towards the front of the house, from whence were now coming the sounds of many voices and the slamming of many car doors. They heard the front screen door bang. It banged again. Whiskey's muffled barking drifted across the garden from the barn. Roberto's men quietly pushed the longest table ever into the shade of the arbor, swept up the last of their sawdust, gathered up their tools and unused lumber, and left the scene.

"Maybe we should go see what all the yelling is about?" said Morgan, feeling mildly concerned they might be missing something.

"Dunno."

A moment later Tinker exploded through the kitchen door. With one hand over her brow to shade her eyes from the sun, she scanned the piazza, then the gardens, then the barnyard. "Julie! Jul-ee!" she called repeatedly.

"What's up? Who's here?" asked Kit, rising to his feet.

Tinker ignored him and barked again. "Julie! Dammit, Julie, where did you get yourself off to now?" Muttering to herself, she turned and ran around the corner of the house towards what was sounding now like a fairly hostile altercation out front.

Kit, having changed his mind about the possible significance of this noise, leapt up and took off after her, calling out, "Tinker! Wait! Thinker! Who's here? What's going on?"

Morgan stayed put, keeping one eye on the kitchen door to see who would pop out next, and the other on the remains of her muffin. She tried, but failed, to make out what was being shouted out front. It seemed only a part of the general cacophony. As she licked the last of the buttered cinnamon off her fingers, the shouting abruptly ended. Four car doors slammed in succession. A motor revved. There was a squeal of tires and a crunch of gravel, after which comparative quiet reigned again. Kit returned at a slow walk, grinning and twirling his moustache like some old Hollywood villain.

"What was that about?"

"Tourists," he said evenly, settling down again and reaching for his coffee, which was now cold.

"What did they want?"

"Drinks. Lunch. You know. A carload of half-drunk people, and it's not even eleven o'clock in the morning. They didn't speak much English. They were upset because the sign down on the road doesn't say the tasting room is closed today. Stuff happens." He shrugged.

"Why were they looking for Julie and Rachel?"

"Because tourists are Julie's responsibility. Didn't I say that? Julie runs the tasting room, does some PR. Rachel is does backup, stands in for her when she's not otherwise engaged." Kit grinned, perhaps a little gleefully. "Indie was so pissed. Apparently this bunch was very aggressive, bowled right into the house without a by-your-leave. And when they didn't find a host or hostess waiting for them, they started banging on the walls for service, as if this were a pub." He snorted with amusement. "You can imagine how that went over with all the chaos in the kitchen. Indie was ready to kill Rachel. Apparently she was supposed to have posted a 'closed' sign down on the highway. And Tinker was mad because Julie had disappeared. Tinker hates dealing with boozy tourists. Anyway, Rickie and Julie finally did came down from upstairs and got rid of the interlopers. Rachel's probably down at the winery, doing winery things." He laughed. "I doubt they'll be back . . . ever. Such drama."

"Does this happen often?"

"Didn't used to. Buckthorn's becoming a little better known, I guess. Too bad Whiskey wasn't on duty. The dogs would have them off the front veranda, or at least out of the house. Oh, look. Here comes more entertainment."

Two figures were making their way slowly through the vegetable garden, which Morgan observed was often used as a shortcut between barn and piazza. They were carrying a long extension ladder; its ropes dragging along the ground. Mork, Julie's youngest and the taller of the two figures, led the way in his in big black work boots, stomping through a patch of defunct English peas. At the back end of the ladder, struggling to support its weight, came the much smaller Emma, his wife, still wearing her chef's apron. They were quarreling, as Emma kept dropping her end in the dirt. Then she tripped, and fell. The ladder hit her in the face. She twisted her wrist. Mork cursed loudly, and the dogs, having escaped from their incarceration when these two had left the barn, started barking as they quarreled, circling, sniffing, and generally getting in the way. Emma, distraught and embarrassed, but happily not horribly wounded, began to cry. Abandoning her end of the ladder, she fled towards the guest cottages. Dennis, at this point, appeared, gesticulating and shouting at his son as he came towards him. He picked up Emma's end of the ladder and proceeded to haul it, and Mork, back to the barn, berating his son continuously. Julie, Mork's mother, popped out of the kitchen door and stood, wiping her hands on her jeans, observing. Then she called out, "Emma! Emma! Wait, Sweetie!" and took off at a run after her daughter-in-law, artfully scooping up on the way a tearful Lucy, who was now adrift by herself between the arbor and the kitchen garden.

"Family tensions rising," Kit remarked. "Don't you just love parties? This is only going to get worse. How about a stroll down to the winery? Might be calmer down there."

Wishful thinking.

"You can't always git what you wa-ant. . ." The Stones blared out across the vineyards to a whooshing passacaglia of high pressure hoses. Various voices called orders over a din of thumps and clangs and clatters and whirrs.

"Somebody, turn off that wretched music!"

A winery at work, thought Morgan as they approached the stone building. They went round to the front to take a look at what was going on with the scaffolding. Turned out to be an almost completed new addition—Julie's new tasting room.

"It certainly makes the place feel very contemporary," said Morgan as she and Kit pressed their noses against the long plate-glass front wall. "You can taste wines with a gorgeous view of the vineyards. Very peaceful. Like being outdoors. I wonder if this glass wall opens up. No, I'll bet it's air-conditioned in there."

"Well, I like that bottle display. Very up-scale. I'd bet Phil did the design. Must have cost a pretty penny. Buckthorn must be doing well. Oh, look! Julie finally got herself a gift shop. She's wanted one for years."

"What a beautiful tasting bar! Mike, eat your heart out," said Morgan, comparing in her mind's eye the sleek brass and marble affair inside the new tasting room with her favorite funky bar back home in Quarry Canyon. "I'd love to see what vintages they're planning to offer. I wonder if that door over there leads through to the winery floor. I'll bet it does. For tours, you know."

"Let's see if we can get in," said Kit.

The main entrance to the tasting room, however, was locked tight, so they walked around to the crush pad, which turned out to be nothing more than a cemented area off the side of the winery. It white canvas roof was still dripping after some power-washing. No one was around. The loud music had been silenced. Morgan and Kit paused a moment before making their way through all the equipment, which Kit said was being readied for harvest and crush. Plastic buckets, bins, and tubs of all sizes were stacked everywhere. Along the far side of the crush pad, between the old winery and the entrance to the wine caves, on the other side of the loading dock, they saw dozens of new oak barrels. There was also a large collection of leftover staves and metal barrel hoops.

"Hey, Mom." Talies waved as a forklift appeared from behind the stone winery. "Check this out!" He drove the forklift slowly towards a tower of empty half-ton plastic bins, inserted the arms of the fork into the middle of the tower, and then elevated half a dozen bins into the air. He carefully shifted into reverse and backed up, bins in the air, circled some squat metal tanks and a mess of canvas hoses, and lowered his cargo onto a different tower of bins. "They let me practice with the empties during break," he called out. "If I get good, Rachel said I can drive this thing during crush. Sweet, huh?"

"Well, be careful, dear," said Morgan.

"Come on. We can get in this way," said Kit, jumping onto the loading dock and opening a small door adjacent to the rolling overhead ones. "Hard to believe how this operation has changed since I spent time up here."

Inside the winery the air felt noticeably cooler and the lighting was dim. Kit pushed a button and one of the overhead doors groaned upwards. Sunshine glinted on the spotless winery floor. Glancing around the interior, Morgan was surprised at how industrial everything looked. Her eyes landed immediately on an orderly rank of shining stainless steel tanks, each one rising twenty or thirty feet towards the rafters. Along the tops of these tanks was a long metal catwalk. There were many smaller tanks in the work area as well, of varying size and shape, and a cluster of ten-foot high redwood tanks on platforms, strategically placed, Morgan noticed, so they would be seen from the bar in the new tasting room. The redwood tanks, Kit explained, had once belonged to Big Eddie himself. At the far end of the winery floor was an open stairway spiraling upwards to a long balcony, and along the back of this balcony were half a dozen closed office doors. Below the balcony was another glass wall, which closed off some workrooms and a lab. In the center of the work floor was a string of six or eight open-topped, rectangular vats—empty. And everywhere there were pipes and spigots, valves, computer monitors, fancy dials, hoses—so many hoses! And not a speck of dust, even vine leaf or squashed berry, anywhere.

"This hardly looks like a boutique operation," remarked Morgan gazing into the shadows of the cavernous winery.

A door in the glass wall under the balcony opened and out came two workers in white lab coats and hair nets, pushing a rolling cart filled with clanking equipment. They halted between parallel rows of oak barrels lying on their sides, just inside one of the rolling doors, and near where Morgan and Kit were standing. Immediately the workers began banging open the bung holes, one for each barrel, and collecting samples of wine using a glass pipette. Each wine sample was put into a test tube and labeled, then returned to the rolling cart. A notation was chalked on the source barrel. Beyond the barrels was a row of four or five medium-sized, ten-foot high, closed-top white metal tanks. Each one, Morgan noticed, had a submarine-like hatch at floor level, and above each hatch hung an official-looking sign in red and white proclaiming, "Danger! Confined Space! Entry by Permit Only."

Morgan tapped Kit's elbow and pointed to a sign. "What's so dangerous in there? Claustrophobia maybe? And why would anyone want to go in?" And the moment she said this, a human, arrayed in scuba gear and breathing apparatus, and wearing bright blue rubber boots and a wet suit, emerged from a hatch. Water gushed out when the hatch opened. Then the diver turned and dragged out a fire hose then a long-handled scrub brush. Morgan felt as if she were observing a creature from another world emerge from an alien ship, rather than someone working on the floor of a modern winery.

"Fumes," responded Kit, following her gaze. "Those tanks are for carbonic maceration—think Beaujolais. It's a closed-lid process. I heard last night that Eddie and Rachel have been playing around with it. The more traditional maceration of the must happens in the open vats back there. Both processes emit gases— some hydrogen sulfides and lots of carbon dioxide. You can smell the sulfide easily. It's that rotten egg smell. So people don't usually stick around and breathe in much. But the carbon dioxide is odorless, and since it's heavier than air, it tends to sit at the bottom of those lidded tanks. I guess most of it escapes if they leave the hatches open long enough, but as it's got no smell, you can't really tell whether it's there or not. They go in to scrub down the tank, of course. Rachel makes the cellar rats wear that apparatus to be on the safe side. Believe it or not, people die every year in Wine Country from not being sufficiently careful when they go into closed tanks. Ventilation is crucial, as we talked about before." Then he turned and pointed back towards the steel catwalk over the huge stainless steel tanks. "Believe it or not, people do fall in and drown in the wine too!"

"Sounds Shakespearean."

Kit pulled a face, even as Morgan's mind made the connection. "Oh, now I really understand why they got so upset when the ventilation ducts were obstructed in the caves. Jules wouldn't have known his life was in danger until it was too late."

Kit nodded, adding, "I'm not sure how much danger Jules was actually in, depends on what was going on back in there. As far as I can tell he hadn't yet started his cold soak maceration. And the emissions from barrels and bottles is relatively small, though not insignificant. So. . . . "

"Forgive my ignorance, but what do you mean by 'maceration' and 'must'?"

"Oh, sorry. 'Must' is simply what winemakers call the soupy mix of unfermented grape juice, seeds, skins, bits of stem that produced by the so-called crush. It's what you start with when you're making wine. If you are making a white wine, of course, you'll remove the skins and solids from the juice pretty quickly, since skins are what give wine its color. But if you're making red wine, it's different. The solids are left in the must to macerate anywhere from a few hours to a few days. 'Macerate' simply means 'soften'. That's all. It's what the skins and seeds and stems do when they soak in the juice. And as they soften, the skins transfer color and tannins into what will become the wine. Actually, fermentation can start during maceration. Just depends. Sometimes a winemaker will add some yeast to get things started, or the winemaker may wait for natural yeasts to take up residence and begin to grow. They live on berry skins, as well as in the air around us. Those little yeasties are alive! They consume the sugar in the grape juice and change it into alcohol, emitting as well a bit of gas. It's magical!"

"Like sourdough."

"Yeah, like sourdough. Anyway, you'll find Jules can talk for hours about maceration and all the many ways winemakers manipulate this first step of the process. Rachel too. And Eddie. It's maceration that puts structure into a wine, Jules says. It's also pretty easy to mess up and ruin a whole batch. I do love the smell of it though. Very pungent! Eddie told me last night that Jules has become quite eccentric in his approach. He keeps some open vats near his workroom in the caves. He's been crafting his own private reserve. He and Rachel have grand arguments about it apparently."

Morgan's face became confused, "So that person I saw crawling out of a tank was macerating? Sounds pornographic. Or have I gotten something wrong?"

"Mom! That was Cody," said Talies, sidling up. "He wasn't macerating! What are you talking about? He was cleaning. That's what we cellar rats mostly do—scrub and sanitize. We're getting ready for crush. It starts pretty soon. I've been learning about carbonic maceration. It's different from the open vat process Jules likes. They put in whole clusters of grapes in, not a must. Rachel says the carbonic is a gentler way to make wine, and quicker too. They pump carbon dioxide over the clusters, and somehow, if I'm getting this right, the wine gets made inside the grapes. Weird, huh? Some French guys invented it. Beaujolais mostly. Very low tannins, and the flavor can be thin, I think. But it's ready to bottle and sell by Thanksgiving. Crazy, eh? I heard Kit talking about people getting gassed in closed tanks. It's true! And so Darwinian. But no worries about me. I scrub only the cement maceration vats, although I suppose I might fall in and get stuck in the must. Cody says the must can form a really hard crust. I hope I get to see that." He grinned and went back outside.

As she was listening to her son, Morgan's attention had been drawn towards a movement at the other end of the work floor. She turned to see Rachel and Eddie step out from behind the stainless steel tanks. They were very close together, and locked in conversation. Rachel's hand crept up Eddie's arm, touched his face, caressed his cheek.

Morgan frowned, and alerted Kit to what she saw. Then she asked in a voice louder than necessary, "Why are there so many differently sized tanks in this winery anyway?" Casually they began strolling towards the steel tanks, puzzling loudly about matters of size and material. "Let's see, those are only half the height of those. I wonder if these are what they call 'puncheons'. Why are those redwood? I thought they used oak. Wow! These vats are bigger than old footed bathtubs—spa-sized."

Kit picked up her game, and together they sustained an inane prattle as they paraded up and down the winery floor, peeking into corners and behind fermentation tanks, as they tracked the movements of Eddie and Rachel.

Kit lectured on winemaking, quite unhindered by his own ignorance. Morgan succumbed to the giggles as he manufactured arcane "facts" and told pointless winemaker jokes. Finally, with a rueful grin, his monologue dribbled to a halt. "I don't know what I'm talking about," he said. "If you really want to understand the art of winemaking, you'll need to talk to Jules, or Rachel, or Eddie." Then, as they peered ingenuously down an aisle of vintage redwood tanks, he added, "Well, speak of the devil. . ."

Eddie's arm was embracing Rachel's hips as they leaned over what looked to Morgan like a long steel barrel lying on a mechanized stainless steel hospital bed.

"What is that thing?" she shouted.

Eddie and Rachel jumped apart, threw her a glance, and

moved off. Eddie pulled a cell phone out of his pocket and signaled to Rachel as if an important call had just come in.

"Good feint," whispered Morgan. Kit snorted. Then they too went over to inspect the contraption, and Kit resumed his role as mock tour guide.

"This here, I believe, is a pneumatic membrane wine press," he said. "It might be the only piece of new technology Jules truly likes."

"A wine press? I thought they did it with feet," said Morgan, noticing Rachel and Eddie had once again contrived to disappear into a forest of tanks.

"Only in the movies. This machine's gentler on the berries than even ladies' feet, and a lot more sanitary." Kit twirled the end of his moustache and bounced his eyebrows in the manner of Groucho Marx. "Would you like to see our vibrator table, lady? It's attached to the—ahem—de-stemmer-crusher. It's just outside here."

Morgan giggled and took his arm. Both rolling doors were now wide open. Indie was standing just inside. "It's not really a table table, you know," she said humorlessly, ducking to avoid being splashed by the power-washing of another section of canvas roof. "It's only a kind of conveyor belt that feeds berries and clusters into a de-stemmer-crusher contraption."

"You mean that big thing over there?" Morgan asked, wondering why Indie wasn't up at the Big House, helping with party preparations.

"Yep," Indie said, glancing at Kit, then at where Eddie and Rachel had disappeared. "Berry clusters get dumped onto that belt. It vibrates them along, shaking everything apart so the big stuff we don't want in the must can be removed. You'd be surprised what comes in from the pick—sticks, leaves, dead birds, stones, plastic bottles, bits of trellis wire, fast food bags . . . pretty much anything. We used to depend on our people to keep that stuff out, when they cut the clusters. But Eddie has started using picking machines. The pick goes faster, but it's a lot less controlled. Last year we had to stand next to the belt and sort out a ton of crap. Only berry clusters are supposed to go into that gismo at the end of the belt. It jams up when it has to deal with more than stems and leaves. And this year,

Eddie's going to try out that new whiz-bang wine press I saw you looking at. It's supposed to be very gentle and very clean—good for both reds and whites. Eddie loves technologies. Uncle Jules has high hopes. It has some artificial intelligence built in," she laughed briefly. "We shall see."

"I didn't realize how much goes on in the beginning," said Morgan.

"Yeah, most people don't. Making wine involves a lot of grunt work. If you want to end up with quality in your glass. Not everybody cares. It's easier to mash everything together and let it all macerate—sticks, leaves, bugs, skins, birds. We found a bunch of condoms in the must last year. Go figger." Indie nodded back towards the workrooms under the balcony. "So what's her royal highness up to? I saw Eddie in here a minute ago."

She got no answers from Morgan or Kit however, for suddenly a geyser erupted on the crush pad, as one of the high pressure hose couplings sprang apart. There was a low rumbling and another geyser erupted, from a different section of hose. Water shot everywhere as the still-pumping end of the hose lashed and writhed around like an angry sea monster. A pile of empty plastic buckets went flying. A raincoat-clad cellar rat in fireman's boots stumbled to his knees.

Suddenly Indie shrieked—"Bailey! What are you doing?!" Bailey was swearing loudly, like an adult. A jet of water had pinned him to the conveyor belt on the vibrating table. He fought to keep his balance. A moment later, there was a loud mechanical screech and the conveyor belt started to shake, and then to move. Somehow Bailey's arm became trapped under the belt. Slowly he was being dragged towards the de-stemmer-crusher.

"Carson! For God's sake do something! He'll be sucked in!" Kit seemed strangely paralyzed.

"Watch out you guys!" cried Tommy, struggling to his feet. "Will somebody switch off that table? I'll get the valve!" He ran to other side of the crush pad. It took him a minute or so to get the water shut off, even as he continued to holler: "Who the hell's been messing with my hoses? What happened to those couplings? They were tight this morning." Still grumbling he headed towards Bailey, who was not only drenched, but screaming in earnest as the rattling conveyor pulled him forward. Tommy flipped the power switch on the table. Nothing happened. "Somebody, turn off the friggin' breaker before the kid gets crushed!" Then he managed to get a hold on Bailey, but was having difficulty extracting the boy's arm. "We'll both be electrocuted!" yelled Tommy, as Cody, Jorge, Talies, the green-haired Adena, and several other cellar rats converged at a run. Finally the electricity went off, and Bailey, soaking wet, was rescued. After which an extensive mopping-up action began.

Attracted by all the shouting, Eddie and Rachel magically re-appeared on the winery floor. Rachel was beaming. Eddie's arm encircled her waist. A brief glance told them the crisis had ended. So, with a nod, Eddie drew Rachel back behind the silver tanks. Morgan tried to signal Kit, but Kit's eyes were glued on Indie, who was hustling their soaked and sniffling son into the relative safety of the winery. An odd expression played across Kit's face.

Jules too was attracted by the noise. He stood at the entrance to the wine cave. Behind him was Samantha. And speaking intently into his ear, was an older man whom Morgan did not recognize. Jules nodded and smiled at what this man was saying, even as his eyes followed the drama on the crush pad. Finally, the stranger laid a hand on Jules' shoulder, whispered something in his ear, and headed off towards the parking area in front of the winery. Moments later Morgan heard a motor start.

Jules, followed by Sam, then began working his way across the crush pad towards Morgan and Kit. He paused to say something to Tommy and to take a look at the failed coupling and, then, the silent, now very still, de-stemmer-crusher.

"Who was that old man?" Morgan asked Kit. "He looks like John Steinbeck. That dapper grey moustache, the beard. Big ears. Big nose. Eyebrows." Kit, however, was still focused on Indie and their son.

Indie at this moment looked up and shouted across the winery floor, "Hey Dad. You missed the excitement."

Morgan's head snapped around. Jack, hardly breaking stride, waved at his daughter but marched steadily towards the workrooms under the balcony. He seemed out of place in his dark blue business suit and sun glasses. "You in there, Rachel?" he called. "Great news from New York! . . . Oh. There you are. Didn't see you in the shadows."

Morgan noticed she was alone. Indie was handing Kit a towel. Kit knelt down beside Bailey, dried his hair gently, and soothed him into a grin and a joke. She stepped closer to this little domestic scene. She wanted to hear what they were saying. Kit asked his former wife, "Was that Ev Wolfe with Jules? He's looks so much older, tired too. Is he ill?" Indie, her back towards Morgan, murmured a response.

"Well, he's certainly aged," responded Kit.

"Still best buds though." Indie had turned to gather the wet towels. "Now, go find Grandpa, Bailey. He went back to the labs. Tell him I'll catch him later." Then she whispered something to Kit, just as Eddie reappeared from behind the steel tanks, furtively tucking in his work shirt.

Jules tapped Morgan lightly on her shoulder. "Playing spies?" he whispered.

They watched as Jack clapped Eddie heartily on the back and began explaining something. Morgan glanced at Indie and Kit: they too were watching Eddie and Jack. She saw a shadow wash across Indie's face. She saw Kit frown. She saw Eddie pull out his cell phone, check his messages and text someone as he slowly walked towards the rolling doors and the crush pad outside. Jack started to follow him, but upon seeing Bailey, he circled back towards his grandson and took his hand as they walked towards Jules. Moments later, from behind another tank further down in the row, Rachel reappeared, this time pushing a table loaded with beakers and lab equipment. She made a remark to Jack as their paths crossed.

"Did you pick up those parts?" Jules suddenly barked out across the winery floor, when Eddie came within earshot.

"No worries, Pop," grinned Eddie. "I got 'em. They're in the truck."

"So what are you waiting for? We need that damned mechanism on that table fixed before someone gets seriously hurt. I told you there was a short in it."

"You mean now?"

"What do you think I mean?"

"Can I help too, Uncle Eddie?" Bailey asked, still holding his grandfather's hand.

Eddie glanced at Indie, read permission in her eyes, and replied, "Sure, sure, come along, my young friend. You'll dry off quicker outside. I've got a box for you to carry. You can be my assistant during this little operation." Morgan saw a smile play at the corners of Indie's mouth as Eddie and Bailey trotted off together. Then Indie whispered something to Kit, turned, and left the winery. Kit absently twisted the end of his moustache as his eyes followed his ex-wife.

"So, how are the berries up at Mustard Seed? Are they ready yet?" Jules asked Jack as they stepped together onto the loading dock to observe the clean-up activities going forth on the crush pad.

"Ripening fast. Rachel said she'll do the brix for me in her lab. Hope you don't mind. I know you keep her pretty busy."

Jules scowled slightly, but said only, "Rachel said the auction went well. Hope your flight home was acceptable. She said she's had a lot of calls, by the way."

"Good! The auction went great! I enlisted a couple of new admirers for Buckthorn wines." Morgan didn't catch everything they said as Jack preened, but she did hear something about "five-star restaurant placements."

A few minutes later Eddie and Bailey were back, bearing tools and parts. They set to work immediately disassembling the ailing de-stemmer-crusher. The crew on the crush pad wandered over to watch, and possibly to help. Talies crowded towards the center of activity, while Kit, having returned to her side, prodded Morgan to join them as well. She did. She liked mechanical things, and, in fact, found this repair operation surprisingly interesting.

"Okay, Bailey, now hand me that small wrench, and we'll see if we can get this baby up and running again." Eddie's deeply masculine voice dripped authority. He looked over at his father in the doorway with a grin like Little Jack Horner's. There followed some definite clanks, a rattle, a bit of a hum, then silence. "Anybody seen Tinker?" he said in disgust with himself. "She's the one who usually gets this damned machine to work!"

Someone said that Tinker was up at the Big House, helping Rickie. So, with a groan, Eddie asked for a different wrench and made a different adjustment. "OK. Now try it," he called back over his shoulder. There was a louder clank, some more humming, and finally a cheer went up, as the de-stemmer-crusher vibrated, even purred. Somebody tossed a cluster of grapes onto the belt and everyone watched as the cluster was sucked into the contraption and bits of stem and crushed grapes went flying in opposite directions.

By the time this was over, despite being under the canvas sun shade, Morgan felt sweaty, hot, and thirsty. What time was it, she wondered? Hunger gnawed in her gut. Kit had disappeared again. Then she saw him, on the other side of winery floor, talking again with Indie. She watched as he laid a hand on her arm and nodded towards the outdoors. Indie nodded back, and they left the winery together. Morgan frowned.

The piercing screech of a red-tailed hawk defending its territory echoed off the palisade, and suddenly Morgan felt very much the outsider here, a stranger, alone in the midst of the swirl of old relationships and conflicting interests. She witnessed many tensions, but understood very little about them. Who should she be watching? What should she be watching for? And what was Kit up to? She did not like at all the way he looked at Indie. She needed a reliable guide.

She became aware of someone standing at her elbow.

9 TÊTE-À-TÊTE

Kit and Indie huffed in silence up the switchbacks towards Poison Oak. Their faces were flushed. The air was still. Sounds from both winery and piazza seemed miles away. The sun, nearing its zenith, shone hot and wrapped them in films of perspiration.

"Slow down! I need to catch my breath," shouted Indie, dropping behind.

Kit was happy to sit on a rock and wait for her. He gazed across the valley floor where the grapes were fast growing sweet. Images from his marriage bubbled into his memory, like hot steam from one of the local fumaroles. He and Indie had had their bad times for sure, and he was used to going through the list of them as he lay in bed in the middle of the night, dry-eyed, focused on the pain and guilt of their divorce. Making that list, he found, helped him decompress. Now, up here at Buckthorn on the palisade, he was remembering the good times too—Bailey, a wonderfully curious baby; raucous family outings to the beach when Bailey was a toddler; the sense of exhaustion that came after hours of laughter; the comforts of the marriage bed; their soft cocoon-like existence in this valley; and, of course, Jules and Rickie and the all-absorbing romance of growing grapes and making wine. Waves of nostalgia washed over him, like waves rolling endlessly onto a sandy beach. As he waited for Indie to catch up, he thought of all this and watched the tiny figures below in the valley, trolling the vineyards, stopping to check leaves for signs of disease, tasting the berries and judging their readiness for harvest. He saw Bailey and Uncle Jules walking hand in hand along a track. It was hard to believe that anything truly dangerous, certainly nothing life-threatening, could ever happen in a place so quiet, so familiar, so idyllic, so deeply peaceful.

And yet . . . and yet. Kit was well aware that feelings can lie, that they often do lie. He knew he should be on guard. But the situation seemed so difficult here, and he felt a surge of gladness that he'd had the patience to wait for Morgan before coming to Buckthorn. At least now he wasn't alone amongst the ambiguities and veiled threats. He knew he could rely on her solid sense. It felt good knowing someone was definitely on his side! Kit smiled to himself.

Droplets of sweat rolled down Indie's cheeks as she rounded the bend; she was breathing hard. But she didn't stop when she came up to Kit; she went right on by, taking the path up to the entrance of the old cinnabar mine, eager to reach that bench in the shade of that oak. Kit followed her, musing about how familiar Indie might be with the mine's network of tunnels. He'd no reason to believe her to be in total ignorance of their existence, but he couldn't remember her ever talking about them. He wondered whether she knew about that side tunnel that had landed them in the storage closet. It seemed in such good condition that it must have been fixed up recently Then, when he actually sat down next to his ex-wife, Kit quite forgot to ask about it.

"Drink?" Indie said taking a small water bottle out of her pocket.

"Yes, thanks."

Their fingers touched and lingered briefly when she passed it to him, and when he passed it back.

"Should have worn my hat."

"So, Carson, you want to talk?" Her tone carried a challenge.

Kit stiffened. "What's with the 'Carson' bit?" he said. "You know I hate that name. Can't you call me 'Kit' like everybody else?"

"It's your name! And you do know that Kit Carson was a despicable racist," she replied. "He killed Indians for a living. I have always found it unbelievable you actually want people to associate you with him."

"He wasn't such a bad fellow. Got along rather well with the Native Americans in fact. His first two wives were Indian, his third was Mexican. Where do you get this stuff?"

"Our son. He came home from school pretty upset about it. I told him 'Kit' was just your nickname, a bad joke, but it didn't help."

"Geeze! Why not tell him the real deal about Kit Carson instead of the pop fiction version? Must you always be so politically correct? We have discussed this before."

Indie shrugged. Kit's nickname was indeed an old bone of contention.

"Wish you'd help me out with this, instead of pretending you don't know anything," Kit went on. "Kit Carson was an interesting guy, an admirable sort even. And the West was a different kind of place a hundred and fifty years ago. Things looked differently than they do today. India, you do know that, don't you? Why do you like yanking my chain so much?"

Indie rolled her eyes.

"Fact is, I'm proud to bear the man's name. Kit Carson was a responsible man, trustworthy. Yes, he killed some Indians, but all Indians were not innocent and peace-loving people back then. They were a warrior people, a people at war, and they often acted like people at war. Indians killed settlers. You do know that. They scalped their enemies. They abducted white children. It wasn't all nice-y, nice-y, on either side. Kit Carson wasn't a racist, but neither was he into ethnic cleansing either. To say he was is an anachronism. He fought a duel with a Frenchman in order to marry his first wife. She was Arapaho. She bore him two children whom he loved very, very much. When his first wife died, he married a Cheyenne woman. But you know this!"

Indie glared at him, defiantly. "Oh, shut up, Mr. I-Always-Have-to-Be-Right. I don't care what you say—I am not calling you 'Kit' anymore!"

Kit groaned. He had done it again—taken the bait. She had him on the defensive again. He needed to practice patience, needed to let go of the old arguments. He sat quietly beside her and dug back into his mind for his long-buried reservoir of Buddhist training. Then he simply sat and followed his breath, in, out, in, out, trying to set aside his irritation with the woman next to him, to wait for his poisonous emotions to drain away.

"So?" Indie eyed him steadily. "I really hate it when you do that."

In. Out. In. Out. "Mmm. Shall we start again?"

Indie sucked her cheeks and considered it. "Okay," she said at last. "So if it wasn't to fight like old times, why did you drag me up here? It's a little hot to be climbing cliffs. What do ya wanna talk about?"

"Well, I was watching you down there in the winery this morning . . ."

"So?"

"So I wondered. Is something on between you and Eddie?"

"What do you mean, me and Eddie?"

"Don't play dumb. I saw the way you watched him with Rachel. You know I don't care who you see. I was just wondering, that's all."

Indie began to laugh. "Oh my gawd, Carson! I do not believe it. You're jealous! Well, my, my, my."

Kit's face grew hot. Was he jealous? Well, so what if he was. After all, Indie still felt like his wife, although he knew very well that she wasn't—not officially anyway. Feeling a bit embarrassed, he groaned. "No," he lied, aware that Indie wouldn't believe him anyway. "No, I'm not jealous. I simply wanted to . . . to understand what's going on at Buckthorn. To understand people's relationships. That's all. So I can do what you asked me to do. Remember?"

"You are hopeless, Carson Jalesco. You do understand that, don't you?"

Kit let it pass and assumed instead a more neutral stance, that of investigating cop.

"Eddie's very lonely, you know?" Indie added. "He misses Nicole—a lot. Breaks my heart. He's a sweet man. I like him. I like him very much in fact. One day he'll be a rich man too. Poor Eddie, he needs to find a good mother for those motherless children. You know? And Bailey, well, he could use a father on a day-to-day basis. It's something he's never really had."

Her words stung. And Kit realized suddenly that Indie had

meant them to.

"Did you see how good Eddie is with Bailey?" she went on, teasingly, her eyes monitoring the expressions on Kit's face. "Did you see how he encouraged Bailey to help him, and all? I certainly could do worse for a husband, than Eddie—much worse."

"But you're first cousins."

"Once removed. So what?"

"So you can't marry him. It's against the law."

Indie rolled her eyes. "Oh, get with it, Carson Jalesco. This is California, honey, and I've checked the law. Are you afraid Bailey might have a three-eyed little sister with horns and hemophilia?" She snorted back a giggle and playfully punched his arm. "Boy, Carson! I sure got ya goin'!"

Kit felt annoyed again. He took a few more deep breaths. "Just trying to sort things out," he mumbled, pulling on his moustache and trying to set his cop-self back on track.

"Well, you make one hopeless sort of a detective," Indie said, her voice dripping with mockery. "Anyway, I told you what's going on. It's that selfish bitch of a winemaker. All you need to do is catch her at one of her tricks."

"Wait a minute." Kit raised an eyebrow. "I think I've just figured out what you have against Rachel. What you've always had. You think she's after Eddie!"

"Cripe! You are hopeless! And you've got a filthy mind. Despite appearances, sweetie pie, Eddie would never go for her! Trust me. I know. There's other stuff going on. So stick to the issue, hon. Remember I can always un-invite you as easily as I invited you up here." She looked down and began picking dirt from under a fingernail. "And that lady friend of yours? She reminds me of a raptor. Red eyes, long red nails, always staring at you. Makes me feel like prey. And that son with the weird name? Taliesin. My god! I mean, really! You told me he'd get the filth on Rachel. I'm sorry, he doesn't look capable of that. A bit wet behind the ears, isn't he?"

Kit was more than a little displeased with the direction she was taking. This lady was protesting too much. "Don't be unkind, Indie. Remember you asked us to find out what's going on and to protect your uncle as best we could. And that's what we're trying to do. By the way, I told Jules all about why we're here, and he's okay with it, so you can't un-invite us. After all, he's still in charge at Buckthorn, not you."

Indie pouted, but she let the matter drop, for the moment.

"Now," Kit continued. "I'd like to know about any evidence you have for Rachel's being behind what's going on up here, because something is going on, and it's definitely not what Jules told us—careless work behavior, my eye. But why should he lie? Why he should he pretend he's not concerned? He ought to be concerned by these quote-unquote events, intentional or accidental. And I'd like to know more about that near miss in the City. Why was Jules so anxious to get away? What did the cops find out? I mean, I presume someone's investigating the van crash since there was an injury, if not a death. What makes you so sure the van was aiming for your uncle? He says it wasn't. And he was there. You weren't."

"You're a fool, Carson Jalesco, if you believe what Uncle Jules says. He is concerned, very concerned. Trust me. He just can't bear believing his precious winemaker is responsible. That's all."

"You aren't answering my questions."

Indie glared at him. Her hostility was palpable.

Kit waited for her to continue. Finally, she did, although her tone was distinctly patronizing. "She's always around. When something happens, there she is. First on the scene. Or she's in the background right around a corner somewhere. Always. And you didn't see what happened in San Francisco either."

He didn't take the bait this time, however. He'd already told Indie about what he'd seen, and not seen. "So are you telling me Rachel was in the City that night too?" Kit asked. Indie looked daggers at him, but maintained silence. Kit went on. "Jules is at least partly right—it is pointless trying to get the police involved. There's isn't any evidence to go on. Not if Jules steadfastly refuses tell them what he knows. And Rachel does work here after all; 'being around' is in her job description, you might say."

"You're missing the point, Carson, again. She is up to something. I can feel it. She's arrogant. Manipulative. And selfish. She's got an agenda. You can bet on that. And she's playing Uncle Jules for a fool. She's playing Eddie too. Dad agrees with me. You just keep on watching. You'll see!"

"So tell me, when did the string of incidents that concern you actually begin?"

"I told you, on the phone."

"Tell me again, please."

Surprisingly, Indie took a deep breath and told him again, sort of. "A few months ago. No, maybe it was half a year ago. No, things were definitely different somewhere after New Year's, I think." She sighed, then listed once more the half dozen so-called attempts on her uncle's life that Kit already knew about. As she spoke, her anger with him seemed to dissipate. "I think it's wearing him down," she said in conclusion. "Uncle Jules looks really, really tired. Don't you agree? Aunt Rickie looks tired too. She doesn't say much, but I know she's very concerned. I do worry about them. You know?"

"I know," he said gently.

"I don't think he's well either. And that whole business about his brother has reared up again. Remember all that?"

"Umm. What do you mean, 'Reared up again'?"

"Well, you remember what Uncle Jules promised his brother, don't you? What happened just before he went off to Korea the second time, towards the end of the war. Nonna was pregnant. And you know how Nonna is. She never let that promise thing actually drop. Usually Uncle Jules doesn't respond if she brings it up. But now, everybody's talking about it."

"And what is 'that promise thing' exactly? My memory is not specific."

"Oh, you know—that if Grandpa got killed in the war, then Grandpa's half of Buckthorn would go to Dad. Didn't happen. Uncle Jules wound up with everything. And he's kept it all for himself, all these years. He promised not to let that happen. They had made a pact."

"Wait a minute. Wasn't your uncle just a boy when his brother died? About Bailey's age now? And was not your Great Grandfather still alive and kicking. He lived into the 1960s, didn't he? And when he died, he left Buckthorn to his only living son. What's so horrible in that? I gather nothing was actually written down about this so-called pact. And even if it had been, Jules was only a kid then. He wouldn't have had the power to execute any sort of legal document, if that's what you think, or Nonna thinks, happened." Kit paused wondering whether or not this statement was in fact correct; then he went on. "So what's the real deal? Money? Buckthorn must be worth millions of dollars today. And I suspect your father thinks he deserves half of it. And that he deserves it because of something two boys said to one another more than half a century ago?"

Indie shrugged.

"Surely there should be a statute of limitations on boyhood promises. Is your dad threatening to sue Jules over this thing? I hope he's got a good lawyer. And what does this have to do with Rachel?"

"Oh, shut up, Carson. It's not about money. It's about honor—about fairness."

"You sound like Jules now, with his ethical wine speech."

"No. I mean it. Actually Nonna says the fair thing would have been for Big Eddie to leave Buckthorn in its entirety to my father, not to my uncle. That never made sense, she says. After all, my grandfather was Big Eddie's oldest son, his first born. And my father was his first born. That's how it works, Nonna says. It's called 'prime and gender' or something like that."

"Oh come on, Indie. Since when do you listen to what Nonna says? You make it sound like a Shakespearean play, with two lines of succession fighting over the throne of England. But this is California and the Twenty-first Century. Uncle Jules inherited Buckthorn fair and square from his father, from your grandfather. And you can't say Jules hasn't been generous and fair to your side of the family over the years. He gave Nonna that house of hers—for her lifetime, if I recall rightly. And doesn't she also have some sort of annuity too? And Jules gave your dad a house and Mustard Seed as well, didn't he? I don't know if that was a lifetime lease or a real property transfer, but for goodness sake, Indie, this isn't the Middle Ages! I'm certain Big Eddie did what he thought was best for Buckthorn in the long run, and that what he did was entirely legal. I cannot imagine him leaving half of Buckthorn to your dad who was—what?—maybe eighteen when Big Eddie passed on?"

"Geeze you are an ass, Carson Jalesco. Legal isn't the point! Never was. Nonna's always said it's about a promise made and a promise kept. Uncle Jules got hold of Buckthorn, and he should have shared it with my father, no matter what the legal beagles say. He should have done what he promised his brother he would do. End of story. Think about it! His only brother dies fighting up Pork Chop Hill for the good of the country—he's a war hero! Nonna is left behind, all alone to bring up his only son, my father. And all she gets out of it is some pittance of an allowance and a lousy place to live for a while. That's shameful. Uncle Jules may be sweet, but he inherited the whole estate! How does that even approach being fair!" She gave Kit an icy look. "But I guess that runs in the family."

"What runs in the family?"

"Theft. Lack of fairness. Single motherhood."

"Sorry?"

"You're hopeless, Carson. Nonna! Me! We're both single moms. We both got screwed. And that broken promise? That's called theft, plain and simple. Now Uncle Jules has a chance to fix it at last. He's revising his trust again. Did you know that? For his birthday, he says. Getting his papers in order, etcetera. Nonna told him straight out, now was the time to make everything straight. I heard her tell him to leave Buckthorn to Dad, in its entirety, to make up for all those lost years. Or at least to leave half of it to Dad. Wow! You should have seen Uncle Jules blow his stack! He was so angry! He told her in no uncertain terms to butt out of his business. But Nonna was marvelous, the way she completely ignored him and just talked about how the family's honor was at stake."

Indie took another swig from her water bottle. Then she scooted down the bench towards Kit and offered it to him again. "I will let you in on a big secret, Carson Jalesco. In spite of all the crap from Nonna, I sometimes wonder whether Dad actually wants Buckthorn at all, or any part of it. Don't get me wrong here. I do believe in my heart Dad could run Buckthorn just fine. But I think he'd be happier if he didn't have to. Do you realize he's almost seventy years old? He should be slowing down, not gearing up." She frowned as if surprised by her own statement, then went on. "Of course, if Dad were to inherit Buckthorn, or his share of it, he might turn right around and pass it over to my brothers and me. Shoot! None of us wants a winery. I'm not saying we don't enjoy it up here. It's really nice. And none of us minds helping out, sometimes. But doing this for the rest of our lives? No way! On the other hand, like you say, Buckthorn is worth many millions of dollars. Now I could see Dad, or any of my brothers, or me, selling this place." She nodded to herself agreeing with herself. "That kind of money would be very nice to have."

Kit sat silently on the bench, looking out across Buckthorn Valley and sipping from the water bottle, as he thought about what Indie had said, measuring her story about a broken promise against the recent threats to Jules' life. Something was missing. But what? "Tomorrow is Jules' birthday," he remarked. "Is he going to make an announcement about this trust revision at the party?"

"Everybody thinks he is, but nobody actually knows. Eddie is convinced that he and Julie and Tinker will become joint owners of Buckthorn when Uncle Jules passes—or abdicates his throne, if you will. I don't know what'll happen to Nonna, or Dad. And I do worry about them. They've both lived up here for their entire lives, so he'd better make some provisions. I think that's probably why Nonna dredged up that promise thing. She's afraid she'll get screwed in the end. Dad too. Poor Dad. Eddie says Uncle Jules would never, ever pass any part of Buckthorn to my dad. Dad does okay with his winemaking, but he really is a terrible businessman. Did I tell you he nearly lost Mustard Seed to the bank a couple of years ago? Uncle Jules was livid; he almost didn't cover Dad's loan payment."

"I thought you said your father's ventures were doing well."

"Right now, maybe. But Dad brags a lot. It's hard to tell sometimes. And anyway, everybody takes out loans when they need to replant a vineyard or buy some new equipment. Cash poor is what they say about us wine growers. Dad messed up a whole vintage once, experimenting with some new scheme of his. And a couple of years ago he actually lost hundreds of gallons of wine. I never understood how one "loses" wine. But it just disappeared. You know? Poof! Magic. He never explained to me what happened. And his finances were pretty dicey for a long time. Dad said he learned his lesson. You know, Carson, I'd say deep down Uncle

Jules hates my father. Doesn't trust him one iota, anyways. Although. . . . Well, obviously he likes him well enough to keep him around the place. Sometimes I think it must have to do with what happened after Mom died. But Uncle Jules sure doesn't like my step-mom. Can't blame him—I don't like my step-mom. We certainly have that in common. But you know all that stuff! Gail hasn't been up to Buckthorn in ages. Did you realize that? They're sort of separated. I mean, I'm pretty sure she and Dad are still officially married, but they haven't lived together in years! That's weird isn't it? That I wouldn't know my own dad's marital status?"

Kit nodded. He'd been wondering whether or not Jack's second wife would put in an appearance for this birthday party. He'd be happy if she didn't. Gail's ice-queen personality always sent shivers down his spine.

"So, how long have these family discussions about Jules' trust revision been going on?" he asked, trying to bring her back to the topic at hand.

"Maybe since last Christmas? The family was all up here then. And I remember one night at dinner Uncle Jules started rambling on about what he'd like to happen with Buckthorn after he dies. He didn't get very far with that though, because everybody started bickering immediately about what they wanted. You know how we are. And then Nonna brings up that old promise thing. Which somebody says—I don't recall exactly who—but someone says that promise didn't matter anymore. And Dad says it ought to matter. And Julie says something about changing Buckthorn's business plan. And then . . . well you don't really want to know all this crap, do you? Anyway, it made for a pretty terrible Christmas. I got so confused! I mean, we're such a big family, and everybody's got their own opinions. Even old Bowie piped up. I couldn't believe it. My dear unreliable brother has no idea what he's talking about when it comes to vineyards. And he knows nothing about winemaking, or wine. Then somebody—maybe it was Aaron—or maybe it was Phil. Somebody anyway suggested Uncle Jules should just sell out. Go into one of those retirement places. Take a cruise around the world. It's a lot less hassle to split up cash. Wow, was that not well received! Dad and Dennis and Eddie really got into it then. I mean really, really got into it! It was like World War Three! I left when

Nonna started shouting it was about the honor of the vineyards, the honor of the vineyards, not about the money! I think Uncle Jules agreed with her, in a way. But he just sat there listening as if he were Yoda. You know? Like I said, it was awful. Since then, it's never really been the same around here."

Indie sighed and studied her cuticles, biting away a tiny bit of loose skin before looking up again. "Actually, you are right, Carson. That wasn't last Christmas. It was maybe the Christmas before that. I don't know. Time! It confuses me. Mostly I think Uncle Jules simply wanted us all to talk about it. You know? The Future—with a capital 'T' and a capital 'F'. And I don't think Uncle Jules knows what he wants either. You know?" She looked up at the sky, then out across the valley floor. "Who knows? Maybe the stuff that's been happening around here since Easter doesn't have anything at all to do with any of that. You know? But I'm still scared for Uncle Jules."

Kit had some difficulty keeping his growing annoyance with his ex-wife at bay. He was so tired of the way Indie always told her stories, skipping around, being inconsistent, vague. And the lies she told. The exaggerations. One never knew. It was difficult to parse what she actually meant.

"Tell me again, when did the series of threats start? Last Christmas? Or the one before?"

"Umm. I know it was right after a big dinner. We all had had a lot to drink, as usual. Uncle Jules got so drunk he collapsed right onto flagstones while we were eating. Did I tell you about that? Or maybe that was Thanksgiving. Anyway, the doctors said he wasn't drunk, that he'd just had a little stroke. They kept him in the hospital for a few of days, 'under observation'. Gave him a pile of meds. Scared us all half to death. Gawd! You should have seen Tinker! She got herself so seriously stressed out. Well, you know how weird she gets sometimes when she's stressed, absolutely manic. Phil actually put her in the hospital for a while."

"So you're saying Jules' fall was not due to a 'dirty trick' that time? Only a trick of fate?"

"Maybe. But you know how Uncle Jules has always been so healthy? He doesn't have high blood pressure. Nothing like that. No heart problems. No COPD. No diabetes. It was so sudden.

And afterwards he was fine. So I don't know. I remember looking it up on the web."

"Looking what up on the web?"

"Stroke. So I asked Uncle Jules about that old heater back in the caves. I thought maybe he'd had it on that morning. Well he did. Did you know that carbon monoxide poisoning can bring on strokes?"

"So you're telling me that Jules' stroke was caused by someone tampering with his space heater?"

"Possibly. Does that feel right? And there was that letter last fall too."

"Last fall? What letter?"

"Oh, yeah. Well, that did happen around Thanksgiving. I remember that exactly. Uncle Jules wouldn't show the letter to anyone—or maybe only to Aunt Rickie—but I could tell something in it worried him, really worried him. Aunt Rickie claimed she didn't know what was in the letter, but she was probably lying. Anyway, nobody actually believed she didn't know. Tinker told me later the letter had to do with a bunch of money Uncle Jules withdrew from his bank account. There could have been a cashier's check in it. Tinker said he took out a lot money! She didn't know what he did with it. It made us all wonder. But there was this holiday stuff going on at the time. . . . Oh, I don't care about the money particularly. But something wasn't right about it, Carson. I knew you could figure it out. That's why I thought about calling you."

And Indie did in fact look upset. Her eyes locked onto Kit's, even as he was trying to stay focused on clarifying what had happened, and when. Nothing added up, and as Indie talked on and on, events seemed only to morph into one another. He lost track of what she was saying. Was she making it up as she went along? Had her mind always been such a mess? In the end, he was catching only words and phrases—"Bailey" and "his future" and "smokescreen" and "blackmail." When she said "blackmail" Kit's ears perked up.

Then it was Indie who grew quiet. She stared at him. "So? What do you think?" she asked, after a rather long moment.

"How much?"

"What?"

"How much money was that check for?"

"Oh that. I'm not sure there actually was a check. Tinker does the accounts. I think she said two hundred and fifty grand was taken out. She said she asked him about it. She said Uncle Jules said he was buying another vineyard. Nobody believed him."

"Why not?"

"Because Buckthorn already owns all the good land in this valley. There's nothing to buy."

Kit made a mental note to ask Jules about this.

"Did you know Dad is handling Buckthorn's marketing now?" Indie asked him next.

Her question was such a non-sequitur that Kit blinked. "How's that going then?"

"Oh fine. He's damned good. Who knew? Maybe Dad's found his niche. Anyway, he said the New York wine auction was a Big Success. He sold cases and cases and cases. But Uncle Jules won't give him any credit. Aunt Julie says Dad's too good, whatever that means." Her words drew slowly to a halt as she looked deep into Kit's very blue eyes.

Then she leaned over and kissed him, passionately, on the mouth.

Surprising himself, Kit kissed her back.

"Oh. . ." Indie pulled away, paused briefly, then suddenly jumped up and ran down the slope towards the Big House, her golden hair flying in the sunshine.

Kit couldn't move. He felt confused. Tears welled in his eyes. Finally, he too rose off the bench and followed his ex-wife down the palisade to where a path cut off towards the tank house. He stopped at the crossroads.

A figure was hurrying up the path towards him. Clearly a woman. She was wearing a summery dress. Red. Flowery. The light glinting from sunset made it glow redder. She was holding a cellphone to her ear.

Kit blushed deeply, and lifted a hand to his lips. He felt like a total fool. A guilty fool at that. What if Morgan had seen what happened?

Then, from a different part of his mind came a small voice—

Morgan doesn't wear dresses. She doesn't even own one. Who is this woman on the path?

Suddenly Kit felt afraid, very afraid.

10 IT'S PARTY TIME

Morgan leaned against the door frame of their little bedroom in the tank house, watching Kit put on a clean shirt and adjust his belt. As they had walked back together along the path, she'd asked what happened during his tête-à-tête with Indie, but all the answer she got was "nothing." Now, studying his freshly washed and newly shorn face, she didn't believe him. Although cheerful, he seemed distracted, inwardly focused, willing to speak only of trivialities.

"Shouldn't we have a strategy for this party?" Morgan asked at one point. "We're here to keep Jules safe. So how are we going to do that? There will be all sorts of people milling about, family as well as folks we don't know, certainly that I don't know at all. Things could get a bit tricky."

Kit shrugged. It was as if he no longer believed in imminent perils to Uncle Jules. "Whatever you think," he said, bending towards the tiny mirror over the little bathroom sink and clipping the ends of his drooping moustache. He barely glanced at her. Neither question nor statement provoked anything other than grunts, or a cryptic "not now." And her gorgeous red dress? The one that Artie, that everyone, always loved? The dress that had hung hidden in the back of her closet since her husband's death? Kit hardly noticed it at all. Something had definitely happened.

Finally, Morgan gave up, determining to attend the birthday party on her own, and create her own strategy to keep Jules safe. And she meant to enjoy herself too, while keeping her eyes and ears open. Kit could do as he liked. "Catch you later," she said, when he went off to make a couple of phone calls "for work."

The party was well underway. She spotted most of the adult Romanos she'd met over the last twenty-four hours. The others were strangers—neighbors? friends? late arriving family? She had no idea. People were standing around in groups, chatting in the shade of market umbrellas that the caterers had positioned over serving tables. Chairs had been dragged off the long veranda and arranged for conversations, somewhat away from the food tables. Under the flowery arbor stretched the recently constructed banquet tables, now covered under a rainbow of tablecloths and garlanded with grapevines and roses. There was enough pottery and silver and glassware on them to serve a small army.

Three caterers, dressed in black aprons and white chef hats, hovered over the grill pit—messing with the fire, painting meats with marinades, turning sizzling legs of lamb, half chickens, dripping racks of ribs, loins of beef and pork. Cooked meats and vegetables had been piled onto colorful platters and set on serving tables along with a cornucopia of salad greens, pastas, Tuscan beans, and fruit compote. There was a raw oyster bar. A table that held only breads. And another with only rounds of cheese and bowls of raw vegetables. Servers snaked among the guests offering finger food and glasses of wine, so much wine!

Jules was sat alone, on the far side of the banquet table, in the shade of the arbor. He used a pitcher to refill his tumbler with red wine and as he sipped, gazed about among his guests. He nodded to one or another of them, but if anyone made as if to come towards him, he waved them back into the crowd. Children buzzed around—laughing, calling to one another, bouncing among the adults, busy with their own affairs. Morgan watched Julie, then Tinker, then Paul, purposefully work the guests—greeting each one with kisses or hugs, chatting a moment, then moving on to the next. Emma and Mork reappeared, this time with a smaller ladder. They busied themselves hanging some sort of rolled thing-y among the leaves of the arbor.

She saw Dennis arrive, then Phil Sasaki, leading his toddling granddaughter by the hand—Desidera, the frilly princess. They went over to Jules, greeted him, conversed for a moment, then wandered back into the crowd. Many glasses of wine were poured. More people appeared. Shouts, waves, and high-fives punctuated the rising noise level. Conversations morphed from friendly to passionate to hostile, and back again. The increasingly crowded piazza displayed all the marks of a successful party.

Despite her red dress, no one paused to say "hello" to Morgan. In fact, no one paid her much attention at all. Just as well, Morgan thought to herself. She needed to observe what was going on, rather than participate in it. Gradually she eased herself closer to Jules, who appeared to be waiting for something, or someone. Or perhaps he was simply observing the company, the interplay of friends and family. Morgan regarded the faces in the growing crowd, memorizing them as best she could, while straining to catch the bits of conversation that swirled around her. Goodwill and family cheer dominated the surface of this scene, but she noticed tensions too, roiling underneath. Jules refilled his wine glass several times from the pitcher in front of him. Each time he nodded grimly, as if carrying on an internal argument with himself. Although the afternoon sun shone brightly and the piazza buzzed, something in the atmosphere reminded Morgan of the dark expectant silence that had preceded that strange magic show in the City. She couldn't put her finger on what was wrong, but when Jules looked up, she caught his eye and sent him a protective smile. No worries, she wanted to say. I'm here.

Indie's brother River and his partner Paul, who hosted Buckthorn's San Francisco tasting room, were still setting up their wine table, smack in the middle of the piazza. She watched as they unpacked cases of bottles, uncorked them, and decanted dark reds and golden whites into a mish-mash of colored crockery pitchers. She tuned her ears to the murmur of their voices. They were tasting the wine from each bottle before emptying it into a pitcher. Was that what they were whispering about? Tasting notes? They looked conspiratorial.

"So pick 'em up, please!" River said, when the pile of drawn corks suddenly spilled onto the flagstones. "We need to get rid of the evidence anyway."

Laughing, Paul picked up one cork. He took aim and tossed it into the array of empty wine glasses, as if trying to make a basket from the far end of the court. He tossed another, and another. He missed one shot entirely, nearly hitting a guest on the neck. Then he retrieved that cork and tossed it again, landing his shot this time.

"Stop that, you idiot. I'm not joking around," said River. "Eddie specifically said to get rid of all these plastic corks, or he'll have another stroke!" River began stuffing the drawn corks into his own pockets. When his pockets became full, he began putting them into a box under the table. Meanwhile Paul was still tossing corks into glasses. He made most of his shots.

"Stop it, Paul!" River said again, stealing a glance at his Uncle Jules. "Put them into this box. I'll go get a garbage bag." River started towards the kitchen. Paul ran after him and stuffed some corks down the back of his shirt. He laughed so hard at River's resulting contortions, that he knocked three bottles of wine onto the flagstones. Everyone turned to look. A caterer ran over to clean up the mess.

"That isn't funny at all," growled River as the party resumed. "What are you going to do if he gets curious and comes over? There will be hell to pay."

Paul settled slightly, although every once in a while, as if to assert his independence, he landed a cork in an empty glass. Morgan heard someone make a disparaging remark about the "plastic wars." She watched as River batted off an attempt by Cody and his sandy-haired cousin, Jonathan, Eddie's oldest, to hi-jack a couple of unopened bottles from one of the wine cases.

"Oh no you don't, my friends," said River. "If you cellar rats want to drink, Rachel says you're to sit up here with the grown-ups, like civilized persons. She wants no nonsense in the caves to-night."

Jonathan laughed, stole two bottles, and sprinted around the corner of the house. Cody shrugged, selected an unopened bottle and a corkscrew, and ambled over to the table where his sister Megan was sitting, pouting in front of a large bowl of pasta. She was nibbling on a carrot.

"I can't believe someone made lobster ravioli," she whined. "They know I'm a vegetarian! And look at all that meat on the grill! What are they thinking?! What am I supposed to eat?"

Grinning, Cody displayed his stolen bottle.

"That'll definitely help!" Megan began peeling off the foil.

"Hey!" cried River, appearing beside Megan and making a grab for the bottle before she could jab it with the corkscrew.

"Hey yourself! This is mine!" Megan pulled away her bottle.

They struggled briefly.

River managed to get hold of the corkscrew, and then the still unopened bottle. Politely, he traded it for an open one.

"That was close!" Morgan heard him whisper to Paul.

Paul stuck out his tongue and threw a cork at one of the dogs asleep in the shade of the arbor.

I wonder what this deal with corks is about, Morgan wondered to herself. I should ask Kit about it. River's very uptight. She looked around for Kit. So how long could it take to make a few phone calls?

She saw Jack and his mother, Irene, arrive. Then Bailey appeared. But not Kit. And not Indie. Dennis was talking with his dark-haired nephew, Yoko, and his niece, Adena of the green hair. Morgan sighed. Such strange names! She saw Eddie finally, locked in animated discussion with his cousin Bowie and Bowie's wife, the very pregnant Kiko. Emma and Mork had joined a group of their contemporaries—cousins maybe, or locals.

Children circled on the fringes of the party crowd, making forays to steal tasty nuggets. Some of the dogs, now loose, were playing cheerfully with Zoe's kittens. Aaron and Jennifer, Indie's brother and his wife, the ones from Los Angeles, made a noisy entrance. She noticed that they failed utterly to give so much as a glance at either their son Cody, or his sister, Megan. She watched Phil Sasaki drag his granddaughter Desidera out from under a table and readjust her princess dress. She noticed that, from time to time, Rickie or Julie would appear at the kitchen door to gaze across the crowd.

Rachel arrived, herding along four of the cellar rats, each one carefully carrying a case of Buckthorn Reserve. Talies among them. After delivering the cases to River and Paul, the rats all went for the food, noisily heaping plates and taking over one end of the long banquet table. Meanwhile, Rachel cut her way through the crowd towards Eddie, her face beaming. Both Tinker and Jess came and went. The noise level rose. Another group of guests—strangers to

Morgan—appeared from the corner of the Big House and headed directly towards Jules. Kit did not appear.

Suddenly a string of curses erupt from a group of older men, congregated near the cheese table. "Goddam that friggin' bastard! The valley needs another AVA about as much as it needs an eight-lane freeway!" Morgan could not identify the speaker. She sighed—she tried to remember what AVA stood for. Jack, after parking his mother in a lawn chair under the arbor and getting her some grilled chicken to eat, joined this group. Something he said to them roused their voices to anger. People turned. Conversations momentarily ceased. Other joined the AVA group. More shouting erupted. Emotions spilled like wine on the flagstones. Jack climbed on his soapbox.

Morgan wished she could to hear what he was saying, but his back was towards her. So, trying to be stealthy, she slipped behind a pair of elderly strangers, a man and a woman, who had just arrived and were tottering towards Jules. They completely ignored the commotion. When they got a look at their faced, and she recognized the man—he was a cleaned-up Ev Wolfe, dressed now in straw boater and shiny blue suspenders. The woman must be his wife—tall, straight of back, wide-hipped, and elegant in a long white linen dress and coat. She too wore a hat—broad-brimmed, flower-trimmed. Morgan glanced over her shoulder—Jack was still haranguing about something. It was difficult to watch in all directions at once.

Paul offered her a glass of wine. Then, nodding to River, she headed for a different listening post, one from which she might keep her eyes and ears on both Jules and Jack. She sipped her wine—fragrant with citrus, dry, not too alcoholic. Now she had something else to ask Kit about—this AVA thing as well as the business with the corks. Then it came to her—"AVA" stood for "American Viticultural Area"—a designation of terroir. So why all the passion? Or was she being naïve?

She watched as the elegant woman in the flower-trimmed sun hat bend to kiss Jules. He smiled fondly up at her. "Ah, Lizzy" he was saying. "So glad you could make my celebration." Then, strangely, Lizzy reached over and with both hands began pulling on Jules' ear lobes. First one, then the other. As if his ear lobes were bell chords in an old church. Over, and over and over, she pulled them, counting out loud—". . . ten, eleven, twelve . . . thirty-two, thirty-three, thirty-four. . . ." The assembly grew quiet as she went on. They began to count with her. ". . . seventy-eight, seventy-nine, eighty!" A roar went up. Ev, grinning, pounded Jules on the back, until Jules sputtered and coughed.

"Stop, Ev . . . please. Between you and that dear wife of yours, I'll die before I get to my cake!" Grinning, Jules coughed again. He rubbed his sore ears. His forehead furrowed. "I've a few too many years on me for this kind of ritual thing."

Lizzy kissed him again. "Oh, stop fussing," she said. "A good pulling of the lobes is more likely to improve your hearing than to kill you. Cheer up. All will be well yet!"

Something in Lizzy's teasing tone sent a shiver down Morgan's spine. She must ask Kit about this ear lobe business too. So where was this man? Her eyes roamed across the piazza, hunting for Kit, for Indie, and for Rachel too—all had disappeared. Then she laughed at herself, regained control, and turned again towards Jules.

Ev was standing behind now, patting his shoulder. Suddenly Ev pulled a large bottle from behind his back, a Jeroboam of sparkling wine. He plumped it down in front of his friend, proclaiming, a bit loudly, "Tradition. Tradition. Oo-la-la how my darling girl does love those old traditions! Drink up, my friend! The bubbles promote longevity! And a long, long rest of your life, Birthday Boy!" He kissed his old friend on both cheeks, then grabbed back the Jeroboam and planted several more sloppy kisses squarely on its foil.

Jules laughed as he said, "Now what are you up to, old friend?"

"Oh, have you not heard? That's the latest fraud prevention technology. The vintner's DNA on the foils." Ev laughed too and sat down beside Jules. He shooed away his wife and began whispering something very intently into Jules' ear. Lizzy shook her head, poured herself a glass of wine, and went off to join her friends.

As she watched, Morgan thought about Ev. He'd been Jules' best friend since childhood, according to Kit. What did he know

148

about the string of so-called accidents? Could she trust what he said? Where did his loyalty lie? Hard to say. After all, Ev is Rachel's grandfather. It might be useful to talk with him.

Indie appeared at the corner of the house, scanned the crowd. Then she cut swiftly through the crowd and broke up her uncle's tête-à-tête with Ev. Something in her body language made Morgan wonder whether Indie needed for some reason to separate these two. Something was definitely going on there. She watched Ev get onto his feet, and let Indie drag him off to the kitchen garden. She watched as they stood talking and gesticulating broadly—first, out towards the vineyards in the valley and, then, up towards Poison Oak and the ridgeline. Ev shook his head. He nodded. She glanced at Jules and saw the shadow pass over his face as he too watched their conference. Then the pair disappeared, walked rapidly around the house and out of sight. Morgan considered learning to lip read; she wished she could read thoughts too! Jules looked around and caught Morgan's eye. Morgan smiled. Jules smiled back. He nodded in the direction the pair had gone. Morgan nodded back. Then she bit her lip, took another sip of wine, and gazed again around the piazza, thinking.

Her thoughts were interrupted however as a tide of strangers streamed around the house, all of them bearing more gifts and more bottles. Happy shouts arose. Jules' expression became almost beatific. He rose to his feet at last, and greeted them each with kisses and hugs. Coals to Newcastle, Morgan said to herself as gifts piled up on the banquet table. The strangers went off to find food and drink. Jules sat down again.

Suddenly Jules slapped the side of his neck. Morgan heard him grumble, "Tiresome bees." She wondered if Jules had his epinephrine in his pocket. She couldn't recall who was supposed to have moved the bee hives. They were still there though, in a row, thirty or fifty feet beyond the arbor. A server stopped to refill Jules' wine pitcher. Indie had returned. She stood in the kitchen doorway, scanned the crowd, then retreated. Meanwhile Jules himself began gathering together his gift wines. He presented them to River and Paul for uncorking. She watched him taste the wine in each bottle, then distribute bottles among his guests.

Rickie stomped out of the kitchen, marshalling before her an army of children, each bearing yet another platter of food. Dogs rushed around, got underfoot, begged for handouts, scavenged for fallen treats. The team of caterers worked the grill and the carving boards. The sun beat down on the arbor and the rainbow of market umbrellas across the piazza. Jules mopped the sweat from his neck and returned to his seat.

Morgan decided it was time to fill her own plate, to find a glass of water. She looked around for Kit, for Ev, for Talies. Then she sat down next to young Samantha. Sam, she had discovered, was surprisingly well informed about winery matters. So she asked her about the so-called closure controversy, which pitted natural cork against plastic. Then she asked about the blood sport of designating a new AVA. Sam revealed that her Uncle Eddie had brought the proposal for a new Buckthorn Valley AVA designation. Jules had been vigorously opposed.

"Don't you think it's odd," said Sam, "that the Federal Bureau of Alcohol Tobacco and Firearms—the BATF—gets final say on AVAs? I mean, they know like nothing about soil types or fog levels, let alone all that microclimate stuff. Dad told me the BATF actually used the phone book to define the Napa County AVA. How strange is that?!"

Then Sam rose and strolled off to the dessert table.

11 FUN AND GAMES

Gradually the shadows lengthened and the heat of the day dissipated. Morgan finally began to relaxed, her belly content with the home-made salami. She drained her wine glass and let down her guard. Jules seemed safe, playing with his grandchildren. Eddie's twins had found an old rubber whoopee cushion and were trying, amid gales of laughter, to insert it under their grandpa's rump. Jules let them succeed, then gently removed it and began demonstrating its musical qualities to a growing audience of small gigglers. Next, they embarked on a game of keep-away, with Jules holding the pink whoopee cushion over his head and the kids leaping up as they tried to grab it. Finally, Jules himself placed the cushion carefully onto his seat and ever so slowly lowered himself down, producing a noise that was significantly rude. The kids collapsed in ecstasies of glee.

As Morgan watched all this merriment, she pondered how much about this large family was hidden from her. They did seem to like one another, to enjoy simply being together, but there were also signs of stress, and enough sparks of conflict to ignite a rather massive wildfire. She considered whether or not to finish off Jules' bottle of gift wine.

Her thoughts were interrupted by a loud ripping sound, rather like that made when the limb of an old tree began to break and fall. A kind of moan echoed across the piazza. Conversations ceased and head's whirled towards the sounds. Morgan's eyes leapt immediately to Jules, and she watched in horror as a heavy canvas banner slowly first unfurled and then fell out of the leafy arbor. On it was painted an innocent enough message—"Buon Compleanno! Happy Birthday!" Then one end of the heavy pole that weighted the bottom of the banner got stuck for a moment in the vines, making its opposite swing down at an awkward angle. There was a sudden crack, and with an awful sound, half the pole hit Jules precisely on the top of his skull. The old man wobbled. He nearly toppled off his seat. Blood streamed down his cheek. His face grew deathly pale. Morgan jumped up to give assistance, only to stop. Emma was already at his side.

"Geeze, Grandpa, what did you do?!" Morgan heard her cry out, as if being hit on the head was his fault. Emma carefully extricated him from the tangle of heavy fabric and wood, then handed him a handful of paper napkins to mop the blood. "I guess we kind of miscalculated how this was going to work," she said. Mork ran up, growling angry words at his young wife. Then Mork and Emma gathered up the mess and carted it off to the barn, leaving Jules holding a wad of napkins to his head. Rickie meanwhile had slammed out the kitchen door and was stomping as rapidly as she could across the piazza. Her own anger was palpable. Jules sat there dazed.

Morgan stood rigidly in place, holding the bottle of gift wine and watching the scene play out. Emma's casualness surprised her. As did Mork's response, not to mention their apparent disregard for Jules' wellbeing. Rickie seemed more angry at the victim than the perpetrators. Most guests had paused briefly when the accident happened, but none had come to Jules' rescue, and all quickly returned to their party concerns. What was she not understanding here?

"Whoa there—that's the good stuff," said Eddie, scooping the gift bottle out of Morgan's hand. "You don't want to spill that! Did you not notice what's in this bottle?" He set the half-empty wine bottle down in the center of the table. "This is a 1989 Yquem! If I were you, I'd hang on to what's left until cake time. It goes really well with cake. You may sit down now too. You're gawping. Dad's fine! Only a scratch. Here, let me pour you some of this less fancy wine." Eddie refilled first Morgan's wine glass, then his own, from a wine pitcher.

"Believe it or not," he went on, "a couple of Jack's boys made that banner, must be twenty years ago. Someone hangs it up there every year. One of the pulleys must have broken. Don't look so worried! Dad's a tough old bird. A little bonk on the head won't hurt him. And he should have known better than to sit in that spot. Nine times out of ten the damn banner falls. So predictable!"

Eddie too was blaming Jules for the accident, Morgan thought. It made no sense. Did he not care that his father could have been killed? And if the banner fell so regularly, why doesn't someone fix it? Or hang it in a safer location rather than right over Jules? He'd been sitting in that seat all afternoon. Were they all out to get him?

"Tommy! Eddie!" cried Julie, jumping up from her seat at the far end of the table. "We forgot the birthday chair!" She dashed off towards the barn.

"Catch you later." Eddie disappeared in the wake of his sister, Tommy after him.

"Wasn't 1989 the year the big earthquake knocked down the freeways in San Francisco?" said someone behind Morgan as party resumed.

"Zoe!!? Where's Zoe?"

"Well, that's an out and out lie!"

"Kiko, love, please put the tray down."

"No!!"

"I'd kill if anyone said that about my wines."

"Has anybody seen Zoe? Is she with Bailey?"

"Don't know. Where is Bailey?"

"Don't tell me that. I know what works in this business!"

"Not possible!"

"I use only new American oak for the malolactic ferment."

"Will someone PUH-LEEZE bring more chairs!"

"Two million five!? But there's no soil there."

A child wailed. Someone picked it up.

Two dogs began quarreling over a rib bone. The pasta table was upset as people tried to separate them.

"Zoe!? Where are all the children?"

"Goddammit all to hell!!"

Morgan's ears rang. What idiot said the louder the party, the better the party? She looked around—and where was Kit? Should she go hunt for him? Probably not. The grill sizzled with barbeque—ribs, chicken, garden vegetables—tomatoes, eggplant, zucchini, artichokes. They were calling to her. If only she hadn't eaten so much salami already. Could she at least squeeze in a small grilled tomato?

She never got that chance.

From around the corner of the house, dancing slowly across the flagstones, came Tommy, Ben, and Zoe, leading a pack of little ones jangling their tambourines. Each dancer was dressed in a red and white striped gondolier's shirt. Tommy and Ben were loosely harnessed with ribbons to the front of an old wooden handcart heaved along by Eddie, his face glistening with sweat. On the handcart reposed an ornately carved, dark wood chair; its seat, arms, and back upholstered in plush red velvet. "Make way! Make way! The Birthday Chair is here!" chanted the whole entourage. "Make way for the Birthday Chair! Grandpa! Nonno! Come sit on the Birthday Chair and be crowned with the red and the gold of Buckthorn Estate."

Family and guests joined the chant as the procession came to a rattling halt in front of the vine and rose bedecked banquet tables. Eddie and Tommy hoisted the big birthday chair off the cart, and then, with help from River and Paul, passed it over the crowd and installed it in the place of honor between the two adjoining banquet tables. A place, Morgan noted, that was well away from where the banner had fallen. Everyone seemed to know what would happen next. The crowd parted like the Red Sea to make way for Eddie's five-year-old twins—Josh and Ellie—each now crowned with a wreath of red and white roses. Between them, like little ring-bearers at a wedding, they carried a bed pillow on which sat a home-made red and gold cardboard crown encircled by tiny fairy lights. This crown itself was quite tall and decorated with grapevines. Behind the twins, herding them gently along, walked Aunt Tinker, beaming. As the twins transported the big crown to Jules, the crowd broke into an enthusiastic, although somewhat off-key, rendition of the happy birthday song—some singing in Italian, the rest, in English. Grinning widely, Jules peeled the blood stained napkins off his head and crowned himself. The he kissed each of the twins, and accepted their escort to his ceremonial throne.

As he lowered himself onto the chair, a long, musically sibilant raspberry rang across the courtyard. The crowd groaned appropriately, then broke into gales of laughter as Jules, with the greatest of solemnity, stiffly pushed himself back up on his feet and removed the offending item from under the velvet chair cushion. He held it high over his head and boomed with all the drama he could muster, "Ah, what fools these mortals be . . ." Then he re-inflated the now flattened whoopee cushion, stepped on it, and produced a long sibilant encore, much to the crowd's delight. "Dearest friends," he said, "after all these years I fear my family still has insufficient respect for my graying head! Just look at me." And with that, he removed his crown and allowed Tinker to wrap a huge gauze band around his wounded skull. Then he replaced the crown on his bandaged head, adjusted the grapevines out of his eyes, and sat down.

"Cake! Cake! Cake!" People began to chant. "We want cake!"

Morgan felt a tap on her arm. "Ah, there you are," she said, smiling up at Kit. But Kit didn't stay. He merely stole Morgan's empty wine glass, filled it from the pitcher, and popped a slice of her salami into his mouth before disappearing back into the crowd.

"Cake! Cake! Cake!" The chant grew louder, more insistent, a bit impatient.

Next came the roar of a tractor, which appeared slowly around the corner of the house, dragging behind it a home-made, vine-covered float, in the middle of which was an extremely large, dark purple, three-tiered cake. It was the largest cake Morgan had ever seen. She half expected a naked lady to jump out. Thankfully that didn't happen. Instead, little LED candles on a huge, golden candelabra behind the cake began to twinkle. And behind this candelabra hung another banner, this one bright blue and green. The lettering looked professional—"*Oggi hai un anno in più, ma sei come il buon vino!*" Fortunately Morgan heard someone whisper a translation—"Today you are one year older, but you are like a good wine–better with age!" Nice, she thought. Marching on either side of the float came an honor guard of cellar rats, beating on red and white drums and wearing traditional Tuscan costumes—tight black leggings, yellow leather boots, loose fitting long-sleeved shirts, red tunics, floppy black cloth hats.

Morgan clapped her hands and waved at drummer Talies, wondering if the next offering would be a Buckthorn version of the famous Pallio, Siena's annual bareback horse race, or maybe there'd be a barrel race. She caught sight of Kit, standing at the far end of the arbor, whispering urgently to Indie. She frowned, and stared at them.

The float halted in the center of the piazza, and there followed a lengthy, quite elaborate, cake serving ceremony. Jack wandered by, still dressed in suit and tie, and designer sunglasses. "It's amazing what these Los Angeles folks dream up, isn't it? All performance though, very little in the way of real style." He leaned in front of Morgan for the pitcher of wine and filled two wine glasses. One he handed to Morgan. The other he raised to his own lips, remarking in an off-hand way, "I heard the price of gold is up this year."

"What?"

A strange look filled Jack's eyes. He frowned as he swirled and sniffed the wine. His expression grew sour. He took a sip, then rolled the wine tentatively across his tongue, as if to distinguish its flavors. Then, instead of swallowing what he held in his mouth, he spat it down onto the flagstone a few inches from his own foot. He proceeded to clear his throat loudly, cough something up, and spat a second time. "Ugh! This stuff is terrible! Tastes foul! Smells like crap! Wish I could get my hands on its cork. . . . How can you drink this plonk?" he said to Morgan as he splashed the rest of the wine onto the flagstones.

"You rude bastard!!" hissed Dennis, appearing at Jack's elbow. "That's Buckthorn Estate Reserve you're drinking. Not some plonk. And believe me, it's not corked!" As Dennis spoke, he tugged Jack around and faced him squarely. Glaring. Puffing. Preening for a fight. Morgan realized both men were completely inebriated. Both had been drinking since breakfast.

"Who said 'corked'? Who said 'plonk'? Not me, bro. What I said was your so-called Reserve tastes like Crap," responded Jack, puffing in return, and preening too. "And it's distinctly boring crap too! Bleh! Awful!" Jack looked around and waved an arm towards

Eddie, motioning him over. "Hey, man, get over here!" He called. "We need your opinion on somethin'."

Eddie ambled over. He seemed tired after hauling the handcart from the barn. Moreover he looked as if he'd heard this particular quarrel before. Sighing he poured two more glasses of wine from the pitcher in question, handing one of them to Dennis. Eddie swirled the wine , sniffed it, and took a sip. He rolled the wine around in his mouth, chewed it briefly, and swallowed. "Mmm," he grunted. "I think your buds are corroded, Jackie my boy. That's your problem. Quite blasted, from all the drink you've consumed today. This here ain't bad at all, an amusing little wine, if I do say so myself." He produced a smarmy sort of grin that offended both Dennis and Jack. "Not a big wine, however. But if you're calling it 'crap', I say bring on The Crap. Pretty little amusement."

Dennis couldn't stopper himself. "My gawd man! You've gotta be joking—just an amusement?! This is Buckthorn's best! And it is not crap at all. It's poetry! Poetry in a bottle! Last year's gold medal winner, by the way! And, like our Jackie boy says, the value of gold is up!" Dennis grinned like a proud papa.

Jack sneered. "You're full of it, my friend. This vino ain't poetry. It's doggerel. Bad doggerel at that. Plain ordinary, stinkin' crapola plonk from the House of Cheap-o Wine." Then to demonstrate, he poured himself half a glass of wine, swished it briefly in his mouth, and made a face as if he were being forced to taste a brew comprised of rotting egg and compost pile. Needless to say he did not swallow. Instead he faked a cough, blew out his cheeks and sprayed his mouthful of red wine onto the flagstones. The splatter hit Dennis's formerly spotless baby blue plimsolls. "Ugh! Awful! Or should I say, 'offal'?" Jack began laughing hysterically.

"Like I said, your palate's blasted, man." responded Dennis calmly. "This vino's golden!" And to demonstrate the truth of his statement, he emptied what was left of the wine in the disputed pitcher into his own glass and guzzled it down a few gulps. "Yummy!" He wiped his mouth on his wrist. "I rest my case." Somewhat irrelevantly he then asked, "Say, has either of you seen Buckthorn's bottom line recently? Cases are literally flying out the doors! On wings of pure gold! People love this Buckthorn Reserve. And they're putting their mouths on the money too . . . I mean their moneys on their mouths . . . um, where their mouths. . . err, something. Oh yeah! Buckthorn wines will be everywhere in a flash! Boxes of it. Cases of it. In the big box stores at last! Trust me. I know what I'm talking about."

"Horseshit!" responded Jack. "I was the one at the Manhattan wine auction last week, not you. And this crappy little red isn't what the people were buying. You'd better check the label on that bottom line of yours."

"Well, you are both wrong!" smirked Eddie. "This here vino isn't now—or ever was—the Buckthorn Reserve at all, or some cheap plonk from the big box either! Jackie my boy, the wine you have been reviling is—was your very own Mustard Seed Cabernet Sauvignon!" He laughed unkindly. "Trust me! I knows my wines. Like my friend Dennis here says, your mouth is completely blasted! You could be drinking Jack and Coke for all your buds are worth at the moment."

Jack glared at his cousin. "What are you talking about? I never drink Jack and Coke. You think I don't recognize my own wine? Well, you know nothing! Nothing about anything—wines or winemaking—or even Tennessee whiskey! Neither of you do . . . I mean, both of you . . . I mean . . . another load of your voodoo, isn't it?"

"Dad! Stop! This is a birthday party." River, the peace-maker, laid a large hand on Jack's arm.

But Jack was too angry to be calmed down. He shook off his son's hand and continued his verbal assault. Words spat from his mouth like the wine he claimed to hate. He laughed drunkenly. Then, he turned back to the table and refilled his glass from a different pitcher, took a loud slurping gulp into his mouth, held it there for a moment as his eyes shifted back and forth between Dennis and Eddie, came to a decision, and spat his mouthful of wine into Dennis's face. "And that's what I think of your Buckthorn's Reserve!" Morgan, who had been slowly stepping back from this spitting contest, leapt out of range.

"You rude son-of-a-bitch," muttered Dennis angrily, wiping his face on his shirttail. Eddie looked like he was about to pop.

Whatever hackles are, his were definitely up. He flexed the fingers on his left hand, sucked in his breath. His face grew red, and redder.

Jack sneered at them both. "Jesus, Mary, and Joseph! Buckthorn has finally lost touch with reality. You know, Eddie my boy, I should have known, when you came up with all those damned plastic stoppers—they're suffocating your wines—that's what's going on! And I saw you, burying those cow horns of manure in the moonlight, suckered once more by the lovely Rachel. Hah-hah-hah! No wonder your wines are tasting like compost! Next thing, you'll be out there, dancing naked in the moonlight and howling like a goddam werewolf! You really ought to get a grip, my friend. Try some of . . . of my all natural 2017 Pinot Gris. Oh I know you were pulling my leg just now. I know that because my reds are still in their barrels. Hah-hah-hah. I haven't started bottling them yet!" Jack cackled madly as if he'd made a wonderful joke.

Eddie looked as if he was about to be sick. "Well, I tasted the acidifier in your last so-called natural cuvée, I can tell you that."

"So now you say I adulterate my wines? I'll be damned! Another of your damned lies!"

River kept trying to distract his father, but kept failing.

"Boys! Boys!" said Rickie, setting a tray of cake slices on the table. "Have some cake. Be friends."

"Wait a minute," said Eddie, ignoring both his mother and his nephew, as his temperature approached boiling. "I resent the whole direction of this conversation! I happen to be Operations Manager at Buckthorn Estate, not you, brother-in-law! You just sell the stuff!" Eddie looked daggers at Dennis. "You need to keep your place, sir." Then he turned to Jack and launched another torrent of abuse. "And if you have any complaints about my winemaking, you can come and talk to me, in my office, during office hours! Maybe you'll learn something. And the wine you just spat at Dennis here, is Buckthorn Reserve. No question about that. I poured it in that pitcher myself. And it's some of the best Buckthorn has ever produced. A damn sight better than that . . . that pop you make. You're the one who uses voodoo. Moreover, biodynamics is science, pal! Not like your hide-bound Neolithic fermentation process! Get with it. Your Mustard Seed plonk is nothing but murk and sediment. And your latest cuvée is . . . is . . . it's undrinkable! And you massacre trees to plug your bottles. Jesus, Mary, and Joseph yourself, man! How can you claim to be environmentally sensitive? Your wines are basically un-stable. Admit it. Your customers send them back, by the caseload!!"

Eddie paused to draw a ragged breath; then he continued. "Moreover, plastic corks have nothing to do with . . . with . . . with anything! This year's Best of the Valley went for a thousand bucks a case, and it was all stoppered with plastic. Did you realize that? And if at some point I do decide to expand this operation, I will expand it. Buckthorn Wines will be everywhere, but only if I choose them to be everywhere. We'll go global pretty soon. Sell Buckthorn wines in Australia. In Brazil! In Italy even! Wine is still the future of this valley. It's the only future! And you can put that in your damned pipe and smoke it till you're higher than six Eiffel Towers, all stacked on top of on another!"

"Boys! Boys!" said Rickie, trying once more to make peace. "Take it easy! Please. Have this conversation later. Okay? Now is the time to celebrate. Zoe, come over here, honey. I want you to do something for me."

Eddie by this time was panting on the outside and seething on the inside, but he did at last take a small step back from the fray. "Sorry Mom. Those two get right under my skin. Neither of them actually knows anything about winemaking." Morgan watched Eddie pick up a napkin and mop the sweat on his neck, and his forehead. Rickie eyed him as if gauging his sanity. She prodded young Zoe towards her father.

"Ouch! Where did those damned things come from?" said Eddie slapping away a bee, as Zoe tugged on his hand. He bent down to her. She whispered something in his ear. The he allowed himself to be pulled out of the fray by his eight-year-old daughter, shooting hostile looks over his shoulder as they disappeared together towards the barn.

"You're both wrong—and Eddie is too, I'm afraid," said Jules, who, like Rickie had materialized as the three-way exchange had grown louder and louder. Jules placed a hand on Dennis's arm, then on Jack's, separating them as well as calming them down. "Like I always say, 'wine is only wine', boys. It's what you like that matters. It's about satisfying yourself, and perhaps satisfying those you care about too, your family, your friends. That's where the integrity lies. Buckthorn makes good honest wines from the good honest grapes that we grow in our own vineyards. We let good honest yeasts do their work, stopper our bottles with good honest corks. Sometimes we may use plastic for wines that are intended to be drunk immediately, but that's not the norm. I'm not fond of plastics, which is why for reds that need many years to develop, we always cork with cork. Wine needs to breathe. The tannins need to mellow. You know that! Wine is alive! If we lose sight of what winemaking is really about, we should get out of this business. Winemaking isn't about competition or money. And it's not an 'investment strategy' either. You know, as I get older, I am learning to hate the whole wine business." Jules eyes flashed between Jack and Dennis. He peered deeply into their eyes, as if trying to read their souls, or perhaps to plant new seeds of integrity.

"No, no you don't hate the wine business," said Rickie intervening. "I won't let you say that. The wine business is your life. It's always been. And you love Buckthorn. You're not happy unless you're out there, in the vineyards with Roberto, or in the winery with Rachel, putting in your two cents. And it's your two cents, my dear, that's the real gold around here. And whatever your sons may say, you still manage this place." She caressed his cheek and kissed him on the mouth. "Now, Master Jack and Master Dennis, settle your feathers, and be friends again. You both know, as do I, what all this quarrelling is really about. And I am certain it will all be resolved very soon. Now, you!" she said to her husband, "Have you made that decision yet, mio caro? You do need to make it soon, before this family tears itself apart." Then she kissed him again, on the cheek, and stepped aside for Indie to bestow upon her uncle a bottle of 18-year-old scotch, tied with a big red bow.

"Here you are, Uncle Jules! Happy Birthday from me!" she said, kissing him on his cheek. "Maybe we've all had a little too much wine today?"

Rickie quickly removed her gift bottle from Jules' hand and poured a liberal amount of scotch into a fresh wine glass and handed it to Jack. "Here, dear. This will take the fight out of you."

"Dad," said Indie to Jack. "Can you come with me, please? I

need your help."

"My daughter summon-eth," said Jack, tossing back his scotch. "But for the record, my daughter's lovely hair is part of Buckthorn's golden legacy too. A queen this one. I'm thinking of naming my new cuvée for her. What do you think? One day I predict, she shall be Queen of Buckthorn! Mark my words. Then you'll see the real gold rush."

"Dad, you're very, very drunk," murmured Indie, leading him away.

They had barely taken a breath when Whiskey, the dog, tore across the garden towards the house, barking the bark Morgan now recognized as has stranger-alert. The other dogs tore right behind him. They made a terrible din and formed a noisy line at the edge of the flagstones to confront the gang of overly merry tourists, who came trailing slowly towards the party from the front the house, looking as if they meant to join in the festivities. Julie, who had been watching them from the kitchen doorway, stepped out onto the veranda, and summarily ejected the interlopers. She stood there, waiting until the sounds of their motors diminished in the distance, then came down into the piazza and joined a group of her friends to laugh, eat cake, and watch Jules open presents.

Morgan sighed and returned to her former post in the shade of the arbor near where Jules was holding court. Ev had reappeared. Rachel was gone again. Kit returned briefly, then disappeared again. Talies was nowhere in sight. The dogs returned to the barn. Kids began to swarm. Then another group of guests arrived. They apologized for being late and deposited their presents and bottles of wine in front of Jules. Zoe and Eddie returned from the barn—Zoe with one arm around the neck of Rickie's gentle white German Shepherd; her father lugged a wash basket crawling with kittens.

Morgan noticed her own exhaustion and decided she'd like a glass of water. As she climbed the few steps towards the kitchen, her eyes caught sight of Irene in an old rocker at the farthest end of the veranda. Irene's usually down-turned mouth had flattened into a thin-lipped smile as Jack held towards her a tiny glass of wine and a soup plate loaded with purple cake. They were conversing softly. Morgan stopped for a moment outside the kitchen door and tried to pick up their words. She watched as Irene shook her head and said something else to her son, but all she could make out were the words—"should marry him." The rest was drowned out by the general party babble. Jack moved away. Irene looked up and caught Morgan's eye. She nodded to Morgan and sat up taller in the rocker, as if sending a mysterious signal of mutual complicity. Then, Irene's left cheek twitched, as if she were attempting a real smile.

Tinker bolted across the piazza, up the veranda steps, and slammed past Morgan into the kitchen. Her face was contorted with weeping. Rickie hobbled after her daughter, stabbing the flagstones with her stick, frowning, and shaking her head.

Whiskey began to bark again.

A child cried.

"Carry on, people. My sister's just being a little over-sensitive." Julie's words rang across the piazza.

Morgan watched Irene's face change into a leer. Then, oddly, the old lady saluted her, lifting her wine glass in a gesture of defiance, if not outright insult. Morgan failed to decode the message. And, in fact, she didn't want to. Instead, she turned away from the old lady and went into the kitchen. Tinker was gone. Morgan drank a large glass of cold water from the tap, found herself some ice, refilled her glass from the tap, and went back to her post outside. As she re-crossed the veranda, she glanced back towards where Irene had been sitting. But Irene too was gone, although her chair continued to rock gently back and forth.

"Where have you been?" Morgan said, swatting away a bee as she slid into the chair next to Kit. Kit was wolfing a plateful of lobster ravioli with pesto and cream and fresh tomato, making little grunts of pleasure. "You missed all the fun," she said, eyeing him closely.

Then she reached over, stole a ravioli, and dropped it into her up-turned mouth.

.

12 THE GOATS GET OUT

The sun dropped to the ridgeline. The crowd mellowed—so much food, so much wine, so much excitement. Morgan leaned back into her seat and played with Fred's soft Labrador ears as the dog's head lay on her lap. Although she'd witnessed plenty of tension, anger, and rudeness during the afternoon, she'd also witnessed little to confirm the presence within this family of truly lethal animosity directed at Jules. Kit had gone off again—she knew not where. Perhaps her fears for Jules were misplaced, although the weekend was far from over.

For a moment peace reigned. Small groups chatted amiably, their chairs and benches pulled together, faces animated, hands and arms waving about as they talked earnestly about the Future of the Valley, the wine business, Buckthorn, the labor shortage, kids and schools, climate change, housing development, the entertainment industry, Art, and The End of Things as They Used To Be. Others, like Morgan, sat or stood by themselves in the late afternoon sunshine, taking a break from party time to check their phones, update social media pages, even catch forty winks. Parents rocked little ones on their laps, encouraging drooping heads to nap before the evening's entertainment began.

Irene, back in her rocker, which had been carried down into the shade of the arbor, had actually fallen fast asleep. Her chin was dropped on to her chest, her body listed slightly to the left. Cody arrived, swatted a bee away from her neck, and leaned down to whisper something in her ear. Nonna startled awake, then smiled that thin smile of hers and shook off a dream. She opened one eye and stared at her great grandson as if she'd never seen him before.

Dogs dozed under the tables, or snuffled half-heartedly for scraps dropped during the afternoon's gluttony. Morgan felt her own body droop, her eyes yearned to close. A breeze kicked up. She stifled a yawn, and looked around for coffee, rousing herself to duty. Patting Fred's head, she lifted it off her lap, got up, stretched, and let her eyes sweep across the scene on the piazza. She found herself seeking, unsuccessfully, Indie's golden braid, Kit's wild West moustache. Jules was nearby, however, talking rather seriously to Jack. She moved softly in their direction.

"Hey people! Wake up!" Bowie called as he led a trio of musicians—two guitars and a saxophone—up onto the veranda where a drummer was already arranging his gear. "Come on everybody! Let's dance out the kinks!"

Adult enthusiasm seemed muted, but the children cheered and lined up in front of the veranda to watch the band get ready. From the kitchen, Angel and Jess and Julie and Adena appeared, bearing trays of lemonade, spritzers, and iced tea as well as more slices of cake. The catering team, having cleared the luncheon detritus, began—to Morgan's delight—setting up an espresso bar. Emma propelled Lucy and Desidera, whining and complaining, into the house for naps.

Kit reappeared at Morgan's side as the band swung into a jazzy version of "Sesame Street."

"Dance?" he asked.

"You must be kidding."

Eddie, looking a bit worse for wear, grabbed at Rachel's arm as she passed through the crowd with a tray of wine pitchers.

"Hey, don't! You'll make me spill."

"Oh, come on. You're not a servant here—or a daughter—yet," he leered. "Dance with me!" But Rachel hissed him away; he was still less than sober. Bailey too refused to dance, with his mother. Indie too was back; she laid claim to Uncle Jules, as the band shifted both tune and tempo. Now, Ev coaxed Rickie onto the flagstones, sedately waltzing her around the margin of the piazza. Mork, still wearing his Tuscan outfit, waltzed Zoe crazily in circles, counting one-two-three, one-two-three quite loudly and somewhat out of time until Zoe fell over giggling. Tommy madly whirled his cousin Jess. Neither Cody nor his sister knew how to waltz, so they simply bounced and waved their arms around. Bowie and his very pregnant wife took a turn. Eddie cut in on Jules, who responded smoothly by taking Rachel for his partner. River and Paul displayed expert dips and twirls. As the music became jazzier, even Sam began to dance, with Bailey. And finally, Morgan danced with Kit. Indeed, the whole piazza was suddenly a-stir with couples and threesomes, kids and dogs, all moving to their different internal rhythms and tunes.

Suddenly BANG! Pop! BANG!

Someone screamed.

Musicians and dancers halted.

Kids began shrieked and ran in circles, or fell to the floor on their stomachs, their arms protecting their heads.

More explosions—Pop! Pop! BANG! Pop! Bang! BANG!

Kit swung around looking for the shooter, preparing to fight.

Morgan's heart pounded in her ears.

Dogs barked excitedly.

Ben and Angel began to laugh, hysterically. "Geeze people!" Ben shouted over the screams and snaps and bangs. "Where's your sense of humor?"

"Ben!" Eddie stormed across the piazza towards his son. "Goddammit! I told you not to even think about tossing those snaps. No worries, folks, it's only Ben!" he shouted. He took his sixteen year old firmly by the elbow and steered him towards the house. Ben and Angel were still laughing, but Eddie's face was furious.

"Geeze, Dad, lighten up. You're hurting me."

Angel stared after them, and casually flipped the few remaining snaps into the crowd. Pop! . . . Pop! . . . Pop! . . . BANG!

"What are you staring at?" Bailey asked Sam, as he jumped on an unexploded bang-snap. Pop! "Don't you wanna dance anymore?"

The snaps however seemed to end almost everyone's desire to dance, although the band played on—a stately version of the happy birthday song, with variations. Morgan smiled, thinking of the band that played as the Titanic sank. Finally, Bowie signaled for them stop, had a conference with one of the musicians, and a few minutes later they had modulated into a set of boring old show tunes. Morgan noticed that Jules had captured Rickie off the dance floor and held her tightly by the hand as they retreated towards the banquet tables. The general atmosphere deflated.

"Gee, that was fun," whispered Morgan to Kit.

"Yeah. A blast," said Kit, frowning at Bailey still jumping on defunct snaps hoping for an explosion. He exchanged a wordless shrug with Indie. Fred nuzzled his head under Morgan's hand. As she ruffled his ear and the dog dropped to his haunches, his large eyes dark and soulful, protective.

"Come on, people," somebody cried. "It was only a joke! Maybe a dumb joke. Don't be so serious." But the mood had shifted, and people had grown tired. A contingent of the neighbors and friends took the opportunity to bid adieu to their hosts and depart. Finally, only family, caterers, and a few cellar rats remained.

"What happens now?" Morgan asked Kit.

Kit muttered something about a family of jokesters. Talies sat down next to his mother and began describing the antics at Cody's birthday a few weeks earlier. How they'd hooked a bubble machine to one of the fermentation tanks, and how, when Cody had gone in to swab it down, they'd pumped in masses of bubbles, like a mountain of frog spawn he said. Cody's breathing apparatus had not appreciated the bubbles, and Cody was spluttering when he crawled out the hatch, covered with pinkish foam, looking more like a Michelin man than a worker in a wine cellar. But he'd survived, not much worse for wear. Even Rachel had laughed. "These guys are seriously nuts, Mom," Talies concluded. "Jokesters, every last one of them. Kind of wish I'd thought of those snap-bangs myself."

Kit scowled.

"Cody could have been hurt," pointed out Morgan.

Talies shrugged. "Aw, you need to lighten up, Mom. Seemed like a good idea at the time. And it was really funny! There's still some bubble stuff left—maybe we'll go get it. These people look half dead, don't you think?"

"Just tired," said his mother.

"I think things are quite lively enough," said Kit, flicking something off the back of his neck. "Don't these bees ever give up?"

"Well, they live right over there." Morgan nodded towards the line of beehives beyond the arbor. Suddenly, Whiskey rocketed out from under the veranda and took off for the barn, barking his little heart out. A moment later Fred took off after him, also barking. So did the rest of pack. But it wasn't a stranger alert this time—this time it was goats!

Two young goats, still draped in ribbons and bells, tore across the piazza chased by dogs. They upset several market umbrellas as well as a large bucket of melting ice. Suddenly two goats became half a dozen goats, then a dozen. Goats and dogs mingled chasing one another round and round the pizza, through the garden, and then out into the vineyards.

"Who let the goats out?!" someone moaned.

Paul shrieked a long whistle.

"Get those animals back where they belong!"

Children careened by, and Mork, and Tommy. Julie watched from the veranda, hands on hips. Morgan murmured something about never a dull moment. "What the Devil?! They're heading for my wine cave!" Jules shoved away from the table and took off at a slow trot around the house and out onto the road to the winery, whistling instructions to his dogs and shouting to Roberto and Jorge for assistance.

"You old fool! Let the young men get them," shouted Rickie. "Go after him, Eddie! You too Dennis, and Phil. He probably left the doors to the wine cave open."

The men jogged after Jules. Talies took off at a sprint, yelling. "Shit! We'll have to re-wash everything if the goats make it to the crush pad!" Cody and Ben and Rachel and Tommy sprinted in his wake.

"Who was supposed to close up?" someone asked.

Kit and Morgan strolled around to the front of the house, where they could watch what was going on, alert, ready to help if trouble ensued.

"Now what?" Tinker asked, appearing on the front veranda with her sister. It wasn't long before Jorge and Roberto returned, dragging with them four of the escaped goats. Eddie followed, having captured two more. Ben had one. Phil, another. Meanwhile the dogs continued to bark and race around as if they, not the humans, were actually in charge. Gradually, the last of the goats were being herded towards the pen.

"Is that Dad out there?" asked Tinker as Jules emerged from a vineyard, gripping a small goat by its collar, green ribbons still dangling from its horns. Jules was limping. And he seemed to be struggling. "Is he okay? He doesn't look okay. Dad?" she called. "Need some help?"

As Jules tottered across the track between the garden and the goat pen, the family turned to look. He paused, wavered slowly back and forth, let go of his goat, clutched his chest, and dropped to the ground. The goat strolled into the garden to munch on string beans. Tinker broke into a run towards her father. Rickie stomped across the piazza, leaning heavily on her stick, calling for Roberto. In a moment half a dozen family had converged on the fallen patriarch. They soon had him sitting up, on the ground. Jules was wheezing badly, gasping, coughing, pounding on his on chest.

Rickie returned to her seat, her eyes anxious. "Overdone it again, the old fool," she muttered, watching as Tinker fished through her father's pockets for his inhaler, and the epi-pen.

"He can't breathe!" Tinker shouted. "For God's sake, somebody call 911?!"

Kit took off at a run, preparing to perform CPR. Morgan dialed 911.

After that, things seemed to move very slowly. Most of the family simply stood around, holding their collective breaths, waiting for the meds to kick in. Finally Jules raised one arm and waved to his family. Fifteen minutes after that, Jorge arrived with the tractor and Jules was hoisted onto the little wagon that had borne his birthday cake, and driven carefully back to the Big House. When they closer, Morgan could see that Jules' eyes were swollen and red, his breathing still uneven. Tinker hovered by her father's side with more epinephrine at the ready. Rickie began instructing Indie where to find the oxygen apparatus.

"Was it a bee?" Rickie asked Jules when he had regained enough composure to talk again.

He shrugged. "Don't think so," he mumbled. "Maybe something I ate. Hit me real quick. Was there shellfish in anything? That has done it before."

"We don't serve shellfish, Dad," said Julie. "It must have been Tinker's damned bees."

"Megan said there was lobster in the raviolis," put in Cody, helpfully. "She wouldn't eat any, but he might have. Was the lobster bad?"

"No. Not 'bad' as in 'poisoned'," explained Rickie. "Your uncle's very, very allergic, that's all."

Jules shrugged, "I don't know . . ." He looked exhausted.

"Could have been running after goats," added Morgan approaching the wagon. "I had a girlfriend with terrible asthma as a kid. For her, playing tag set off an attack. Can be a combination of factors. I called 911. Shouldn't they be here by now? You ought to be checked out."

"Don't worry. I'll be fine," said Jules. "It takes a long time for the emergency crew to get out here. I just need to lie down for a while." And with that, he allowed Tinker and Eddie to help him up the back steps and into the house. Rickie stomped along behind with her cane, muttering under her breath. She looked and sounded more angry than sympathetic.

Everyone else returned to the piazza, but then as they began to relax, a siren wailed in the distance. Shoot! thought Morgan to herself, now the EMTs arrive.

But it wasn't the EMTs. The vehicle that pulled up to the back veranda was big and black; it looked more like a hearse than an ambulance. A young man wearing a dark suit, dark glasses, and a slightly tattered top hat climbed out of the driver's seat. Another young man, similarly dressed, opened the rear of the vehicle and together they began extracting a stretcher. Morgan recognized neither one, while the band, which had been sitting quietly during the goat excitement started to play a Dixieland rendition of the Funeral March.

"Someone called to take away a body?" asked the first man in an excessively deep voice.

"Yoko! Tommy!" Julie sounded horrified. "Have you no sense at all?"

170

"What? It's a party thing, Aunt Julie," said Tommy in his regular voice.

"Did we miss something?" asked Yoko.

"You're timing is terrible!" responded Julie. "Your grandfather nearly died a few minutes ago!"

She was interrupted by a noise and a flash of light in the vines of the arbor. Heads turned. The fairy lights had flipped on again. The band stopped playing, and the entire courtyard grew silent, for what they saw was not an array of pretty lights in the gathering dusk, but rather little lights carefully arranged to spell out — "U R A DEAD MAN NOW".

Morgan's jaw dropped.

"Jesus!" she heard Yoko whisper to his cousin Tommy. "Did you do that? Pretty tasteless!"

"Believe me—I did not."

"Then who did?"

A shiver ran down Morgan's spine.

It took some time for things to settle down after that, but eventually they did. The dogs returned to their resting positions under the tables. The younger children were teased into carrying dirty dishes into the kitchen where the caterers washed them up. The band began playing relatively subdued pop songs and light jazz. Dennis disconnected the offending lights and removed them. River and Paul went off to the barn for some torches and installed them as dusk settled on the piazza. Even Jules reappeared, looking subdued and paler than usual. Tired, but cheerful, he called for a scotch as Rickie and Indie fussed, fruitlessly urging him to return to his bed.

Yet another carload of tourists arrived at the front door, but were quickly rebuffed. Julie fumed again about the sign, confessing to her own partial responsibility for the earlier intrusions, but blaming anyone and everyone, including the ghost of Big Eddie and the local police, for this last occurrence. Yoko and Tommy were forgiven their undertaker gaff. A chastened Ben reappeared, and he and Angel crept off into the vineyards blanket in hand, declaring they meant to watch the constellations come out. Morgan, her feet on Kit's lap, watched them depart, noting that Sam was following stealthily in their wake. The rest of the children, at least those who refused to be herded off to bed, were allowed to stay up, even as they spun and fell giggling on one another like over-wound tops.

"Has anybody seen Dennis?" Julie called from the kitchen doorway. "If he turns up, someone tell him to get down there and fix that entrance sign once and for all. Take it down if he has to, cover it with plywood."

A voice called through the gathering darkness that Dennis was out front, in fact, going at it again with Eddie out front by the cars.

"Dylan, honey," sighed Julie to her shaggy headed nephew, "Would you mind asking your Uncle Dennis to come see me, please?" Before Dylan could however fulfill this request, shouts exploded at the other side of the house.

Julie groaned, turned, and headed back through the kitchen towards the front door.

Kit jumped up, knocking Morgan's legs to the flagstones, and also headed for the noise. The children, suddenly revived by it, chased one another around the corner of the house to see what was happening out front. Dogs barked and took off, again. In fact, most of the family, who had been lolling around, roused themselves and went to see what was happening. Morgan helped Rickie out of her chair, then followed the troops. And behind them all came Jules.

What they found out front were two grown men rolling in the gravel, struggling to pin one another, and shouting blasphemies that better belonged in an Elizabethan play.

"Hey! Stop it!!" said Kit, trying to pull the two apart.

Growling and puffing, Bowie and Jack wrestled Dennis to a standing position. Bowie swore loudly, as he gripped Dennis' left arm to steady him. "Get a-hold of yourself, bro!" He ducked to avoid being punched. Blood dripped from Dennis' nose. His good shirt was torn. Jack handed him a neatly folded handkerchief, which Dennis used to wrap his bruised fist.

Meanwhile Eddie was simply sitting on the ground, rubbing at his jaw while Whiskey and Dewey and Little Lupo crowded round to see if dogs might make it better. "Way to go, big boy!" said Rachel, offering Eddie her sweatshirt. "Anything broke? Ugh,

172

your eye looks bad." And indeed Eddie's eye was already swelling, as was his lower lip.

"Boys! This is too much!" exclaimed Rickie, stomping around the corner of the house. "You're acting like ten-year-olds! Are you still drunk?" She looked, Morgan noted, beaten, defeated. Her words did little to soothe the anger that had broken out. The two men stared daggers at one another, growling like thoroughly irritated bulls pawing the dust. Neither man uttered a cogent word.

"Okay now," said Kit, his hands raised like a traffic cop's to keep the fighters apart. "It's over. Please, everyone, please. Go back to what you were doing. . . . What the hell is wrong with you guys?"

Tinker stood at the corner of the house; Phil's arm encircled her waist. Morgan saw tears roll down her cheeks. Samantha materialized. "Mom? What's going on?" she said in a small voice, tentatively patting her mother's shoulder. "Are you okay? Is Uncle Eddie hurt?" Tinker and Phil simply reached out and gathered their whimpering daughter into their arms.

Jack had by now stepped up onto the veranda and was contemplating the scene with an oddly self-satisfied expression, rather like a cat's after being caught tearing viciously into the Thanksgiving Turkey—all innocence and pride for its own cleverness. Morgan began to wonder how much Jack had had to do with what had been going on—the goats, the hearse, the bees, the falling banner, the warning in the arbor.

Jules seemed very, very tired. He climbed up the front steps of the house very slowly, leaning his weight on the handrails. Then he lowered himself into one of the porch chairs. His hands clung to the arms of the chair as he stared at his son and his son-in law, his mouth in a grim line. Although the physical fighting had ended, tension hung palpably in the air. Even the dogs felt it, and were quiet. Aida padded up the front steps and lay her large head in Jules' lap. Gradually, Jules released his death grip on the arms of his chair and began stroking her slowly as he pondered his family.

Finally, Eddie pushed himself off the ground and stood up. He glanced at Rachel, who had never once lifted her eyes from his form, and silently scowled at his parents. His eyes moved for a moment to Indie, then to his sister Julie, who were both watching from the front door of the house. "I'm not doing this anymore, folks," he called out as if he'd just made some sort of decision. "Dad, you and Dennis can run Buckthorn yourselves. I'm done!" And then he turned and marched up the road before anyone could say anything.

"Dad," called Tommy running after him. "Wait. I'm coming with you."

Then Rachel, without a word, followed them.

"I suppose you think Rachel's going to come with you wherever you're going, and be your winemaker!" shouted Indie at their retreating backs. "Trust me. That's not going to happen."

Eddie kept on walking.

Jack's cat-like grin grew wider.

"Wow!" said Talies to his mother. "What's that about?!"

Kit tapped Morgan's other shoulder. "Come on. Let's get out of here too. Don't worry—he'll be back. He's done this before. You coming with us, Talies?"

"No. Can't." returned Talies. "I promised to do a magic show down at the wine caves for the kids tonight. You guys should come on down—in an hour or so, before it gets really dark."

"Okay. We'll be there," said Morgan. Kit produced a non-committal grunt.

Finding themselves alone at last, Kit and Morgan found a couple of chairs at a corner of the piazza. They sat down in relief, and began bringing each other up to date on their party experiences. Kit left a few things out, of course. But so did Morgan, although she did confess to finding this Romano clan a little hard to take. She told him that Paul and River had offered her a lift back to Quarry Canyon the next morning, and that she was going to accept their offer. She promised to return to Buckthorn by the end of the week, if Kit still needed her.

"I'm beginning to think," she added, reaching down to massage her foot, which was still sore after their descent through the Hobbit Hole. "This family doesn't need an investigator so much as it needs a mediator, or two. They're their own worst enemies. Anyway, I want to check on a few things in our library. Naeve said she'd help me."

"Okay. But I wish we could talk about this in the morning," replied Kit. "There's too much going on in my head right now for me to think about anything else!"

"Okay. In the morning. If you go with me to Tally's magic show now."

13 DISAPPEARING ACTS

It was almost dark by the time Talies gathered up the kids and began walking them towards the winery for his magic show. By the time Kit and Morgan joined the parade, they were talking about parrots.

"Dylan!" Talies called to Cody's scruffy ten year old cousin, who was marching beside Bailey. "Did you bring your parrot?"

"What parrot? I don't have any parrot."

"Well that's good. Parrots aren't allowed in magic shows anymore."

"Why not?" asked Bailey.

I like parrots," piped up Zoe. "I like red parrots."

"Because parrots are trouble. If they figure out how any of the tricks is done, they can't keep their bills shut."

"What do you mean?" said Dylan.

"I mean," said Talies, "a parrot always gives tricks away." The rest of the kids stepped closer to Talies so they could hear him better. "And when the parrot tells the audience how stuff is done," Talies continued, "it ruins the magic."

"What do you mean?"

"But I like to know how stuff is done," piped another little voice.

"I know. Everybody does," said Talies. "But most people, if they figure out a trick, keep their bills shut."

"People don't have bills," pointed out Zoe.

"Well parrots do," said Talies with a straight face. "Even red ones. Once I pulled my rabbit out of a hat, and my darned parrot started squawking—'The rabbit was under the table all along,' that bird said. 'The hat doesn't have a real top.' And bam! No more magic. And there was the time I cut a lady in half . . ."

"Do you really cut ladies in half?" asked Dylan, his eyes wide.

"Of course he does," responded Cody. "But it doesn't hurt them, because it's an illusion."

"What's an illusion?"

"Same as a trick," explained the all-knowing Bailey.

"Can I hold your rabbit?" asked Zoe, taking Talies' hand. "Please?"

"I didn't bring my rabbit with me this time," said Talies. "Or my parrot. That's my point. That parrot was too annoying—I couldn't do even a simple card trick without that big-mouthed parrot figuring it out and then telling the audience. He was too smart."

"But you do have a rabbit, don't you?" asked Zoe.

"Oh, sure. All magicians have rabbits."

"I love rabbits. They're so soft," said Zoe. "I held a rabbit once."

"But, kids, I have to tell you something," said Talies shifting back on topic. "That parrot wasn't nearly as smart as he thought he was. Once I took him on a party boat—you do know what a party boat is, don't you?"

Several of the kids nodded. Someone shouted, "It's a big flat boat with an awning to keep off the sun, like on Lake Shasta. Everybody drinks a lot on party boats."

"Naw," said somebody else. "It's any old boat with a party on it, like on McCovey Cove near the ballpark. Some of 'em are just kayaks."

"Naw, not kayaks. You can't have a party in a kayak!"

"Yes you can! You can have a party in anything. My parents have parties in inner tubes on the Russian River."

"All right, all right, let me tell the story, will you?" interrupted Talies. "So I brought along my parrot to help me with some tricks."

"Like an assistant?"

"Yeah. But that parrot got right up to his old ways—figuring out tricks and then telling the audience. I couldn't get him to stop! I tried to fool him a few times, but, like I said, he was too smart. Anyways, right in the middle of the show, this storm comes up. Big storm. Out of nowhere. It gets very dark. The wind starts to blow. The waves get higher, and higher. And before you know it, a big wave hits the party boat we're on and the boat flips over. And sinks!"

"Oh no . . . " said Zoe, squeezing Talies' hand.

"No worries. Nobody got hurt. Everybody jumped overboard. All the guests knew how to swim. Anyway, the boat wasn't far from shore."

"What happened to your parrot?"

"Did it swim too?"

"No. Parrots don't swim. They fly. The parrot was fine. It flew!"

"Did you jump in?"

"Were you scared?"

"I was scared. But I jumped in anyways. I didn't have to swim much though, because I grabbed this board that was floating by. From the shipwreck, you know? I climbed on top of it, and then the parrot flew down and sat next to me. We floated along for a while. And for once the parrot didn't say anything. I could hardly believe it. Very unusual for him, because, like I said, my parrot did like to talk! But instead of talking, turns out he was thinking."

"Well, I think he was quiet because he was scared," said Zoe.

"We'd be scared," chorused Josh and Ellie.

"Maybe he was cold."

"Maybe he was wet."

"Maybe he was hungry!"

"No. Because then he stopped being quiet. And he said he'd been thinking. Want to know what he said he was thinking about?"

"Yes! Tell us!" chorused the bigger kids, anticipating a punch line.

"He said—'Okay. I give up. What did you do with the boat?'"

Ben and Jonathan groaned loudly. Morgan rolled her eyes. Kit gave a snort.

"I don't get it," said Zoe.

"Us neither," added Josh and Ellie.

"Me neither," complained Dylan. "The boat sank, didn't it?"

Bailey groaned and poked his cousin. "Don't be dumb! The parrot thought it was a trick when the boat sank. Get it? Like making a rabbit disappear by putting it into a hat. Don't you get it?"

"Oh," said Dylan, poking Bailey back.

"I still don't get it," said Zoe.

"Us neither," repeated Josh and Ellie

"You guys are hopeless!" said Bailey. Then with some help from Dylan, he explained the joke, again. The twins never did get it.

"I got it," said Zoe finally. "But I don't think it's funny."

"I think it's an okay joke, Talies," said Bailey, ever the diplomat. "I sort of liked it even. But that parrot doesn't seem so smart to me. I mean, he thought you made the boat disappear? How stupid is that?"

"Well, I liked it," said Dylan, poking Bailey again. "Will you show us how to make things disappear, Tally?"

"Maybe. But remember, kids, this is a magic show. Which means if you should see how one of my tricks is done during my performance, don't go opening your bills like my parrot. Okay?"

"Okay," they all yelled as Talies led them across the crush pad to the cave entrance, where he flipped a switch and flooded the area with light. He and his friends had earlier created a small performance space here in front of the big oak door. He pointed the children towards some planks where they could sit and have a good view of the show. Behind these planks was a semi-circle of plastic chairs and overturned barrels for the adults. After the goat chase, however, someone had locked the cave entrance, so Talies found the key and threw open the door. A draft of cold air emerged.

"Wait here, kids," he said. "Sam, would you like to be my assistant?"

"I'd be honored, sir." She followed Talies into the cave.

Talies had previously piled his magician's gear just inside the cave. First, he donned his costume—a long, black, star-studded wizard's cape. Actually it was one of several Algerian burnooses he'd found in a costume shop in San Francisco's Castro District. Then he put on a black bowler hat that made his ears stick out, and a pair of mirrored wire-rimmed glasses. He handed Sam another black burnoose, although hers had no painted-on stars. With its huge drooping hood, she looked like a character out of Dickens. He made her exchange her pink and yellow running shoes for a pair of black rubber boots, the kind cellar rats wore when they hosed down the floors. "Your shoes are distracting," he explained.

He gave Sam some instructions and asked her to carry a folding tea tray table and a box of balloons out to the performance space. As she gathered these together, he opened a small case of his own magic gear, put some items into his pockets, slipped on a pair of tight fitting bright white gloves, and draped a red feather boa around Sam's shoulders. They stepped outside together. Sam began setting up the tray table, while Talies climbed onto a stool and redirected the outdoor flood lamps so they would shine as one, making them into a single spotlight for his performance. Various adults, with and without children drifted in, and found seats.

"So, what do you think, kids?" Talies asked his audience as he adjusted and readjusted Sam's boa to achieve various funny affects. "Do you like this on Sam, or not? I think she ought wear it all the time. Don't you?" Sam paraded up and down as if she were a runway model, trying their shouted suggestions. Meanwhile, Talies arranged a dark curtain around the legs of his tray table. When he was nearly finished, Sam tried draping her feather boa humorously around his neck. He tossed it off, laughing, and rushed back into the wine cave. "Forgot something very important," he called over his shoulder. "My magician's wand!" Emerging from the cave a minute later, he waved a standard issue black wand and back and forth in grand arcs, then used it as a pointer to rearrange the assembling audience so the littlest ones could sit up front. Several were still hovering in front of his tray table.

"Please take your seats, kids," he said at one point. "If you stand this close you won't be able to see what my hands are doing. Hey, Bailey, would you come up here a minute? There's something funny going on with your ear." Bailey ran up, fiddling with the bottom of his right ear to see what the matter with it.

"No. Your other ear," said Talies. "You left something there." And he pulled out a shiny quarter. "You'll want this next time your dad takes you into Calistoga. Anybody else lose a quarter?"

To shouts of "I lost one!" and "Do me! Do me!" Talies strolled among his audience, retrieving quarters from ears, elbows, socks and passing them back to their reputed owners. It was an excellent way to raise the level of excitement.

Everything must come to an end however. Talies indicated there were no more coins to found, so he and Sam switched to blowing up colored balloons and twisting them into various wearable shapes. He kept up a continuous patter, larded with terrible jokes until everyone in the audience, even Rachel, was decorated with a floppy crown of lavender, pink, baby blue, or green. Several balloons popped, making the children scream. Bailey jumped on his, rather liking the loud noise. When several others decided to join in, Talies decided it was time to start the real magic show.

Morgan and Kit, who had found seats on some plastic buckets towards the back of the group, leaned up against a large wine barrel, or puncheon, and prepared to enjoy themselves as they surveyed the audience. Most of the vineyard crew had turned up by this time, along with their families. Eddie had appeared, a nasty looking bruise on his cheek, somewhat chastened but ready to be forgiven. He nodded stiffly to Rachel, then to Indie, and took a seat near his twins. The lights of the Sasaki house on the ridgeline glowed into the darkness. Tinker did not seem to be at the show, but Phil had arrived, a sleepy Desidera on his shoulder. And a contingent of merry cellar rats turned up, each carrying an empty berry bucket to sit on. They dropped their buckets beside the performance area and immediately began disrupting Talies' patter.

"Hey, man, I didn't know you were a magician. Can we play too?" said Tommy, his arm around a girl Morgan did not recognize.

"Yeah, do some of those quarter tricks for us, will ya?" called Adena. "We could use the change!"

"Look behind my ears," offered her brother, Mork, approaching Talies and lifting his hair off his ears. "I'll take it in gold Doubloons, please."

"Where's your rabbit, man?" called out Bobby, one of the cellar rats from town.

"Probably under this little table," responded Mork, poking

his head through the curtain Talies had so carefully arranged. The tray crashed to the ground. "Oops. Sorry, man," he muttered, and turned to the audience to shout helpfully, "Nothing under here except a mess of balloons!" He promptly stole a balloon, blew it up, and jumped on it.

Sam glared at her cousin. "Shouldn't you make them all sit down? We need to get started, don't we?"

Talies merely re-assembled his tray table and re-adjusted its curtain before gently chastising his friend "Okay guys, could you all take your seats back there? The little kids need to be able to see, and we need to get this show on the road."

As the audience finally settled down again, Talies waved his wand in a grand arc. "Now watch what happens in my magic circle of light," he said, and pulled an enormous bouquet of red and yellow flowers from the end of his magic wand. He presented the bouquet, with a flourish, to Zoe, who giggled and lowered her eyes.

"I'll start with a few card tricks to get you in the mood. Now remember, kids, if you already know how a card trick works, don't be like that old parrot of mine—don't open your bills about what you know." He winked at Bailey.

Morgan tapped Kit's arm and nodded towards Jules, who was slowly making his way around the audience towards the cave entrance. He was wearing only an old pair of bedroom slippers, some baggy striped pajama pants, and a tee-shirt. Indie too had noticed her uncle. She quickly captured him, draped a blanket around his shoulder, and indicated he should take a seat on a pair of overturned berry lugs. Jules decided to comply. He nodded to Eddie, and motioned for Josh and Ellie to come sit on their grandpa's lap.

Somewhere on the ridge an owl hooted.

And so began Talies' first Buckthorn magic show.

He pulled out all the stops. Most of his tricks were sufficiently well practiced to amaze the younger children, and amuse the older ones. His peers from the winery pretended to be unimpressed, keeping up their disruptive banter with comments like, "I saw that" or a "Not so clever, Mr. Magic Man" or "I saw you pull that card out of your sock!"

"Parrots!" hissed Talies, winking at the children. Still, all in all, Morgan judged her son's delivery to be surprisingly smooth, and most of his tricks did seem to go more or less as planned. He palmed quarters well, and made small items appear and disappear miraculously. At one point, he actually pounded a plastic cork right through the tray table, using the side of a small wooden corkscrew as a hammer. Although it took him a few tries to get this trick to work, in the end both cork and corkscrew landed with a solid thunk! under the table and left no visible hole in the tray. Several adults even clapped.

Half an hour later Talies was teaching his audience how to win at the shell game. He positioned Bailey and Zoe and Dylan to be his shills in front of the little table. Suddenly the twins jumped off Jules' lap and ran to the table too. As soon as he was unburdened, Morgan noticed Jules slipping quietly towards the cave, pausing only to whisper something to his oldest daughter. Indie, who was hovering near the cave's entrance, followed him through the oak door.

Talies' next teaching moment involved a small "magic" box, which as he demonstrated had two, not one, compartments in it. This so-called secret compartment allowed the "magician" to control what the audience would see after the big abracadabra. "It's really just a simple little box. Ask Santa to bring you one next Christmas," he told them. "And this next one, you may have seen on tv. It takes a bit more skill." Then he pulled a red silk scarf out of a pocket inside his cloak, and stuffed the silk with his index finger into his left fist as he held both arms out in front of himself. The kids leaned forward, rapt; the cellar rats rolled their eyes and made scornful comments—they knew perfectly well what was coming, or at least they thought they did.

"There," said Talies, moving his fist in a grand arc so the whole audience could see. "Now, where do think my scarf is?"

"In your fist, idiot," came a shout from the back.

"Yeah, in your fist."

"No. It's not," said someone else. "You've disappeared it somewhere."

"Yeah, it's probably under the table, in the balloons!" said Bobby.

Ignoring them, Talies opened his fist and held up a hen's egg.

"Hmm," he said. "Looks like my pretty scarf has turned into an egg. What do you think, kids?"

There followed a chorus of outrageous ideas.

"Wait," said Talies, as if he'd just had an idea. "I think I know where my scarf went." And he drew a red silk scarf out of his sleeve.

This was met with some cheers, and laughter, and, finally, applause.

"So, would you like to learn how this trick is done?"

The audience shouted their willingness to learn the secret.

"Okay. First, you need two identical silk scarves." Grinning, he pulled a second red silk scarf out of his other sleeve and flapped it at his audience.

Wait a minute, thought Morgan—that's three scarves!

As she puzzled about the number of scarves, she spotted Indie rushing out of the wine cave, her face visibly puffed, tear streaked. Several of the other adults also turned and stared. Rachel stood up, moved swiftly across the back of the audience, then, stepping around Indie, disappeared back into the wine cave. Morgan nudged Kit and nodded towards this action. "What's that all about?" she whispered.

Kit shrugged and shook his head. "Just some stupid nonsense," he said. "I'll go check in a minute. I saw this scarf routine in Vegas once. I'm interested to see how Talies manages it." So Morgan returned her attention to her son's scarf trick, and kept only half an eye on the woman sniveling in the shadowed cave door.

"Next you need to make yourself a hollow egg shell," Talies was saying. "Like this." He held up an egg. "This is a real egg. You take a little knife and poke a little hole in the shell. Not too small though, because you have to blow out the yolk, and the white. It can get a little messy, so I'll show you how to do it later, if you want. You do this before the show, of course, and you try never to let the audience see the little hole. Be careful when you put it into your hand so you don't break the shell. Oops!" he dropped the little pieces of shell into the bowl Sam held out. "Good thing I made a backup."

Wait a minute, thought Morgan. Shouldn't there have been a

scarf in that hollow egg?

"So—when I stuff the silk scarf into my fist, you see it's really going through the little hole and into the hollow eggshell. Like this. Then I give a little twist and open my hand. All the audience sees is the egg." He chuckled. "No hole, because the hole points away from them. And, no scarf. Right? So where is that scarf?"

"Up your sleeve!" cried Bailey, feeling quite sure of his ground.

"Shh... Don't be a parrot," said Talies under his breath.

Someone shouted from the back row, "In the egg?"

"Well, let's take a look," continued Talies smoothly. "You're both right, of course! There is a scarf up my sleeve." He pulled out another red silk scarf and waved it around. "I put this up my sleeve before the show. And there's the scarf I stuffed into the eggshell. Let's get that one too." He opened his hand, displayed the egg, and carefully picked a red scarf out through the little hole. He waved both red scarves in the air. "So, that's how this trick is done, my friends. Who wants to try?"

"Me! Me!" This kids all shouted as one. "Let me try!" Bailey jumped up. Kit rolled his eyes for Morgan's benefit, and grinned, but held up his hand and stopped Bailey from coming forward. "Wait a minute," said Talies. "I didn't do something quite right. Let me see. . . . Ah, yes, that's it. Now watch me do the trick again, please . . ." And so he began the trick again, moving around so everyone got a good look at how he stuffed the scarf into the egg hidden inside his fist. "Wait, I was supposed to use my magic wand here. I forgot about that. . . . Now, where did I put that wand?" He poked through the pockets of his magic cloak. "Ah, here it is!" Grinning, he tapped his wand on the fist, which was still holding the scarf-stuffed egg, once, twice, three times "Of course, you do realize, this wand won't work unless you say the magic word, don't you? So, all together now . . ."

"Abracadabra!!" everyone screamed.

He sure does milk his audience, thought Morgan. I wonder where he learned that. Talies slowly opened his fist and displayed what everyone expected to see—the eggshell. But as he pointed out the little hole into which he'd stuffed his silk scarf, a puzzled look dawned. "Wait a minute, kids! Something has gone wrong again! This isn't a hole! I mean not a real hole!" He held the egg up and squinted into what looked from the audience's perspective like a hole. "This is a fake hole." And with that, he peeled a little black sticker off the eggshell and held it up for all to see. Then Sam passed him a cereal bowl and he cracked the egg into it. "Anybody for an omelet?"

Bailey's mouth dropped open. Even the cellar rats blinked. Finally everyone clapped and cheered. Sam remained mute beside Talies.

So smooth, thought Morgan with a smile. She had quite missed the substitution.

"Oh, well," Talies continued, in mock sorrow, as he covered the bowl with one, two red scarves, then a third, pulled from his left sleeve. "Guess I'll just have to work on this trick a bit more." Sighing, he turned and began setting up another card trick.

Morgan too turned, to whisper in Kit's ear about the scarf trick, but to her surprise Kit himself was gone. Finally her eyes found him, in the shadows by the open cave door. Kit was actually holding Indie in his arms, and soothing her tears. Morgan watched him lead her back into the winery, where they disappeared from view. As they had passed behind where she was sitting, Morgan had overheard Indie telling Kit, once more, that Rachel could not be trusted. She looked around for Rachel. Was Rachel still back in the wine cave? A cold chill washed over her.

By the time Morgan's attention returned to the magic show, Talies was doing some sort of pick-a-card-any-card trick. The show went on for another half hour, and by the time it was over, Morgan had decided to accept that offer of a ride from River. Her thoughts were interrupted by the sound of a crash, and the tinkle of broken glass. "Oh no!" she groaned silently, her mind leaping to yesterday's crashing barrels. Enough! Tomorrow! Quarry Canyon here I come. For sure!

Talies too heard the crash, and turned in time to see Cody and Eddie and Julie, all hurry into the wine cave. They barely avoided colliding with a stony-faced Rachel, on her way out. "Don't bother," Rachel said coolly. "It was just me. I tripped over a hose and knocked into one of those stupid pumps, and a whole box of pipettes." She snorted in derision. "You don't really want to go back in there—Jules is in a foul mood. I don't think he feels well. I told him to go back to the house, and get into bed. And to put some shoes on!"

The audience took the crash as a signal that the magic show was over. She watched as they gathered up their children and dispersed towards the parking lot or along one of the tracks through the vineyards. Morgan decided to wait for Jules, meaning to walk him back to the Big House, be sure he was safe. She leaned back against the wine puncheon and watched as Talies and Sam packed up. Good riddance to Kit, she thought, and whatever he's up to. She felt tired, grateful for a few minutes of peace and quiet. She glanced towards the ridge above the cave entrance, and the house where Tinker and her family lived. Their lights were on, a beacon of sorts. And as she stared at it, an idea began to form in her mind.

"Jules?" Morgan called into the cave. Everyone but Talies and Sam had gone home. "Are you in here? Are you all right?"

Silence.

She flipped on a light and headed down the tunnel towards Jules' workroom and the wine library. She kicked some hoses back under the barrels and stooped to right the pump, wondering why Rachel hadn't picked it up. She gathered up some scattered pieces of broken pipettes, and placed the glass in an open box someone had left on a barrel top.

The solid oak-paneled door into Jules' workroom was closed, but a shaft of light shown under it. She tapped. No answer. She tapped again and tried the handle. The door opened easily. Jules' workroom was a wide space at the dead-end of the tunnel. Along the forward walls of the work space were double stacked wine barrels in their cradles, and some open vats. Between the rows was a long plank table. At the far end were racks and racks of bottles— the so-called library.

"Anybody in here?"

The workroom was deserted. She touched the bung hole on one of the barrels. It was plugged tight, but dark with splashed wine. The wood felt moist. The table was covered with a mess of papers and some odd pieces of winemaking equipment as well as the kind of pipette Kit had called a wine thief. On top of the papers sat a pair of unwashed glasses and an empty whiskey bottle. She glanced at the open cellar books and then noticed that two old kitchen chairs had been pushed back from the work table. One of them was turned towards a small drop-leaf desk, somewhat hidden behind a cement vat. On top of this desk stood an unopened bottle of scotch. Five small sherry casks were stacked in a corner.

Jules' work area seemed dark and dirty compared with the neatly white-washed main wine caves. Its floor was only packed dirt. It's walls, hewn from the original rock. The diamond-shaped wooden wine racks of the library climbed from floor to ceiling. A metal grate had been loosely drawn across the front of these racks. Morgan flipped on another light, and studied this so-called library, for a minute or two. There must be hundreds, if not thousands, of bottles here, she thought. But Jules himself had gone away. So she turned out the lights, closed the workroom door, and returned to the cave entrance. There she found Talies, back in his normal clothes and ready to leave.

"No, I didn't see Jules come out of the cave," he told his mother in response to her question. "But I was busy with my performance."

Morgan concluded that the old man must have taken Rachel's advice and gone back to his bed. Probably came down for a few bottles from the library to celebrate his birthday, and forgotten to turn out the light. She waited outside the cave as Talies closed and locked the big oak door. He hung the key on a high hook hidden in a crack behind the door frame.

Security was obviously not a major deal here at Buckthorn. But, why should it be, in this remote valley?

"Good night, dear," she said, hugging her son. "I'm going home in the morning. Check on a few things. Paul and River will drive me. I'll let you know if or when I'm coming back. Good show, by the way. The children seemed to enjoy it."

14 SEARCH PARTY

Morgan's plan collapsed the next morning, shortly after she and Kit arrived at the Big House in search of breakfast. They had found the kitchen overflowing with Romanos, most of them gathered around the long table, although there were not enough seats for everyone. Bailey and Samantha sat side by side on the floor next to the hall door, knees pulled under their chins. Bailey's eyes were as round as his round, wire rimmed, glasses. Kit ruffled his hair as he entered the room. Morgan, having dropped her weekend bag on the veranda, was hurrying down the hall checking texts and emails. She nearly plowed into Kit's back.

"River's car is outside," she murmured, looking down at her phone. "I guess I didn't miss my ride after all." Then she looked up, and blinked. "Well, Good morning everyone!" Her cheery note seemed oddly out of tune. "What's going on?" she whispered to Kit.

"She wants to know what's going on," Kit repeated into the silent room. "So do I. I figured you'd all be sleeping in after that party. Something happen?"

Rickie looked up as Kit and Morgan entered the room. She was sitting towards at the head of the table, hands folded around a cup of tea, shoulders hunched, gray hair uncombed, face looking as worn out as her brown wool robe. Her children, her grandchildren, her nieces and her nephews turned towards them too. At the other end of the table, sat Nonna stirring sugar into her tea. Indie stood motionless near the restaurant style range, holding a plate of buttered toast. Her face was streaky with tears. One could have cut the tension in the room with a dull knife.

For a long minute, no-one said a word.

Whiskey whimpered in his sleep. Fred opened his eyes.

Tinker, robot-like, spooned soft scrambled eggs from her plate into Desidera's bowl.

"Gramma! 'Nuff . . . I said 'nuff! Don't want more." Desidera pushed her bowl away, knocking a glass of orange juice to the floor.

The crash woke Whiskey. "Woof!" he woofed. The rest of the dogs, stationed around the room, also started barking.

"Quiet, dogs!" sounded Aaron's voice on the other side of the room

Morgan stepped around the people to find some coffee.

"Hush, Whiskey," said Rickie patting him. "Hush now, or I'll put you out."

"So what's going on?" Kit asked again, looking from face to face. "Tell us what's happened." His tone acknowledged the fear and anxiety reflected in their faces. Everyone seemed a little in shock.

Slowly Rickie said with something between a groan and a sigh, "He's gone. Jules is gone."

"Gone where?"

"We don't know. He's simply missing."

"Missing?" Morgan repeated, giving careful stress to the word. "Perhaps he got up early. Took a long walk somewhere, or a drive, or went into town for breakfast. Surely he's not actually missing."

Rickie shook her head. "No. He is missing. I feel it." She pounded her chest. "Here. He's gone. He was taken away from us. Something bad happened."

Her words hung in the air until a rising, very human, whimper cut through the silence. "Oooo . . . He's been kidnapped, hasn't he? I knew it. He's been hurt." Tinker began a rapid descent into hysteria.

"Mom," said Jess, taking the spoon out of her mother's hand, then reaching for Desidera. "Settle down, Mom. Here let me have the baby."

And with that, the room erupted. Everyone began talking at once, and Morgan found it impossible to understand what any one person was saying. Kit dragged a chair into the kitchen from the hallway and sat down at the table beside Rickie. "Now, please tell us," he said to her, "exactly what happened? When did you last see Jules?" His quiet police detective's voice seemed to calm the room. Everyone focused on what Rickie had to say.

"He didn't sleep in his bed last night," she said first.

"But that's not so unusual, Mom," put in Julie who was sitting on the other side of the table. "Dad sometimes sleeps in one of the guest rooms, doesn't he? Or on that little cot down in his workroom. It's a lot cooler down there. . . ." Her eyes expressed hope as she looked over her shoulder towards Morgan and explained, "Their bedroom is under the eaves. It gets very still up there, and very hot sometimes. Dad doesn't breathe well. We've tried but he refuses to put in an air conditioner."

"Is this true?" Kit asked Rickie.

Rickie nodded. "Last night was different though. He wasn't well. Anyway, he always tells me where he's going. He would have said, if he was going to sleep in the caves. I suppose there's a chance he got up very early, and is lying outside somewhere— sick—hurt—worse. I've yelled myself hoarse already, and I called his phone. All his meds are upstairs."

Tinker began whimpering again. "Oh my God, Mom. You think he's dead, don't you?"

"Don't go there, Tink," said Julie. "Please, not now. Get a-hold of yourself, sister. Nobody knows what's happened, yet." Her eyes pleaded with Kit. "Can't you and Morgan do something? Or tell us what to do?"

Jess stared at her mother, watching as she grew increasingly agitated. "Shall I go get Dad for you, Mom?" Jess stood up, the baby across her shoulder. "I don't think he's left for work yet. I can easily go up to the house." Tinker was chewing on her knuckle, and was so thoroughly absorbed in her own effort not to dissolve into hysteria, that she failed to respond to her daughter.

"Just stay where you are, dear," Rickie said to her granddaughter. "Don't go running off. Your mother needs you, as do your own daughters." She turned to Kit and Morgan. The look on her face silently begging their help.

"Mommy . . ." whimpered Desidera. "I gotta go poo-poo."

"Here. I'll take you, sweetie," said Emma scooping the little girl out of her high chair. "Come on. Come with me."

"Rachel and Eddie went down to the winery fifteen minutes ago to look for him," put in Dennis, who was sitting between Kiko and Jennifer. "We should wait for them to get back before we before we do anything more. Hopefully they won't be too long. Maybe he's down in his workroom, as good as gold. In the meantime, people, please try to hold it together. And how about us all having some breakfast? I'm sure the kids are hungry. I know I am. Indie, that toast must be cold by now."

"Here, let me have that," said Julie, taking the plate from Indie and putting it into the oven to warm. She passed around the coffee pot. "Orange juice anyone? Ben? Dylan? Tommy? Zoe, dear. Adena, will you get out some cereal or something, and some bowls. Bowie, you could get the jams out of the fridge. Jen, maybe you could pour the kids some milk?" The children remained strangely quiet as the adults gradually came to life in their service. "Megan, do you know where Cody and Ben are? We haven't seen either one of them this morning."

"They probably spent the night down in the dorms," replied Megan. "There was a kind of party down there last night. I didn't get back until one, and they were still going at it when I left."

"And Yoko? Was he down there too?" asked Dennis, as if everyone suddenly felt it necessary to take attendance.

"Didn't come in until three, Dad." said Mork. "He was bartending for some people over in Healdsburg. I doubt we'll see him before this afternoon. I've gotta go get to work, you know. Mom, Dad, how much longer do you need me to be here? I'm sure Grampa will turn up."

"Hang in with us a bit longer, please," said Dennis.

"Here, do something useful." Julie handed her youngest son the toast plate. "I didn't mean eat it, honey. I meant pass it around." She stepped over to her mother and began massaging her shoulders. "Did anyone look for Dad down in the guest cottages? Doesn't he sometimes sleep down there?"

"Of course, we looked there," replied Rickie.

"How about the barns?" Julie continued.

"Jorge and Roberto already looked in the obvious places, before I called you all together," said Rickie. "I called Roberto as soon as I knew he was missing. He called Ev. The vineyard crew's out now going through the fields. I know Roberto will call me, if he finds anything. Ev suggested Lizzy ask around town, see if anyone's seen him since last night, although I doubt that'll do much good. The old fool's truck is still parked outside." As the furrows on her brow deepened, Rickie's eyes caught Morgan's. "My guess is he put a foot into one of those holes that girl makes, and he's broken something."

"Zoe, take the twins and Lucy outside please, and the dogs," said Eddie, as he and Rachel re-entered the kitchen. "Get them to help you feed the goats. And take Dylan with you too, and Bailey, if you can find him." He hadn't noticed Bailey sitting on the floor next to Sam.

As the children departed on their assigned tasks, Tinker broke into a barely controlled howl. "Ooo Eddie, Dad's dead, isn't he? Ooo I can see it in your face. You found him! Our father is dead!" She whined and whimpered and repeated herself until Jess too started sniveling.

"Tinker! Jess!" said Julie with a marked lack of sympathy. "Control yourselves."

"No. I didn't find him. Dad wasn't in either the winery or the cave," said Eddie, much annoyed by his sister's tendency to take refuge from trouble in hysteria. "Rachel and I walked up and down all the tunnels back in there too. He's not in his workroom. In fact, it was closed up tight. The cellar team say they haven't seen him in the winery either. His truck's still parked outside, so he must be around here somewhere."

"Did you actually go into the library and look around?" asked Kit.

"Of course we did," put in Rachel. "He wasn't there."

Morgan raised an eyebrow and caught Kit's eye. He nodded. They were both thinking about the secret door into the Hobbit Hole, but that seemed like a difficult climb for a tired, if not sick, old man in bedroom slippers.

"And when was the last time either of you saw Jules?" Kit asked.

"Well, same as you probably," replied Rachel. "Jules was at the magic show. And then we saw him go into the cave. He seemed fine to me. I followed him, thinking I'd update him on Jack's New York trip. I've been going over the sales figures, but Jules seemed preoccupied last night, and pretty tired. He didn't want to talk about them, so we had a scotch together. Our glasses are still there—I looked specifically."

"And what was he doing when you were with him?" asked Kit.

"I don't actually know, but he had pulled down some bottles of wine and seemed to be reviewing his tasting notes. Indie was on her way out. She was upset about something. Maybe you should ask her."

"I was trying to help," interrupted Indie. "He should have been in bed."

"Well, I can agree with that," said Rachel. "I said the same thing. But I needed some guidance about what he wanted me to do with that wine guy. I suppose I'll have to wing it now."

Kit looked around the room and asked, "So—did anyone see Jules leave the cave last night?"

No one said anything.

"Well, I sure didn't," said Rachel firmly. "He was pouring himself another scotch when I left him."

"And what time was that?"

Rachel shrugged. "Don't know. Talies was doing some card trick. What time was that, Tal?"

Talies, who had just arrived, was leaning quietly in the hallway door, hands in his pockets. He shrugged. "I don't know. I did a lot of card tricks last night—which one?"

"How should I know? They all look the same to me." Rachel sounded defensive.

"All I know," Talies continued, "is Mom and I buttoned things up around ten-thirty. You went back into the cave, Mom. What did you see?"

Morgan shrugged. "No sign of Jules, although his light was on. I called out." But something she recalled didn't quite match up with what Rachel had been saying.

Kit sighed. "It would help to have a good time frame. Indie and I both saw Rachel exit the wine cave, but as I don't wear a watch any more. . . . " Dennis put in that he thought Rachel left about quarter to ten. Yoko thought it more like 9:30 or 9:35—he'd been making a video on his phone of the magic act to post on the web."

"That's cool," said Talies. "Could you check the time mark on the video?"

"Great idea!" All eyes turned to Yoko as he fiddled with his phone "9:04. No. That's not the right one. Can't be. Right, I forgot. I deleted several videos. Sorry." He looked up. "Doesn't seem to be here."

"Nine-oh-four seems right to me," said Rachel. "Anyway, Jules was fine when I left. I can't stand around here debating; I've really got to go. I have to get things ready for Frye. He likes to arrive ahead of schedule, to catch me out I suppose." She hurried away.

"Fine. Good-bye," said Kit. "We'll talk later." He turned back to the family. "All right, here's the question one more time— who actually saw Jules leave the cave? Or, to put it another way— did anyone see Jules outside the cave after, say, nine o'clock last night? Somebody must have."

But nobody had anything helpful or concrete to add.

"This is so odd," said Morgan in a puzzled voice. "I was in the audience. You were there too, Kit. And Indie, and Rachel. And most of the rest of you were there too. So if he came out during the show, which he must have done, how did we all miss him? It's like he became invisible."

Silence lay upon the room.

After a long pause, she went on. "Logically," she went on, "if nobody saw Jules leave, then he must still be in there. Right? I know, Eddie, that you and Rachel have looked, but I'd feel better if Kit and I took another gander. Don't you think so, Kit? I might have missed something last night—I wasn't looking for a body, that's for sure. Although that was a pretty big crash. Does anyone remember whether that crash came before or after Rachel left the cave?"

"Before."

"After. Definitely after."

"I dunno," said Talies. "I really wasn't paying attention."

"And there are other ways to leave the cave, besides the front door," added Kit. "There's the old mine shaft. A bit treacherous for an old man though . . ."

"No way," interrupted Julie. "I know what you mean. But it makes no sense. If Dad went up the shaft, what would he do when he came out that little hobbit door in the middle of the palisade? Walk down again? He'd still have to pass us as we watched the show. In his slippers? I don't think so. Why would he do that?"

"Yeah. I forgot, he was wearing his slippers, and pajamas," put in Tinker. "And it's a long climb up that old shaft, in the dark. We used to do it as kids, but I seriously doubt Dad could make it, now. And he wasn't well last night. But I suppose it wouldn't hurt to look. Just, why not come out the front? On the other hand, if the shaft is the way he went out, then somebody must have helped him. I told you he was kidnapped. That makes sense."

"Or it's where he's stuck," said Dennis. "Or he's hurt himself. But I agree, why would he do that? And who would kidnap Dad?" Dennis's question hung over the kitchen like the noxious smell of badly burned bacon.

Kit pulled on his moustache and stared at Indie, whose eyes had once again begun to leak.

"Perhaps we should call the police," said Morgan.

"No." said Rickie firmly. "We'll wait. We'll wait and see what Roberto and Jorge find. Meanwhile, you two young people should go search the caves and the tunnels again—all of them this time."

Suddenly Rachel reappeared in the kitchen doorway. She was breathing hard.

"Has he turned up?" chimed several voices.

"No. I forgot to tell you something. I ran all the way back."

Eddie stared at her.

"His rifle is gone. It's usually behind that stack of casks by his desk. For the mountain lions, you know," she added for benefit of Kit and Morgan. "Maybe he took it with him?"

Rickie drew a ragged breath then said, "Kit dear, would you please organize a search of the barrel tunnels and the shaft, as soon as possible? See if that old fool is in the caves. Or if there are any signs of his having gone out somehow. I mean, if he heard something . . . maybe he did go up the shaft, to see what it was. He doesn't always think about consequences, you know. There's a map of those tunnels in one of his drawers upstairs. And take some blankets and some water with you, and some chocolate, and one of his puffers."

"Dad, I want to come," came a small voice from the floor. "Sam too. Uncle Jules showed us about the mine shaft. We'll find him!"

"He did what?! You are not allowed in those tunnels!" Indie was aghast. Rickie shook her head in disbelief.

"Me too," said Zoe, who had quietly crept back into the kitchen, Fluff in her arms. "I want to come too."

"Sorry, kids," said Kit. "You all need to stay here for the time being. Morgan and I will do this ourselves. We don't want you getting hurt. Talies, would you join us? Bring a flashlight. We could use you."

"I doubt he's in the cave," said Talies as the three of them hurried down the road to the winery. "Cody and I were all over it this morning. And you know that storage closet off the main barrel room?" Morgan nodded. "Well, it was bolted on the cave side of the door. I've watched enough television to know that if he went out that way, that bolt would be open."

Morgan said nothing.

"But we went up the shaft anyways," Talies went on. "And at the top we found another problem. Somebody's put locks up there, on the outside. You can't open the grates from inside, you know? I really think he had to have come out the regular way, through the main door."

"But, Tal, nobody saw him come out that way, and we were all right there," said Morgan.

"That's the thing," said Talies. "I've been thinking— it could well have been a trick of the light. What was he wearing? Do you remember?"

"Slippers," replied Morgan. "Baggy pajamas. And maybe

some sort of blanket thing around his shoulders."

"Mmm," said Talies. "I did adjust the floodlights outside the cave to shine a very bright 'spotlight of attention' on my tray table—that's what magicians call it because it makes the surrounding area look darker than ordinary, sets up the kind of high contrast dark-light situation that tricks your eyes. Remember how Jorge used it during his show? I wonder if Jules put on the other burnoose I had. It was black, like Sam's. I'll bet he did. It would be much better than holding a blanket around your shoulders to stay warm. Anyway, if he was wearing that, then I'd say he could have walked right out of the cave and nobody would have seen him go. We should check to see if that burnoose is where it should be."

Kit shook his head. "No, sorry. I was there, and I was watching that door, so was your mother. If Jules walked out, one of us would have seen him, whatever the color his clothes were."

"Not so sure about you," murmured Morgan to herself. "Your attention was definitely being diverted by someone else." But she didn't press the point. Out loud she said only, "Talies, you'll have to explain how this dark-light thing works for me sometime. It seems counter-intuitive."

"I'm not making this up, Mom. Next time we're home, I'll do a demo. It is a strange phenomenon though. A real—miracle, you might say."

"I don't believe in miracles," growled Kit. "I only believe what I see. I want to go see for myself what's in that old mine tunnel. Coming, Morgan?"

"Yes."

Talies came along too, although he was pretty sure they wouldn't find Jules. They worked out a search plan as they walked, failing to notice they were being quietly followed by Sam, the stealthy stalker, as well as Bailey, and Zoe. Fluff had remained behind. And these three were laying their own plans.

Kit, Morgan, and Talies spent more than an hour climbing up and down the main mine shaft as well as many of its side tunnels. They repositioned fallen sections of framing as they went, and got turned around several times even though they were trying to use Jules' old tunnel map. Their search was tense, dirty, and fruitless.

As Talies had said, they found no sign that Jules had gone out this way, and, when they did finally work their way up to the hobbit hole gate, the locks seemed inaccessible from inside. They gave it up. Either Jules had had a strong assistant, or Talies's theory was correct. Or perhaps there was a third way, as yet unknown. At any rate, they agreed: valuable time and a great deal of energy had been wasted, and they were no closer to solving the mystery of Jules' whereabouts.

They also did a quick search of Jules' workroom and the wine library, even though Eddie and Rachel had already been through these areas. Not surprisingly, they found no clues to where Jules might be, although they did find, behind the barrels, the old camp bed he used for naps. It looked more or less like a dog's bed—but whether or not Jules had slept there recently none could tell. Nor did they find the missing rifle or Talies' third burnoose. Finally the three detectives strolled up and down the barrel-lined tunnels of the wine cave, convincing themselves that Jules was not lying under one of the barrel cradles, hurt, or worse."

By the time they re-emerged onto the crush pad, all three felt frustrated, thirsty, and ready for a rest. Sam and Bailey and Zoe were waiting for them, grinning broadly.

"Hey, old man," said Kit rubbing his son's head. "What are you three monkeys up to? You look smug. Did Uncle Jules turn up while we were busy looking for him?"

"No," said Sam. "Nonna says she'll call the police if we don't find him in the cave. While you were in the tunnels, we were in Grandpa's workroom. We discovered some things. Actually, Bailey did the best discovering."

Bailey held up a pair of yellow and white striped pajama bottoms he'd found under one of the barrel cradles. A thin line of dried blood ran down a pant leg. Sam exhibited a pair of broken reading glasses she'd found under Jules' work table. She claimed they belonged to her grandfather. And Zoe showed them a handful of torn paper scraps she'd picked up in the workroom.

"So—what do you think?" asked Sam. "Did we do good?"

"You did well," said Kit, staring at the blood stained pants. "The old trickster," he muttered to himself. "I wonder if that's really his blood. Or a rat's. We should get it tested. So, he must have changed clothes. . . ."

"He probably put on that burnoose and just walked out, like I said," added Talies.

"So what's next?" said Morgan. "Should we search the vineyards?"

"No, I don't think that'll be necessary," said Kit. "Rickie said Roberto and his people are working on that. I'll defer to them."

"And I gotta get back to work," muttered Talies turning to leave.

Suddenly Bailey blurted out, "I know where Uncle Jules is! I'll go get him. Meet you back at the Big House." And he tore off before his father could say anything, much less stop him.

Bailey was wrong.

15 AT ALICE'S MOON DOG DINER

"Smoke and mirrors," said Morgan as she and Kit and Talies crossed the crush pad. "I agree, there must be a third way out."

Kit stroked his moustache. "Well, I certainly didn't see him leave by the big door, and Indie says she didn't either."

"But if he did, and even if he didn't, somebody must have seen something!" said Morgan, feeling annoyed with herself for missing Jules' exit. "And I wonder what time it is. I wonder if I missed my ride. They probably left without me. Maybe we should head back to the house."

Kit nodded. "And my knee is killing me. I could really use some quiet sit-down time about now—emphasis on the 'quiet.' Did we ever get any breakfast? And we need to figure out a follow up plan. We need to check with everyone who was at the show last night. Wait a sec, I have an idea." And with a couple of texts, he found out five things. First, that Jules had not turned up. Second, that Bailey had gone off on his bike. Third, that Nonna had taken the children to her place for lunch. Fourth, that Eddie had already driven into town and talked to police, who had declared that as a competent adult Jules hadn't been gone long enough to be labeled "missing." And fifth, that Rickie and Tinker were alone together in the kitchen, simply waiting.

"Well I'm going to Nonna's too, for lunch. Come on, Sam," announced Zoe. "And then I'm going to see what Fluff is doing." Morgan and Kit watched them trot off down the road.

When they were gone, Kit said, "And I know a place where you and I, my dear, can get something to eat. And have a good talk. Just the two of us." He winked at her, and grinned. "I know I haven't told you yet what Irene told me when I cornered her at the party last night."

Minutes later they were heading down the Silverado Trail towards Alice's Moon Dog Diner. Kit broke into song as he swung into the graveled parking lot.

Little darling, it's been years since I've been here.

Here comes the sun. Here comes the sun. And it's all right.

The old place looked exactly as he remembered it—shiny and silver, little curtains on the windows, faded posters from the Forties. Alice, however, had moved up to her daughter's place in Shasta, and Ning was now in charge. But the all-day breakfast deal was the same—omelets with piles of bacon and cheese, bottomless cups of coffee. And Ning, like Alice before her, let her customers sit for as long as they wanted to in the booths. Kit was still whistling as they slid onto the vinyl benches of a back booth. The diner was nearly empty.

"What time is it?" Kit asked the waitress, as he flipped through selections on the table-sized jukebox.

"Two thirty, sir. If you want much more than hot coffee, iced tea, or a coke, you'd better order quick. Ning goes on break at three. Takes her kid down to her mom's in Napa City and doesn't get back till almost four. In the meantime, all you get is me, those pies over there, and maybe some egg salad, if there's any left. So . . . what'll it be?"

They ate omelets, which were fluffy and fresh and accompanied by a whole plate of crispy bacon. After food, two aspirins, and three cups of coffee, Kit's knee felt much better. Morgan stuck to iced tea. She was on her third glass of it when he got around to telling her about Irene.

"She looks older, a lot older in fact. Sort of marinated. Her arthritis seems worse. But her attitude's like I remember—bitter, slightly toxic, like the berries of an old Mountain Ash tree. Memory seems okay, although a bit vague around the edges." Kit smiled as the waitress topped up his coffee. "So . . . I learned two things of interest. First—Irene does not believe in this so-called dirty tricks campaign against Jules. She won't say why, but she doesn't. She was not at all amused by the practical jokes and other nonsense at the party yesterday, I should add. Nor has she changed her views on either Tinker or Indie. She thinks they're both frivolous and prone to exaggeration. I'd have to agree. I think I told you, she and Indie never got along well. On the other hand, Irene does seem to be getting along better with Jules these days, despite all her nagging about that promise business. I don't know. Maybe she and Jules called a truce. Did I tell you I saw them talking together yesterday like best pals? It seemed strange to me."

Kit grinned, and reached across the table to hijack Morgan's penultimate strip of bacon.

"Don't you dare," she said, slapping his hand. "I wonder what Irene thinks about Jules' disappearance last night. She seemed very quiet this morning."

"Couldn't say. Maybe you should go talk with her about that when we get back," said Kit, making a second, also unsuccessful, heist attempt. "Anyway, the other thing I learned is perhaps of greater moment—I learned her side of the story about that promise Jules supposedly made to his brother way back when."

Morgan nodded.

"She says it was more than a verbal promise. She claims there's an actual written agreement between Jules and his brother, an agreement witnessed by Big Eddie himself."

"Did she show it to you?"

"No. She didn't even know if she had it any more, although she described it to me—a single page of blue tissue-y paper, hand written, three signatures at the bottom. She was vague about the date though. I pressed her. She thought it was right after she and Eddie got married, which would make it 1952. Just before Eddie went to Korea, I might add."

Morgan considered this. "Does the timing make a real difference?" she asked him. "Was this agreement like as a sort of will, in case Eddie was killed?" She waited to hear the rest of Kit's narrative.

"I don't know," Kit said. "Jules was pretty young at the time. Anyway, Irene told me the split was to be fifty-fifty—half to Jules and his descendants, and half to herself and their descendants. I assume she was pregnant with Jack. And this part is truly weird—at the time the agreement was supposedly made, she claims to have promised never to marry again if Eddie Jr. was killed in the war. I'd not heard this bit before, but perhaps it explains why she was so upset when Jack married. Clearly, she doesn't approve of divorce. But maybe she believed that remarriage—either hers or Jack's— would somehow cancel out that agreement about Buckthorn."

"I don't see why."

"I don't either, but we need to get a hold of this elusive document."

"If it exists."

"Yeah. If it exists. Anyway, I gather she's fed this story to Jack for his entire life, Jules too. Jules, of course, tells the story a bit differently. And the two versions have some inconsistencies. For one thing, Jules has never mentioned in my hearing that there was ever a written agreement."

"And I recall Jules saying he was ten when his brother was killed," put in Morgan. "That stuck with me because that was Tally's age when Artie died. But the dates don't work—he must have been older. He just turned eighty. Wasn't Pork Chop Hill in '53? Also, I don't recall Jules mentioning anything about a document either, for what that's worth. But I'd like to see it—if it exists. Do you think Irene and Jules are both beginning to lose some memory? Memory is not a terribly robust phenomenon, and memories can be created as well as modified by repeated suggestions. People start believing their own stories, their own lies. Happens all the time. Anyway, I find it hard to believe that some broken promise made so long ago has a whole lot to do with those incidents that we came here to investigate. Surely you're not suggesting Irene is behind them. I find that really hard to believe, don't you?"

"Umm. I agree. It seems unlikely that Irene herself could be doing those things."

"But her son might? Urged on by his mother's stories. On the other hand, I got the impression Jack's not around all that much. Maybe we should try to check alibis. Or are you thinking they used that promise to somehow intimidate Jules? Blackmail maybe? But I can't see that either. Uncle Jules doesn't seem the type to be intimidated. Perhaps it's a red herring."

They kicked around ideas for a while longer but came to no real conclusions.

"Irene said something else that knocked me over," said Kit finally. "She said if Eddie married Indie, she'd consider that old agreement fulfilled."

Morgan stifled a snort of laughter. "Well it would solve some things, wouldn't it? I mean, how would you feel if Indie married Eddie? Maybe you should encourage that idea. At least then Indie might stop harassing you."

Kit frowned. His mouth shaped a word, but nothing came out.

"You should see your face right now," chortled Morgan. "I mean I wish you could see your face! O my, I shouldn't laugh at you, but it does feel like we're coming out of a long dark tunnel somehow—oh, excuse the reference," she put her hand over her mouth to stifle another laugh. "We're not getting anywhere, are we? Maybe I don't understand what's going on at Buckthorn, I don't know these people, but then . . . " She failed to finish the sentence as they both had simultaneously become aware of grinning stupidly at one another.

Kit rolled his eyes. "Well, we should get back. See whether Bailey's turned up. I certainly hope he found Jules. Although I can't imagine what that boy is thinking. I admit, this whole thing makes me a little crazy. But thank you for indulging me about lunch, and thanks too for the aspirin, and the laughs. I feel much better than I did."

"You're welcome. It happens to the best of us. I mean, this feeling of being a little crazy happens to the best of us." And with this she reached across the table for Kit's hand. "If Jules isn't back by the time we return, I want to spend a few minutes in his workroom. Who knows? Maybe that old document is in there somewhere, maybe I can find it now that I know what color it is! And I want to check a few other things. Then I want to go back to Quarry Canyon . . . for a couple of days. Tally said I could borrow his car. And you, my friend, should talk some more to Indie, about . . . about, well . . . stuff."

As they climbed up into Kit's big vehicle, Morgan was still

giggling at the look her last suggestion had produced on Kit's face. They stopped again at the viewpoint on top of the ridge. This time, however, instead of marking the beauty of summer in Buckthorn Valley, he simply leaned over and kissed her, long and hard.

"I'd like to be a winemaker," Sam was telling Talies when Kit and Morgan walked onto the winery floor. "But not like Rachel. She's mean."

Talies was only half listening to her as he rolled the empty barrels down a metal track and adjusted them to sit bung-hole-up for steam cleaning. "If you want to be useful, you could move those buckets and that pump out of the way. I'm gonna blast these babies with hot water in a minute. Hand me the wand, would you?" He re-positioned the steam machine and stuffed the wand into the first bung hole, and steadied it as he fiddled with the connector. "Want to try?"

"Sure," said Sam. "I'll do the next one. Did you see how Rachel treated Mr. Frye this morning? She really told him off, I thought. I heard her say not to come around here anymore."

"You have to be careful with this beast," continued Talies. "The steam's really hot. And you don't want the wand to come popping out when it's under pressure. What's her thing with Frye?"

"Dunno. Uncle Eddie hates him. So does Grandpa." Sam grinned. "I think he doesn't like our wines." She jumped back as Talies loosed a blast of steam into the barrel. "How long do you do that for?" she asked.

"Not long. In fact, that's enough." He turned off the steam and removed the wand from the barrel and passed the apparatus over to Sam and watched as she fixed it into the bung hole of the next barrel in line.

"And why do we do this?" she asked as he rolled his barrel over to drain.

"Gets all the crap out of the barrel. And the steam kills the bacteria and molds that get into the wood. Then it's okay to re-use the barrels. Here, let me see if you got it tight." He wiggled the wand Sam had placed on her barrel and gave the connector another turn. "Pretty good. Ready to give her a blast?"

"Yeah! Ow!" Sam sucked the burn on her finger.

"Have to keep your hands away. Steam's hot!"

"I'm not stupid. Just made a mistake. I'm going to take the course in enology at high school next year. Uncle Eddie says if I do well in the course, I can join the cellar team next summer."

"Cool," said Talies, rolling over her blasted barrel and watching the hot water drip into the pan below the track. "Oh—Hi, Mom!" he called to Morgan. "Just showing my new assistant here the ropes on steam cleaning. You guys better stand clear. This process gets hot, and wet. You should've seen me do this my first time! The steam line got loose and danced around like a damned cobra gone crazy! Burnt my neck!"

Kit raised an eyebrow. "I've never heard Samantha talk so much to anyone," he remarked softly to Morgan as they stood back.

"She looks tense," said Morgan nodding back over her shoulder as Rachel rushed across the winery floor, stopping briefly to check on Talies and Sam.

"Be careful!" Rachel said before spitting a few more instructions. "When you're done with those, take them out to the crush pad for the cooper to inspect for cracks. Then do the barrels over there. And don't forget to top up the water level in the steamer. When you you're done, go help Ben and Cody finish racking those reds. We bottle next week. I'd help, but I'm running late after that Frye confrontation. Fine time the old man chose to take off! Have you seen Eddie?"

"I wonder what happened between Rachel and Frye," said Morgan softly to Kit.

"Ah, I was looking for you, Rach," said Eddie stepping through the open door of the loading dock waving a fat manila envelope. His eyes absorbed the presence of Kit and Morgan as he continued to speak. "I picked up that info you wanted on the development north of the lake when I was in town. Not sure there's enough to convince the planning board to deny that application. Want to see?" Rachel nodded and they turned to walk back to the lab behind the stainless steel tanks.

As they disappeared, Indie came storming into the winery. She was in full freak-out mode. "Has anyone seen Bailey?! I can't find him anywhere! He never came back! I've looked and looked and looked. I can't believe he's gone too!"

"He was going somewhere on his bike when he left this morning," put in Kit. "He'll show up. Don't worry."

"First Jules. Now Bailey. Why on earth shouldn't I worry?" She wrapped her long braid around one hand and knotted it on top of her head. She shrieked as Talies blasted steam into another barrel. "Jesus, Mary, and Joseph! You gotta go find our son, Kit! I can't stand much more of this!"

Talies handed the wand to Sam and strolled over to Indie. "I saw Bailey this morning too, after the three of us searched the mine shaft. He was acting a little odd, even for Bailey. He asked me whether the forty-niners ever found gold around here. I said I had no idea. Then he went tearing off. I don't where, but I'd bet he's okay."

"The gold rush was mostly in the Sierra hills, east of here," said Kit.

"But what about the Cinnabar thing?" put in Morgan. "Don't you remember what Jules said? Find Cinnabar and you find Quicksilver, and sometimes Gold?"

"I doubt that's what Bailey was talking about," replied Kit.

"Didn't Jules tell us these hills were riddled with mines?"

"What are you two talking about?" shrieked Indie. "What mines? I thought there was only the one."

"Oh, calm down, Indie. Let's you and me go see what's going on at the Big House," said Kit, putting his arm around Indie's shoulder. "Bailey said he knew where Uncle Jules was. Maybe he's back by now." He threw a wink over his shoulder at Morgan, indicating that now would be a good time for her to go to Jules' workroom.

Morgan quickly nodded her agreement. Then waited as Kit took Indie away, complaining she went. "It's all Rachel's fault really," Indie said. "She's trying to get her hands on Buckthorn. You should ask her about that ravioli fiasco too. She's the one who brought that dish. I remember her saying it was her grandmother's recipe. My ass! Lobster is what I think made Uncle Jules sick."

Sam, wand in hand, stared after them.

"Piece of work," muttered Talies, and went back to steam

cleaning. "No! Dump the pan down the drain, Sam, not on the floor, or you'll find yourself mopping again," he said.

Morgan dug into her jeans for her cell phone. As she did so, her fingers touched the crumpled scraps of paper Zoe had handed her that morning. If only those scraps had been blue! She sighed. Time to get to work. With any luck the cellar rats would stay busy racking wine and steaming barrels for the next few hours.

She sent her message to Kit: "Going home when done here. Text if Bailey's back."

Morgan sighed, wondering what she was going to find in the cave, if anything.

She passed an old, hand-operated grape press and three open cement vats along one wall as she hurried down that tunnel that led to Jules' workroom. The vats she now knew were used for primary fermentation. In a deep niche on the other side of the tunnel were several piles of medium-sized whiskey casks as well several stacks of barrels marked "Special Reserve." All this seemed to confirm that Jules did make his own wines; her eyes scanned the walls and ceiling for signs of the ventilation system.

At the end of the tunnel behind an oak door lay the workroom. Her attention was drawn immediately to the mess of papers and small equipment on his work table. She stared at the pieces of small equipment, much of it old, possibly antique. Then she found a brand new chemistry set, and a digital scale. She set these aside and began sorting through papers. She found plenty of bills and receipts and letters too, several in French, most seemed business related—letters from lawyers, medical stuff, tax information, real estate notices, as well as various announcements, forms, and even some award certificates from winemaking associations. It was hard to know which to look at closely. She added the most interesting of these to her pile of cellar books. She didn't have time at the moment to read through everything that looked interesting.

Under the work table was a box of freshly printed wine labels, as well as some mailing tubes containing survey maps, both old and recent. These she looked at quickly, then put them back in their tubes, and added several of the tubes to her growing pile of stuff to take home. She shook out books she found, on winemaking and on local history and geology, hoping that a hidden letter or a forgotten note, or even some blue paper, might fall out. No luck. Next she spent almost half an hour exploring the wine library at the back of the workroom. Fortunately, the sliding metal security gate had been left open. The wine racks held hundreds, perhaps thousands, of dusty bottles, some many decades old. She hunted through the bottles to get a feel for what was there, and even climbed up a folding ladder to inspect what she couldn't see from the floor. There she discovered a stash of old whiskeys, mostly scotches. She'd looked behind Jules' collection of large sized bottles—magnums, Jeroboams, and even a few Methuselahs of champagne. She tenderly fingered various bottles, including his Brunello, imagining what it might be like to taste what was inside them. Next she searched around the workroom itself, into the corners, behind furniture, and under pieces of winemaking gear, barrels, and casks. She pulled open the drawers of Jules' drop-leaf desk, but found no sign of an agreement on blue paper. She also found no rifle and no hidden, third way out of the wine cave, only dust, dirt, damp, and mouse droppings.

Finally she sat down in an ancient, mouse-eaten stuffed chair to think. She stared at the little ferns and bits of moss growing out of the hard-packed earthen floor back in a corner. Imagining that Jules himself probably sat in this chair often, she dug into its crevices and looked under the seat cushion, but again there was nothing but crumbs and dirt, a pencil, a broken cork, and some pieces of ram's horn. Leaving no stone unturned, she took a second look at the little desk, looking this time for secret drawers. She did find some old photos and at the back of the bottom desk drawer, and some extra asthma inhalers, a couple of epi-pens, a small bottle of heart pills, and some baby aspirin. She also found, oddly, a wallet stuffed with hundred dollar bills. She counted the money—more than twenty grand! She replaced the money into the wallet and the wallet in the drawer, then got down on her knees to look under the desk. She poked behind several stacks of wine cases and discovered several more bits of ram's horn as well as several dirty glass tumblers, broken. Finally, she crawled up the ladder again and peered into various air ducts as well as the ventilation fans that circulated fresh air through this end of the cave. All seemed in good working order; no sign of being stuffed with rags. Had she missed anything? She took another look around, then packed up what she wanted to take with her in the army duffle bag she'd found under Jules camp bed and lugged it out to Talies's beat-up hatchback. No one was around to ask questions, fortunately.

Before starting the car, Morgan texted her two friends in Quarry Canyon—Naeve Casey, a well-connected San Francisco lawyer; and Izzy Folger, who ran the bookshop on the downtown plaza. Izzy was a bit erratic, but brave, and solidly sensible. She made arrangements to meet them both at Formerly's, for supper and a good long talk. She found herself looking forward to sleeping in her very own bed, snuggled up next to her own yellow cat, Max, sleeping on what had been Artie's pillow. It seemed so long since she'd been home, yet in fact it had been only a few days.

16 QUARRY CANYON AGAIN

The road home tunneled through the redwoods, then climbed towards the eastern shoulder of Mount Tamalpais, curved around, and finally dropped down into Quarry Canyon itself, Morgan's delightful hometown. From the top of Mount Tam one could look west to the cold Pacific Ocean as well as south towards the iconic Golden Gate Bridge, whose red towers were often buried in fog, or east into Quarry Canyon. It was nearly seven by the time Morgan arrived in town. Rosie's cafe on the downtown plaza, which served both breakfast and lunch, was closed, and Izzy was out in front of her shop, Books for All Reasons, resupplying the bargain book display. Geronimo, Izzy's sweet-eyed black Lab, lay on the sidewalk nearby, leashed to a parking meter. Morgan tooted and waved as she drove by. Izzy returned her wave. Geronimo simply lifted his head and slapped his tail.

Morgan did not go directly to Formerly's, where she would be meeting her girlfriends for drinks and supper. Instead she swung right and drove the few blocks to the public library, where she hoped to find Olivia—the head librarian and her boss. Olivia often came into work on Sundays although the library was officially closed for the day. Indeed, Olivia's red Prius was parked in front of the building. Morgan pulled in next to it and got out.

"Olivia?" she called, unlocking the front door of the library. She dropped the duffle bag of Jules' maps, papers, and cellar books on the circulation desk.

"Back here," came the familiar voice. "I thought you were away until next weekend, Morgan."

"I am," Morgan said, removing a stack of books and files from the chair in Olivia's office and sitting down. "I just popped back to look up a few things. I'm glad you're here. I could use some help."

"What are you looking for, dear?"

Olivia always reminded Morgan of a friendly witch—twinkling eyes, wrinkled brow, gray hair in a ratty bun at the back of her head, bare feet. Olivia also possessed an uncannily acute mind that knew every detail of, not only her own library's holdings, but also those of every other well stocked Bay Area library.

Morgan explained what she wanted. Olivia agreed that most old maps were not digitized and thus unavailable online. The largest collection she knew of was held in the local history archives of UC Berkeley's Bancroft Library. "But check what we've got first. You might get lucky," she advised.

Lucky my eye, thought Morgan—she knows exactly what we have. She's just being coy about it. "Great! Point me in the direction." And soon Morgan was seated at a big table in the library's atrium, surrounded by map tubes and property survey books as well as several old atlases of Northern California. She felt a bit as if she were sitting among the long lost scrolls of the ancient library at Alexandria.

It seemed no time at all before Olivia called out, "I'm turning out the lights back here. Lock up when you leave. Good luck with your search. Don't stay too late."

Morgan smiled to herself. She had located what she wanted and was making copies. Then she spent another half an hour or so squinting at handwritten nineteenth century labels and then scrolling through computer databases. Finally she replaced all the materials she'd taken from the basement archives, repacked her duffle bag adding in the copies, and headed off to meet Naeve and Izzy for dinner.

On a whim, she left her car parked where it was in front of the library and took the path through Old Mill Park along the creek towards the downtown plaza. She loved the heavy scent of redwoods as well as the musical gurgle of the park's year-round stream. Over her head, a wisp of fog darkened the new moon. Contentment wrapped around her like a warm blanket, a feeling improved by a certain smugness about the results of her map search. Fingers crossed, she felt herself well on the path to understanding the source for all the tension surrounding Jules. Then she passed where the path turned and climbed the Crossways Steps. Her sense of contentment quickly slipped away as she remembered the story of young Justin who had been murdered on these steps and her roll in all that. Morgan sighed, wishing she'd been able to help stave off the boy's death. At least she'd done something to help heal the town after it happened. And here she was now, working on another investigation, with possibly another young boy to worry about—Bailey. Fingers crossed again that Kit's son would be restored to them, alive and well. But there was the old man too to worry about. She felt less sanguine about him. She hoped she wasn't too late.

"Hey Mike," she called to the bald-headed man behind the bar. "Kitchen still open?"

"For you, it's always open," grinned Mike. "What'll you have?"

"A Pinot Grigio while I wait for Naeve and Izzy, please. No, on second thought, make that a cucumber martini." She flopped into one of the stuffed chairs under the open window and stared across the plaza pondering what she'd discovered at the library.

Izzy was soon striding across the plaza towards her, Geronimo bounding unleashed out in front.

"Over here," she waved. Morgan rose to embrace her friend. "Good to see you!"

"You too, girlfriend. And you, you foolish creature," said Izzy, giving her dog's rump a gentle push with her foot. "Get yourself all the way under the table or you'll have your tail stepped on." They watched as the big dog slowly turned himself around and around, then settled again, with his nose resting on Izzy's shoe.

"So, how's it going in wine country? You and handsome Mr. Kit getting along okay with this whole ex-in-law crowd?" Izzy tucked some wisps of dark hair behind an ear. "Ooh, I'll have one of those too please," she said as Mike placed a martini glass in front of Morgan.

"Me too," put in Naeve Casey, parking a small wheeled overnight bag in the corner. She gave Morgan a peck on the cheek. "I'm bushed! Just flew in from DC. And that shuttle from the airport was grotesquely slow." Naeve slipped off her four inch heels and sat down, curling aher legs under her. "Did you guys order anything to eat yet? I'm famished. Nothing since breakfast except peanuts and stale crackers. I could use one of Mike's rib eyes."

"Go for it, girl. Want to split a pizza, Morgan?"

"Actually," said Morgan. "I've been dreaming about Mike's gigantic Caesar salad with a piece of roasted salmon on top. I'd split one of those with you, if you like."

"Okay. Shall we get a bottle to go with? Or a pitcher of martinis?"

As they waited for their food to appear, they sipped their drinks and chatted lazily like the three old friends they were, catching up on family, friends, and local politics.

"I saw Hugh O'Connor at the planning board meeting Thursday night," said Izzy. "He's finally going to open that little French restaurant on the plaza. He came in for his liquor license."

"Good for him! He's such a talented chef."

"Yeah. It'll be nice to have something slightly more upscale than Mike's version of home cookin'. Speaking of which, here comes our food."

"Did you hear that some of the pines on the mountain are showing signs of more bark beetle infestation?"

"Shoot! Hope it doesn't mean more wildfires."

"How's your mom, Iz? Doing any better?"

"A little. But now Giles is driving me crazy, getting ready for the Art and Wine Fest next month. Wasn't that where you and Kit met a couple of years ago?" They chatted on and relaxed together until finally Izzy and Naeve steered the conversation to Kit and Buckthorn, peppering Morgan with questions.

"So, what news, girlfriend? Find out who done what yet?"

"And how are you and Kit getting along?"

"Is that ex-wife of his fomenting more trouble?"

"How's the endangered uncle?"

"Anything else happen?"

"Anybody dead?"

"Anything we can do to help?"

Morgan did her best to answer her friends' rapid fire of questions. "Nobody's dead, yet," she concluded. "Maybe we'll be able to forestall that. Although Jules did suffer some mysterious attack during his birthday party—possibly an allergic reaction, or a small stroke. Unclear etiology. And last night he disappeared right in front of us. That was pretty strange. Nobody saw him go, and we were all sitting right there. Now nobody will admit either to knowing where he is. Then this morning, Kit's son disappeared. Or at least that's what people were saying when I left. He went off on his bike somewhere. Claimed to know where Jules was. He'd been gone only half a day or so but Indie was already frantic. Rickie was anxious too. I left Kit trying to settle them down. I can't stop thinking however about Bailey. Before he disappeared, he and a couple of the kids found some pajama pants Jules had been wearing the night before. They said the pants were stuck up under one of the barrel cradles back in the wine cave. And they had blood on them."

"Sounds dramatic," said Izzy.

"I know," replied Morgan. "A bit too dramatic, isn't it? Feels like something out of a book. And this family does likes practical jokes too. There were several during Jules' birthday party. It's hard to know what take seriously. Neither Kit nor I am sure what's going." Then Morgan went on to describe the agreement between two brothers about the future ownership of Buckthorn. Her friends' eyes grew wide.

Finally, she brought her monologue to a close. "It's funny. I keep thinking Jules and Bailey will just walk through the door—you know?—with a perfectly sensible explanation for where they've been. It's hard for me to believe something really bad has happened to them, On the other hand, Rickie, did send her son Eddie into town to see if the cops would list the old man as a 'missing person'. I'm not sure how that worked out. The cops didn't want to declare him missing at first. Seemed to believe that adults have a perfect right to disappear from time to time. If you'll excuse me a moment, I ought to text Kit."

As she fussed with her phone, Naeve ordered a pitcher of ice water, to dilute the alcohol in their systems. When Morgan looked up again, Naeve asked, "How are Kit's conflicts of interest coming along? Didn't you say he was concerned his investigative skills might be compromised by his knowing everyone so well? Afraid he'd miss things, or not catch their lies. Has he overstepped? How about conflicting loyalties?"

Morgan shrugged and poured some ice water into her empty martini glass. "Hard to say. He's not been at his best. He feels very much a part of this family. Told me that Jules is some sort of cousin of his mother. And he seems a bit too sure in his opinions about these people. I'm taking everything he says with a large grain of salt."

Morgan frowned, and pursed her lips. "And he seems to be getting along better than I expected with Indie. I don't know what I expected. I try not to think about this too much. I'm finding them both hard to read. Frankly, I feel I've been put in an awkward situation. It's good to get away from all those Romanos for a while. Be able to think. Oh, you'll never guess what else Kit did. He hired Talies on as an intern! And nobody told me! Tally went up to Buckthorn a few weeks ago. Kit has had him working undercover, believe it or not, as a cellar rat! You could have knocked me over with a feather when I saw Tally in the wine caves. He was racking wine, and driving a fork lift!"

"Goodness!" her friends chorused.

"Kit's idea was that Tally should keep an eye on the winemaker. Her name is Rachel Suttermann."

"Suttermann?" said Naeve.

"Yeah, I was led to believe she's related to the Sutter of Sutter's Mill," replied Morgan.

"Dam my eyes," said Izzy.

"Indie has been claiming that Rachel is behind these incidents we're investigating. And it does get interesting. . . ." Morgan then spent the next hour or so laying out for her friends the people and the business at Buckthorn, including some of the conflicts of interest within the family and the tug of war over Jules' threatened trust revisions.

"Those old estates up in wine country are worth a pile of money these days," remarked Naeve when Morgan was finishing.

"Do you think it's all about the money?"

"Of course it is," said Morgan, suddenly remembering that she'd failed to mention Jules' horde of cash.

"Or, money and sex," added Izzy. "Always a lethal combination. Do you think Indie embellished her fears about a threat to attract Kit's attention? It's a little strange how you say that family ignores the things she told Kit about, except for her cousin of course. Why do they call her Tinker? Is that really her birth name?"

Morgan said she had no idea.

Geronimo whimpered in his sleep, then cut a long, slow stinker. "Ugh. Excuse you, beast," said Izzy. "Would you excuse us please? It may be time for a short walk."

"My intuition is that it will all come down to Jules and his trust, in the end," said Morgan to Naeve, as Izzy encouraged her dog out the door of Formerly's. "I do wish I could get hold of that old agreement we've been told about, and I would love to know what, if any changes, he's planning for his trust. He acts very mysterious. His sister-in-law, Irene, nags on and on about this promise, as she calls it—a promise she says Jules made to his brother before his brother went to off to Korea, where he was killed. The details seem to change every time I hear the story. And Jules was quite young. Sometimes he claims not to remember what happened, and other times he seems to. I don't know what's going on. I've got to go have tea with Irene when I get back to Buckthorn and probe some more. Would there be any sort of public record that would help? I couldn't get access from our library here."

Naeve nodded thoughtfully. "Only if a formal agreement was drawn up. I can usually get into the requisite databases. He might have executed a trust agreement we could see; and I can find out who owns which pieces of property in Buckthorn Valley. I could check real estate recent transfers. That might prove interesting. I'll take tomorrow off. Stop by, hopefully I'll find something to help."

"Oh, thank you! And can we check Jack's property holdings too? I'm curious about the status of his Mustard Seed vineyard? I have some maps in the car."

"Catch me up, guys. I want to be in on this," said Izzy, plumping down again in her big chair. And so they caught her up and made their plans. And Izzy promised to watch over Max when Morgan returned to Buckthorn.

"Where'd you leave Geronimo?" asked Naeve.

"Big lout wouldn't do anything . . . umm . . . productive. So I tied him to that bench over there. He'll be fine." Their eyes followed her point to where the big black Lab was sitting prettily on his haunches, paws crossed, on the seat of the park bench in the plaza, staring at them, pleading to join them. They laughed as he slapped his feathered tail.

As the evening wore on, the three friends shared more town and family news until Izzy started yawning. Then Naeve yawned. Then Morgan. "It is getting late!" Morgan said. "I've kept you dear people out too long."

Her phone buzzed as a message came in.

"Oh dear," Morgan's eyes flicked between her friends. "Kit says Bailey's not back yet, but they found his bike. The police are all super occupied by some sort of hostage thing at a campground outside Calistoga, but they did agreed to put out one of those Amber Alerts for missing children, to cell phones and freeway signs. And they released photos to the tv news."

"So the police are taking this disappearance more seriously," remarked Izzy.

Naeve pushed herself up and prepared to leave. "Well, see you tomorrow, girlfriends. Get some sleep."

"Poor Kit," murmured Izzy, staring at the ringless fourth finger of Morgan's left hand. "He must be half crazed by now. He'll need you, Morgan. More than ever."

Morgan glanced down at own hand and wondered, briefly, whether to return her wedding ring to her finger when she got home, or not.

17 THEORIES AND DISCOVERIES

Although Kit was doing his best to avoid Indie while Morgan was away, they did run into each other Tuesday morning. Kit was walking from the tank house towards the winery. She was going the other way. They stood and talked.

"You look like you haven't been sleeping," Kit began.

"I haven't. Are you?"

He asked if there was any news of Jules or Bailey.

"Nothing. I'm really getting scared, Carson. First Uncle Jules disappears. Now our kid. What's happening? Who's doing this? Who'll be next? Who'd want to hurt either one of them? I keep having these visions of Bailey, buried under a collapsed mine tunnel somewhere. Screaming. Uncle Jules is lying dead nearby. Am I going crazy?"

"Just try to stay calm, dear. I don't know where Bailey is. But I know that kid is not a risk taker. He wouldn't go down into the mine shaft. My gut tells me he's okay. If he, or your Uncle Jules, was kidnapped, we'd have heard something by now. Anyway, I am very sure neither one is lying in a mine tunnel, or in the wine cave. Morgan and I did a thorough search before she left. So thorough, I messed up my knee again."

"You get no sympathy from me about that knee, Carson. You and your famous detecting—but somebody's been in those tunnels. I just came from up there. That old mine is near where Roberto found Bailey's bike—near that falling down shack Jules uses as a blind during hunting season. Did you know where I mean?"

Kit nodded. "I know."

"Well, did you also know the locks on the gate into mine shaft is broken? That gate, and the one inside too, is standing wide open?"

Kit looked sheepish. "I . . . umm . . ."

Indie stared at him. "You did know? But you weren't going to say?"

"Not exactly. Fact is, it was me. I went up again last night. Wanted to see how secure those locks were."

"And. . ."

"They're not secure. The latch devices are junk. I fiddled them both easily. And that little device above the door? It's a joke. I must have left the gate open. Hope no animals got in. Anyway . . . although I suppose Bailey could have gotten into the mine tunnels, if he really wanted to, I don't think he did. He'd have had to stand on something to get at the mechanism, and I saw no evidence he did that. Still, I went in. Took another long look around. By the way, I also found that both of those locks can be opened from inside, although that's not so easy either."

"Oh damn you! Damn. Damn. Damn."

"Hang on. Didn't you hear what I said? I found no evidence that either Jules or Bailey is in those tunnels now, dead or alive. I seriously doubt Bailey ever went in. I also said any tallish adult could easily get in, from the palisade side. So that suggests to me that someone could have used the shaft. . . say, to sabotage the barrel racks or stop up the ventilation system and then disappear out the same way. But I do not believe that Jules left the cave that way the other night. He's an old man! So I've come around to Talies' idea that Jules simply came out the main entrance Saturday night, and nobody saw him because we were all focused on the damned magic show. Talies had some cognitive explanation for why it happened as it did, although I don't buy it. Still, I think we need to move on."

As he rattled on, Indie's eyes had collapsed into an angry squint. Finally, she screamed at him, "You don't get it, do you? You never got it!" She began pummeling him on his chest to emphasize her words. "Rachel's . . . behind . . . it! . . . Rachel's . . . behind . . . everything! I bet she's got Uncle Jules and Bailey drugged, stashed somewhere. Like in her damned mobile home. Have you looked there?"

"Oh, stop it!" Kit said, capturing her wrists. "You are being crazy now."

"I am not! Rachel's wanted to get rid of Uncle Jules for a long time! She'd like him dead! Want to know why?"

"Sure. Why?"

"So she can get her hands on Buckthorn. Why do you think she wants to marry Eddie?! Have you seen the way she looks at him? Uncle Jules knows what she's up to. That's why he's revising his damned trust! And Eddie's been in love with Rachel since we were kids! He does whatever she wants him to. She's a sly one. Completely self-serving."

Kit dropped her wrists, even as Indie ranted on. "And she's got Bailey too. Hidden him somewhere. He's lying somewhere tied up on a bed. You need to get into her mobile home, Carson. Break in if you have to. I'll bet that's where Bailey is! Uncle Jules too."

Kit frowned, but said nothing. Indie was sounding like a bad TV show.

"The trouble with Uncle Jules is," Indie went on, "he always thinks the best of people. Like Rachel, for example. In his eyes, that girl can do no wrong . . . except when the subject of her marrying Eddie comes up." Indie scoffed. "And our Uncle Jules takes enormous risks . . . I bet he did climb up out the mine shaft, in the middle of night, in his bedroom slippers. And when he came out, there she was. At the top. Waiting. It's like a game for her. Except this time, she's deadly serious. Why do you think we've never been friends?"

Kit finally interrupted. "Stop this, Indie. Some of what you say makes a sort of sense, but a lot of it is pure garbage! Why should Uncle Jules be upset if Eddie and Rachel married? Everybody says she's like a daughter to him." He stopped himself suddenly, scratched his ear, and touched his moustache. Then his blue eyes grew wide. "Is that the problem here?"

"What?"

"I just had this really weird idea. Could Rachel be your

uncle's daughter?" He stared at her. "No wonder he wouldn't want Eddie to marry her."

"Oh, gawd, Carson," Indie groaned. "You are so thick."

"No, that's too weird."

"Wait a minute." Indie barked suddenly. "I know where he is."

"Where who is?"

"At his fishing camp on Lake Berryessa. I bet. I bet that's where they've taken him."

"Taken who? Bailey?"

"No. Uncle Jules, you idiot."

"What fishing camp?"

"Don't you remember? We went there once, years ago. But it isn't really a fishing camp anymore. It's a terroir now. Uncle Jules tested the soils. Said he was gonna plant vines. It's hard to get to, though. I'm gonna ask Bowie to do a fly over on his way back to LA. And Bowie's leaving this morning!" With that she tore off towards the Big House to catch her brother.

Kit stared after Indie, admiring her golden braid. It was like a horse's tail, flying out behind her as she sprinted towards the finish line. He sighed, turned slowly, and continued down the track to the winery, thinking. Talies wanted to show him some data he had uncovered. And he wondered whether or not Talies had found anyone who'd seen Jules leave the cave Saturday night.

As it happened, Talies wanted to talk about something else.

"So—what do you know about blending wine?" Talies asked Kit as they sat down under the olive trees with their coffee mugs.

"Not much. Except that many of the wines people prefer are actually varietal blends. Champagnes. Chardonnays. Even Cabernets." Kit grinned. "Indie and I used to make a darned good kitchen-sink red after some of those Romano get-togethers."

"Well, I didn't know squat about blending before I started this job, but I'm learning. It's is a big piece of what Rachel does. It happens before they bottle, so she's into it now. Takes a good nose and a good palate, a bit of patience, and a bit of knowledge about how the individual varietals mature over time, she told me. Wine is magic in a bottle, Jules says. Winemakers make all sorts of blends.

Sometimes they even mimic the great wines of the past, although it's helpful to have an actual bottle for comparison rather than relying on tasting notes in some moldy cellar book. Then it came to me. That's what a wine library is for. Gotta get the chemistries right of course, watch the maceration and the ferment and stuff, watch like the proverbial hawk, manage the oxygen, manage the sugar, manage time spent on the lees, et cetera, et cetera. But a good wine library is key to making a good blend. And guess what Buckthorn has?"

"A good wine library?"

"Yep!"

"Where are you going with this, Tal? Blending is commonplace. It's part of the reason people hire consultants."

"True, but not like this." Talies lowered his coffee mug and leaned across the picnic table as if about to reveal a deep conspiracy. "I found some really interesting labels hidden back in Rachel's lab. And some stamped corks, and foils too. I got to thinking. So I went into Buckthorn's inventory database and did some calculations. Actually it took me a while. I lost precious sleep in the process, but I'm pretty sure—not only does Buckthorn sell more cases of wine than it produces, but also they've been selling wines nobody makes anymore—like that 1973 Montelena Chardonnay. The one they made the film about. You know—the blind tasting in France."

"How is that possible?" asked Kit.

"Well, it is, and it isn't."

"Are we talking wine fraud here?"

Talies nodded slowly. "Yessir. Right here in River City, sir. And I think Rachel, with her talented palate, is the perp. Or one of the perps. If she has help, my money would be on Indie's father— good old Jack. He has no ethics to speak of. And I now know for sure that he sold more cases of last year's Estate Reserve on his New York trip than Buckthorn actually bottled."

"Sounds like magic to me."

"Don't be upset, sir, but there is no such thing as magic," said Talies seriously. "That's the main thing I learned over the past year as I worked up my party tricks."

"I'm not upset. And I did know that about magic. I simply

haven't always understood how the apparent magic works."

"How about I go get my computer and meet you in the tank house in half an hour. Or should I wait until Mom gets back?"

Kit did not want to wait. He and Talies spent the next few hours head to head over Talies' laptop, as two big fans roared behind them, keeping them cool. Kit was not at first certain what to make of the information Talies had developed. To what extent was what happened, fraud? To what extent was Buckthorn pushing the limits of integrity by blending estate grown grapes with non-estate grown grapes in order to turn a profit? And who besides Rachel knew what was going on? Who even cared? Jules surely did. But Eddie? Or Dennis? Anyone? And, then, how did this scheme relate to the series of so-called accidents that all seemed to focus on Jules? And did it relate to the disappearance of Jules, or Bailey? Could wine fraud provide a motive for murder? Kit felt pleased about his placing Talies in the winery. He had to admit, Talies had accomplished something he himself would never have thought to attempt. Even if it had entered his mind, which it hadn't. He realized suddenly that he'd heard so much about the integrity of Buckthorn's wines over the years, that to look for signs of fraud would seem like madness. But there it was. What else had he missed?

He wanted to tell Morgan about it, but he didn't want to talk about wine fraud over the phone, much less use a text messenger. He'd wait. See what else he could learn in the meantime. He had so many questions. After Talies returned to work in the winery, Kit headed for the Big House to see if he could find some answers.

When he arrived, he found only Sam, sitting at the kitchen table, polishing off a bowl of vegetable soup. He poured himself another coffee and sat down across from her. She looked up.

"I heard that you'll be taking an enology course next year at the high school," he began.

She nodded sagely and went on eating.

"What other courses?"

"Art, American history, pre-calc, programming, and either Italian or French."

"Which interests you most?"

"Enology."

The look she gave him as she answered his questions made Kit feel stupid, but he persisted, in deliberately dumb and dumber mode. He was seeking a perch from which to make real conversation. "Do you play any sports? Soccer?"

Sam shook her head, kept her eyes on her food. "I hate sports."

"Do you think it would that be okay if I made myself a sandwich?" he asked, giving up and getting up.

Samantha shrugged. "Fine with me." She watched him assemble his sandwich—toast the bread, spread the mayo, slice some ham off the bone, try to locate the mustard.

"Behind the milk," Sam said, after Kit had removed a dozen bottles and jars, unstacked a leaning tower of plastic containers, and knocked over a sippy cup of red juice. "Uncle Bowie flew up to the camp this morning," she volunteered. "Aunt Indie thought Grandpa and Bailey might be there. Mom wanted to go along, but Uncle Bowie wouldn't let her—she gets sick on small planes. He called when he was done, said he didn't see anyone. Said the road's closed, or something—being paved, or something. He didn't think anybody could have driven in. Do you know where my grandpa is? Or Bailey?"

"No, I don't," said Kit, surprised by Sam's sudden volubility. He took a large bite of his sandwich.

"Do you think they're okay?"

Kit said he didn't know and took another bite of sandwich. "Tell me about this place on Berryessa. Have you been there? What's it like?"

"It's nice. I like it. There's a little beach and a dock. I swim sometimes. Grandpa fishes. Last time we dug around and took soil samples. I guess he's planning a new vineyard, though it'd be pretty hard to get to. There are mountain lions around there, Grandpa says. That's why he won't let Whiskey come along. He always takes his rifle. Have you never been there?"

"Indie says I have, but I don't remember it. Is there a cabin? Running water? Flush toilets?"

"Oh, sure. It's a nice place. Got an outdoor shower and stuff. Kitchen's rough. The generator gets cranky sometimes. Grandpa refuses to put in Wi-Fi. My phone's spotty. Worse than here. It's okay though. I read books. Grandpa and Gramma go there when it gets too hot here. I hate all the motor boats on the reservoir. But most don't get as far north as the cabin. I guess the lake's down a lot since the drought. We weren't supposed to flush the toilets very often, last time." She grinned, and stopped talking.

"Oh please, go on," said Kit. "I'm interested. And it's nice hearing what you have to say. You were such a little thing last time I saw you."

Sam gave him a withering look.

Indie came into the kitchen from the flagstone piazza. "Do you know where your Uncle Jack's gotten to?" she asked Sam. "I haven't seen him since yesterday, and he doesn't answer his phone." She acknowledged Kit's presence. "I'm wondering if Dad has Bailey with him. Have either of you heard from Jack?"

Kit literally threw his hands into the air. "I cannot keep track of this family! Like, for example, where have you been since you rushed off this morning?"

"Me? With Julie. Keeping busy. She wants to open her new tasting room before Labor Day. She and Rachel are choosing the wines." She paused, snickering. "Rachel wouldn't let her put out anything Andrew Frye called 'plonk'. He really rocked her self-confidence. And by the way, Bowie did fly over Berryessa. Did you hear what he saw?"

"Actually, Sam told me—nothing!"

"See? You do know things. Aunt Rickie's getting more and more worried, and she seems very angry about something too. Maybe it's the cops. They told her to be patient, and she told them Uncle Jules doesn't have his pills. Shit. I wish this weren't happening." Indie sat down at the table, laid her head on her arms, and turned on the tears. Sam reached over and patted Indie's arm.

"They'll find them, Aunt Indie," Sam said. "Don't cry. Come on, let's go find Mom."

Kit watched them walk out to the garden, where Tinker and Desidera, both in wide-brimmed straw hats, were busy among the tomato plants. Tinker was bringing in the harvest. Desidera was "helping" as only a three-year-old can help, which means she was eating cherry tomatoes.

Out beyond the garden, bees buzzed around their hives,

which still had not been moved. The summer sun beat down. Grapes ripened. Kit sat quietly and thought. Finally he got up and carried his empty plate and Sam's empty soup bowl to the sink and ran water on them.

Somewhere a phone was ringing. It rang and rang and rang. Only gradually did he recognize the ring as his own. He answered it. "No . . . Okay. I'll be there."

18 TWO OLD WOMEN

Morgan dropped Talies's hatchback at a service station in Healdsburg. That was where Kit picked her up. As they drove back to Buckthorn, they brought each other up to date. Kit told her the police had finally taken the disappearance of both Jules and Bailey seriously, but there was no news yet regarding their whereabouts. He described Talies' discovery of possible wine fraud, but did not mention his meet-ups with Indie, or his fruitless re-exploration of the mine tunnels. Morgan summarized the results of her research— the quilt of real estate transactions in the valley, the Nineteenth Century map of area mines, and Naeve's failed effort to locate any evidence that Jules had recently changed his trust, adding that this lack of evidence was inconclusive since state databases could take months to update. They speculated how these discoveries might fit together, but drew no conclusions.

By this time they'd finished, they were back at Buckthorn. Kit pulled up outside Irene's place and they sat quietly in the vehicle for a few minutes, watching Eddie's twins busy with buckets and shovels in the dirt under the old apple tree. The yard was still a tumble of rusting tools and broken toys and overgrown flower beds, although the plastic play gym looked a little less lopsided. The twins chirped and chattered like fledgling birds. Suddenly they jumped up, flapped their wings, and ran, giggling, through the open gate and across the road towards Julie and Dennis's place.

"Hey! Wild children! Where do you think you're going?" shouted Irene from the porch swing. The twins ignored her, chasing one another around the corner of their aunt's house. A screen door slammed. The laughter faded. Irene returned to her knitting.

Morgan climbed out of Kit's large vehicle and pushed open the unlatched gate. "Good morning, Irene," she said looking up at her.

"Good morning," echoed Kit following her through the gate.

Morgan smiled broadly at the old lady as they went up the front steps. Today she was wearing a dark red bibbed apron over her long black dress, and had pinned her grey hair into a messy knot on top of her head. A pair of reading glasses hung around Irene's neck on a cord. Her feet, in sturdy tie shoes, rested on a low wooden stool in front of the swing. She pushed herself slowly back and forth, as she nodded to them and used her knitting needle to indicate where she wanted them to sit. Irene's expression was stern, her mouth as straight and thin as a ruled line. She looked neither happy nor unhappy to see them. Kit opened with some small talk, to loosen her up, but Irene refused to play. Her answers were cryptic. She didn't like gossip, she said. She preferred silence, or simple direct statements. When Kit asked for her thoughts on Jules' disappearance, she said only, "I told you what I think about those kinds of things. What more do you want?"

Next, Morgan had a go. "It was really my idea to stop here this morning, Irene," she said. "I was hoping for a cup of tea. I was hoping we might get to know one another a little better."

"All right. I'll get you some tea. But before I do, tell me why you're really here."

Morgan nodded. "Point taken," she said. "Well, you've lived at Buckthorn your whole life, haven't you?"

"Mmm," said the old lady, rocking slowly back and forth and continuing to knit. Suddenly, she took both needles into one hand and with the other lifted up her glasses and laid them on the middle of her nose. Kit and Morgan watched in silence as she counted the stitches in her last row, glanced across the road to see if the children had reappeared (they had not), and completed a complex dance movement with both knitting needles. When she returned to her straight knit one purl one pattern, Irene gave a well-practiced wiggle to her nose, which dropped her glasses back onto her chest.

Then she looked up at them as if to say she was ready to resume their conversation.

Morgan would have liked to ask what she was knitting, but instead said, "You must know Jules and Rickie pretty well."

"Of course I do. What are you getting at?"

"Well, Kit did tell me what you thought about several of these so-called accidents. But there have been more than just those few. So I've been wondering how the whole series strikes you. Do you find it unusual? Or do these sorts of accident happen to Jules all the time? Jules does always seem to be the target."

Irene was knitting rapidly, but her eyes had locked onto Morgan's. "Hard to say. I mind my own business." She paused, watched the twins race back across the road, laughing at something as they returned to their dirt pile. Her needles clicked. Morgan and Kit waited. "Jules never had a van jump a curb at him before. His asthma seems worse. And the accidents have become more frequent. There have always been accidents, of course, but Jules hasn't always seemed like the target. The large volume of spilled wine this year seems a bit unusual. Is that the kind of thing you're asking about?"

"Yes," said Morgan. "Thank you."

More silence. More clicking. More thinking.

Finally Kit asked, "Did you locate that old agreement, by the way?"

Irene shrugged. "I looked for it. Someone removed it from my desk."

"Who?" Morgan couldn't help herself.

"I'd say if I knew."

"Are you certain it was in your desk? Jules told us it was a verbal promise. Are you sure a document exists?" he said. "Memories, even seemingly clear ones, can morph into something quite different from what really happened. You must be aware of that."

The look Irene shot him could have been the spear of a Masai warrior aimed at the heart of a lion on the veldt. "It exists," she said.

On instinct Morgan shifted a micro-unit to the left to avoid being hit by another figurative spear as she asked, "And what exactly did this agreement say?"

More silence. More knitting. More thinking.

"Simply that if my Eduardo died while doing his duty, that his brother Jules would deed half of Buckthorn to me, our child, and our descendants."

"And how did you get hold of this agreement?"

"Eduardo sent it to me, of course. After I wrote him about the baby. He said he and his brother had signed in blood. You probably think this is an exaggeration, but there were dark fingerprints on the paper and the signatures were smeared. My Eduardo was most concerned about our welfare."

"So was this agreement in a letter? Or with a letter? I'd love to see it."

"I haven't looked at Eduardo's letters in years. They're mostly in a box in the attic—eaten by mice. However I distinctly remember putting the one with the agreement in it into my desk. It was on blue paper. Jack has probably 'organized' it into some box. He 'organizes' everything around here. Usually that means he throws things away. Or good as. When he's done organizing, I can't find a thing."

Irene lifted her glasses onto her nose again and made that dancing movement with her knitting needles again.

"I thought . . ." Morgan stopped herself, and took a minute or two to consider her words. It made no sense that Jack would simply throw out a document that gave him half of Buckthorn. What was the possibility that Irene herself had "exaggerated" that agreement into physical existence? She began again. "You have a free ninety-nine year lease on this house, don't you? Same as Jack's cottage? And his vineyard?"

"That was my father-in-law's doing. I'm ninety-two years old. What happens in seven years? Jack and I will be put out on the street, that's what. Leased property is not the same as owned property, young lady." She glanced at the twins. "Children! Stop throwing dirt. Now!"

"Is that what worries you?" asked Morgan. "Losing your home when you turn ninety-nine?"

Irene shot another spear across the veldt. Morgan ducked.

"How would you feel?," said Irene. "If your brother-in-law

reneged on a promise? Jules is head of this family. He has responsibility. My son agrees. So do my grandchildren. So does everyone. I'm old fashioned, young woman. I believe honorable men keep promises."

"But Jules was so young when this one was made . . . ten years old? thirteen?"

"Age is irrelevant. Children must learn to keep promises too. Otherwise we're not civilized. Now, I promised you tea."

"Oh, that's all right. Don't bother yourself. We're fine, aren't we Kit? And we do need to be going."

Irene however would hear none of this. She lay her knitting aside and rose slowly to her feet. "Please keep an eye on the children for me," she said before turning towards the door. "I'll be back in ten minutes with the tray."

"May I help you?" said Morgan starting to rise.

"No. You are guests." Her tone brooked no argument.

While she had gone, Morgan and Kit simply sat quietly and watched the children, who were back once more to digging and chirping and chattering like bird babies. "I thought she would be different," Morgan whispered to Kit after a while. "Less talkative."

Irene pushed open the screen door and wheeled out a small serving cart on which sat a pot of tea, a bowl of sugar substitute, a small milk pitcher in the shape of a cow, and three unmatched tea cups, three spoons, no saucers. She poured tea into the cups, and handed one to Morgan and one to Kit. Then she picked up the remaining cup and stood before them to say, "My nephew Eduardo needs a wife. I lie awake nights worrying about those motherless children—the twins especially, and young Zoe. I would appreciate your help solving this problem, which I do think important." She looked Kit in the eye.

He frowned.

"Yes, I'm talking to you," she continued. "Now that you and my granddaughter are no longer married, I'd like you to release her to young Eduardo. I believe they will get along well, and your son Bailey will have a full-time father for a change. In return for your help, after they have married, I will consider Jules' promise fulfilled, since my granddaughter and his son will share equally in ownership of Buckthorn upon Jules' death. I've spoken to Jules and Jack about this. They agree. Don't say anything now. Just drink your tea and think on it. This marriage would be good for the family. None of us is getting younger."

Kit stared at her in disbelief, while Morgan worked to stifle her giggles. Unfazed, Irene turned towards Morgan and said, "I expect you to use whatever influence you have with this man to make it happen. And thank you both for coming to see me." Then, without another word, Irene drank down her tepid tea, placed her empty cup on the serving cart, returned to her swing seat, and took up her needles. She glanced at the twins to make sure they were safe. Clearly, as far as Irene was concerned, both the visit and the discussion were over.

Kit heaved a great sigh as they closed the front gate and climbed back into his vehicle. "I don't know where to begin."

"Well, I liked her. But is she mad?" said Morgan.

"Yes, and no."

Morgan finally released her giggles. "Poor old you," she spluttered. "You should have seen the look on your face when she asked you to 'release Indie'! It was like . . . like . . . like nothing I've ever seen before. Or maybe that's how you'd look if the wicked old witch suddenly turned into a brown toad, right before your eyes. Abracadabra! Poof!" She laughed again. "Oh, Kit. Where is your sense of humor? Don't frown so!"

"I don't think it's all that funny," Kit pouted. "Imagine me trying to convince Indie to do anything." He however did allow himself a small smile. "We learned nothing from her, did we? I mean nothing. At least, I didn't. And she certainly said nothing that might help us find either Bailey or Jules."

"Oh, but Irene did help. One just needs to put what she said into context."

Kit stopped the car abruptly and turned towards her. "And how exactly do we do that?"

"Well, you drive, and I'll explain. It's complicated, and there are still some missing pieces. I'll need to talk with Rickie though."

Kit nodded and began to drive slowly down the road towards the Big House, and Morgan told him as quickly as she could what she'd found in Jules' cellar books—not only tasting notes, but also a duplicate set of books recording how much wine Buckthorn produced and how much was sold and how Jules had balanced these accounts with a third column of figures reflecting wine dumped—or spilled. The records went back to when Rachel joined the winery, and they seemed to confirm what Talies had discovered. They also confirmed that despite appearances Jules was keeping closely tracking not only Rachel's activities, but also the activities of all the Romanos involved with winery operations. The cellar books provided motive for blackmail, if not murder.

Kit stopped again and turned towards Morgan. He told her about Talies' ugly suggestion that Rachel had been attempting to make a wine that would pass for the '73 Montelena Chardonnay, a wine now selling for over ten grand a bottle, what few bottles there were left. He did not know whether or not Rachel had succeeded in imitating that blend. Nor whether she, or anyone from Buckthorn, had ever tried to sell a fraudulent bottle. They discussed this, agreeing in the end neither of them knew what Rachel was planning to do, or who else might be involved. Morgan's mind jumped to the wallet of cash she'd found hidden in Jules' desk, then to Indie's announcement regarding the disappearance of a great deal of money from the Buckthorn accounts.

And none of this could explain the disappearance of Bailey. Or why Jules would leave those cellar books lying out in plain sight? What exactly had Jules been up to? Then they arrived almost simultaneously at the notion that since Jules went missing, there had been no more threatening accidents at Buckthorn.

"It's as if the show was suddenly somehow cancelled," suggested Morgan.

Then an idea surfaced.

"I see what's been bothering me," she said quietly, half to herself and half to Kit. "Those threats may have been diversionary, distractions from something more important. So many of them, coming so fast upon each other, one doesn't have time to take them in, to get a bigger picture."

Finally Kit started driving again, and as they drew up in front of the Big House, Morgan turned to him and remarked. "It's like a magic show, isn't it? Things aren't what they seem at first, but there's no time to think about what just happened, because something else happens immediately. One loses focus. One's attention is forced to jump around. And yet, each trick has to have been set up ahead of time, and the audience must be invited in to see the show. Very clever!"

"You may be right, but I can't focus on what you're saying. The important thing now is to find Bailey," Kit said. "Forget about wine fraud. Forget about what Jules thinks he's doing. Forget about where Jules is! Forget about who owns which vineyard. Forget about what Rickie knows, or doesn't know, or Rachel or Jack or Indie or any of them. What's important is Bailey. I've got to find him."

"I know. Find Bailey," agreed Morgan.

"And I don't even know where to start!" Kit groaned.

"Well, it may seem strange, but I was rather hoping Bailey would find us," remarked Morgan gently.

"What do you mean?! What if . . . I can't bear to think about might have happened to him."

As they climbed out in front of the Big House, Kit was so upset, he nearly cried. Strung out on emotion and completely out of ideas, he stood there, staring woefully at Morgan. Simultaneously, they became aware of a pair of voices approaching through the leafy rows of the ripening vineyard. "Jack's back at any rate," Kit whispered as they sank into a crouch behind the big SUV.

"I can't see. Is that Indie with him?" whispered Morgan. "Can you hear what they're arguing about? Something about Bailey?"

Jack and Indie were indeed arguing, but there was no mention of Bailey.

"I don't trust her, Dad," Indie was saying. "He swore to me she'd never do anything like that. You know she's got an agenda."

"Are they talking about Rachel?" whispered Morgan.

"Shh," hissed Kit.

"She's got power, Dad. Remember the time she deliberately destroyed our new cultivator for steep slope vineyards?"

Kit nodded silently. He clearly remembered that cultivator business. It had happened shortly after Rachel had taken up with a bunch of crazy environmental activists.

"Uncle Jules knew about it too, and he just let it happen. He let her get away with it," Indie continued.

"Are you saying he deserves what happened to him? I liked your first idea better, my dear daughter. Tinker's a friggin' busy body. You know how she gets. And Julie's not the brightest light in the firmament either."

Unfortunately that was all Kit and Morgan would hear of this conversation, for the pair turned at the end of the row and headed back the way they had come. Their words faded into an unintelligible static, leaving only the sounds of buzzing insects, wind in the olive trees, and grinding machines in the distance.

"Was that Rachel they were talking about?" Morgan said as they stood up.

"Possibly. Although it was one of Roberto's crew who actually flipped that cultivator. A bad scene."

Morgan's face puckered with frustration. "Yeah. That's exactly what my problem is with this business—too many possibilities, so much we don't know. But I want to ask Rickie a few questions. Would you like to come in with me? Or go work out how we find Bailey?"

Kit opted to follow Morgan into the Big House.

Rickie was upstairs, alone in the hallway, in an old cane-seat chair rocking her body slowly back and forth, frowning as she stared out the window towards Poison Oak. She looked tired, defeated, old.

"Oh, hello," she said, turning as they came up the stairs. Then, in an unsuccessful effort at brightness, she added, "Any news of Jules yet? Or the boy? He had no right, you know. Makes me very angry!"

"No. No news yet. I'm sorry to say," replied Morgan evenly. "We just stopped by to ask you a few questions. Would that be okay?"

"Of course."

Morgan got right to the point. "This promise business—to split Buckthorn between the two families. Why now? What's your take on why it's become such an issue, now?"

Rickie sighed, and shook her head. "Irene can be such a nag. You know once, ten, twenty years ago, Jules tried to make right by her. He tried to find his father's map of the original holdings, as they stood after the war. You know, before his brother went off to Korea, when she claims Jules made that promise. Nearly three quarters of a century ago! She makes me so angry. She doesn't know how to let go. No luck finding Big Eddie's map though. He even went down to the County. No luck there either. Someone told him all those old maps were long gone—lost in the flood of '86, I think it was. A foolish errand anyway. He tried to tell her that she and Jack had already received their shares of Buckthorn—their homes, that vineyard. But she wouldn't buy it. She wanted half of what he and I had built—Buckthorn as it is, not as it was. So he stopped trying to make her happy. Told me once, he doesn't in fact remember ever making that promise anyway. Never signed anything 'in blood'. Although if you asked me, that part sounds like something a boy would do." She stopped rocking and looked first Morgan in the eye, then Kit. "She probably made the whole thing up years ago. That's what I think. I don't know what got her started. But she's told that story so many times, she's come to believe her own lies. Her whole family believes her too. So does Jules for that matter. He tells me—just because he doesn't remember, doesn't mean it didn't happen." She looked out the window again, and began rocking her body back and forth again.

"There are some things that happened in the past that no one can fix," Rickie continued. "Not ever! I get so tired of it. Were you aware that Jules changed the wording of his father's original grant to them, just to satisfy her? She couldn't get it through her brain that a ninety-nine year lease was plenty long enough. She kept saying she'd be thrown out of her house if she lived ninety-nine years, which isn't how it works. Anyway, now both she, and Jack too, have lifetime grants of their properties. Makes no difference to Irene, or Jack. Just an excuse to go on and on about how dishonorable Jules is. How unfair he's been to them. It does get under his skin. It grinds on him. He's obsessed by it. There'll be trouble in the end. He'll do something. He does love Buckthorn though. It's his life! Who would have imagined that what we built would come to this? That crazy old woman is going to break his heart! She needs to let go!"

Rickie paused. Kit and Morgan didn't move, sensing she had more to say. "Jack is another kettle of fish entirely. Jules worries that he'll up and sell off anything he owns, to some developer or one of those German beer producers. He's too fond of money. Jules doesn't trust poor Tinker either, or Phil, for that matter. Phil doesn't want to run a winery, he just wants to design things, build things. And Tinker? Well, my poor Tinker—one day that switch in her brain will simply stay flipped forever. She'll become completely manic and give away whatever she owns. She's very sweet, but you can't trust her. Anyway, she and Phil don't care about farming grapes, or making wine. Not really. He's right about that, my husband is. He used to talk about deed restrictions. You know—to stop inconsistent development, to keep the vineyards always vineyards. La-La-La! I haven't heard much about that lately." She shook her head and rocked some more. "Past mistakes. Money. People. The world is mad, you know. It's all Jules thinks about anymore. Something he calls Honor. Integrity. Well, you can't take any of it with you in the end, I say." She harrumphed and rocked on. Minutes passed.

"So what are Uncle Jules' plans for Buckthorn," Kit said finally. "I mean, for after he's gone? He never got around to telling the family about how he intended to change the trust, did he? I've asked him, but can't get a straight answer. Surely Eddie and Julie are poised to inherit the family business, aren't they? They appear to be very interested in carrying on the tradition."

"Oh, I told Jules, go ahead and give them the vineyards and the winery. And give some of it to Jack too, if he wants it. And do something for Tinker of course. But stop making such a fuss! Stop trying to fix the past and control the future. Both of those are just like wine—they'll turn to vinegar when you least expect. Let your kids figure it out, I say to him. You can't control life from the grave. It's a waste of time and energy to try. But he won't listen to me. Oh, no. We argue about it, a lot. He has some very wrong-headed ideas in that old brain of his! He makes me so mad! Half the time I don't know what he's up to. And I don't want to know either! Neither of us has much time left on this earth!"

"How much do you think Buckthorn is worth . . . ballpark?" asked Morgan.

"Goodness! I don't know. We own more than a hundred and fifty acres down here on the valley floor, but the old fool has been on a buying spree for the past few years—hillsides, large parcels in a couple of different valleys, and then there's the old camp at the lake. I tell him it's quite mad to be buying land at our age. But he just smiles and smiles and does what he wants." Rickie stopped rocking. "As for how much this is all worth? I'd say millions—millions and millions. Way too much money. And that trust of his is more trouble than it's worth. Out of date for one thing. The whole family quarrels about it constantly, about final distributions, about various riders he thinks he needs. Everybody wants more and more and more. That's why Dennis and Eddie came to blows the other night, but you've probably figured that out. Eddie's got a terrible temper. Got it from me, I suppose. Still hasn't learned to control his. I control mine by simply closing off my ears."

"So what kinds of riders does he want?" asked Morgan.

"Can't remember. Everybody in this family has ideas. Even some who aren't in the family. And every one of them wants to have his or her own way, can't bear to think someone else would get more than they will. Madness!"

"Do you think any of them is behind Jules' disappearance?" asked Kit quickly.

"Oh, gracious no! Someone from the family? Someone we know? Not possible."

"Then, what do you think has happened to him?" asked Morgan.

"I thought I made myself clear. Nobody's kidnapped him. Why would anyone do that? This isn't the movies. This is just us. What worries me is that the old fool is lying somewhere, hurt or injured . . . or dead. He is eighty years old! And he's in worse shape than he lets on. Tinker has tried to get him to carry one of those emergency call button things, but he absolutely refuses. Chances are he'll turn up soon, with some damned story. But I don't really know, do I? Although the longer this goes on. . . . I did finally let Irene have her way, you know. Despite how she behaves, I think she cares about him. Eddie put in the report with the cops, and they sent out one of those alerts to the freeway signs. So now Jules has his name in lights," she added sourly. "Nothing's happened, though. Except the cops are proved right again—Jules isn't really missing."

"Are you aware," asked Morgan, "that there has been an offer to purchase Buckthorn?"

"Now where did you hear that piece of nonsense?" Fear and anger washed across Rickie's face.

"A friend of mine told me," said Morgan. "She's sort of in the business. There are some very large corporate buyers active in Wine Country at the moment. Several are making bids significantly over market value. We did a little homework, and I think the company after Buckthorn may be a limited liability company, quite possibly a front for a New Jersey billionaire rumored to use unethical methods. It struck us that might explain Jules' disappearance. You know, to put pressure on."

Rickie blanched. She seemed genuinely surprised. "Buckthorn? On the auction block? An outsider? A billionaire? Jules would certainly have said something to me, if he knew. Of course, we do hear of such things in the County. It's appalling. I realize Wine Country is changing; some folks treat winemaking like it's any other profit-making business—squeeze out all the money you can, then move on—as if it were an out-of-date textile mill, or a coal mine. I'm unwilling to believe that Jules would ever condone such an end for Buckthorn. Buckthorn is our life!"

"Sellers don't always have a choice," remarked Kit.

Morgan, who was now wondering how the revelation of a little wine fraud might play with such a buyer, asked, "So tell me, how much wine does Buckthorn actually produce per acre of vineyard."

Rickie seemed taken a-back. "Difficult to say. It depends."

"Depends on what?"

"On lots of things. How close together you plant rows. How many times you put your berries through the press. There are so many variables, including of course plain old weather."

"So, you're saying there's no easy equivalency—nothing like X number of acres yields Y number of cases of wine?"

"That's right. But I'm sure Rachel keeps excellent records. If you want to know, why not ask her?"

"I will," said Morgan.

"And there's also that other interesting variable," Rickie went on, warming to the subject. "Many wineries stretch their estate production by cutting it with juice from elsewhere —the Central Valley for example. There are rules for this here in Wine Country, although Buckthorn has immunity from several of the most restrictive ones—we've been around long enough to be 'grandfathered' under the law. You can imagine how the percentage of foreign juice in a blend might affect any calculation of an estate's annual production." She shook her head, smiling tightly.

"And let me say something else. Last year the boys, that is Ed, Dennis, Jack, and Jules too, quarreled endlessly on this very topic. They could not come to any agreement, other than agreeing to disagree. And I don't know where Buckthorn stands now. Remember, I did catch Jules buying up more vineyard—some of it outside our AVA. On the other hand, Dennis expostulates loudly that as long as a Buckthorn wine tastes like a Buckthorn wine, it doesn't matter where the grapes are grown—Timbuktu or right up there." She waggled a finger towards Poison Oak. "I try to stay out of it. But Jules? He gets exercised enough to have a heart attack!"

"Interesting," murmured Kit.

"Just let me say this," Rickie said, rolling her eyes across the vineyards outside. "This younger generation, and we, the older one, don't think the same way about many things. Dennis, Ed, Julie, and to some extent Jack, all believe strongly in maximizing profits. Jules gets livid when they talk like that. Not that he doesn't expect the winery to pay its own way, mind you, but it's different for him. We didn't have so many options when we were young, and running a winery can be a rocky ride. We took life more seriously than they do now, and in other ways, a lot less seriously. The winery has always been, however, our life. It's not the same for the younger generation." She turned again and looked both Morgan and Kit in the eye. "I don't know what Jules has gone and done this time. And I don't know where that old fool is hiding himself, or where your boy is either. I probably should, but I don't. And I don't like their disappearing like this."

"My boy?" said Kit, catching on her words. "You mean Bailey? You think Bailey is with Jules? Well now, that is interesting."

But Rickie wasn't listening to him. She had risen from her chair and was leaning out the window, staring. Her face had grown pale. Her mouth had fallen open. Her breathing became harsh. She looked as if she'd seen a ghost. A real ghost.

19 GHOSTS

Actually there were two ghosts. The taller was an old man wearing a ratty, wide-brimmed straw hat, rather like Tinker's garden hat. The other was a boy, in dire need of a haircut and fresh clothes. The boy was rubbing his glasses on his dirty shirt front as he followed the old man across the gravel.

A deep stillness filled that upstairs room as the two figures walked slowly towards the house. Recognition dawned among the watchers. A cold shiver ran down Morgan's spine. Her eyes widened. Her breath became shallow and ragged. She blinked to defeat her welling tears. Kit's face broke into a spectacular grin. He jumped up and yelled out the window. Rickie simply gasped, something rather crude, and reached for her cane. Then all three watchers moved rapidly down the front stairs, out the screen door, and onto the veranda.

As soon as he replaced his spectacles, Bailey too began moving, faster than anyone. He ran up the steps onto the veranda and straight into his father's giant bear hug, their intersection sent both crashing into a happy pile at the top of the front steps. Jules stopped below on the gravel, his eyes riveted on Rickie as she stomped her way across the veranda, stopping at the top of the steps, now made impassible thanks to the prone and babbling bodies of Kit and Bailey. The expression on her face passed rapidly between anger and joy and back to anger. With her free hand she smeared away a tear. "You damned old fool!" she shouted down at

Jules. "I thought you were dead in a ditch somewhere! I'll kill you myself if you ever do that again! And I mean it!"

Morgan found herself grinning so hard she had to hang onto the screen door, nearly pulling it off its hinges. For a moment all she could do was gawp.

Rickie quickly defaulted to her commander's voice. "Get up here. All of you. Right now! Get into the house!" She tapped Kit's shoulder with her cane, indicating he and Bailey should remove themselves from the steps to allow Jules space to climb. This turned out to be an awkward move as Bailey refused to let go of his father's neck. Finally, however, Rickie got a grip on her husband's elbow, turned him into the house, and marched everyone down the corridor to the kitchen, where she immediately began issuing another stream of instructions and commentary. "Sit. Don't talk. Eat. You look terrible! I don't want to know anything about what you've done until you're cleaned up!" She stomped around the kitchen loading the table with bowls and plates of food, glasses of water, juice. She plunked a large unlabeled bottle of red wine in front of Jules. "And stop looking so amused, you've been a fool! I mean it! And I am really, really mad!"

"Oh sit down, sit down, yourself," said Jules soothingly, patting the chair next to him. "Sit here, next to me. I need to tell you what I've gone and done." He looked as if he would burst with his news.

"Oh no you don't. You're the devil incarnate! You're not going to say anything about anything right now. You're going to eat first. Then you're going to sleep. And you look horrible! Filthy. What have the pair of you been up to. You look like Lazarus recently risen. You need a wash! What the devil happened to you? No. I didn't say that. Don't tell me anything, yet. Wash. Eat. Rest. Then you will tell me everything."

"It's only a bit of dust, *cara mia*. Nothing to worry about. Still, I s'pose we could use a bit of a wash. You sit down. Come on, boy, we need to go wash."

Rickie frowned, her eyes hardened as she glued them to her husband's figure, as if he were an illusion, as if he would disappear again if she shifted her gaze for a moment. Morgan had a vision of Rickie chaining Jules to his chair. Meanwhile Jules leaned towards his wife, who was by this point sitting on the proffered chair, and pressed her hand, smiled into her eyes, then poured and offered her a glass of wine. "I won't disappear again," he said, reading her mind. "I promise. Now come along, Bailey. Loosen that grip on your dad. Let's get at least the top layer of dirt off." Jules helped Bailey off his father's lap; then, hand in hand, the two "ghosts" made their way down the hall towards a hot shower for each.

"Well!" said Morgan turning to Kit, who was staring after them. "Can't wait to hear this story. I wonder how much of it we got right."

"I'll call the others—let them know he's back," said Kit suddenly all business. "And the sheriff's office as well."

Rickie remained in her seat, silent, frowning, unmoved, lost in thought.

Dusk had fallen by the time everyone was assembled at the long table out under the arbor to listen to Jules' tale of adventure. Once again the fairy lights were twinkling, although this time with no strange message. Bailey had quickly wearied of the attention—the hugs, kisses, the greetings, the expressions of wonder and delight—and had slipped away to join the other kids on the back veranda, where Zoe was displaying Fred's new puppies in her doll buggy. The puppies, excited by their buggy ride, kept scrambling up and dropping over the sides, hitting the floor with surprised squeaks. Recovering from their falls, they scattered hither and yon, while Fred and the delighted children worked to gather them back together. Bailey had already begged permission to keep one of the puppies, and was now trying to decide which tumbling ball of fur his parents would be least able to resist.

Morgan pulled her eyes back to the drama unfolding at the table under the arbor. Kit, his hands steepled under his chin, was sitting next to her. On his other side sat Indie. And across from them, Jules and Rickie. All around sat or stood most of the other Romanos, eager to hear the story. Indeed, River and Paul had jumped into their car as soon as they received Kit's phone call. Even the Southern California contingent was present—virtually— thanks to Cody and Talies who had opened a video link on someone's laptop. Bowie had already promised to fly any of the

Los Angeles based family up to Buckthorn the following weekend. Jack had walked Irene down the road that afternoon, while Jules was napping. And most of Buckthorn's staff had turned up too, including Rachel and the majority of the cellar rats. Roberto, Jorge, and the vineyard team had filed in ten minutes ago. Even Ev and Lizzy Wolf had come by—bearing a huge mess of strawberries, a sheet cake, and a flagon of lemonade.

"I am flattered," said Jules, his eyes roaming their faces. "So many of you to hear my sordid little tale."

"Estamos contentos de que estés bien, Patrón," said Roberto.

"*Muchas gracias, mis amigos.* I do feel well. And I am sorry for the trouble and worry I caused."

"They're pleased you are home again, dear," said Rickie, patting her husband's hand. She glanced towards her grandchildren and the puppies, and added, almost as an afterthought, "Bailey too."

"How'd you manage to get over to the camp, Dad? You didn't take the truck," said Eddie. "Bowie looped around in his plane on Monday, on his way back to LA. He said the place looked deserted. The road was closed."

"Well, that's probably true, when he flew over. I confess. Ev was my co-conspirator for much of this." He tossed a sheepish grin at his long-time friend. "He dropped me off in the dark of night. And on Sunday he brought the boy over! That was something of a surprise! Good thing that old Corolla, the one I keep at the camp, was still running. The boy and I left early on Monday, before they closed Steele Canyon Road for the paving. We went to Sacramento. Spent a couple of days up there, doing business mostly. When we got back, the road was closed off. Thank heaven for boats."

"But why the secrecy? Ev knew we were looking for you, and for Bailey too, but he pretended he didn't know where you were," put in Kit. "I don't get it."

"Yeah, Dad. You up and disappear in the middle of the night? What were you thinking?" added Julie.

"And you didn't even tell Mom . . . or me!" Tinker's tone was distinctly accusatory.

"You kidnapped Bailey!!" said Indie in disbelief. "Why??"

Jules flinched. Rickie looked grim. He patted her hand. "It's complicated," he said, shaking his head sadly.

Morgan leaned forward. "So why not tell them? Did you accomplish everything you wanted to?"

Jules winked at her, then turned to his family. He looked uncomfortable, but not apologetic. He harrumphed. "I didn't need any more butting in. I knew what I had to do. Although I didn't reckon on the boy. Luckily he wasn't any trouble. He nearly finished The Three Musketeers while waiting around for me."

"And what have you done, Dad?" Julie visibly bracing herself.

"We're more than ready, Dad," added Eddie.

"It's a long story."

Murmurs rose around the table, then quickly subsided into silence, everyone expecting the worst.

"I am eighty years old," he began, "I've been feeling my age, more than you know. It's time to settle the future for Buckthorn. But then, you are all aware of that." He gazed around the table, his eyes lingering on each of his children in turn; then he looked at Jack and Irene and Indie and finally at Roberto and Rachel and Ev and Lizzy. Finally his gaze came to rest on Rickie's face. Her expression was wary. The little muscles around her mouth quivered slightly.

The old man spoke slowly, with many long pauses. He seemed exhausted, although at the same time cheerful, if not proud of himself. He straightened his back, raised his chin defiantly, and told them about the doctor visits. The family had been more or less aware of these visits, and the tests, although Jules had been quite cryptic about results, even with Rickie. "I wanted to be sure," he said. "To decide for myself what I wanted to do about the cancer, how long I had. I still feel well, but my stamina's begun to decline. There are treatments, even when the disease is as advanced as mine." Ignoring their gasps and groans, he carried through bravely. "Perhaps if I were forty again," he said, "but I'm not. And my systems seem to all breaking down at once. Treatment would likely kill me, possibly sooner than the disease. I don't want to linger, a wreck and a burden." He shrugged and rolled his eyes, then asked them to be quiet until he got through everything. Irene harrumphed loudly. Rickie scowled, murmuring something unsympathetic.

"So I needed to resolve a few matters, before I could take it easy like the doctors said I should. You all know what I'm talking about—Buckthorn. Now, I've listened to what each of you has had to say, but, in the end, Buckthorn's my job. My last job. Perhaps my most important job. I have no intention of leaving my family in a state of war over it." He turned his eyes pointedly towards the Eddie's still swollen, slightly green cheek. Then he frowned at both Dennis and Jack. "It's an understatement to say your quarreling doesn't make me happy. Look no further than yourselves to understand why I decided to keep what I was doing a secret. Do remember I built Buckthorn and I still own it. And I am not dead yet!" His expression turned icy. Rickie remained silent, but she looked explosive. Morgan shivered. Had Jules put Buckthorn on the auction block?

Jules spent nearly an hour talking. First, he explained how he had placed deed restrictions on all of Buckthorn's valley acres, and purchase options on the few remaining vineyards he did not own. A couple of quiet cheers went up. Next he told them how he had resolved Irene's anxiety about outliving her 99-year lease by simply making her the owner of her house and of Jack's, and, with no apology at all, he rejected any further discussion or nagging about that long ago promise to his dead brother, a promise his lawyer claimed could have no standing in court. He looked straight at Irene when he said this. Her face fell several millimeters as she took in defeat.

He went on: "I loved and admired my brother, but we were very different people. Indeed, had my brother lived, I doubt I would have made a good a team for Buckthorn. Hi might have made a good manager, but I would have done something else with my life. When I was a boy, I dreamed of building rockets. I dreamed about going to the moon! But my father grew grapes and made wine, and when the time came, that seemed like the only reasonable choice for me too."

"I didn't know that, Dad," said Eddie.

"Well, there's a lot you don't know. Don't ever assume. That's a pretty good rule to live by."

Morgan watched Jules watching his son, and his other children. She could only guess what was passing through his mind.

After that, Jules began by describing various real estate

dealings. Then he said, "You may be surprised to learn I considered putting Buckthorn Estate on the auction block too."

Morgan leaned a fraction of an inch forward, while the eyes of several around that table grew wide with horror, or a measure of delight. Jules himself chuckled, although without amusement. "Yes, I considered it—I seriously considered it. But in the end, I didn't. So relax, everyone. I opted for deed restrictions instead, including, by the way, on Jack's Mustard Seed vineyard and on Poison Oak, and Tinker and Phil's spread up there on the ridge—that view is worth preserving. I made allowances for construction of several more family homes and outbuildings, but no castles, no sprawling subdivisions, no resorts, no spas, no big tourist attractions, and, except for a few modest tasting rooms, no retail either. These restrictions go forever, so don't try to be clever and challenge them. You'll just waste your money. Rickie and I have discussed doing these restrictions for years. And it turns out, I'm pretty good at real estate speculation. Last week, I closed a substantial deal with a gold reclamation company in Montana that wanted the Berryessa camp. Indeed, most of the land I've bought over the last few years has now been sold. Profits were good."

With his eyes resting on Rachel, he went on. "I know your feelings, my dear. How could I not? Gold mine tailings are hazardous. But be assured, I did my best with the lawyers to ensure their operation won't pollute our watersheds, lakes, or land—at least not too badly. And the new owner's application has already been approved by the State, so don't waste your time trying to stop something you can do nothing about."

Rachel's face grew red. She spluttered something, rose to her feet, and began to move away. Eddie caught her arm as she stepped around him. Hissing something in her ear, he held her in place to hear for the rest of what Jules had to say.

"You may or may not be aware that by restricting future development on Buckthorn Estate," Jules said, "I have also limited its monetary value. That's one reason I did it, of course. But I also needed a source of cash. Hence my land speculation career. I wanted the money to fund some college tuitions for the next generation of Romanos. My grandchildren will have options besides making wine."

As his listeners took this in, he paused, reached for the pitcher, and poured himself a glass of wine. He sat for a few minutes silently swirling, sniffing, and sipping. Finally, he looked up. "You're probably asking yourselves right now—so what happens to Buckthorn when the old man dies? Who'll get the family business? Well, I do feel a bit like a magician here." He winked at Talies. "Thank you for a useful idea, young man. You suggested how I might saw this lady into pieces, and still keep her whole! So here's the way it will go—Julie, Eddie, Tinker, and Jack will each receive about one quarter of the Buckthorn vineyards along with a quarter share in the winemaking operation. I realize that's less than some of you hoped for, and, Dennis, you'll have to share with your wife. It should be enough so each of you can have your own operation. That's about all the vineyard my dad started with in the Central Valley, and it's more than three times the size of our family's vineyard in Tuscany. Bigger isn't better!"

"Is he mad?" whispered Dennis to Julie.

With a glance at them, Jules continued. "And don't forget, when my parents arrived here they had to tear out the walnuts, and the prune trees, and the buckthorn. You won't have to do that. The four of you are also free to decide among yourselves how, or even whether, you want to work together. Like I said, you can start separate boutique operations, or you can form a cooperative, or even sell your share to one of the other three." He looked directly at Tinker as he said this. "Whatever arrangement you want. You may even choose to raise olives. Or flowers. Or simply watch the birds. I no longer care. I don't want to be involved. But remember, your deed has certain restrictions, so you'd better read them. Oh, and in addition to this, I plan to divide the bulk of the money from my recent land sales equally among the four of you too. But not all of it. I'm no Lear. Your mother and I will be supporting ourselves, and there are those tuitions to pay. I had the vineyards surveyed this past spring. We can look at the maps together, although I reserve the final say about who gets what. I aim to finalize these distributions over the next few weeks."

Jules rested his eyes for a moment on Rickie, whose expression was now under tight control. He squeezed her hand. "The Big House and its immediate environs will stay with me *e mia cara Ricarda* for the time being. In other words, we're not going to live with any one of you, or make a load of trouble. Who knows what the future will bring. Perhaps I'll ask Phil here to build us a new, smaller house. Which is another reason I will need a bit of ready cash."

Jules cast his eyes around his family and friends, nodding and smiling at some, shaking his head or frowning at others. He even lifted his eyebrow once or twice, to acknowledge a response. He looked, Morgan thought, very pleased with himself. The rest of his family, however—with the exception of Tinker who had begun to cry—remained inscrutable as they each considered their options, or whispered among themselves. Jack grinned broadly. Dennis frowned. Jules topped up his wine glass and offered to refill Rickie's.

After several minutes he started to speak once more. "I'm sure I haven't answered all your questions. There will be time for that, although not an eternity. I do hope your futures seem clearer. I hope too I've reduced the likelihood of quarrels. Roberto, my old friend, I assume you and your workers will stay on, but that will be at the will of the new owners. If they don't want you, Ev said he'd hire you, and your team, in a flash. And finally, as soon as we are through crush, this old lady here and I are going away. I bought us some cruise tickets! We'll be back by Christmas. But before we go, I'll have the lawyers put everything into writing. And now, I'm tired. You're all dismissed. But not you Rachel my dear, I have something to say to you, but in private. Would you come see me first thing in the morning?"

As friends and family began to disperse, Morgan leaned forward. "I still have some questions," she said.

"Ah, yes," replied Jules, as if he knew what she was going to ask. "But let's wait until these people leave. Tinker, Indie, would you to stay, and Rickie too, if you don't mind."

It was quite dark by the time the six of them sat alone.

"It's about what brought us here in the first place," said Morgan. "Why I asked you to go away for a while."

"You knew?" Kit was more than a little surprised. Indie and Tinker simply stared at her. Rickie folded her hands in her lap, and focused on maintaining control of her emotions.

"There were no accidents while you were away." Morgan went on. "But then why should there be? I don't understand, though, your decision to steal Bailey away too. Did you think we were fools? I was pretty sure you had him with you. . . ."

Jules drummed his fingers on the table as he scrutinized their faces. "Oh, you're not fools," he said. "And I admit I've been parsimonious with the truth. And Bailey? Well, Bailey just happened. But once Ev brought him to me, I couldn't very well send him home, could I? Buckthorn isn't a single simple story. No family is. There's much going on here. Many strands of life braided together. No outsider can unwind them all. The conflicts, the lies, and the out and out frauds. . . . They can undermine the myth of trusting in one's family." He made a motion with his hand to silence his wife and his younger daughter as well as his niece. "There comes a time for decisions to be made—by one man, alone—without interruption or argument. My own decisions have been complicated by my illness of course. I needed a diversionary strategy. As magicians say, a little misdirection. It seemed necessary anyway, if I wanted to accomplish my own tricks. The rags in the ventilation ducts, for example. That did happen once, but it was many years ago, and I myself was the culprit." He laughed briefly. "I was only a boy, doing a job I didn't understand, and I was severely reprimanded by my father for creating a dangerous situation. He was about to start the maceration. He became furious with me about what I had let happen, so furious that he missed the sweet spot in the primary ferment and ruined a whole batch of wine. The memory of that is what gave me the idea. Ev was my co-conspirator. He helped stuff the ducts, then locked me in and skedaddled up the mine shaft. I knew Rachel would find me. And I did exaggerate my danger, and in the excitement that followed I simply slipped the bolt on the door I showed you, and no one suspected a thing. After that it became easy to manufacture incidents."

"Meanwhile, I had found Rachel indulging in her own bit of trickery. That's why I had to create those spills, to cover her inventory discrepancies. And one thing led to another." He shook his head sadly. "Not everyone believed in my little scheme of course. Certainly not you, Rickie. That's why I decided to bring in a couple of detectives. I let the cats out of the bag very gently, but suddenly, everybody bought into the idea that my life was in danger. Kit, my boy, the presence of you and your lady kept everyone busy worrying, and making up theories. They became so focused on what you two were up to that nobody seemed to notice little old me. It was quite amazing!"

"What about the van, Dad?" said Tinker. "I thought it actually hit you! How'd you manage that? You do realize I haven't slept in weeks!"

"Well, now, that was a real accident. And your response was perfect, dear. I merely saw an opportunity and adapted. I did sit down pretty hard on that curb however. Sam of course has kept her mouth shut about what she saw. And you, dear Tinker, I knew if I extracted a promise from you to say nothing about it, you'd carry the news far and wide, including some wicked version back to Indie. You're so predictably ornery, my dear daughter." He paused briefly. "And by the way, you have been taking your meds, haven't you?"

"You're horrible! I hate you!" screamed Tinker, jumping up and running towards the house. Rickie followed, brandishing her cane and yelling back over her shoulder, "Jules, you've gone too far!"

"Come back!" Jules called. "I'm sorry! Tink! You were perfectly perfect that night! And you did a wonderful job calming your mother. She was going to forbid my ever going into San Francisco again."

Tinker however had already slammed through the kitchen door. She did not return. Nor did Rickie. Jules bowed his head in frustration, for a moment. Then with a sigh, he looked up at Kit and Morgan, and winked, unrepentant. "I did think I was done for when I saw Kit in that crowd."

"What about the asthma attack at your party? That was real. Wasn't it?" Indie broke in.

"It was. Although I played it up—a bit. I did get stung while running after those damned goats. Fortunately, everyone came to my rescue. I, of course, blamed the lobster ravioli, because that seemed more provocative—that someone we knew might bring me food that could kill. I do wish Tinker would at least think about moving her hives away from where her old papà likes to sit."

"And Bailey? Why kidnap him? You haven't said much about his role," asked Kit. "Gave you no thought to his parents' feelings?"

"Ah yes, Bailey . . . Quite an observant boy, and so smart. But rather like that old parrot Talies talks about. He guessed about those mine tunnels—I have been using them, with some frequency. Roberto found him asleep in my old hunting blind, near what Morgan calls the hobbit door." Jules chuckled. "Fortunately, the boy isn't tall enough to fiddle the locks on the security gate yet. I'm not sure why he got it in his head to wait for me up there. Roberto found him and took him to Ev. An insightful move, I thought. You see, Roberto had figured out many months ago that Ev and I were up to something, and whatever it was, he didn't want to ruin it. He was right about the wild boar, by the way. One of his men shot a big one up on the ridge. It was rooting around close to Poison Oak. I took it as another opportunity in my little game, so to speak."

"You mean you cut the wires yourself?" said Kit.

Jules smiled.

"And Bailey?"

"Ah . . . your boy was rather insistent about making sure I was all right. He refused to go back to his mother's, so finally Ev drove him over to the camp. And once Bailey knew where I was— well, like I said, I couldn't risk his giving me away before I was done. Awkward, but we did have fun. I doubt Bailey had any idea what I was really doing at the camp, other than escaping the heat of the valley, that is. We fished. He helped me collect assay samples. And he rode along to Sacramento. I squeezed out a promise to keep our adventures secret until I gave him the signal."

"I know I encouraged you to disappear for a while just to be safe," put in Morgan. "But, really, who was going to stop you from doing what you wanted with your own property? Was all that secrecy and play acting really necessary?"

"Just say I've become a bit paranoid. Blame my tumor. And I couldn't afford to let word of the gold mining deal get out. My dear Rachel would have alerted her environmentalist friends. . . ." He shook his head slowly. "She's enough to break one's heart, isn't she? Real talent, but so idealistic. She has trouble seeing the forest for the trees."

"I had the opportunity to go over her production and sales data," added Morgan before she could stop herself. "I know you know what she was doing. Those cellar books you left behind . . . they detail some interesting discrepancies."

"Hmm. Yes. It was not a good decision to adulterate the cuvée with non-estate grown juice. I suspect she was trying to save Jack's reputation. He will need to stop selling cases of wine that don't officially exist. I'll be talking to him. He'll get in over his head one day. I did what I could to muddy the data with all those spills, but my poor Rachel . . . lacks basic good sense sometimes. And that biodynamic business? She has tried many ways to get Eddie to adopt her theories, including seduction."

Indie sucked in her breath and stared at her uncle, then at Kit. "But . . . I . . . I" she spluttered, unable to say more.

Jules rubbed the stubble on his chin, declaring he had no more to say on that topic. Instead he reached around behind his seat and pulled several bottles out of a case that was sitting on the flagstones. According to their labels, the bottles held a fifty year old Brunello. "I thought about steaming off these labels," he said with A smile. "But I got lazy. I think we should just drink it up. It's pretty good. And you can't go to jail for what you keep in the family."

Indie, who had been remarkably quiet, finally opened her mouth. "Rachel made this. Right?"

"Yes. She did. And it's quite magical. I gather she was planning to distribute it through our new tasting room. I had to put the kibosh on that." He popped a cork—a real cork—and poured out four glasses. "See what you think," he said, handing around the glasses, then lifting his own. "And here's to the purple magic. To the good wines of Buckthorn. Long may they thrive. I am going to miss this!"

Kit and Morgan talked until three in the morning, arguing about the roles of Indie and Tinker, Rachel and Uncle Jules in what had happened. Kit grappled with his own biases, but held firm to his conviction that Rickie and Jules were trustworthy, quite denying that Jules' had done anything less than noble with regard to Bailey. Morgan disagreed, claiming that many of Jules' actions were essentially unethical, if not downright mean, and that there could be no excuse at all for keeping Bailey incognito for days. She maintained Jules still knew more than he was letting on, that even now he could be lying to them. Although Jules had acknowledged his own responsibility, she was convinced he was still protecting someone. She supported these views by revealing what Naeve had discovered in the birth records—to whit, that Rachel's birth father was listed as "unknown." Did Ev perhaps know who the father was? Did Jules? Then she floated an idea that startled Kit. "It would explain a lot of Jules' behavior, if he himself was Rachel's father," she said.

Kit, as she expected, went ballistic. "That's not possible! Uncle Jules is not that sort of person! And he would never lie to me. Rachel? His own daughter? I would certainly know if that were true. What are you thinking? What would Rickie think?" And he steadfastly refused to budge from this position.

So, in the end, Morgan said no more, taking small comfort in the fact that no one had been injured or hurt, much less killed, by the events they'd come to investigate, and that probably Jules' various changes to the ownership of Buckthorn properties reduced the possibility of disgruntled heirs. But she wasn't sanguine about the future. Nor was Kit for that matter. They both lay awake most of the night.

The next morning they lingered over coffee talking with Jules before heading back to the Bay Area.

"I still don't get it," Kit said to him. "You had no real need for Morgan and me up here—you knew there was no real danger. Look at what you made us go through. And why put Talies on your cellar team? You have plenty of winery staff without him. I don't like being played as a fool."

Jules did look a bit uncomfortable at this. He eyed them both warily, first the one then the other. "I suppose I wanted to see for myself," he said, with an expression like a truant schoolboy after being collared by the principal.

"See what?" asked Morgan less than sweetly.

"See how Indie behaved in the presence of you two."

"Indie? You thought she was involved?" Kit obviously had not a clue what Jules was getting at.

"No. No. That's not what I mean. I was curious how you and Indie still felt about one another. And what she felt about you and Morgan, as a couple. That's all."

"But we're divorced!"

"I know that, boy. But she was so insistent to have you up here, it made me wonder."

This comment made Morgan nod knowingly. It was interesting to have her own jealous suspicion confirmed by Jules.

"It was Irene's idea," Jules went on. "She's been promoting a match between your Indie and my Eddie for a while now."

Kit looked horrified. "And you thought I might be jealous of such a match? Geeze!"

Jules shrugged. "Well, I wanted to understand the lay of that land."

Morgan of course fully understood what Jules was saying, but found his methods devious, overly cunning. There was an arrogance about them too. The arrogance of a great magician setting up his mark. She did not appreciate being anyone's 'mark'. Or maybe this was yet one more misdirection. Kit seemed completely taken in.

"I told Irene," Jules continued slowly, "I thought a match between Eddie and Indie could be a decent idea. They've been pals since childhood, and recently I have seen a spark between them. It would be good for the kids too. And good for Buckthorn." He fixed his eyes on Kit for a moment; then lifted them and smiled charmingly at Morgan.

You old snake, Morgan thought to herself. You're pretending again, aren't you? Why don't you come out and say it? This isn't about a match between Eddie and Indie at all. You don't really care that it might upset Kit. In fact, you want that match to happen because you were afraid your own son might just go marry Rachel, his own half-sister! But she only smiled charmingly back, and said nothing about any of that.

Jules had gone on. ". . . And then you, my dear boy, you called and invited yourself to my birthday party, wanting to investigate what Indie told you about." He emitted a half laugh.

"You were so anxious because Indie was so anxious. Is it any wonder I wondered how you felt about her? But I try to keep an open mind—and I wanted to meet your lovely friend too. I wanted to get to know her, and her son. Well, I've been satisfied, on all counts. Morgan here is a better match for you than Indie ever was. Need I say more? I will inform Irene tomorrow that her plans for the wedding can be laid, after our cruise, of course—I do like Christmas weddings. Hope you both will come up for the celebration. I'm sure Indie and Eddie would appreciate your presence."

Kit rolled his eyes at Morgan, but she hardly noticed, being hard at work trying not to show her outrage at the old man's patronizing words. Morgan shrugged nonchalantly, thinking two can play this game. "We'll let you know," she said, smiling sweetly. "By the way, Talies tells me he's staying on through crush. I hope that's all right with you."

Jules nodded. "Fine with me. Despite Rachel's complaints about his abilities, he's a good boy. Smart. And I enjoy his enthusiasm. That black burnoose by the way was a stroke of pure genius, if I do say so myself. Nobody noticed me, not even the magician himself, when I came out of the cave." Suddenly Jules began to cough, pounding his chest as if he'd swallowed his coffee down the wrong pipe.

Later, as Morgan and Kit drove out of the valley, Morgan remarked, "That speech of Jules' to his family? It was pretty amazing. I thought when we first got here that he would turn out to be just another charming old guy victimized by his family. He is charming, of course. I mean, he can be charming, but he's a cunning SOB, isn't he? Hard-nosed, my mother would say, and an arrogant bastard! He doesn't seem to mind hurting or insulting people at all, even his own family. Particularly his own family. And he does like to get his own way. Has he always been like this?"

"Mmm. Now that you mention it. And you stop noticing after a while. He is a self-centered, control freak. Maybe gotten a little worse with age. Didn't he say he had a brain tumor? That can exaggerate some personality traits. Or maybe he's just hearing the suck of the grave. Indie takes after him, a little. Rachel too, now that I think about it. You may well be right about his being her father. Does make a kind of sense."

They drove in silence onto the Richmond-San Rafael Bridge. Halfway across, Kit asked, "How about stopping at my place in Novato? We could swim in the pool this afternoon. Throw something on the grill. I'd love if you stayed the night. I'm finding I rather like having you around."

Morgan didn't respond immediately, but as they came to the end of the bridge and the fork in the road, she took the exit north, towards Novato, smiling to herself.

20 END GAME

Two weeks later Uncle Jules was dead.

Eddie found the old man on the floor of his workroom in front of the wine library about seven in the morning. Rickie had sent him to get Jules' opinion about whether Buckthorn should take two or three tables at the next Art and Wine Fest. Instead, Eddie just stared at his father, lying there in a pool of blood and wine, surrounded by broken bottles, including, he noticed, several bottles of the 2008 Cabernet Sauvignon Estate Reserve, along with what he believed to be the last three bottles of his grandfather's Brunello, vintage 1952. A great loss!

Eddie looked around, noticing that in fact well over a dozen bottles had fallen off the library's wine racks and been smashed. For a moment he considered reassembling the pieces so he could properly log the breakage, but in the end he chose not to do so, even though he had plenty of time. Eddie did, however, pause to right one of his father's straight-backed kitchen chairs, which had both been moved away from the work table and tipped over. And he righted the folding ladder that his father sometimes used to reach the top shelves of the library. That ladder had fallen against a tower of empty wine casks, toppling it over too. He began to re-stack the casks. One had rolled under his father's work table. He fished it out, along with some scraps of blue paper, which he stuffed into his pocket. Another cask had fallen onto the table top and sent a pair of crystal tumblers as well as an empty Scotch bottle scuttling across the packed earthen floor of the workroom. Both tumblers and bottle had broken. He kicked the broken glass into a sort of pile with his foot. Jules' lovely wine thief, hand-made on the Island of Murano near Venice, had also fallen to the floor, but miraculously escaped damage, not even a chip. He laid it gently on the work table next to an unopened bottle of single malt.

He pondered what to do next. Should he go look for Dennis? That didn't seem like a good idea. Should he get his mother? No— she had probably gone back to sleep, and what could she do anyway? He considered calling Roberto, but decided not to get him involved. Rachel? She couldn't do anything. He looked down at his father. He looked thoroughly dead—extremely pale, absolutely still, no motion whatsoever. No urgency now about him. After a few minutes, Eddie left the cave and walked out on the crush pad, where he knew there was a good cell phone signal. He dialed 911. Then, satisfied with his own coolness under pressure, he strolled back across the crush pad and returned to his father's workroom to wait. He didn't like the idea of leaving his father's body alone.

He'd watched enough television to know not to mess around with a corpse, so he didn't touch the body. Anyway, the thought of doing so made him feel squeamish. In fact, Eddie felt squeamish just thinking about the idea of looking at his father's body. So, to pass the time, he sent his eyes roving across the top shelf of the wine library, totting up in his head the value of the now fairly rare vintages that lay up there. He noted some empty spaces from which bottles had fallen, including a Jeroboam. Behind those Jeroboams his father kept his cache of good Scotch. Eddie could make out at least four more bottles of single malt undisturbed in the shadows. Jules had lived under the illusion that nobody knew about his cache of fine scotches, but of course everybody did. Eddie returned the unopened bottle of single malt on the work table back among its peers, hoping to avoid impertinent questions, questions like How much had his father been drinking when he fell? He didn't use his father's ladder to reach where the scotch was kept: he was tall enough to simply put it into position. While he was at it, he pulled some neighboring wine bottles and rearranged them to hide the whiskey cache. The top shelf now looked a little ragged, so, without thinking much, he began to straighten things up, twirling bottles so they lay symmetrically, humming a tune from "Cavaliere Rusticana" as he worked. He stood back and admired his work. Then he tossed half a dozen more bottles to the floor, stomping on those that didn't smash immediately and then watching as the wine mixed with his father's blood and disappeared into the packed earthen floor. He moved more bottles around, forming a neat pattern of empty spots in the library that might disguise the area that had interested his father. Laughing softly, he turned and pushed the remaining large pieces of glass onto the previous pile. He added a piece of bottle with its scotch label. He cut his finger. It bled a little. Sucking at the cut, he kicked the whole pile of broken glass into a dark corner, and looked around for a broom.

"No need for anyone else to get hurt," he said out loud to the empty room. For some reason, his father's fondness for scotch whiskey had always made him uncomfortable. He hoped his father hadn't been too drunk when he fell. He leaned against the little drop leaf desk, and put his hands into the pockets of his jeans to survey the room again, wondering how long he would have to wait for someone official to appear. Feeling the bits of paper in his pocket, he pulled them out and uncrunched them. There was some writing; he wished he had his reading glasses. Shrugging, Eddie crumpled the bits of paper into a ball and shoved it back into his pocket. Only then did he see the waste basket, upside down, empty, in the corner behind his father's desk. He frowned.

At this point, two policemen arrived, calling out his name as they came down the barrel tunnel from the cave's entrance. Eddie explained that his father had slipped, probably while climbing up onto the chair to take down a bottle, or to add one. He said his father was sometimes stubborn about using the ladder, which Tinker had given him because she thought it would be safer than a chair. His father was old, he told the cops. They'd just celebrated his eightieth birthday. His balance was not good. His head had probably come down on the corner of the work table. The table too was old, solid oak, stained with wine; he'd cut his own finger picking up a piece of broken glass and that had bled on the table too. The policemen both nodded sagely and looked at the corner Eddie was pointing at. It had been knocked into many times. The woman cop went outside to call in for someone to pick up the body. Then they'd all three sat down in the workroom and argued about the latest NFL draft picks.

Indie's call woke Kit up. It was nearly eleven in the morning. She sounded strangely calm. There had been another accident, she told him. Uncle Jules had fallen off a ladder. Nobody had been around, so nobody knew exactly what happened, or when, but he was dead now. No, Kit didn't need to rush up to Buckthorn. She simply thought he ought to know. She'd text him when the family made up its mind about funeral arrangements. Everyone was still arguing about what to do out in the kitchen, she told him. The cops had just left. They'd taken away his body. They couldn't bury him anyway, until the coroner released it. No word on when that was going to be.

Talies had been there when the cops arrived, around eight-thirty. He'd immediately called Morgan, even though all he knew was that Jules was dead and Rachel was screaming at everyone, making them work as if nothing had happened. Wine waits for no man, she'd said. Wine doesn't care who dies; the bottle truck will be at Buckthorn in four days. So, when Kit turned up in Morgan's kitchen around noon, she was prepared.

"I couldn't go back to sleep after Indie called," Kit said. Morgan nodded, handed him a mug of coffee, and sat down across from him at the kitchen table. Outside the sky was clear and blue, not a wisp of fog. A breeze rattled through the redwoods on the steep slope above her house. An adolescent Blue Jay squawked from a nearby branch. Max the yellow cat looked up from his morning toilette and blinked in the sun, as if to say to that Jay, "Your racket is irrelevant, Bird."

"Do you think we should drive up, even though Indie said not to?" Kit asked. Morgan adjusted a curl behind one ear, then rested her chin on a palm, and gazed at this man across from her. She frowned, and bit her lip, thinking what to say. Max growled softly as he bit into a burr buried in the fur of his back leg. "I can't believe Uncle Jules is really dead," she said finally. "I feel as if we'll find him still sitting out under the arbor with a bottle of his good red wine. You know?"

"Death is like that."

"Yeah. I know. 'Magical thinking' my shrink called it. I've been thinking a lot about Buckthorn over the past two weeks. Funny. I wasn't the least surprised when Talies told me that Jules was dead. He said he wasn't surprised either. In fact, Tal said nobody in the family seemed surprised. How could that be? Was everyone worn out by the constant barrage of false accidents? Waiting for the real one? Of course, Talies and I agree, Jules' death wasn't an accident."

Kit was noncommittal, at first. "I wonder what the cops think."

"He didn't have heart problems. He had cancer. I suppose he might have collapsed. But he was getting around quite well when we left him not long ago; and he wasn't to start treatment until he got back from that cruise."

"That's what I heard."

"And speaking of 'heart', when Talies called me this morning, nobody had yet had the heart yet to tell either Tinker, or Rickie. I suppose they must know by now."

Kit cocked his head thoughtfully. "Now you mention it, I was surprised when Indie called me. I thought we'd put to bed all those fake accidents. Like you say, I suppose this could have been a real accident . . . but that seems unlikely. Death after falling off a chair? And it's a lousy way to commit suicide . . . anyway, he'd bought those cruise tickets. Where did we go wrong? What did we miss? If you and Talies saw this coming, shouldn't I have seen it coming too? And prevented it . . . somehow?"

Morgan refilled her coffee mug and watched the cream swirl in its caffeinated blackness. "Speak for yourself," she said, taking a few sips. "I wasn't as sure as you when we left that the Uncle Jules' story was finished. You've known the Romanos a long time, and it's no wonder you have a lot more trust in them than I do. I've been waiting, I suppose, for the other shoe about to drop. I've been thinking about Buckthorn a lot since we got back, and in the end I don't think either Indie or Tinker was making everything up. I think they both sensed something we didn't, or maybe they knew something they didn't want to talk about. And I can't get it out of my mind that Jules was covering for someone. Someone who had to be very close to him. Someone he was willing to take the risk for. Someone he was willing to die for. Why do we keep believing what people tell us? And who said Jules' death was an accident anyway?"

"Well, Eddie did. Indie said Eddie found him. He told her it was an accident, and that's what he said to the police too."

"But why should we believe Eddie? Think about it, Kit. Think about how that family responded when Jules disappeared in the middle of the night. I knew he hadn't been kidnapped, because I'd told him he needed to disappear. But I was just playing along. I didn't know exactly where he was, of course. But I find it interesting that nobody thought to distrust my behavior. In fact, several people jumped to the conclusion he was dead already."

"Rickie didn't."

"That's true."

"And she did ask the police to put out that amber alert."

"Under duress. But, yes, she did," replied Morgan, suddenly feeling more sure of her ground. "However I had the distinct feeling she didn't expect anything to come of it. Was that because she too knew, or suspected, that Jules hadn't been kidnapped? That he wasn't dead? In fact, I think she knew he was fine. Or maybe that was only a good guess? Anyway, did you notice how angry she became? The way she looked at Jules when he turned up with Bailey? I think she had that amber alert put out to keep her family happy. I think, like me, she was simply playing along and then the game got out of control. She was really pissed off at him. I think she felt he set her up. And then, when she learned he'd let Ev into the secret . . . . oh, that really made her mad! Then he turns up? As good as gold, one might say, with yet another unsupported story. And did you notice how Jules treated the disappearance of Bailey? He made that sound like a lark. And everyone bought into it immediately, relieved both of them were back. And claiming responsibility for all those faked accidents? Hmm. . . ."

"But I thought at the time," put in Kit, "that Bailey's disappearance was pure Bailey, not some part of a scheme. The kid wants to be a hero. Jules then used it as another so-called opportunity, like he did with that van thing."

Morgan pouted. "We are still missing something. I've been trying ever since we got back to sort the real accidents from Jules' managed ones. I'm almost there, but there was so much going on. Hard not to become confused. One thing I am sure of is—we must stop trusting Jules' versions. He lies, Kit. He leaves things out. He crafts his stories for his own ends. It must be very annoying to live with him."

"But why lie to us? To me? I always thought of him, and Rickie too, as some of the most trustworthy human beings alive. And he seemed actually merry the night he sat everyone down and confessed to everything."

"That's it! That's what has been bothering me. He acted like a kid who'd finally figured out how to get away with something he desperately wanted. And let's not believe he confessed to everything."

"What?"

"Well," Morgan paused, sucking on her lips. "There's the Rachel thing. I'd bet my cat's life that Jules is her biological father. Easy enough to check. I wonder what he was meaning to do for her in the end. And I did rather expect it to be a so-called hunting accident."

"A what?" Kit leaned across the table as if he hadn't quite heard what she said.

"The gun," she said. "The one that went missing. I don't like loose weapons lying around, although I suppose someone must have found it by now, and put it somewhere. You know—to keep it out of harm's way. But why didn't he say anything about the gun either? He obviously took it somewhere."

"Or maybe Rachel did. Or Rickie? Or Tinker?"

Morgan frowned again, and picked up her cell phone, which had begun vibrating with great insistence. "Slow down, dear! You're breaking up," she hurried outside where reception was better. As she opened the screen door, Max raced between her legs into the kitchen, a headless mouse in his jaws. Kit watched her disappear around the corner of the house.

Ten minutes later, she was back, an overnight bag slung over her shoulder. "That was Talies. There's been another death up at Buckthorn. I'm ready. Would you like to take your big suburban, or shall I drive my little hybrid?"

They rode in silence most of the way. Morgan drove. She took the faster route, and they arrived in under two hours. She pulled up and parked on the gravel in front of the Big House next to some pickup trucks. It seemed unusually quiet when they stepped out into the sunlight.

Quickly, they checked the house, then the piazza. "They're probably still down at the cabins," Morgan said. "I wonder where all the dogs are. I suppose someone has called the police. Talies said he'd text me when they arrive, but I haven't heard from him at all."

"This is not going to be fun, you know," said Kit.

"I know."

"Daddy!!" Bailey careened into his father's arms.

"Bailey seems fine," Morgan murmured.

"Mommy said she knew you'd come. So did I. I snuck out to watch for you. All the other kids are in the barn with Jess. Aunt Rickie is dead! Did you know? She got shot! They wouldn't let us see her. Everybody's all weepy. I was scared! But I'm okay now. Tinker and Sam are on guard, and everybody just talks and talks. Sam has Uncle Jules' gun! She won't let anybody in!"

"Slow down, Bailey. Morgan and I need to go down there, but I'd prefer you stayed out of it for now, if there's a gun somewhere. In fact, would you go back to the barn and stay there with Jess? Would you do that for me? Is your mother down at the cabins?"

Bailey nodded.

"Is everybody down at the cabins?" asked Morgan.

Baily nodded again.

"The dogs too?" said Kit.

"No. Eddie locked them up in the barn. With the kids. Little Lupo and Fred didn't want to go into the barn all! But Zoe got the puppies, then Fred followed her and them to the barn. Lupo did too. Wasn't that smart? Uncle Eddie told Zoe to take care of the little ones, but Mom said Jess should do that. I escaped. I'm not little!"

"Well, I'm glad Eddie and Mom have some sense," said Kit. "You might help Zoe with the puppies, or Jess with the kids. I'm sure they can use your help."

"Okay. It's pretty boring up here by myself."

"Where's Nonna? And Grandpa Jack? Are they down at the cabins too?" asked Morgan as the three of them hurried towards the barn.

"Yeah. They're there too," replied Bailey.

"Okay. You stay put in that barn this time, mister, until I come get you," said Kit. "And, please, make sure the other kids stay put too. Make sure the doors are closed, and bolted. And don't let anyone in unless I tell you it's okay." Bailey nodded solemnly and gave a little salute. "I'm being serious, Bailey. You must do what I say."

"I know. It's like 'shelter in place' at school, isn't it?"

Kit smiled grimly. "Gawd! What is the world coming to?" he muttered under his breath as he and Morgan hurried past the tank house towards the row of guest cabins under the palisade. "I wonder if we'll find Rachel and Ev down there too."

Morgan made no response. She was wondering just how close to the truth she had finally come.

There were six cabins along the creek under the palisades, each one tiny, and each one painted a different pastel color. The late afternoon sun slanted across the valley, highlighting their tin roofs. The family was gathered at a long picnic table in the shade of a live oak. They were all there, sitting or standing, talking quietly among themselves. Eddie sat alone at one end of the table, studying some pieces of paper laid out in front of him on the table. Talies was there too. Fifty feet away, on the stoop of one of the cabins, sat Tinker and Sam, "on guard" as Bailey had said. The missing rifle lay across Sam's knees, held down like a barrier by one of her hands. Her other hand was placed solidly, but tenderly, on her mother's shoulder, holding her down as well. The door to the cabin was closed. Tinker was leaning forward, her face in her hands. She was crying quietly.

Sam noticed Kit and Morgan immediately. "Finally!" she called out. "Good!"

"Stay back," Kit said to Morgan. "I'll go. I need to get that gun."

Sam seemed relieved and gave the gun up without a word. Phil, who had been hovering on the margins of the picnic table group, ran over to his wife and took her in his arms. Kit waved Morgan forward and handed the gun to her. Morgan passed the rifle to Talies, who broke open its action and extracted the remaining cartridge. "Is it okay if we open the door?" Kit said to Sam.

"If you want. It's not very nice. I wouldn't let anyone else in."

"I just want to take a look. I won't go in. Did someone call the police?"

"Uncle Eddie did."

He nodded, pushed open the cabin door, scanned the room, stared briefly at Rickie's body, then closed the door gently. His face was grim.

Meanwhile Morgan had gone to see what Eddie was doing. "What are you frowning at?" she asked.

"Just one of dad's 'to do' lists," Eddie replied, shaking his head. "I found it this morning, back in his workroom. He loves this damned blue paper," he said, scoffing briefly. "I thought for a second, you know, it was going to be that old agreement Nonna has been going on about. But it's not, of course. Just 'tell Ev, tell Rachel, sulfites, tickets, barrel staves'. I thought there might be something I should take care of. But I have no idea what this all means? More of Dad's hocus-pocus, I suppose."

Morgan nodded and moved over to Sam, who had started to shake as soon as Kit had taken the gun. She put her arm around the girl and walked her away from the cabin. "You've done well," she said.

"Thank you." Sam's voice quaked.

"Let's get you a glass of water, and a cool place to sit."

Sam nodded in agreement.

"Can you tell me what happened here?" asked Morgan.

"I followed Mom down here when we found out where Gram had gone. Gram kept saying over and over, 'I couldn't help it. I couldn't help it. I deserve to die too.' I saw her. She was just sitting in there on the chair next to the bed, with one end of the rifle on the floor and the other under her chin. It was horrible! Mom tried to take the gun away. She got hold of it, but then it just went off. Mom screamed and screamed and screamed. It took me a long time to get her to come outside with me and just sit down and stop screaming."

"I am so sorry, Sam. I am so sorry about both your grandparents. They were good people. And your poor mom! That must have been terrible for her. But you are one amazing young woman, Sam. I am so proud to know you."

At this point the police arrived, sirens blasting as their cars bumped down the dirt track from the Big House and pulled up near the picnic table. Four officers climbed out. Kit had worked with one of them before, a tall middle-aged African American woman. He haled her, and immediately they began to confer, while the other officers looked around the scene for a minute then got down to business.

Morgan and Kit did not stick around; they were soon back on the road to home.

"What happened to Rachel? I didn't see her anywhere," said Kit.

"Talies told me she left this morning. Said a simple good-bye to everyone at the winery, and she was gone. Ev took her to the airport. She's flying to France—Bordeaux, then St. Emilion. She got a grant from the Wine Institute over there. Jules set the whole thing up. He funded her Institute grant, and then set up a trust fund to fund her living expenses. I doubt she'll be back in California soon, if ever. When Rickie found out about this, she became furious. She thought their money should have all gone to her children, not to Jules' illegitimate daughter."

"What?"

"Oh, didn't I tell you Jules had had an affair with Rachel's mother shortly after Ev's son died? I think it was leukemia, wasn't it?"

Kit grunted. "How did Talies find this out?"

"Talies, bless his heart, had a long talk with Ev, who was feeling guilty about keeping quiet. I knew we should have gone to speak with him ourselves. Anyway, he confirmed what Naeve and I already suspected from the birth records. He just filled in a few gaps."

"I never would have thought of talking with Ev."

"It puts an interesting gloss on the rivalry between Indie and Rachel, doesn't it? I wonder how Rachel felt when Jules told her he was her real father. Sam said she thinks he told Rickie about it right after he got back from the camp, but waited until only a few days ago before telling the whole family, probably wanted to confirm the arrangements before saying anything. He told the family he wanted everyone to understand that Rachel was part of the family too, and entitled to a piece of Buckthorn. Poor Rickie, I wonder if she ever suspected."

"And how is Sam?"

"She's upset. It's such a sad story really. But Sam pieced a lot of things together for me. She'd make a good spy! Knows how to stay in the background and observe. She overheard her grandmother telling Tinker how angry she was with Jules and his plans. Apparently Jules when returned home, he intended to split Buckthorn five ways instead of four. Rickie threatened all kinds of havoc if he did that. So he had to figure something else out, quick. Remember how he asked Rachel to meet privately with him after that long confession? He and Rachel probably worked out the plan. It was a better plan than what he originally had in mind, since it not only solved Jules' desire to give his other daughter a share of Buckthorn, but also removed her from further involvement with the wine fraud she'd gotten herself into with Jack. Jack, you realize, was selling more wine than Buckthorn produced and keeping the change? I'll bet he was encouraging her to fake some of those blends too."

"And that's why Jules was faking those accidents that drained off a lot of wine."

"Right. Anyway, the story Rickie gave Tinker, and that Sam overheard, was that she and Jules were down in the caves last night, in the wine library drinking scotch together and arguing about Rachel and wine fraud and the inheritance, even where their cruise was supposed to go. They finished off one bottle of scotch and Jules decided to get another one. He climbed onto a chair but couldn't reach what he wanted, so he decided to use the ladder. Fumbling around I suppose, while Rickie steamed. She told Tinker that she was so angry with him that she deliberately tipped him off the ladder after he handed her the new bottle of scotch. He fell and hit his head on the work table, and then she hit him with a Jeroboam of Cabernet and finished him off with her cane. Then she held him in her arms while he died.

When she sobered up, she sent Eddie down to the clean up the mess and stomped off to the cabins with the gun. I suspect she intended to kill herself. She was interrupted however by Tinker, of course, who was herself being carefully watched by Sam, which is how Sam overheard her grandmother. Sam, you see, was watching Tinker because she knew her meds were out of balance, and she was determined to keep her mother out of trouble until Phil could get her to the doctor. Tinker suffers from bipolar disorder. Irene told me that on our first night here. She said you knew."

Kit nodded. "I do, but we're all used to it."

"Umm. Irene told me if Tinker doesn't sleep, she gets a little wild, unpredictable. She said Rickie's a little the same way. I don't know if that has anything to do with what happened, but it certainly couldn't have helped. Neither of them was at her best. Anyway—when Tinker tried to get the gun away from her mother, it went off. Poor Tinker. She became convinced she murdered her own mother. Sam was a little unclear about what happened next, it went so fast. She knew however that she had to get hold of that gun and to keep it out of her mother's hands. An amazing girl. Very astute. And brave."

They rode in silence for a while as Kit absorbed the story. At last, Morgan said, "It was the dogs, you know. That was interesting."

"The dogs?"

"Yes, Whiskey and Fred picked up on something that indicated all was not right with Rickie and Tinker. I've heard dogs can smell certain mental episodes coming on. Anyway, they led the whole pack around the estate very early this morning, waking up the family and leading them down to the cabins. Like something out of a book. Without them there might have been two more deaths!"

Kit blinked. "My head is spinning. I'm still trying to take in all those lies Jules told us. Is there anything you haven't figured out, Morgan?"

"Well, yes. Yes, there is. . . . Why is she called Tinker? I couldn't figure that out."

Kit laughed out loud. "It's short for 'Tinkerbell'. You know, the fairy in Peter Pan. Tinker's birth name is Ricarda, after her mother. But Jules told me, a long time ago, that when he first saw his new baby girl, she just grinned up at him, her eyes twinkling. She was utterly magical, he said. All he could think of was sparkly little Tinkerbell, with her wings and her wand, zipping around as fast as a dragonfly in that cartoon movie, leaving behind a trail of pixie dust. So that's what he has called her, from the beginning. He said he wasn't going to have two Rickies in the family. One was more than enough!"

DISCUSSION QUESTIONS

Terroir is the second book in a series of Morgan Kendall mysteries, a series designed not only to entertain readers but also to encourage discussion of important contemporary issues that have an ethical twist. *Fog*, the first book in this series, takes up questions of the death penalty and child molestation, two issues that continue to feed headlines. Neither issue is easy or comfortable to navigate. With its more humorous tone, *Terroir* may strike some readers as a less emotional read. It takes on the issue of conflicts of interest, which affect several characters as well as various tensions between them. The ethics of such conflict may be shrugged off at first, but often have an insidious long-term effect that can undermine any individual's ability to be objective and rational when making decisions that involve the well-being of others, particularly when these conflicts are hidden. Below are a few questions to get readers thinking.

1. What is meant by conflict of interest? Describe a few different examples of the conflicts of interest you have encountered in your life. Some people argue that conflicts of interest are inevitable. To what extent is a "conflict of interest" simply another name for having a predisposed bias for or against something? To what extent is a conflict of interest quite different from "bias"?

2. Many of us go through some form of "conflict of interest"

training at our places of work. What conflicts have you recognized in your life? How do these relate to the type of conflicts described in *Terroir*? Why might it be a conflict of interest for a doctor to treat her own family member? Or for a lawyer to represent his best friend? How does one neutralize the impact of a conflict of interest?

3. When *Terroir* opens, Kit is explaining to Morgan that his conflicts of interest could impact his investigations at Buckthorn. What does he mean? What sorts of impact does he foresee? What does he want Morgan to do for him? To what extent is it possible for her to help him? By the end of the book, do you think Kit's conflicts resolved or evolved?

3. Describe the conflicts of interest displayed by some of the other characters in this tale. For example: Jules, Irene, Indie, Rachel, Ev Wolfe, Talies, Morgan herself.

4. Talies claims that an understanding magic can help a detective do a better job. What does he mean? And do you think he is right? And how does this magic theme relate to the problem of conflicts of interest?

5. Is it possible to see "wine fraud" as a conflict of interest?